DEATH
BY
DESIGN

A Bailey Davis Vampire Intrigue
M.D. Kenney

DEDICATION

For my husband, Jonathan, whose tireless support and constant praise helps me to realize I can dream.

CONTENTS

ACKNOWLEDGMENTS

I would like to thank my mother, Diane Boyer, for her endless editorial expertise and kind words. My gratitude also extends to Jennifer Hitchcock, Megan Kenney, and Nancy Lucas who's creative eye and boundless talents on and off the computer broaden Bailey's world. To my editor, Carol Gaskin, who helped transform my ideas into cohesive thoughts. And to one of my oldest and dearest friends, Linda Surles, who forced me to watch the original Nosferatu film decades ago–introducing me to all things vampyre.

Finally, a special thank you to all of my loved ones who are constants in my life. You know who you are.

FULBLOOD FAMILY TREE

Carla (f) b. 3023 bce d. 2399 bce

Line to continue

Arabet II (f) b. 3550 bce Egypt d. 2523 bce Yucatan

Dancil (m) b. 5996 bce Egypt d. 2523 bce Egypt

m 5368 bce

Karah C. (f) b. 5915 bce Sudan d. 1257 bce Egypt

Alleah C. (f) b. 9460 bce Europe d. 2120 bce Egypt

m 6003 bce

Perithomas C. (m) b. 7960 bce Sudan d. 2523 bce Egypt

Kas C. (m) b. 5871 bce Sudan d. 78 Syria

m 5220 bce

Sanji (f) b. 5639 bce Egypt d. 3060 bce Egypt

Reneb C. (m) b. 3250 bce Egypt d. 527 bce Yucatan

m 2314 bce

Tansi (f) 3250 bce Yucatan d. 2225 Yucatan

m 1988 bce to Reneb

Sari (f) b. 2186 bce Yucatan d. 650 bce

Nefereli C. b. 4284 bce Egypt d. 2654 bce Egypt

Line to continue

Zor C. (f) b. 4756 bce Egypt d. 962 Spain

Batz Chan b. 2640 bce Yucatan d. 527 bce Yucatan

m 962 bce

Ah Kin C. (f) b. 2523 bce Yucatan d. ?

m 2535 bce

Buhi (m) b. 2351 bce Yucatan d. 1906 bce Mexico

Taki C. (m) b. 3150 bce Yucatan d. 12 bce Yucatan

Paletra (m) b. 1980 bce Yucatan d. 1731 bce Yucatan

Jannan C. (f) b. 1941 bce Yucatan d. 299 Spain

m 3 bce

Sati (m) b. 1620 bce Yucatan d. 305 Spain

Dedan's 2nd G. Grandfather; Line to continue

3 other children died at birth

Ix C. (f) b. 543 bce Yucatan d. ?

m 306? bce

Unknown

Jaaf (m) b. 62 Yucatan d. 615 Spain

Tam C. (f) b. 1551 bce Yucatan d. 654 Yucatan

Eliz C. (f) b. 164 Yucatan d. 1659 England

Tor (m) b. 215 Yucatan d. 1436 France

Xainfe C. (m) b. 54 Spain

m 69

Bethe H. (f) b. 126 bce France?

Tunia C. (f) b. 150 bce. Olympia?

Cacon (m) b. 106 bce. Olympia?

Santi (m) b. 26 Rome?

Jacob (m) b. 139? Rome

Isabel C. (f) b. 3427 France d. 1295 Paris

Line to continue

m 339

Cravin C. (m) b. 762 Poitou d. 1295 Paris

Seethe (m) b. 910 Tours

Line to Continue?

m 1273

Marc (m) b. 1290 Paris d. 2002 America?

m 1433

Agnes (f) b. 1399? Rome

Beatria C. (f) b. 1283 Paris

Margot (f) b. 1526 London d. 1862 Vienna

Edward II C. (m) b. 1530 London

Alan (m) b. 1532 Copenhagen

Edward H. (m) b. 1516 England d. 1589 Paris

m 1524

Albin (m) b. 1540 Copenhagen d. 1541 Copenhagen

Amelia C. (f) b. 1545 Paris

William C. (m) b. 1589 Denmark d. 1960 S. Carolina

Jacques (m) b. 1478 Paris d. 1490 Paris

Marguerite C. (f) b. 1506 Paris

Line to continue

m 2011

2 other children stillborn or died in birth

m 1628

Lines to continue

Martha C. (f) b. 1606 London

m 1672

Edward III C. (m) b. 1626 London

Caroline (f) b. 1679 Boston d. 1680 Boston

William II (m) b. 1772 Boston d. 1863 Gettysburg

Mary C. (f) b. 1778 New York

Charles H. (m) b. 1826 New York

Jasmine C. (f) b. 1962 Oak Park d. 1980 Oak Park

Emilie (Bailey) C. (f) b. 1978 Oak Park

m 1851

Line to continue

Legend

Bce- Before Common Era
C.- Centurion
H- Human
(m)- Male (f)- Female
b.- Birth d.- Death
—— Marriage/Mate
—— Offspring/Siblings

Ahkin
Arabet & Reneb Line
Bailey's Family

PROLOGUE

October, 1295-Ile de la Cité, Paris, France

The visions of endless suffering tormented his mind: the bloodied and trampled earth, the bloated and distorted bodies of countless thousands. He could still smell the stench of the eviscerated and hear the buzzing flies fighting for position over festering wounds, knowing that the dreaded maggots would soon follow. He squeezed his eyes shut and shook his head in an attempt to erase the brutal images, but knew it was a wasted gesture. He would not soon forget, if ever, the cost of war.

Although bone tired, filthy and half starved, Sethe hadn't fed in weeks. He'd had plenty of opportunities to choose amongst the weak and dying along the way–people who could no longer defend themselves, ragged and displaced, roaming from the violence that never seemed to end. Normally he would revel in that violence and partake in their human misery. After all, most people considered him a tyrant and a murderer at the very least. But even he could no longer stomach further bloodshed, at least for a time, not even to feed. He dragged himself onward, continually torn between needing the sustenance and not wanting to waste an instant by stopping on his long voyage. And he could smell that he was close–so close–to finally being home after twenty-five years of traveling and fighting.

Joining forces with his family's longtime friend and ally, King Louis IX, to liberate Jerusalem from the infidels who had ruled the city for years had seemed the appropriate thing to do at the time. Especially with his father's endless and irksome nagging about honor and duty, two things he couldn't care less about. But he knew that he needed to keep up the pretense of normality. His family's rank and position in society had been at stake. His

1

older brother, Gabriel, had fought valiantly to suppress several local revolts in the south led by the Nobleman, Pierre Mauclerc, and eventually secured Poitou for the crown. Thus, Sethe had no choice but to go, leaving his financial affairs, his friends, but most importantly, the search for *his* Isabol, behind.

Sethe had spent five long years hunting for her after waking up one awful morning in Barcelona to find his rooms in shambles, and Isabol and all of her belongings gone. She had snuck out while he was sleeping off another drunken night that had ended badly with another woman–possibly two–involved, and a physical altercation by the look of it. He couldn't remember or care in the least, but knew that Isabol would pay a costly price for her betrayal when she was finally found. Sethe had thought of her almost every moment of every day since Barcelona, yearning to see her lovely face–hating her, yet loving her–leaving him more crazed by the day.

After scouring the countryside far and wide, Sethe had eventually gone crawling back to his family, mateless and miserable. But he had never stopped looking for his lost lover. Not for an instant. He had not been able to walk down the street without scrutinizing every woman for iridescent tendrils of strawberry curls. He could imagine them escaping from her barbette, and the way they looked cascading down her back when she released them from their bindings, and how those silky curls felt wrapped within his grasp. He remembered her translucent emerald eyes, which held the knowledge of her years on earth, outlined by impossibly long and thick dark eyelashes. He visualized her elegant stature–how she moved in her expensive linens, and how she looked without them on. He saw her at every mass, in every shop, at every gathering, and even in battle. He had even forced his burghers to keep a rendering of her beautiful face posted for all to see in their shops as a constant reminder of his search. One time he thought he had spotted her in London, but the hair turned out to belong to a whore, which only infuriated him further, until he'd taken out his anger on her frail and repulsive body.

"*Merci, monsieur. Avez-vous des aliments?*" He spun on the beggar, shocked that he had not sensed another presence on this desolate road into town. The peasant was certainly desperate for food if he was begging from a large, filthy stranger in the dead of night.

"*Déplacez hors de ma façon, vous sale mendicant!*" He pushed past the man. Sethe had no patience for the poor, unlike the late King Louis, who had constantly stopped to give money and aid to the wretched–much to his annoyance. That had been one of the reasons it took over a full year for the Crusaders to reach Tunisia.

Tunis, a wasteland shithole he had helped to capture and secure from the Emir Abû Zakariya Yahyâ and the rest of the Hafsids in power. But it had been just the first hurdle to cross on their march to Jerusalem, a fruitless and unsatisfactory journey that started with high expectations, but instead had been filled with despair and death. They had lost hundreds from the fighting and hundreds more from the black bile, including the king himself. Not even their Christian God could save them from the scorching heat, starvation, and sickness that seemed to follow them throughout their journey.

Yet Sethe had killed hundreds, and for the first several years it proved to be a very powerful aphrodisiac to be able to maim and torture without consequence. He had gorged and reveled in the blood of his and his God's enemies. Believing the infidels and blasphemers were even less deserving than the fate that had finally befallen them. He did it partially for the glory of his God, but mostly he took pleasure in his total control of the lives of others. He was also interested, almost clinically, to see just how far and how long humans could withstand his cruelty. To his utter disappointment, he was often dissatisfied with the outcome, except for a very few strong-willed ones. And, of course, he did run into his own kind, but he steered clear of those. He wanted nothing to do with an actual challenge.

As the years passed, the fighting became mundane, and his devout beliefs began to dissipate as the end never seemed within their grasp. He grew tired of the drudgery of war that he had so reveled in only a few short years before. The filth, the stench, the dying and suffering *slowly* began to erode his constant anger, leaving only a hollow emptiness within his soul. He soon began to think only of home and resuming his search for Isabol who had never, even for a minute, left his mind. So early one morning, almost twenty-four years after the futile endeavor had begun, Sethe found he had his fill of the bloodshed and left his command. He had abandoned his soldiers, his prisoners, and his whores without hesitation and started the long journey home.

A sudden cramping arose in his belly, one like he had not felt since he was stranded without food at the battle of Carthage several years before. Without hesitation he grabbed the peasant, ignoring his stench, and sank his fangs into the man's neck. As the hot flow welled onto his tongue Sethe realized that this was what he needed, and he drank in heaping gulps while suppressing the man's windpipe to keep him from calling out. Eventually he unlatched and discovered he had all but drained the wretched fellow. With his newfound strength, he easily lifted the beggar and carried him into a thatch of trees by a nearby farm. With any luck he would not be discovered for many days. He erased the man's memories just in case, then resumed his steadfast walk home.

Sethe wanted to vomit by the side of the road when he thought about the beggar, who had smelled of rotten meat and filth. Only a desperate man would feed from such a creature. Moreover, the nourishment he received from the feeding would only last a short while because the man was malnourished and unhealthy. It had hardly seemed worth the trouble, and now the vile taste of the beggar would not leave his tongue.

Hah, he laughed, then grimaced. He looked and smelled no better than the peasant. He surveyed his tattered cyclas, which was once royal blue velvet but now hung on his bony shoulders with no luster and no embellishments. He dreamed of soaking in a wooden basin with herb-scented hot water for the next several days. Unlike so many of his contemporaries, he was usually fastidiously clean, not believing for a second that evil spirits lurked in the water of one's bath. He continued his appraisal. His mail hung in broken pieces off his body, and his mantle was long gone, along with his stockings and linen. His shoes were worn and too small, scavenged from a dead farmer somewhere in Aragon. Bare headed, his lengthy, greasy hair continually stuck to his brow and itched from the lice acquired during his journey. His beard grew long and shabby, and his once meticulous hands and nails were cracked, filthy, and torn. Wouldn't his family be surprised at the sight of him? The thought almost had him smiling.

It had been years since he had last heard from them. Correspondence had been virtually nonexistent while he was traveling and fighting from one savage land to the next. Sethe thought about his privileged background and the contrast the last decades had shown him. Sometime within his years away, he had learned to appreciate the niceties that came with rank and title that he had previously taken for granted, even dared to scoff at. He never thought he would miss them so. Born and raised by one of the most powerful families in all of France, he was a noble by birth and inheritance. His brother was a

Centurion, and his parents were part of the ruling class of their Guild. Sethe was the last to prove himself worthy, and coming home defeated would be a humiliation he was not looking forward to.

As he trudged onward he could feel himself getting close to the outer walls of the city. He had long dreamed of once again seeing the incredible ramparts that Phillippe Auguste had built. The Louvre was the last and final section that protected the grand city of Paris from its enemies. The stone magnificence stood an amazing nine meters in height, and at the very least, three meters thick and was celebrated throughout France, being duplicated all over Europe. Or so he had been told.

Sethe sucked in a breath at seeing the massive double walled fortification standing before him. He all but fell to his knees and cried out at the beautiful sight and the men who were guarding the entrance to his beloved city. But as he approached Porte Barbette, he grew hesitant and lingered in the shadows. He was supposed to be fighting for his Christian God; he suddenly realized he would be immediately executed for desertion if found back in Paris without his garrison or proper papers of leave. This fact made him want to weep. He had traveled hundreds of leagues, and to be turned away at the gate was a possibility he would not even entertain.

Dawn was quickly approaching; he had to find a way in soon. He could easily jump over the wall, but needed a secluded spot where he wouldn't be seen by the *gardien*. He walked south for several minutes until he happened upon the river. Several men had been stationed at the corner towers to watch the river for possible infiltrators. He paused to think, and then backtracked until he found a dark area between two towers that would suit his needs perfectly. All he required were a couple of seconds. He backed up and flew at the wall, clearing it by a full meter.

Once inside, he viewed the transformation with stunned disbelief as the city began to waken. Apprentices and journeymen were already out cleaning the beautifully maintained cobblestone streets. The stench was tolerable, even on this unusually warm autumn morning, although he could tell that the new sewers that ran along the curbs were not very effective, and he had to jump over the clogged waste every so often.

He couldn't believe his own eyes as he walked through a newly developed area, lined with magnificent stone and plaster maisons and chateaus that stretched well into the sky, blocking out the morning sun. He had never seen such luxury within a city. These palaces were usually reserved for country living alone. He walked past servants who were out cleaning paths, maintaining gardens, and preparing the breaking of the fast for their masters. Mesmerized, he slowly travelled south towards the sections of the city he hoped he would clearly remember.

As Sethe took his time navigating the new and unfamiliar streets, the city transformed yet again. The widened avenues and new squares now filled with people. Hundreds were out conducting business, shopping, or just strolling and enjoying the beautiful morning. Artists demonstrated their talents and were selling their wares. Poets entertained passersby with their alliterations. Squealing children ran around and played. Women wore luxurious linens and veils with golden thread, and men boasted elegant silk tunics with intricate details. Even the servants were clean and well dressed. Pilgrims, who had flocked to the city in hordes to worship at Notre Dame, Sainte-Chapelle, and Saint-Denis Basilica, were dressed conservatively, but wore clean woolen or linen robes, the women in unfashionable wimples and men in simple leggings and skull caps.

He passed an unfamiliar market where colorful flowers, luxurious textiles, live fowl, salted and dried meats, breads of all types and flavors, and exotic spices from all over the continent and beyond were being traded and sold. One merchant was hawking the esteemed cabbage of Senlis, whose leaves smelled like heaven itself. Lentils, turnips, apples, plums, pears, and even quince were available to any Parisian who could afford them. He felt a pang of hunger as he passed stall after stall of aromatic foodstuffs. It had been years since he had indulged in a decent meal.

After receiving several looks of disgust, and pointed at by a group of privileged children, Sethe decided that he needed to clean himself and find some proper clothing before he was thrown out of this new and improved civilized Paris. He quickly continued towards the older section of town, where he found the more familiar narrow paths, some paved, others still dirt, and half-timbered domiciles lining both sides of the streets. By the time he had reached a more recognizable area it was mid-morning, and his energy was quickly waning.

It didn't take long for Sethe to find what he was looking for, and turned left into a stretch of alley he could barely squeeze himself through. He stopped and breathed deeply. The warm breeze held the stink of waste, human excrement, and despair. Beggars slept in doorways or anywhere they could lay their heads. The wailing of hungry infants penetrated the otherwise quiet morning. Now he smiled. This was the Paris he remembered and loved. He had a particular destination in mind, and hoped and prayed the place was still in business.

He stopped in front of a familiar red door, now worn; the wash had peeled, pitted, and flaked off onto the stone entry. He pounded several times but heard no movement, however he knew they were there. He could smell them inside. Finally, a tattered and grimy lace window covering swayed in the opening above his head and then he heard footsteps.

"Attendez, je serai là!" An old woman with yellowing and missing teeth came to the door. She sneered at his appearance and smell, but he thought that she was not far behind him in the grooming arena. She tried to shoo him away until he spoke. Of course, he had the voice, speech and manners of a noble, which quickly caught her attention.

"Excusez-moi, but I am searching for Mademoiselle Marie Michele."

The woman's eyes widened and she crossed herself several times. He wouldn't have been surprised if she'd fallen to her knees, invoking the Holy Trinity. She started speaking very fast in a language he couldn't decipher.

"Madame, de pardon, en anglais ou en français, veuillez."

She seemed to compose herself and relax somewhat. "Mademoiselle Marie is dead!" She told him. "She was attacked and torn apart by an animal on this very street." The woman crossed herself once more.

He feigned horror at the news, but became very suspicious. His kind did not die easily, so he decided to tap into the old woman's mind. As he dove into her psyche, he saw her discover the body of Marie lying in a pool of blood, her mangled and twisted corpse almost unrecognizable. Thankfully, he also discovered that the vision had been planted. He felt relieved because he had a fondness for the whore. Well, as close as he could possibly get to caring. And he needed her help.

He scrubbed the old woman's mind and quickly left in search of Marie. He knew she would most certainly have taken advantage of the city's newfound wealth. So he made his way to the nearest hostel and was almost thrown out until he flashed his coin. Even a ruffian like himself could get a dram of wine if he had the means. The owner brought a flask filled with the delicious drink and set it in front of him. He downed it in three large gulps, then slowly lowered the flask to the table as he looked around. He opened his mind and read everyone in the place, which was fairly full for the early hour. Humans were so easy to read; so boring. Sure enough, a large man sitting with a friend in the corner had recently visited Marie and her establishment. He thought the whores were first rate and the place clean. Well, well. Marie had certainly moved up in the world. She was now located in an area he was unfamiliar with, but he knew the way. He quickly left, ensuring no one would even remember seeing him enter.

He made his way back the way he had come and found the street he was looking for. Rue Chardonnet was located in the new section of St. Merri, where the maisons were larger than those he had just left, with finer gardens and stylish facades made of brick and stone. He could see servants scurrying to maintain their households and masters. The cobblestone and brick street looked new, and a few servants were out brushing the paths that led to their front doors. He headed for the barns visible beyond the main structures. Crawling over shrubbery and hiding in the shadows like a vagabond, he felt ashamed. A feeling he rarely, if ever, experienced before. This was certainly not the fantasy of returning to his home that he had in mind. He had envisioned a parade down Rue Grande with elegant women waving their flags and coats of arms in his direction, and Isabol at his family domicile, waiting with bated breath for his triumphant return. He expected to be praised, not reviled. This was certainly a sad ending to his commission and long journey. But he couldn't even work up the energy to be angry. He was home, and that was all that mattered.

He crept into Marie's barn, then paused in surprise to admire the assortment of fine horseflesh housed there. The collection must have taken many *livre tournois* to purchase. He found an unoccupied stall where he could rest. Once safely hidden, he waited for the cover of darkness to descend, but fell into a deathlike sleep almost immediately.

Sethe awoke to a scream, but it was not a cry of pain he'd heard, it was one of lust, and that made his cock swell. It had been a long time since he had lain with a woman. He stood and brushed the hay from his tattered clothes, quietly as not to disturb the stable boys. He waited in the shadows at the back of the house until a boy of about nine, dressed neatly in new linen and jumper, came out to the well with a fine porcelain pitcher. When the boy's back was turned, he slipped through the open door.

He found her in an office with vivid blue walls and hangings of women and men in various poses. An enormous fire pit dominated one wall. The wooden floors were smooth to the touch, the furnishings sparse but comfortable and inviting. He was amazed by her fortune. Marie sat with her back to him at a table, reading by the flickering candlelight.

"Well, well, well. Look at what the cat has dragged in." She turned to him, eyes widening. "My God, war has certainly taken the life out of you, Master."

"Hello, Marie. You are as lovely as ever," and he bowed to her out of habit and a touch of respect. "I see you have come up in the world." He gestured to the room with a smirk. "Who exactly did you fuck to get all of this?"

"How dare you!" She whirled toward him for a slap but got within smelling distance and abruptly stopped. She brought her hand to her face to cover her nose, but just as quickly seemed to forget about his unpleasant odor.

"I don't hear from you in over twenty years, and this is what I get on your return? *Simplement obtenir l'enfer hors de ma vue!*" And she pointed to the door.

"I will not leave until I am good and ready. Now I need to feed, bathe, and find some decent clothing." He stood rooted with his arms folded over his chest and his scrawny legs apart. She hesitated, then dipped her head as if to acknowledge his authority and power.

"You know, many things have changed here in Paris since your departure. The city is growing by leaps and bounds, and we are thriving. Over a half of a million souls reside within these walls now. Our kind has also grown. Many come to seek the business that Paris has to offer."

"Yes, I have noticed. And you have certainly taken advantage of the circumstances."

She shrugged and gave him a wicked grin. "But of course. Men will pay handsomely for my services now that there is plenty of coin to go around. My girls are beautiful and clean and well taken care of. And *naturellement* we are all very discreet and are good neighbors." She picked up and rang a little silver bell that sat on her desk. Almost immediately a woman of about nineteen came in dressed in silks, her glorious golden hair tumbling loosely to below her waist. The sight took his breath away just for an instant. He hadn't seen such beauty in years.

"Alix, please take Master Rousseau to my private chambers, bathe him and find some appropriate attire for a nobleman. But first, take him out back and remove and burn his clothing, and cut his filthy hair and beard. And rid him of the awful lice he carries. I will not have that in my home. We will see about feeding him afterwards." With a dismissive wave, Marie turned back to her readings.

He was not used to being treated thus; it was a long time since he'd obeyed someone else's orders. But he tamped his annoyance down and did her bidding. He trailed after the tantalizing Alix who led him to a bench in an alcove out back. She brought a large basin of water and a wrap that she held up in front of him so he could disrobe in privacy. Normally he would have been proud of his physique, but now he was almost embarrassed to display his verminous, skeletal body, however she seemed to not care in the slightest. She fashioned the linen into a loincloth and washed him to remove the first few layers of grime, then brought forth a foul smelling liquid. She spread it on his head and beard, and he almost gagged from the stench. After letting it set for a time, Alix rinsed it off with scalding hot water that the servant boy brought out from the house. She then razored off much of his disheveled beard and trimmed up his hair. Finally, she led him back into the house and up the servants' stairs to Marie's private boudoir.

After soaking in a hot herb-fragrant bath until the water cooled and his skin began to shrivel, he lounged naked in Marie's down-padded bed, patiently waiting for Alix's return. His cock was more than ready for some long overdue attention. But Alix never came, and instead Marie carried a bundle into the room.

"Well, I see you have made yourself at home." She dropped what she had in her arms on a nearby chair. "Here are your clothes."

"I thank you for your kindness. Now come here and give me a proper welcome home, Marie." He held out his hand and she only hesitated for a moment before she grabbed it and was in his arms.

He awoke from his slumber sated and rested. Marie had been very generous with her body as well as her blood. He looked over to where she rested, her dark hair disorderly, lips swollen from contact, arms askew, and breasts popping out of her shift. She was beautiful, he thought, but could not come close to the magnificence of Isabol. How he longed for his Isabol.

Marie shifted, and a droplet of blood dripped from her neck towards the silken head roll. He flit his tongue to the heady morsel and mopped it up. She roused and smiled. Her fangs glistening, she sat up on her elbow.

"You know, your family has left the Left Bank and moved to the new area we call Les Champeaux on the right. Not far from here. They live in one of the largest chateaus in the city on Rue St. Genevieve. Your brother still comes to see me, but very rarely now that he is happily mated."

"Mated? Gabriel is mated?"

"Yes, have you had no correspondence at all when you were away?" He only shook his head in bewilderment.

"It's been years now." Marie told him. "They have two lovely children, Marc and...oh yes, Beatriz. They are of high rank in the Guild and she does many charitable and *Godly* things." Marie swiped her hand over her raven-colored hair and frowned with irritation.

"I cannot believe that he would take a mate." Sethe said. "Gabriel was always so fastidious about women. I've never known him to be serious with anyone."

"Yes, well you haven't seen his wife. She is quite spectacular and annoyingly perfect."

"Really? What is my new sister's name?"

"Isabol."

Sethe froze. The blood in his body rushed to his head and he heard a buzzing sound, as though thousands of bees were trapped in his skull. "What did you say her name was?"

"Isabol." She eyed him strangely as he quickly got up and dressed.

"Describe my new sister to me please." He said it with such venom that Marie flinched in sudden fright. Before she could speak, he spun and grabbed her throat. "I want to know what this woman looks like!" He dropped his hand so she could speak.

"S-she," Marie coughed and held up her palm. "She is of my height with red curly hair and green eyes, and–"

Isabol. He let out a string of obscenities and a strangled cry of despair. His rage was beginning to take control of his body, and he left Marie without a backwards glance, continued down the stairs, and slammed out the front door.

He staggered to the road, driven by a wave of dizzying nausea, as the fury inside of him demanded release. How could this have happened? Isabol and Gabriel? It was unimaginable! He tried desperately not to visualize the two of them in each other's arms but failed, and the torrent of desolation almost brought him to his knees. Did they know? Are they laughing at his childish infatuation?

Dawn was just approaching, and people were beginning to stir. He headed straight for his parents' chateau, which proved to be a country house within the walled city—enormous and ornate, with acres of property, stables, a barn, and other outbuildings. It didn't take him long: now that he was properly fed and rested, he could smell them even inside their domicile. But he didn't pause to relish in his family's success; he craved blood and retribution.

He could just barely smell her essence in a smaller masion out towards the back wall of the property. They were asleep. Together. His vision bled red and it hurt him to breathe. He entered the house through a back door and climbed the stairs straight to their rooms. There he saw a sight he would relive for the rest of his days on earth: *his* flame-haired Isabol naked and curled up in the arms of his brother. Both soundly asleep, oblivious to his presence.

The buzzing in his head grew louder and his vision was quickly tunneling. Before he lost his nerve, he silently swiped the sweat off of his brow, and grabbed for his brother's sword, which lay by his discarded clothing. He strode up to his brother, the Centurion, who opened his eyes wide and met Sethe's livid gaze just as he brought the sword down with all of his might severing Gabriel's head.

Isabol woke up screaming. *"Mon Dieu, qu'avez-vous fait, vous bâtard!"* Her eyes changed to a magnificent gold and fire came out of her hands.

He took one look at her and swiftly brought the blade down on the only true love he had ever known.

He could not feel the flames as they lapped at his robes. He numbly walked into the hallway and went down to the children's rooms without thought, without meaning, without hope. The governess was screaming, so he quickly dispatched her. He turned towards the children without emotion…oh, God. The daughter looked identical to *his* Isabol. And she was sobbing for her mother. He hefted his brother's bloodied sword as his mind swirled with leftover rage and sickness. These wretched children were the spawn of his brother and that traitorous bitch, he silently thought through the buzzing in his head. Saliva dripped from his fangs as he hissed and screamed at the children.

"Faire halte!" He turned to find his father and mother in their nightclothes, both wearing expressions of utter horror.

"What have you done!" His mother raced up the stairs and started shrieking in a strange foreign language.

His father grabbed him, wrenched away the bloodied sword, then threw him aside like a limp rag as he went to the children to calm them down. At his father's direction, one of the servants cast a blanket over the children with shaking hands, and they left the horror of their family's home.

Slowly Sethe's hearing and vision returned, and the realization of what he had done started setting in. His mother came back down the stairs cradling his brothers head in her bloody hands.

"You bastard. Look what you have done to us," she hissed with narrowed eyes.

His father turned to him gravely; his fangs were extended and saliva glistened off of their tips. His eyes were bitter white and reflected the wrath he himself had felt only a short while ago.

"You will leave this domicile and this city forever." He said intently. "You are banned from this family. If I ever see you in or around Paris, you will be killed on sight. If you ever threaten or harm my grandchildren or their descendants in any way, you will be hunted down like the dog you are. You are no longer from the house of Rousseau! *"Vous êtes morts pour nous maintenant!"*

His father turned his back to him for the last time and gave instructions to the Centurions who were now arriving. They murmured, agitated, and all but his father who would never look at him again, glanced his way, ready to pounce if he so much as twitched.

Sethe felt hollow as he watched his mother on the floor, sobbing uncontrollably. He dared not move to console her. She would not meet his eyes as his father gently and lovingly picked her up in his arms and left without a glance in his direction.

He let out a single howl of unadulterated grief…then a moan of devastation, heartbreak, and defeat. But beneath it all, the rage still simmered in his black heart, and he knew that this day had yet to be concluded. The

Centurions surrounded him and the last thing he remembered was pain and regret. But what he kept close to his soul was the revenge he would seek. He would see that Isabol and her spawn paid for this, even if it took the rest of his eternal life to do so.

1

MY LIFE, AS IT WAS

Present Day: The Gold Coast, Chicago, Illinois, USA

"Damn, damn, damn. I can't believe this is happening." I grabbed the heel of my right Nando Muzi shoe, which was wobbly. *Man, these cost me a fortune*, I thought, and they were irreplaceable, considering I'd brought them back, along with a suitcase full of shoes and handbags, from Florence two months earlier. My vices were Italian shoes, hot cars, and McDonald's. I chose to keep the last a secret.

"I'll have to walk gingerly," I mumbled. "Now where is he? How could he possibly take this long to park a car?" Just then, Ron, my assistant, finally rounded the corner.

He glared at me. "Don't ask. Are you prepared for this?"

I smiled at his yellow pants only Ron could pull off as I answered, "Of course."

"Well, you look good in that suit but not as fine as me." He said as he eyed me from head to toe. I was wearing my favorite emerald green Pucci pencil skirt with matching princess jacket and satin cream-colored blouse.

"I never claim to look as good as you, my dear. You, who has his finger on the pulse of Chicago high fashion," I giggled. "Come on, let's get this project."

We were meeting with the Trents, a very wealthy middle-aged couple from London who loved Chicago and wanted a small place by the lake. The small place they purchased was about eight thousand square feet, located on the most prestigious street in the city. Astor Street was lined with historical townhouses and brownstones that boasted elaborate cast-iron gates and hand-carved limestone urns filled with colorful summer annuals.

The neighborhood is known as the Gold Coast, and was developed shortly after the Great Chicago Fire of 1871, when the nouveau riche chose to relocate to the north rather than re-establishing themselves in the Prairie Avenue area just south of the "Loop". Young industrialists and their families built their palaces along the beautiful lakefront and the surrounding area north of Oak Street. The Gold Coast was officially listed on the National Register of Historic Places in 1978 and contains some of the most important historic structures in the city of Chicago.

Ron punched the doorbell at the elaborately detailed gate. A camera located just to the right blinked on.

"Hello, Ms. Davis, please come in," said a man with a British accent. As the buzzer went off, Ron scrambled to open the heavy gate while carrying drawings, the laptop, and a projector.

"Here, let me take something." I grabbed the laptop and maneuvered up the marble steps to the ornately carved mahogany doors.

A short, stocky white-haired man opened the doors to the foyer and welcomed us in. I've seen many beautiful houses as an interior designer, but this one always took my breath away. The four-story limestone Second Empire structure had been built in 1886 for a shipping tycoon and his large family. The house contained six bedrooms, a maid's quarters and guesthouse, five bathrooms, three large parlors, a library, a conservatory, and large kitchen and dining spaces. The interior finishes were exquisite: Louis Comfort Tiffany-designed stained-glass windows, sculpted Carrara marble fireplace mantels imported from Italy, and parquet flooring in exotic woods, among other unique features of this magnificent structure.

The ceilings rose to thirteen feet on the main level, with elaborately carved quarter-sawn oak moldings. The same wood had been used on the lower half of the plastered walls. Black and white marble tiles covered the large foyer floor. Polished bronze sconces with a matching chandelier that adorned the entryway were accented in hand-carved ebony, depicting flying putti.

"Hello, Nathan," I said to the bulky butler.

"Good day, Ms. Davis and Mr. Dandridge. Please follow me. Mr. and Mrs. Trent will meet with you in the kitchen."

Nathan led us past a couple of richly decorated parlors and the large two-level library, then through a huge dining room that needed immediate attention. The ceiling plaster was cracked in areas and spalling off in others. The original oil painting above the hand-carved paneling, now ripped and punctured in spots, needed to be removed and restored. Obviously a water leak from one of the bathrooms above had not been stopped in time to prevent some damage.

While enormous and formal, the house was decorated in a comfortable way. Carol Trent had very refined tastes with a hint of casualness to make the spaces seem elegant yet relaxed. A combination of new and old furnishings complemented the rich Persian carpets and silk window treatments. Modern, impressionistic, and classical art adorned the walls and gave the house an eclectic and interesting feel. *Mrs. Trent certainly didn't need me for the decorating portion of this job*, I thought. *She'd done great job on her own.* We followed Nathan to the back of the house where the more private spaces were located, and where the work would commence.

I had yet to win the extensive work of redesigning the kitchen, dining room, butler's pantry, and buttery, along with adding media and laundry rooms conveniently adjacent to these spaces. We would have to be mindful of the conservatory, which was an important focal point and a well-used room at back of the house.

"Hello, Bailey; hello, Ron." Alan Trent nodded cheerfully while carrying a pot of coffee to the table where his attractive wife was sitting. Alan was tall and dark, with salt and pepper hair receding slightly. He was dressed causally, in khaki slacks and pink polo shirt.

"Hello, please have a seat," said Carol, who was dressed in a cashmere sleeveless sweater and perfectly fitted jeans.

Both Alan and Carol Trent sported the lean, athletic physiques common among wealthy tennis players and golfers. Alan even had one un-tanned hand where his golfing glove frequently sat.

"Hello," Ron and I said simultaneously while he immediately started to set up the presentation we had prepared for the meeting.

"What a beautiful late summer morning,." I said while digging out my drawings.

"Yes, indeed. Would either of you like a cup of coffee?" Mr. Trent offered.

"Yes, thank you." I replied. Ron declined.

By the time I added cream to my coffee, Ron had finished setting up the laptop and projector. I began the meeting by reviewing the programming portion of the project, discussing the design parameters, and finally pitching my development and design statements. I concluded the presentation by representing my ideas visually, showing my three-dimensional rendered models and elevations via multimedia. The Trents seemed impressed, and after an hour of questions, Ron and I left with a retainer check for ten thousand dollars.

Ron beamed once we were on Astor. "Great job, Bailey. They were completely smitten with you."

"Oh, please. It was your saffron yellow slacks, Ron. They looked at your pants and said, "*We have to have those two work on our project!*" We both laughed and gave each other high-fives.

"I'll get the car while you call the dragon lady to give her the good news." Ron said as I dug in my purse for my phone.

"Okay," I said as I watched Ron walk away and turn the corner. I was still amazed at the ability Ron had to read my mind. He was, by far, the best assistant I'd ever had, and I had gone through several in the ten years I had worked for RL Conklin and Partners, one of the most respected design firms in the city, perhaps the country.

I was the manager of the residential division of the company. I had received my Bachelor of Fine Arts degree by twenty and my Master's of Science in Historic Preservation by the tender age of twenty-two. I got my job at Conklin's right after undergraduate school and worked my way up fast from my original position as a designer's assistant. I was lucky that I had a boss who not only encouraged me to go to graduate school, but actually paid for most of my tuition, as long as I put in at least fifteen hours a week of work. That was not a problem.

I loved my job, and I was good at it. My specialty was preservation, so whenever a job came up that involved a historic home, I grabbed it for myself. I wanted to protect the original integrity of these important homes and work within my strict preservation and restoration guidelines, while creating spaces that embraced both the historic quality and the convenience of contemporary living. To me, the "gut job" was a big no-no. Luckily, once educated to the alternatives of total demolition, most of my clients agreed and were very happy with the outcome.

I finally found my phone. As usual it had tumbled to the bottom of my purse. I punched the speed dial for Connie Adams Gardner, my direct boss and the vice president of the company. Connie was a five-foot-ten-inch, fifty-something-year-old who took pride in her gorgeous looks. She came complete with two-inch acrylic nails and double "D" implants. Well, at least we all thought they were implants, but the office was divided, and the pool must be at two grand by now. Too bad no one had the guts to prove it either way.

Connie was an enigma. No one really knew her very well except for the basics. She loved to wear tight clothes that were better suited to a twenty-year-old at a dance club than the head of operations of a major design firm. She lived in a suite at the famed Lake Point Towers, the only building located east of Lake Shore Drive. She smoked, although she tried to hide it, but I could smell the lingering effects on her clothing. Connie had no children, at least she never referred to any, and she was currently married. Or at least she said she was married, but no one seems to have seen this husband. Come to think of it, I didn't think anyone had seen the last two husbands. Connie kept getting married, and each husband was wealthier than the last. She was on her fifth or sixth, who knew for sure? What I did know was that Connie bought herself a new ring after each divorce, and there was so much bling on her fingers it made me wonder. Her mystifying ways have provided office gossips with fodder for years, and no doubt will continue for years to come.

"Hi, Connie, I've got a check," I informed my boss with pride.

"Good job, Davis." Connie always referred to me by my last name in her gravelly voice.

"I think working around the conservatory will be tricky, so we'll need Carl on this job; plus I would like to have Kathy as PM." I wanted to line up the project manager and the general site supervisor positions on the Trent job right away. I liked and respected Carl Kaplin, who was my favorite general contractor on Conklin's team. He was smart, his subs were competent, and he could take orders from a woman. Kathy Harrington was a fifty-five-year-old married woman whose six kids were all grown. She was extremely organized and dedicated to her job, and I thought that anyone who raised six kids without someone maimed or dead deserved total respect. I couldn't imagine having just one, let alone more than a basketball team.

"Let them know, and I'll get the paperwork together and leave it in your box," Connie replied.

"Done." I disconnected just as Ron pulled up. He drove an old beat-up Honda Civic that I hated.

"Don't we pay you enough to buy something decent?"

"No, plus I don't care if this gets beat up. You know city driving is hellacious on cars. Besides, Randy wants to drive the BMW to take clients out to lunch."

Randy was Ron's significant other, an up-and-coming young lawyer who specialized in criminal defense. But why he would need an expensive car to impress those creeps he represented was anyone's guess. I thought. High-end design professionals, on the other hand, needed to make a statement.

"The company should buy you a car so we don't have to be seen in this. It's embarrassing," I stated.

"Not everyone has the funds you do," Ron said in his exaggerated effeminate manner. "Miss Hoity Toity." I laughed. He swiveled his caramel colored eyes my way. "So, did you make Connie happy enough that she won't bite the heads off of infants?"

"I think so, but she was pretty subdued. Do you think she's having marital difficulties again?"

"Honey, when doesn't she have marital difficulties?" Ron exclaimed. "She thinks she's Elizabeth friggin Taylor, for crying out loud!"

I couldn't help but laugh. Ron was right most of the time and especially astute.

"She must have great technique in bed," I said. "And she is beautiful for her age."

"Oh, god, the thought of that makes me want to hurl! Do you know her true age? Come on, Bailey, spill. How old is she?" he pleaded.

"I swear I have no firm proof, but I would guess she's in her fifties."

"Fifties! I would have thought sixties."

"Sixties? Are you kidding me? She can't be that old. Just look at her hands. You can always judge age by the back of someone's hands. Wrinkles can't be hidden there. At least I never heard of anyone getting a hand lift."

"Hmm. I'll have to check that out." Ron maneuvered around a double-parked delivery truck. "I'll have Adam start working on the field measurements and the overview drawings for you to evaluate and mark up," he said, back to business.

"I've been thinking. I would like you to review them first. I believe you're ready to help with the designing." I looked over, and his eyes had widened with pleasure. "Just don't forget the parameters we talked about, and be very mindful of the existing finishes. I want this job to be a portfolio piece for both of us."

"I can't wait to show you my ideas! Thanks so much, Bailey."

"No problem. I think you're prepared to take the next step. How is the studying going?" I asked.

Ron's radiant smile dropped to a grimace, and he visibly blanched. He had been studying for the National Council for Interior Design Qualification exam, for about six months. It was a rigorous, two-day exam that only qualified applicants were eligible to take. Ron's application was accepted after he'd received his bachelor's degree and worked full-time with the company for three years. The exam was scheduled for next week.

He shrugged. "It's going."

"I know you will do a fine job," I said. "Just relax and remember to take the shortcuts that we talked about." He sighed. I reached over and patted his hand. "Don't worry. You'll kick ass."

"I'm nervous as hell."

I felt for him. I knew how difficult the exam was, fewer than forty-five percent of the participants passed the first time around. The exam was a feather in the cap of all interior designers and meant more elite job opportunities and pay raises. Plus, once you passed you could legally call yourself a Registered Interior Designer—at least once you registered with the state professional regulation board in Illinois. Every state's regulation differed.

"It is scary, but everyone is in the same boat, and you are much better prepared than most."

"I know, I know," Ron conceded as he pulled into the parking garage. "I'm going to cram all weekend while Randy is in Vegas at a conference."

The offices of RL Conklin were located on the fifty-fifth and fifty-sixth floors of the Willis Tower, formally known as the Sears Tower. I, along with most of the city of Chicago, will always call it the Sears Tower, no matter what its official name is. Robert Conklin had leased twelve thousand square feet of the prime office space just after 9/11, following the mass exodus of people who were terrified to work in a building that was a possible terrorist target. The space needed work, so the brilliant Robert Conklin negotiated his way into a dirt-cheap, twenty-five year lease that included a large stipend for a complete redesign, as well as a glass elevator and spiral staircase connection between the two levels. Robert Conklin was not only a terrific boss and gifted designer; he was one hell of a businessman. Young designers clamored to become an associate at RL Conklin, and Human Resources received at least thirty resumes a month.

The fifty-sixth floor of Conklin's housed upper management, HR, residential design staff offices and their AutoCAD technicians' cubes, and a couple of large conference rooms. Located at the top level of one of the Tower's aluminum tubes, it provided plenty of natural light. The fifty-fifth level contained the main reception and waiting area, commercial design staff offices and their assistants' cubicles, the materials library, two smaller conference rooms, project management team offices, and a kitchen. Both levels were decorated using high-style design elements and state-of-the-art system furnishings, keeping sustainability in mind.

"I want to stop on fifty-five and check to see if Kathy is around," I said as I fiddled with the broken heel of my shoe.

"Okay, I'll fill in Carrie and Adam," referring to our CAD techs. I nodded and punched in our floor.

The dedicated elevator opened up into a large reception area with frosted glass-paneled walls in various pastel colors, lit from inside with LED lamping. The waiting area furniture was sleek and modern, with white leather cushions and glass framing, sophisticated yet comfortable. The focal point, the circular desk in the center of the space, had a brushed titanium finish with the logo of the company illuminated from behind in colors complementing the glass walls, which cast colorful shadows against the lustrous metal desk. Above the desk, a light-well that broke through the fifty-sixth floor to the roof bathed the whole area with natural light.

We said our hellos to the receptionist, when she looked beyond my shoulder, her face transforming from a welcoming greeting into a mask of disgust. It took all of my will power not to look behind me.

"Crap, look who's coming," she muttered. "I have to take my break now. Talk to you later." And she took off like a bolt of lightning, leaving Ron and me to greet Sammy DeLenaro. *Great,* I thought.

DeLenaro was a horse's ass, to put it mildly, and someone I did not wish to speak to at any time. He was a five-foot-six-inch creep who thought he was God's gift to all women, the design field, and the world in general. He wore a toupee that was the wrong color and badly fit. His clothes often squeezed his chunky physique and frequently bore stains from his last meal. And he had bad breath. Yuck. He constantly hounded me and found a way to insinuate himself into my business and personal space. How his poor downtrodden wife and children put up with him was beyond me. How we put up with him was a bigger question, considering he'd had many complaints lodged against him at work, resulting in no more client interaction. Unfortunately, he was a somewhat competent contract designer who had a tremendous amount of important vendor contacts. So he was hard to fire.

Damn, too late to for us to scurry away. Sammy came strutting up in a caramel-colored polyester suit that was two sizes too small, showing off his basketball-sized gut.

"Hello, Bailey, I hear congratulations are in order. I told you that the Trents would go for those ideas I gave you," he touted as he scooted himself too close. I backed away when his foul breath assaulted my senses. Little did he know that I immediately dismissed his lame concepts.

"Hello, Sammy. Thank you." I said while gritting my teeth. He continued ranting about how wonderful he was, but I was transfixed on his face. Did I see a huge something hanging from his left nostril? I turned to Ron who immediately turned red, and I saw his right temple throb from suppressed laughter. He mumbled his excuses as he turned and sped away towards the CAD technicians' cubicles.

I'm going to kill him, I thought. But I was so riveted on Sammy's precariously hanging problem, debating on whether it would fall off and onto his belly, that I hadn't noticed the small crowd that gathering to check out my reactions, thanks to Ron. I was really going to murder him!

I managed to break eye contact with Sammy and his…problem and made my escape before I said something I would regret. I limped past the laughing crowd to Ron, who was discussing the upcoming Trent project with my CAD technicians.

"Wipe the smirks off of your faces," I ordered as we gathered at the CAD work area. "Ron, that was a mean thing to do to me. I owe you one," I whispered.

"He's so disgusting." Carrie said. "Why does he seem so obsessed with you, Bailey?"

"If you ever find out, let me know so I can do something about it," I replied as Ron and Adam sniggered. "Seriously, who knows, I can handle him though. I'll leave you guys to discuss the Trent project. Ron is the lead on this. I'll check in with you later." I turned to my assistant. "Ron, I'll drive myself to Oak Park this afternoon, which will give you extra time on the new project. And don't forget we need programming for the Rankin job by next Friday. Have Adam help you on that. Are you going to be okay with all of this?"

"I've studied for six months for this damn test. If I'm not ready by now, I never will be." He eyed my anxious face and smiled. "I'm nervous, but I'll be fine, Bailey. Don't worry. Besides, work takes my mind off of it."

"Okay, I'll check in with you later." And we said our goodbyes.

After finding Kathy and explaining the job to her, I went upstairs and ducked into my office because I saw Sammy still lurking about. *Doesn't he have any work to do?* I thought. But immediately began to relax. My large office faced east, so I had a great view of the city with the lake in the distance. I decorated it in peaceful muted greens with exciting hot accents in sienna and ocher. The effects, comforting yet vibrant, always made me happy. I loved my office.

I went to my closet, where I always kept a couple of extra pairs of shoes for emergencies. I placed my new Nando Muzis in a shoebox and made a note to take them in to get the heel repaired this week. I replaced them with a pair of Prada black *peau de soie* pumps.

I had just booted up my computer to read my e-mail messages when Connie strolled in. She had on a white chiffon blouse with ruffled sleeves that tapered at the forearms. The blouse would have been very tasteful if it weren't cut so low in front that if she bent over, her huge breasts would spill out and onto my desk. Her skin-tight black skirt rose about five inches above her knees and the slit much higher than that. To set the outfit off she wore three-inch spiked zebra mules and about two pounds of gold jewelry, including huge hoop earrings but no new rings, so I figured all must be fine on the home front. Hmm, I liked the shoes.

"Davis, congratulations again on the Trent job," she said.

"Thanks, Connie. It's a great project and the house is going to be fabulous when completed."

"Yes, I can just imagine. I'm looking forward to seeing your concepts."

"Ron and I will give you a presentation anytime your schedule will permit. Just shoot me an e-mail," I said as Connie nodded her approval.

"Here's the paperwork for Carl." She handed me an orange file folder. "Did you contact him yet?"

"No, I just got into the office. Traffic was horrible, as usual."

"Well, let me know what he says." And she was gone.

I checked my messages and took care of some paperwork. I sent Carl an e-mail about the upcoming Trent job, and Ron ran in with my revised drawings for my two o'clock appointment in Oak Park.

"I was just about to call you for these," I said.

"I knew you would want to grab some lunch before your appointment, so I thought you would want them. I made a copy for John as well," he added with a raised eyebrow.

"Why the face?" I demanded while Ron eyeballed me. "Like I'm going to jump his bones at the job site with everyone around? Besides, he's married now, and I don't do married men."

"Yeah, right." Ron snorted. "He's gorgeous and sexy and–"

"Come on, that's ancient history," I interrupted. "It's not happening."

"Okay, I'll lay off for now." He winked and left.

"Really," I said to the air. "It's not."

2

THE JOB SITE

oor Ron, I thought as I was getting ready for my appointment in Oak Park. He believed it was necessary to take care of me and arrange my love life, which at the moment was pretty nonexistent. I couldn't remember the last time I had a decent date, let alone had sex. *Wow, how depressing, I'm thirty years old with no prospects.*

I always knew I was odd. Not in the social misfit, or tattooing every square inch of me, or picking my nose in public, odd. I'm just a bit different from everyone else I know. In my thirty years on earth, I've never been sick, not even a sniffle. While my sister battled strep throat and my brother endured another one of his migraines, I just kept on kicking without so much as a sneeze. I've never broken a bone, or had a sprain. I participated in high school softball, soccer, and track, yet I never sustained so much as an infected scratch. Sure, I would get an occasional scrape, but my body practically healed before I could get a Band-aid on. I questioned my parents about this strange phenomenon and they just shrugged me off, so after awhile I stopped asking. My grandmother always said I had a strong constitution, but I just thought I was…weird.

And that's only the tip of the iceberg. Even though my health is off the charts, the most frighteningly strange thing about me, hands down, is my strength. Okay, I'll admit that I'm a bit of a jock. Yes, one of those weirdos who actually likes to work out. But I'm certainly no bodybuilder, and I'm not a superhero either. At least I didn't believe so, but come to think of it, I've never actually tried to leap over a tall building. Not yet, anyway. However, there is one thing I know for sure: I can do things normal people can't.

I've had a pretty ordinary childhood. Caring parents and grandparents who were involved and loving. Two siblings I got along with, well, for the most part. I attended public schools in the suburbs of Chicago, where I played various sports, was in the drama club, and almost made valedictorian. Overall, I was considered a "good girl"–though, much to my mother's horror, I quit playing the piano because I hated it, and I ran away from home once when my father wouldn't let me have a pair of pot-bellied pigs I saw in a pet store. Needless to say, I only made it to the corner before I was dragged home, and I was never allowed to enter another pet store.

So while I was good daughter and student, I wasn't perfect by any means. I got into my share of trouble: sneaking smokes behind our garage, and skipping school on St. Patrick's Day to hop on the "L" for the city. I wasn't the most popular girl in school. That would be reserved for Ashley Corcoran and her group of cheerleaders, who did a lot more than cheering, from what I understand. But I had several circles of friends in differing groups. The jocks I worked out with, the emo's from drama club, several nerds I studied with, and the neighborhood kids who I've known for most of my life. I had plenty of dates and even a couple of serious relationships, but nothing that ever amounted to true love and commitment, at least on their part. In short, I had a pretty normal and somewhat uninteresting childhood. At least until I got to college.

At the age of eighteen, I began getting cramps in my arms, legs, and abdomen. Sometimes so severe I had to miss school. I was away at college in New York so my parents never knew, and I certainly wasn't about to tell them. Of course I thought the worst–cancer, tumors, blood clots. Fortunately, after about six months, and before I made a total ass out of myself by running to the doctor, the cramping stopped. Just like that. Poof, they were gone.

While the pain diminished, my body seemed to transform before my very eyes. My muscles were better defined, and my strength grew more powerful and longer lasting. I'd always been athletic, but my body leaned towards the well rounded, voluptuous type rather than the long, sinewy runner type. That didn't change, my breasts were still large and my hips still full. But my whole stature was now somehow more vigorous, more distinctive, and noticeably agile. I began to run marathons, then triathlons, and barely broke a sweat doing so. I was always careful not to go too fast, and

I pretended to look exhausted, even though I never was. There was no way I wanted the attention, because I knew I wasn't normal. So I purposely lagged with the bulk of the crowd, rarely out of breath and certainly not having much fun. Eventually I gave it up, but my strength never waned. I stopped working out, running, swimming, biking, and purposely ate anything and everything in sight. I sat on my ass studying for days on end, finishing school and earning my degree in only three years. The whole while, I never gained an ounce; I never lost muscle tone or strength. Very scary.

At this point I decided to put my little oddities behind me and concentrate on getting a job and settling into adulthood. Soon I just stopped thinking about my abilities and got on with life.

I got up to primp in my bathroom mirror before I had to leave. I wasn't drop-dead gorgeous but I could hold my own. My hair was a little disheveled, but it was a pretty strawberry-blonde color that came down to my mid-back in thick waves. My large green eyes were probably a bit farther apart than they should be. My lips were nicely sculpted above a rather pointy chin that contained a somewhat large cleft. I had high cheekbones that were still a bit bronzed from the summer sun. My figure ran to the voluptuous athletic rather than the skinny and boney, and my backside was well rounded and toned rather than flat. Unfortunately, most of the men I met tended to like the anorexic, flat-butt look. *Depressing.*

I did attract some interest, but nothing I could take home to dear old mom, that was for sure. And I hated going out to clubs with the girls. They were always loud, hot, and smelled bad. Besides, I wasn't particularly interested in one-night stands. But lately a few of my friends, including Ron, had been rumbling about making a profile for me on one of the matchmaking websites. Yikes. I had to put a kibosh on that soon, before I found myself on some god-awful blind date. I wasn't that desperate yet. *Was I?*

I didn't want to think about my miserable love life any further, so I gathered my things, along with a couple of disks for work over the weekend, and left the office. Free parking came with the job but I wanted to do my part for the environment so I usually took the train to work. However, when I had to go to the suburbs for meetings I liked to drive. I love a great automobile, and I'd really splurged on my latest wheels. The parking attendant pulled up in my new royal blue Mercedes SL convertible.

"This one is awesome, Ms. Davis," he stated. "What a great summer ride."

"I'm having fun with it, thank you."

With the top down and enjoying the unusual sultry late summer sun, I maneuvered through traffic and hopped on the Eisenhower Expressway to Harlem Avenue, wondering how I would feel seeing John Blaine again. We had previously talked on the phone about the Conrad project, but I hadn't seen him in the flesh since our breakup about two years before.

We'd met through a mutual acquaintance in a local blues club. Our instant attraction led to a passionate love affair, and after six weeks I moved into his condo in the Loop. We cohabitated happily for over a year and a half before it started to fall apart. He wanted his independence and his buddies; I wanted an adult relationship. Needless to say, I left, hurt and disillusioned. He persevered, and within three months fell in love and got married. Ouch! Men can really suck sometimes.

I knew there was a possibility we could run into each other someday because of our relationship to the building trades. He was an architect, I was an interior designer; we both worked in the city at prestigious firms. However, I was hoping that day would never come. Apparently I still nursed the hurt, or maybe it was just my pride that was wounded. Either way, I was about to find out.

The Conrad job site was on the north side of Oak Park, an important historic community located about ten miles directly west of the Loop. From Frank Lloyd Wright to Ernest Hemmingway, Oak Park was home to the creative and artistic of the nineteenth century, and its architecture reflects the ingenuity of its inhabitants. I also grew up in the western suburbs, so I was familiar with the area.

As I rounded the corner and glided into the long driveway, I scanned the property. The Conrad house stood well behind a massive cast-iron gate. Several mature maple trees lined the estate just inside the fencing and obscured the majestic three-story Italian Renaissance structure from the street. The expansive property was at least an acre, which encompassed almost a whole city block. It looked like a miniature version of the Breakers in Newport, Rhode Island. Conklin had been hired to create a large addition that would include a new kitchen and media room with a huge master suite above, and a new pool and pool house. The work was about four weeks from completion, if we were lucky. Thank goodness the Conrads were in Europe for the summer and early autumn so they didn't have to put up with the mess of construction.

I changed into my favorite Gucci flats that I kept in the car and checked myself in the mirror. God, I looked terrible. I swiped my lips with color and detangled my locks, which were in need of a good foiling soon. Thankfully, my suit still looked presentable. I preened for the mirror, damn, I was really nervous about this.

I had to navigate around several earth-moving vehicles, along with countless sub-contractors' trucks scattered throughout the front yard. Deep ruts of mud marred the otherwise pristine landscape. I had narrowly missed sliding into several by the time I made it to the backyard, where the work had commenced. I was immediately greeted by Charlie Watkins, our general contractor on the job.

"Hello, Ms. Davis." He extended his hand. "Jake has a couple of questions on the master shower, and we have to meet with the carpenter in about fifteen minutes. Is Mr. Blaine going to meet with us too?" He checked his watch.

"He's supposed to meet with us and the carpenter to talk about the roof pitch of the pool house and some other issues, like the master suite windows. I don't like how they will come together and interfere with the view of the pool. That really should be unobstructed."

"I agree."

"Let's go talk to Jake while we wait."

After we adjusted the shower sprays to the proper height and talked about the location of the vent piping, Charlie and I went back downstairs to our meeting.

The carpenter was there to greet us at the far edge of the new pool, which was in the process of being excavated. We trudged around the piles of dirt to where the pool house was going to be erected and waited for John to show.

Just as I was growing annoyed at his tardiness, he strutted up and stopped beside me. Damn him, he always liked to make an entrance.

"Hello, Mr. Blaine," I said as I offered him my hand.

"Ms. Davis." His eyes bored into mine and he drew very close.

Christ, I thought. *He's got a lot of nerve, and in front of the co-workers too, the jerk.* All eyes were certainly on us. I hastily removed my hand from his clutches, cleared my throat, and looked around. I felt the heat rushing up my neck.

He tore his eyes away from mine to greet the others, which gave me a second to appraise him. His medium height and build appeared more toned than when we were together. His blond hair was cut short in the back, but fell long in the front, hiding his eyebrows. His face was never classically handsome; his brow was a bit too heavy, and his lips were on the thin side. But his grey-blue eyes were striking and friendly, and his face was masculine and chiseled. All in all, he looked a bit tired, but it was clear that he had been doing just fine without me.

He looked back at me and our meeting officially began. After a somewhat heated discussion about the windows, we finally agreed on a course of action. I gave John the set of plans Ron had printed and shoved mine under my arm. As we finished up and I turned to leave, my vision suddenly tunneled and I began to sweat. My breath came in short gasps as I tried desperately it to find my balance. A sudden apparition of a young dark-haired girl swam in front of my eyes. I felt myself stumble and sway over the edge of the pit dug for the new pool, when a firm and steady hand grabbed me before I could tumble into the muddy mess. I was held until I was steady. Much to my dismay and annoyance, I looked up to see John's handsome and smiling face. *Double crap,* I thought. *Why couldn't it have been anybody else?*

"Are you all right?" he asked with what appeared to be true concern.

"Ah, I think so. I just got a little dizzy, thank you—just give me a minute." I bent over and caught my breath. My heart slowly steadied and my vision returned to normal. *Weird,* I thought.

"You can let go of me now," but he didn't release me.

"You look a little pale. Let me walk you to your car?" He started leading me to the front of the property.

"Don't you have to go back to work?" I asked, exasperated. I did not want to be alone with him. We had too much history and way too much chemistry. Not good.

"No, I'm finished for the day. I can work on the drawings from home."

"Oh." God, I'm so lame. I couldn't think of anything to say, so I turned and walked to my car with John following on my heels. I opened my car door, but he stopped me from getting in.

"Listen, Bailey, I'm glad we ran into one another. I've been meaning to call you for some time, but I couldn't get up the nerve."

"Oh really? I thought you had a lot of nerve. Congratulations on your marriage, by the way," I said, trying very hard to keep the bitterness out of my voice.

"I understand if you're still angry with me. I'm sorry about that. I'm sorry about a lot of things. I just wanted to let you know that Carley and I have split."

After my brain finally registered what he'd said, my exclamation was distinct. "Already? That was quick. So why are you telling me this?"

"I miss you," he actually had the gall to say.

"You've got to be kidding me, right? Is this some kind of a test? Am I being filmed or something?" I asked while I looked around.

"It's not a joke, Bailey."

"Oh, really? Maybe you should have thought about this over two years ago. Did you suddenly grow up or something?"

His eyes narrowed. I had finally hit a nerve. Maybe his soon-to-be ex had the same problem with him. "I was hoping we could have a civil conversation. Maybe this isn't the right time. I'll call you." And he was gone.

I felt dumfounded, and I'm afraid I looked the part. After I was able to close my mouth, I got in my car and took off. As if on autopilot, I made my way to Riverside—to my parent's house where I maneuvered into a parking place on the street. I turned off the car and just sat until my heart rate returned to its steady rhythm. Between Jon's declaration and my dizzy spell, I needed to gather my wits before I went into the house.

I couldn't have been any more stunned that John wanted back into my life. Clearly I still had feelings for him as well, otherwise, why all the anger? *Damn.* This was not the romantic future I had in mind. I tried to focus on something else while I got out of the car and started towards the house.

My parents lived in an 1885 Queen Anne with all of the prototypical gingerbread details and wrap-around porches. It contained six bedrooms, five and a half bathrooms, and countless nooks and crannies. I grew up in this house and loved it, but to my dismay, my parents had been making noises about selling and heading south, where snow and ice were all but nonexistent. I couldn't blame them for wanting out of the winter mess here in the city, but still, the thought of them leaving left my gut in knots.

"Is anyone home?" I was hoping that my mother was done with her appointments for the day. "Mom, Dad, is anyone around?"

Damn, I would have to check her clinic around back. My mother was a sex therapist, and much to my distress, she'd opened up a clinic in the large, detached coach house a few years before. "She's an excellent therapist," one of her clients told me once. And I'm sure she was, but I certainly did not need to know any of the details.

I balked at going into her office. My mother's idea of decorating her space was to display some of the tools and art of her trade: a giant Noah's Ark painting where everyone was having sex, including all of the animals; several phallic-looking statues; blurry images of certain body parts. She even had several sexual toys and apparatus on exhibit. I had seen things in her clinic that gave me nightmares. I even walked right into a group session once. Oh man, that was awful. I couldn't look at my mother for a week.

I tentatively walked in and saw her receptionist packing up for the day.

"Hi, Rachel. Is my mom around?"

"Oh hi, sweetie." Rachel always called me that. "She's in the relaxation room, just finishing up with her last appointment."

"Can you just tell her that I'll be in the house? Have a great weekend, Rachel."

I entered through the back door to the kitchen and decided to look around for something to eat. Mom was a good cook and almost always had something left over that I could munch on. I thought about John as I reheated a bowl of homemade soup. What was I going to do when he called? Did I want him back in my life? He had a lot of nerve if he thought I'd was pining away for him these past two years. What an ego, how dare he! I only pined for about six months.

My thoughts were interrupted by the entrance of my mother, Katherine Davis. She still looked good for someone in her mid-fifties, tall and lean, with a well-defined face and thick dark hair that had streaks of white running through it. That afternoon it was pulled back in a ponytail, and she looked comfortable, yet professional in summer white linen pants and a cornflower blue linen blouse that set off her beautiful blue eyes.

"Hi, honey. What a glorious day this has been." I nodded in agreement. She stood next to me and gave me a kiss on the head. "What are you doing in town?"

"I had a meeting over at the Conrad job."

"Oh yes. How is that going?"

"We're still on schedule. Keep your fingers crossed that nothing major happens." I babbled on as I added lemon to my soup. "Um, I saw John today at the site."

My mom froze. John and my mother had gotten along well until he broke my heart. After that she had comforted my damaged psyche for months. She gazed at me with non-judgmental eyes and I loved her for it.

"Was he nice?" she asked.

"Yes, he was perfectly, annoyingly nice. He informed me of his ruined marriage. He's getting divorced." I walked over to the table and sat with my hot soup. She followed and took the seat opposite, her eyebrows raised.

"Already?" she said, now exhibiting her motherly, disapproving tone of voice. I dreaded that tone. "I always thought he rushed into that, so I'm not too surprised." She sat back and looked triumphant.

I grunted in response and dug into my soup so she couldn't ask me any further questions about John. "Yum. This is great."

"Thank you, dear," she said as she bored a hole into me. The hairs on the back of my neck stood. Christ, my mother knew I was in turmoil. It must have been the therapist in her, or she just knew me too well.

"Not to change the subject, but are David and Marny coming Sunday?" I asked. My mother always made Sunday dinner for whoever was around. My older brother, David, and his snobby wife Marny came on occasion. They lived in Highland Park on the North Shore and had three of the worst behaved children on the face of the planet. I always had to brace myself before I saw them.

She must have decided to let me off of the "John" hook, because she replied to my question after several beats. "Yes, Marny called to say they would be here. She's going to bring a salad."

Perfect, I thought. She was not exactly the French Chef.

"How about Kristen and the grandparents?"

"I'm pretty sure they will all be here."

Kristen was my younger sister, who was currently residing at home and working at Denny's on Harlem Avenue. Much to the disappointment of all of us, she'd quit the University of Chicago and run off with a biker for over a year. She'd come back a couple of months before but didn't ditch the boyfriend. Jack kind of grew on you. He was a big leather teddy bear who was afraid of spiders. My parents were accepting of everybody, so it didn't take them long to forgive and forget.

My mother's parents lived in assisted living on Lake Street, about a mile from my parents' house. Shade Tree Living was a beautiful, newly constructed facility that contained apartments, cottages, and a full-scale nursing home, along with a clubhouse, pool, and meeting facilities, so Grandma and Grandpa Carrington were happy and well taken care of.

"Rosa is not going to Maria's this weekend, so we'll bring dessert," I said. "Maybe I can talk her into making flan."

Rosa was my housekeeper. She came to live with me when I bought my place in the city. She'd been the housekeeper of a good client who was moving to Italy, and Rosa didn't want to go. She had a granddaughter here and was just grasping the English language. I couldn't afford her salary, so as a compromise I gave her a small stipend and let her live with me for free while she ran my household. Everyone was happy, especially her granddaughter, Maria, who was glad to see her go because she lived in a cramped two-bedroom apartment with four kids and a rotten husband.

Rosa loved to come for Sunday dinner at my parents' house because there was usually a disaster that occurred or something that entertained her. Funny, most of the time Rosa was involved in the melee in some way, shape or form.

My mom got up to start cooking dinner. "That would be wonderful. But don't let her go to a lot of trouble," she said as she threw the pot of soup onto the stove and started the oven for warming up a loaf of French bread.

"She likes to cook for us. You know how happy it makes her to hear us groan with delight over her cooking." I got up to rinse my empty bowl and put it in the dishwasher. "Is Kristen at work?" I asked.

"No, she and Jack went to Wisconsin for the weekend to a Harley convention or some such thing. They plan on returning before Sunday dinner."

I didn't comment on her tone, but I knew she wasn't too happy about the direction my little sister was taking in her life. Not that anyone could stop her from doing exactly what she wanted. I was hopeful it was a rebellious phase that she would eventually overcome. With any luck, it would be sooner rather than later, for my parents' sake.

Just as I was about to grab my purse to leave, my dad walked in the back door. My parents greeted one another, or I should say, groped one another in a very embarrassing way, before he finally noticed I was there.

"Hi, Dad." I waved.

"Bailey, what a wonderful surprise! What are you doing around these parts?"

My six-foot-two-inch white-haired father was in his last year of work at Rush University Medical Center in the city. Dr. Henry Davis was an excellent thoracic surgeon who had worked so hard over the years that it burnt him out at the relatively young age of sixty. He was very much looking forward to his retirement in the spring. He was still a handsome man, even though his face bore deep laugh lines and worry wrinkles. But his dark eyes reflected gentleness, sensitivity, kindness, and a wealth of knowledge. However, he was often absent-minded, forgetting what my mother asked him to do, as well as a bit sloppy. Mom had to follow him around, cleaning up after him. Amazing, considering he was fastidious at work and never missed a trick.

"I was at the Conrad jobsite and I thought I would come for a visit," I stated as we hugged.

"Well, when you get a chance, come out and see my hibiscus. I ordered a couple of exotics, and they are doing great."

My father had found his real passion after my mother begged him to spend more time at home and less at work. It had only been a few years since he had turned to gardening for his mental therapy, but he certainly had a knack for it. He had won several local awards for his prized flowerbeds and gardening design.

We enjoyed the beautiful flowers while sitting on an old iron bench, soaking in the last vestiges of the late summer sun. The air was filled with the fragrance of early autumn leaves and freshly tilled earth. We relaxed and talked about his upcoming preparation for winter protection of his prized plants, along with a little politics and life in general. I didn't mention John; I didn't want to ruin the pleasure I was having in his company. When Mom called him in for dinner, I realized it was getting late.

I returned to the kitchen to fetch my purse.

"Where is your bracelet?" My mother grabbed my wrist to look for it. My diamond bracelet had been a gift from my paternal grandfather after my grandmother's death in 2000. He'd died the following year, so I cherished the memento and had kept it on every day since then. I would be brokenhearted if it were lost.

"Shit," I grabbed my bare wrist. "It must have fallen off my wrist when I took a tumble at the jobsite. I've been putting off getting the clasp fixed. I have to go find it."

"Are you sure it's not around here somewhere?" my father asked.

"I'll look."

"We'll all look. Come on, Katherine. You check the coach house while I look out back."

"I'll check out front and in my car."

We all hit our assignments. I felt sick with worry. What if I'd lost it? Would my grandmother curse me from the grave? It had been my great-grandmother's originally, and I'd been trusted over the rest of my cousins to keep it in the family. Oh God, I felt as if I were going to vomit. But I bucked up and continued looking. We reconvened in the kitchen after about fifteen minutes.

"No luck?" I questioned with dread. They looked at each other and then at me with sad expressions. "Well, I guess I'd better run to the Conrads' before it gets too dark."

"Bailey, you can't go over there at night. Why don't you stay over and go in the morning?"

"I can't, Mom, thanks, but I have to get home. Rosa has plans for the whole day tomorrow, and I need to be around for the boys." I was referring to my two Boston Terriers, who I adored. "Don't worry, I know where to look; it should only take a minute, and I have a flashlight in the trunk." *Thankfully, I had the code for the Conrads' gate*, I thought.

"I'll come with you," my dad offered.

"Henry, you can't. We have to be at the Darbys' in twenty minutes for cards, and you haven't eaten supper yet." Mom looked torn.

"Well, I'll just have to be late," my father replied.

"No, Dad, just go and have fun. I'll be fine. I'll call you when I find it." When they didn't respond, I added, "I swear," and crossed my heart. They looked a bit more placated when I left, but they still seemed somewhat worried.

What could possibly happen in the middle of Oak Park? I thought as I pulled up to the darkened gate. Still, the expansive and very deserted property with lurking shadows gave me the creeps. It didn't take long before I started to believe that I should have taken my father up on his offer to accompany me.

I steeled my resolve, punched in the code, and watched as the large iron gates cranked open with a groan. I followed the driveway into the darkness beyond and parked where I had before. As I got out of the car, I realized that the neighbors couldn't be seen. Why hadn't I ever noticed that before? And it was deathly quiet. *Now why did I think of that?* I was only giving myself the willies. I shrugged off my worries, opened the trunk, found my flashlight, then proceeded to retrace my steps from earlier that afternoon.

The terrain was even more treacherous at night, but I managed to make it to the backyard without incident. *Hmm, what was that noise? I could have sworn that I heard a scratching sound. Jeez, I'm scaring myself silly.* I took my cell phone out and carried it in my hand, just in case.

I made it to the spot where I almost fell and looked around. Nothing, damn. I moved closer to the ditch where the pool would be poured, shone the beam of light around, and quickly spotted my bracelet sparkling at the bottom of the opening. "Oh, thank god, I found it". It must have fallen off when John had grabbed my arm to keep me from tumbling in. My heart did a little dance at the thought of the contact between the two of us.

"Snap out of it, Bailey!" I chastised myself as I tried to determine how I was going to retrieve my bracelet. The hole was deep, dark, and wet. Yuck. I should just come back on Monday when the crew resumed work. But I immediately dismissed that idea. I would never sleep a wink knowing my precious bracelet could be taken at any time. Nope, I had to do this. I walked back to the car and changed into a pair of old jeans and a t-shirt that I always kept in the trunk in case of site mishaps. It was getting chilly and I had no jacket, but I could deal with that. However much to my dismay, I had no boots. Why didn't I keep a pair of boots handy? Dumb! Rather than ruining my Guccis in the mud, I would have to climb down in bare feet. Double yuck. But at least they could be washed.

Before I charged back to the pool, I called my mom to let her know that I'd found my bracelet. She wanted me to wait and come back with my father in the morning, but I quickly dismissed her concerns and murmured something about my abilities and fortitude. I don't know whether she believed me or not. Come to think of it, I didn't know if I believed me or not.

"Mom, I'll be fine. I saw a ladder that the workmen left, and it will only take me a second to get to it."

"Well, okay, but if I don't hear back in fifteen minutes, I'm sending your father after you."

I hung up, retrieved the ladder, dragged it to the edge of the excavation, and slowly lowered it in. I rolled up my pant legs, and just when I had gathered my resolve to start down, I spotted something in the muck next to my bracelet. It looked long, narrow, and cream in color. Like a white stick. Probably just some garbage the workmen left, the jerks. I made a mental note to talk to Charlie about the workmen cleaning up after themselves.

I gingerly lowered myself down the ladder realizing that I was probably going to ruin my crappy clothes. The mud wall was cold and wet, and large clots of it fell on the ladder rungs. I lost my footing on the last tread and landed on my butt, hard, right on the piece of garbage left by the workman.

"Ouch, that hurt," I reprimanded myself. I was a muddy mess, and I'd lost my flashlight when I fell. After wiping my hands on my jeans, I crawled around in search of the light and found it quickly, thanks to the beam it was still casting, even though it was halfway submerged in the muck. I pried it out and wiped it on my jeans as well. *How on earth am I going to keep my car clean? I'll have to take my jeans off and throw them in the trash when I get out of this hole, and drive home in my underwear. This was one of the dumbest ideas I've had in a while,* I thought, as I scrambled for my bracelet, which I immediately shoved deep in my pocket.

As I was about to climb back up the ladder, I realized that I hadn't missed a rung like I had previously thought. The cheap wooden ladder was broken right in two. No wonder it was left behind.

"Damn! Just great. How am I supposed to get out of here now?" I yelled into the dark night.

I dug into my pocket to retrieve my cell phone when I was rudely reminded of the piece of trash digging into my shin. "What on earth is this, anyway?" I exclaimed as I pulled what appeared to be a long heavy stick out of the mud. I shined the light directly on it and brushed some of the caked dirt away. On closer inspection, it looked like some kind of bone. *A human bone,* I thought, as I flashed backed to my grandfather's anatomy class, where I'd sat in for fun as a child. I'd pretended to be grossed out by the cadavers, but secretly I'd been was fascinated by them.

"What the hell?" I mumbled as the hair on the back of my neck stood up. Suddenly, I heard a sucking sound and I spun to see a lone shadow approaching from behind me. Did I see glowing white eyes? My vision began to tunnel, my heart raced, and I began to sweat for the second time that day. I heard a squish as the intruder landed in the pit with me. The vertigo I was experiencing prevented me from seeing him clearly, until he opened his mouth, and then I began to scream, and that was all I could get out before everything went black.

3

JASMINE ON MY MIND

Jasmine Tandini spotted the stranger across the backyard, standing next to the pool. He was incredibly gorgeous, with dark hair and dimples, and was obviously enjoying her party–especially Heather Gold's tube top, which was slinking down inch by inch. She wondered who he was and why she had never seen him before. Well, she hoped he was impressed. She knew this would be the best party of the summer–her last summer at home.

She still couldn't believe that in only two weeks she would be off to Harvard to start her new life, a life without the relentless eagle-eyed supervision of her parents and their Gestapo mindset.

She was normally never allowed to attend a party, let alone have one. Little did Frank Tandini know that his precious Jasmine was not the shy, conservative, goodie-two-shoes kid that she led all of the adults around her to believe. She did get straight As, was in the Honors Society, and was voted best dressed in school, but she only did those things to keep her parents off of her back. Besides, school was easy for her. She never even had to study much.

"Hey, Jasmine, great party," called Mark Mallory swaying back and forth while manning the keg. He obviously was drinking as much as he was serving.

Friends were also easy to come by. Jasmine had known most of her life that she was somehow different–that people were more attracted to her, more responsive, due to her special gifts. At least that's what her mother called them, because she had them as well. Only her mother was much more powerful, almost frighteningly so. Even though her parents tried to hide most of it from her, Jasmine wasn't fooled. But her unexplained perceptive night vision, her tireless strength, and especially her mind-perception abilities, scared her. Knowing how other people felt gave her a huge advantage at school, but it was increasingly becoming problematic socially. She often felt moody and distant. She hid it well most of the time, but the bouts and headaches were starting to strengthen, and her gifts were becoming harder to hide. She could hardly wait to flee her parents' scrutiny and pursue her real interests: boys and partying, the two things that actually kept her mind off of her so-called gifts.

A raven-haired beauty with large smoky eyes and plump rosy lips, Jasmine never had trouble attracting boys, even without her gifts. The problem was finding ways to get out of the house for rendezvous without being seen. Her father had state-of-the art security as well as bodyguards. She even had her own bodyguard, but he was easy to manipulate, and Jasmine was very quick and stealthy. She never let anyone else know just how fast she could move, because it would certainly scare whoever witnessed her. After all, it even frightened Jasmine. Besides, her bodyguard Derrick was young and cute and often looked the other way if she gave him special favors.

It took months of persuasion to convince her parents to let her stay behind from the annual family trip to their secluded beach house on Sullivan's Island. They had only agreed because Derrick would remain to act as her protector. Between Derrick and Mary Jane, their housekeeper, they thought Jasmine would be safe and sound until their return. She did miss her little sister Emilie, though. Only two years old, she was completely attached to Jasmine. Her mother had to pry Emilie's tiny arms off of her big sister at the airport during their departure.

God, she was finally having fun after a day spent planning, manipulating, and lying her way into having the house to herself. She had disabled the security cameras at about six PM, right after Mary Jane and the gardeners left. They were always around cutting grass, planting flowers, and moving dirt—making a nuisance of themselves. She was dismayed to see that her mother had ordered yet another new flower bed to be planted to the left of the pool. And she knew why: her parents were planning a surprise family party before her departure for college, and she wanted the yard to be in tiptop shape. Jasmine hated family parties. Her aunts and uncles gave her the creeps,

42

and her cousins were nerdy bores. She had overheard her mother talking to Mary Jane about the preparations for her "special night." So Jasmine knew she would just have to deal with a large ditch barely covered by a huge tarp at her party. She hoped no one would see the mess. She wanted everything to be perfect.

With any luck her father wouldn't notice the missing time on the security cameras. If he did, she would just blame it on a thunderstorm or something. She'd managed to talk Mary Jane into visiting her ailing daughter for the weekend, and Derrick was dead asleep from the sedative she'd slipped into his soda a couple of hours earlier. Jasmine would have to go check on him soon. She had locked him in the wine cellar just in case he woke up and caused a stink. But she knew he would never tell her father about this weekend, because she had so much on him it would give her father a stroke. The last thing Derrick or anyone else wanted was to get her dad angry. People went missing when her father got mad.

Jasmine's big old house was perfectly situated for a great party, nestled far back from the road among the maples and pines trees. The ten-foot-tall iron fencing surrounding the large property added a perfect cover from the neighbors. They wouldn't be a problem anyway. The Capallas were at their summer house in Las Vegas and the Drakes were at some family member's anniversary or something in California.

She grinned with satisfaction. Everything was perfect, and everyone was having a great time. On the stereo, Blondie was belting out *Call Me* into the hot summer air while people danced and partied. A few of her friends had already lost some clothing and were enjoying a dip in the pool. The party was very well attended. It wasn't often that you got into the house of Frank Tandini, and everyone who was anyone was going to be there. At first her friends were hesitant to incite her father's wrath, but Jasmine assured them that he would never find out. So not only had they been looking forward to the party, it quickly became the bash of the year.

Jasmine wondered again about the stranger. He was her type: tall, well built, dark, and mysterious. As their eyes momentarily locked, she felt a deep jolt of excitement. She didn't want to appear too eager, though, and she had other things to attend to now. Besides, it was way too early in the evening for her to hook up. So she broke eye contact first, electing to check on Derrick instead.

On her way through the house after glancing at Derrick, who was sleeping like a baby, she was waylaid by Eddie, an ex-boyfriend her father knew nothing about, who offered Jasmine a quick line. As they headed to Jasmine's suite of rooms, rooms that he was very familiar with, Jasmine thought Eddie Walsh had his share of problems, but acquiring good cocaine was not one of them, and she was not about to turn down this opportunity. As they walked through the threshold to her sitting room, Eddie grabbed Jasmine and roughly shoved her up against the wall while sliding his hand up her skirt to find her with no panties on.

"I've missed you. How about one for old time's sake?"

"How about what you promised me first and then we will see?" Jasmine replied.

Eddie backed off and took the precious white powder out of his pants pocket. "Wait until you try this stuff; it's the best I've ever had."

Jasmine offered her makeup mirror for cutting. Eddie had a hypnotic technique with the powder. She was always astounded by his touch with the stuff. He treated it with much more tenderness than he ever did a girlfriend. Well, her, anyway.

They managed to get a couple of lines blown before a large contingent of people descended on the intimate party. Jasmine leaped up in relief. She really didn't want to fight with Eddie tonight. She just wanted the rush and then to get back to her friends—and especially the handsome stranger. Thank goodness Cindi Harding, a beautiful blonde with a large chest, and playful manner, easily distracted Eddie.

It took her a good hour before she got back to the pool area where she had last seen the mysterious stranger. She'd been constantly waylaid to join in on shooting shots and doing bong hits, along with listening to the occasional bit of gossip. The party was certainly heating up; most of the guests were dancing out on the large patio and a few in the pool, sans clothing, of course. The party was going even better than she'd expected. In fact, this was the best party ever.

Just as she was about to head off to get another drink, she felt a presence next to her. She spun to find the handsome stranger standing very close beside her. Startled, she realized she felt an instant physical attraction she had never experienced before, yet she had no idea what he was feeling…strange.

"Who are you, and who let you into my party?"

"I came by myself and I let myself in," he said. "There was no one at the door to stop me. Nice party by the way."

Cocky, she thought. And interesting accent, but both turned her on. "I'm glad you're enjoying it," she replied. "Do I know you?"

"I doubt it, but I would like to get to know you better. Is there somewhere we could go to get a little privacy around here?"

"My, you are bold. What makes you so sure I'm interested?"

"Hmm, call it intuition."

His smirk was infectious, and she couldn't help but laugh. As their eyes met, hers smoldering with lust, she thought she saw his lighten to a bluish white. No, it must have been the lighting around the pool. Or maybe she was too far trashed. But she couldn't shake the fact that she felt turned on by this mysterious stranger.

"I know a place; follow me." She led him though the crowd that had gathered around the pool, then through the house and out the front door to the side driveway.

"Shit, my car is ten deep. Do you have a car here?"

He shook his head as he ran his hand down her neck to her breast and outlined her already hard nipple. She sucked in her breath and immediately decided that she could no longer wait. She grabbed his hand and detoured around the side of the house, through the shrubbery to the back yard, carefully navigating around the new ditch the gardeners had dug.

She could still hear the thumping bass of the music in the distance, but they had not seen or heard anyone else during their trek to the far reaches of the property. At least Jasmine hadn't, entirely focused on the anticipation of their coupling.

She was breathing heavily by the time they made it to the secluded gardener's shed located at the back of the expansive property. Was it exertion or excitement? Jasmine thought the latter was more likely.

"What's your name?" she asked. But before she could finish the question she was thoroughly and savagely kissed. She melted like butter, and it wasn't long before she was struggling to take her clothes off. The stranger lifted her up as if she weighed nothing, then sat her on the potting shelf where he used his mouth to trace every inch of her. By the time he removed his clothes she was panting.

"Please hurry, I need you inside me now" she gasped. The stranger was happy to comply and thrust deeply into her wet and waiting core.

"Oh, god!" Jasmine cried while the first orgasm swept over her. As he came close to reaching his climax, Jasmine could have sworn she saw a glint of glowing blue-white eyes again, but that was crazy, and soon she completely forgot about anything but her pleasure. By the time they reached a final climax together they found themselves outside on the damp grass, breathless. They lay in silence for quite some time, both contemplating their next move. Jasmine was completely sated, but not tired in the least and ready to get back to her friends.

"What did you say your name was?" Jasmine giggled as they got up to search for their clothing.

"Mikel." He smiled broadly. His eyes were a dark molten brown, clearly not the icy blue she thought she saw. "Thanks for the great evening."

"No problem." Jasmine said. "Where are you from? Your accent is nice."

He paused and looked deeply into her eyes. "Far, far away."

Jasmine felt the hair on her arms rise, but shrugged it off. "Oh, I would love to see you again." She returned to the shed to find a pencil and something to write her private number on. A sudden movement caught her eye through the window on the back wall, and her pulse quickened. She couldn't begin to understand the dread that was seeping into every pore of her being. All she knew was that evil was waiting for her just outside the shed window.

"Mikel!" she yelled. "There's someone behind the shed spying on us. Mikel?" Her frantic call went unanswered. She heard nothing, but could sense his breathing. She could almost see the blood running through his veins. So why wasn't he answering her? And why couldn't she read what he was thinking?

"Mikel, are you still out there?"

A huge arm suddenly wrapped around her neck, closing off her breathing. She managed to scream, but it was sharply cut off when the pressure tightened.

"Don't worry, this won't hurt a bit," Mikel was saying in a voice she didn't recognize. She could barely identify with his face either, now elongated with reddish lips and gleaming white teeth that were not right; they couldn't quite fit into his mouth. And his eyes were a startling and frightening blue-white, with pupils so black that she thought he would pull her into them and she would never be seen again. She hadn't been imagining it earlier. *Oh god*, she prayed as terror filled her. Then he bit down on her neck.

Excruciating pain, yet incredible ecstasy enveloped her, and after what felt like an eternity, Mikel roared back as if in bewilderment, his eyes gleaming and her blood dripping from his mouth.

"What the hell"–

But before he could finish, Jasmine kicked him in the groin and sent him flying through the shed door. She knew she had exceptional strength, but she was so astonished by her own force that she almost forgot to run. Almost. As she flew through the door she noticed someone helping Mikel up off the ground. Someone petite, with blond hair and hatred in her bright blue eyes. Her mouth opened to reveal elongated teeth, or were they fangs? Jasmine didn't know or care. She quickly gathered her senses and whipped around them with all the speed she could muster.

She had to get to the house, to safety. What was happening? She cursed herself for doping Derrick. Just as she had her destination in sight, she tripped on the tarp and landed badly on her right ankle in the hole that was to be the new flowerbed. Her calls for help went unanswered over the din of the music, and before she could make her way out, her time was up. She had nowhere to turn as she slowly watched the two predators circle around her for their attack. She managed to land a couple of well-placed blows before she saw the glint of silver and felt a slice of pain in her chest. Then she saw no more.

4

WHO ARE YOU?

I woke up to my very first raging headache with blurry vision and ringing ears. When I could finally focus, everything around me glared stark white and stank of disinfectant. I tried to lift my head, but a firm hand held me back.

A familiar voice rang out. "Henry, she's awake." And my parents came into view. They both looked worried and exhausted, my dad more disheveled than usual.

"What happened?" I managed to croak. "Where am I, and what time is it?"

"They don't know yet," my mom said. "Apparently a neighborhood family was out walking their dogs when one of them noticed the Conrads gate open. They went in to investigate while dialing 911 because the dogs started going crazy, barking and howling. One of them broke off his leash and went directly to you. They ran after him and found him crying by the hole you had fallen into. One of the kids swore he saw a large man jump out of the hole and fly across the yard and over the side gate in one stride. But no one else saw a thing."

My dad said what we all silently thought: "Too many video games, I'm sure."

"I had already sent your dad because you weren't answering your cell phone and we were worried. He arrived at the same time as the ambulance, and as you can imagine, it almost gave him a heart attack." She grabbed his arm and squeezed. As they eyed one another, I could see the tension roll out of them. They turned back to me.

"The police think you may have scared a burglar and he attacked you," Dad chimed in. "You're safe now. You're in the hospital." He clutched my hand and held on tight with tears in his eyes.

"I'm so sorry to worry you. I guess I forgot to close the gate," was all I could get out while my head banged to my heartbeat and the room began to spin. "I feel terrible. My head is killing me, and I feel so weak." What an understatement. I had never felt so awful. As if on cue, a nurse came scurrying in to take my vitals and ask me questions.

"It's nice to see you awake. How are you feeling?"

"Like shit," I moaned.

"Well, that's to be expected. You took a good whack to the head and you have a moderate concussion along with some bumps and bruises that seem to be healing already." She examined my face, lifted my arms, and frowned. "I'll give you some pain medication which should help."

"That's okay, I'll just go home and rest." Everyone in the room protested at once.

"Now, you are going to spend some time with us so we can keep an eye on you," the nurse demanded as she made me swallow a huge pill. "I'll let Dr. Caldwell know you're awake. Call me if you need anything. And you two should let her rest now. We'll take good care of her. Go home and get some sleep." She patted my mom's hand. "Dr. Davis is welcome to come to the nurses' station and take a look at her chart before you leave, with Bailey's permission, of course."

"Of course. What time is it?"

"About a quarter to eight."

"In the morning?" I gasped.

"You've been out for about eleven hours and we were starting to worry a bit, even though the doctor said you may not wake up for awhile." With that, she left the room.

"What about the boys? Rosa had plans today to do some shopping with Maria."

"Don't be concerned. Rosa is taking the boys to Maria's so the kids can play with them. They'll be just fine," said my mom. "Just worry about getting better."

I was just about to nod off and my parents were getting up to leave when I heard a loud bang and then a scream and click-clacking of small nails on a hard floor coming from the hallway, followed by a familiar voice yelling in broken English. My parents went to see what was happening just as the boys bounded in and Jerry jumped on my bed.

"Holy crap, how did you guys get in here?" I was so happy to see my dogs that I didn't care if my head hurt and they would get into big trouble. My parents looked horrified as Rosa and three security guards came running into my room.

"These dogs are not allowed in the hospital," one of the guards yelled as he went for Tom, my seven-month-old, who was sniffing around the room. I knew what that meant, and what happened next evolved in slow motion.

"Don't," I yelled, but I was too late. Tom proceeded to pee on the wall and on the guard who had grabbed him and was currently holding him at arm's length.

"Don't touch, don't touch!" Rosa shrieked as she swatted the guard's hands away. "*Cabrón!*"

Pandemonium ensued. Several nurses' aides came running in just as the dogs decided they wanted to play tag. Someone knocked over my tray and spilled my water and ice all over the floor. I was seeing double, so I just laid back my head and closed my eyes. I was hoping that this was just a nightmare.

"Everyone stop!" my dad finally shouted. Everyone was so amazed that he'd raised his voice that we all immediately froze, even the dogs. "Rosa, you must take the boys out of the hospital. Bailey will be fine. She will probably get to go home tomorrow."

Rosa immediately did as my father demanded, and the guards escorted the menagerie out after we said our goodbyes. The aids stayed to clean up the mess while my parents readjusted my bedding.

"Holy cow, Dad. That was awesome."

"I can take control when I need to," my father said, puffing out his chest a little while he finished tucking me in.

"You guys look pooped. Go home. I'll be fine for a while. Come back tonight after you get some sleep." I could see they were about to protest so I used my splitting headache as an excuse.

I felt relieved when they finally left. I wanted to just relax and try to reconstruct what had happened the previous night when I remembered—my very scary dream. It was hazy, but I managed to recall the girl's—Jasmine's horrifying ordeal. It was so real–as if I was actually there–I could sense her pain. And that thing that attacked her. He was the same monster that was in my childhood nightmares.

The medication suddenly started to kick-in, and I found it hard to focus. I had just closed my eyes for a second when I was woken up by an unfamiliar male voice. Dr. Caldwell performed a thorough exam and quickly left with a squeeze on the shoulder and an assurance I would be just fine. I fell back asleep before the door closed. It wasn't long before another voice penetrated my disjointed dreams.

"I'm so sorry to disturb you, Ms. Davis, but we have to ask you a few questions."

I opened my eyes to find two plain-clothed policemen at the foot of my bed, wearing their badges for all to see.

"What time is it?" I seemed to be fixated with the time.

"Two-thirty."

"In the afternoon? I swear, I just closed my eyes." I struggled to sit up, and the young blond detective came forth to my rescue.

After I was comfortable, the older officer began. "We were hoping you could tell us what happened last night. Start directly after leaving your parents' house, and please don't leave anything out."

"It's all a bit fuzzy, but I'll try." After I explained what I remembered, the blond asked if I could describe the shadowy figure.

"I'm afraid I can't help you out much. It was so dark, and I had fallen and was dizzy. I think it was a man, but I can't even be sure of that." Frustrated, I closed my eyes to think, but I only succeeded in reactivating my headache. "I'm sorry," I said as I massaged my brow.

"It's okay, we'll talk again soon." The older one handed me a card. "By the way, we had to close your job site for further investigation."

"What? For how long? My clients will have to be notified."

"Don't worry, I talked to someone named–he checked his notes–Connie. She's taking care of everything."

Just as they were leaving, the older cop turned back. "Do you remember holding onto a bone?" he asked. I must have looked as though I'd just thought of something, because they came back to my bedside.

"Yes, I do recall that," I said excitedly. "I remember landing on a hard object that I thought was garbage left by the workers, but when I dug it up, it appeared to be some kind of bone. Was it from a big dog?"

They looked at each other and the elder stepped closer. "It was a human bone. They don't know for sure yet, but they think it's a femur." Then his face changed into a smirk. "You know, you were found grasping that bone so tightly that they had to use forceps to pry it out of your hand in the ambulance."

My mouth was still ajar as they left my room. I looked at the card and what stood out to me was the word "homicide". Jesus, I rang for the nurse to give me more drugs. My head was suddenly pounding again, and I needed to go back to sleep, fast.

The next time I woke it was to an unfamiliar doctor probing and prodding. "Ouch, that hurt," I complained.

"Sorry, I was just feeling to see how your swelling is doing. It seems to be stabilized. Your x-rays show no brain swelling, so Dr. Caldwell is going to release you tomorrow. Do you have any questions for me?"

"Yes, when will this headache end?"

"You'll feel much better tomorrow. Just take it easy for the next couple of days. The nurse will give you some instructions, and I'll leave a prescription for some pain medication if you need it." He turned to leave just as a huge arrangement of balloons entered my room. Hidden behind them were Ron, Adam, Carrie, and Connie. I couldn't believe Connie was here. She hated hospitals. Her second husband had had cancer and she'd refused to visit him while he was in the hospital. She was afraid of germs.

"Oh my god, you guys! This is crazy. Did my mom call you?"

"No, I called your cell phone and she answered! She told me everything." Ron studied my face, then gripped my hand with a anxious look. The others gaped, then politely rearranged their expressions, I figured I must look even worse then I felt.

"What the hell happened to you, Davis? Trying to get out of work for a week?" Connie said, as the doctor almost dropped his stethoscope. Connie had on a skin-tight, very low-cut leopard top with painted-on, black cropped pants and five-inch leopard stilettos. She had her weekend makeup on, which meant sparkles and two-inch fake eyelashes. Eyes bulging, the doctor mumbled something about getting home to his wife as he left.

"Very funny." And then I explained the whole story, at least what I could remember.

"Jesus, Bailey! You could have been killed!" Ron exclaimed.

"Do the cops have any leads?" asked Adam.

"I don't think so. I'm sure that I just scared a burglar or something."

Ron and Carrie had made themselves comfortable on my bed. Adam had sprawled contentedly in the wing chair, but Connie was stiffly standing in the middle of the room, careful not to touch anything.

"I was clutching a human bone when they found me." I narrowed my eyes, ready for their reaction. They didn't disappoint me. After several minutes they had calmed down to a reasonable level, and I explained my lack memory of the event.

"So do you think you uncovered something, somebody wants to keep hidden?" Ron didn't look happy.

I shrugged. "For all I know, that bone could be over a hundred years old." We were silent for several minutes.

"Anybody know what time it is?" I asked. I don't know why I was so obsessed with the time. I couldn't seem to find a clock in my room.

"It's about five-fifteen," Carrie replied.

"Hmm. I'm starting to get hungry. I guess that's a good sign. Thanks so much for the balloons. These will cheer me up." I gave a loud yawn, hoping they would take the hint. "I apologize, but they've been pumping me up with pain meds that are knocking me for a loop."

"That's okay, we need to get going anyway," Ron said. "I have studying to do."

"When are they releasing you?" Carrie asked.

"Tomorrow."

"Well, I don't expect to see you this week at work," said Connie. "You just rest up. These guys can cover for you," she pointed to the trio. "Plus, Stacy will be back from vacation on Monday."

"Thanks, Connie, but I have work to do."

"No buts, Davis. Come on, guys, let's get out of this hellhole. It's giving me the creeps."

We said our goodbyes after I promised to take it easy. The food cart came in just as they were leaving. Yuck. I pushed around something that resembled turkey and green beans. The jello wasn't even palatable. Thank goodness my mother arrived shortly after I contemplated digging into something that resembled cherry pie. My father joined us a couple of minutes later carrying goodies.

"Yum, just what the doctor ordered," I said with a mouth full of Big Mac. This is sure to make me feel better." I studied them closely. They seemed well rested but a little tense.

"So what's up?" I tried for small talk, but my father wanted no part of it. He got up and walked to the bed.

"How's your head?" he inquired while prodding my skull.

"Much better. I'm a touch achy but not nearly as bad as before. I'm looking forward to going home tomorrow, that's for sure." I stretched my arms out to prove my strength.

"Who brought you all of these balloons?" my father asked.

"The guys from work. They stopped by earlier."

"How nice," my mother commented. She leaned over to give me an old watch to hold onto so I wouldn't have to worry about the time.

"Thank you."

"Of course dear. I don't know why there's no clock in this room. I took your filthy clothes home to wash. Here are some clean ones and a pair of sneakers that Rosa brought over." She dug into a bag she had brought with her. "I'll just put them in the closet. And your father brought your bracelet over to Klein's for cleaning and repairs before we came over."

"Thank you for everything," I replied "I'm so glad I found it after all of this."

"They'll call you when it's ready for pick-up. We brought your car over to the house so you don't have to deal with that tomorrow. You should have seen your father trying to drive that thing. He barely fit!" She added with a chuckle.

His eyes sparkled. "I really like that car. I looked hot in it. You should have seen all of the sexy looks I got from the girls."

"Oh, brother," my mom said as she rolled her eyes, and we both laughed. "I'm glad you're feeling better, honey. Maybe you can take a shower tonight."

It was past nine by the time they finally left for the evening. I was tired but restless, so I decided to take my mother's hint and shower. It would be good to get up and move around. Perhaps I would feel better getting some blood circulating. I managed to get my feet on the floor and shuffle into the bathroom. Wow, for the first time in my life, I felt a hundred years old. It had to be the painkillers.

I looked at myself in the mirror. "Holy crap!" I yelled. Healing cuts and scrapes on my face; my head was matted with mud, blood, and something green that I think was applied in the hospital. At least I hoped so. I had faded bruising on my neck and arms. What had happened? I couldn't remember getting bruises, and that bothered me. I flexed my arms, back, and legs. I ached a bit, but now that I was up and moving my muscles were loosening up and I was feeling better. I managed to shower with some awful hospital soap that smelled like nail polish remover. I gently shampooed my hair and even managed to brush my teeth, thanks to my mom, who had remembered to bring a toothbrush. By the time I was finished, I looked and felt halfway human.

I turned on the TV, but there wasn't much to choose from. I watched the Cubs play the Giants for a while, but I quickly tired of watching grown men spit and grab their crotches. What was up with that? I decided to read some of the trash magazines Ron had left for me. Jeez, I must be getting old. I hardly knew who anyone was in these things. I put them away and decided to walk around. After about twenty-five trips around my room, I felt utterly bored and itching to get home to my boys.

I laid back down and was just about to fall asleep when I heard a gentle tapping on the door.

"Come back tomorrow," I called. "I'm not buying, it's almost midnight." A large man had the nerve to enter anyway.

"Sorry to disturb you, but I need to speak with you about what happened last night," said a strong male voice from the doorway.

"I already talked to the Oak Park police. Who are you?"

"I'm Detective Declan O'Connor. I'm with the Special Homicide division of the CPD. Can you tell me what happened?" He quietly glided into the room.

Glided? Yep, that's what he did.

"Can I see some identification?" I demanded. "I find it hard to believe Chicago Homicide would be interested in what happened to me, let alone sending someone over at this hour."

He sighed as he dug for his badge and stepped into the light shed by the bedside reading lamp.

I almost gasped out loud as my stomach did flips. He was about six foot one, with long dark curly hair and startling brilliant blue eyes, which were now boring into mine. He had the kind of chiseled face that you would only see in GQ magazine. He had on jeans that fit perfectly, a blue dress shirt under a natural linen jacket, and a blue striped tie that looked like silk. His chocolate colored loafers looked worn, but were polished and spotless. Wow, I didn't know cops were allowed to dress so well. This guy looked positively sexy, in a scary way. Oh my, I was grateful that I wasn't hooked up to a heart monitor, because it would be beeping like crazy. *Crap,* I thought, *I couldn't look worse. Figures.* But at least I no longer smelled.

He shoved his badge in my face and said, "We are interested in any homicide that may have a connection to the Mafia."

"The Mafia? What does this have to do with the Mafia?" I asked with sudden interest.

"Unfortunately, I cannot discuss that with you at this time," he said in a condescending tone. "We are still in the fact-finding stage, and I don't speculate."

"Well, I can't tell you much. Did you talk to the Oak Park detectives? I already gave them a statement."

"I wanted to hear what happened in your own words," he said as those ice blue eyes locked onto mine.

Damn, he was making me uncomfortable. He was gorgeous, but definitely had a bug up his ass about something, which rubbed me the wrong way. I decided to tell him everything I knew so he would leave me alone to get some rest. I took him through the whole episode, at least all that I could remember. Starting from the moment my mom noticed my bracelet was missing.

"Now close your eyes and tell me your story again, but with every feeling and sensation that you had. Even if you think it may be silly or insignificant." He reached to touch me, but I pulled away.

"Are you insane? It's one o'clock in the morning! I'm tired and my head is starting to hurt again, thanks to you. I've told you everything I'm going to tonight. If you want to speak with me more, it will have to be some other time. Goodnight, Detective O'Connor." I snapped off the light with a dramatic flick of the wrist. Did I see his eyes glow? No, of course not, it must be the drugs. But then I felt his hands press against my cheeks and turn my face to look at him. I was so shocked by the ballsy move that I didn't protest, so we stayed in that position for a couple of beats. Eventually I awoke from my stupor.

"Do you mind?"

Startled by my question, he stepped back with a look of total confusion. I doubt any woman had ever dismissed him like that before, so after a time, he closed his mouth and left in a huff. *Too bad,* I thought, *he was a real looker.* And those eyes...they were almost hypnotic.

I tossed and turned for quite some time. My mind raced about the possible connections my attack had to the Mafia. Did a wise guy dump a body at the Conrad's? The thought was ludicrous. But why then was Detective O'Connor involved? I couldn't think of another reason, but my brain was still a little fuzzy. I was exhausted, but too scared to close my eyes because of the off chance I would dream about Jasmine and the monsters again. But as much as I fought it, fatigue combined with the pain medication finally succeeded in putting me into a deep uninterrupted sleep.

5

COME AND MEET THE FAMILY

I woke up at nine o'clock and was relieved to see I was alone. No prodding doctors, no nurses taking my vitals. I got out of bed without feeling dizzy, which I took as a good sign. I wanted to take another shower, but first I did some stretches to work the kinks out. I was amazed how good I felt, so I took a chance and looked at myself in the mirror. Most of the cuts and bruising were already faded. I certainly wasn't used to being laid up, so I didn't find it unusual to see I was as good as new.

I showered, brushed my teeth, and even flossed. After changing into clean clothes and combing the knots out of my locks, I opened the bathroom door to find Ron sitting on my bed.

"Hey, wow. You look better," he said with a frown.

"Don't look so excited to see me, I replied curtly.

"Oh, sorry. I was just surprised to see that your injuries are almost gone." He examined me more closely.

I stepped away from him and flicked my wrist. "I heal fast–I feel as good as new." And I twirled to prove my point.

"Great." He gave me a hug. "Get your things together. I told your parents that I would bring you back to their house. I'll go see about your discharge papers."

I gathered my belongings and sat to wait for my carriage. I needed out of this depressing place fast.

"They'll be here any minute," Ron stated when he returned to my room.

We chatted for about an hour before the nurse came in with the release papers and a wheelchair. I couldn't roll out to the parking lot fast enough. It felt good to be out of the confines of the hospital, and it wasn't long before Ron pulled up to my parents' house.

"Come in for Sunday dinner," I offered.

"Not this time. I have to pick up Randy at the airport." He leaned over and gave me a peck on the cheek.

"Oh, okay. I'll call you in the morning to go over things while I'm out of the office." I got out of his car.

He shook his head. "Always working, aren't you? Just concentrate on your recovery. We can handle things at work."

My dad met me at the door. "Bailey. Your mother and I were wondering when you were going to get here. You're looking a lot better today." He probed my head as I stood in the foyer.

"Okay, Doctor. You can stop the exam. I'm fine. Where's Mother?" I asked, even though I knew she would be cooking up a storm. I maneuvered out of my father's grasp and headed to the kitchen, where sure enough, my mom stood at the stove. I walked up behind her and gave her a big hug.

"Thanks for everything," I said, misty-eyed.

"Oh honey, you're so welcome." She appraised me from head to toe. "You look great today." She gave me her dazzling smile, and returned to whisking a sauce.

"I feel much better, thanks. Mm, that smells great. I'm starved."

"Excellent, it will do you good to have a decent meal for a change. It looks like you've lost weight."

I looked down at my loose jeans.

"I hadn't noticed. I've been working pretty hard lately. I have several large projects going at once. Maybe I forgot to eat a meal or two."

She narrowed her eyes. "Forgot?" She said it like it was a dirty word. "That's ridiculous, Bailey. No one simply *forgets* to eat."

Oh boy, I decided to change the subject. "Is Kristen around?"

Mom slid her blues in my direction, knowing I wanted out of the current conversation. After a couple of beats she sighed.

"I haven't seen her yet. She doesn't even know about what happened to you. I tried to call her cell phone, but she left it here charging."

"She must have forgotten it, again." My sister was a little absent-minded, just like our father.

"When I told Marny, she said she would let David know, but I never heard back from them," Mom continued with a worried expression. "It's unlike them not to call."

"They probably have a lot on their minds, with the kids and all," I said, but I secretly thought that my sister-in-law, the bitch, probably didn't tell him because he certainly would have called me. My mother would likely agree with my assessment, but we never discussed our mutual dislike of Marny. My mother tended to ignore unpleasantness.

"Come and sit down and I'll get you a drink. How about iced tea, or soda?" she asked.

"I'll grab a diet. Thanks."

"Don't be silly, I'm already up. I'll get it for you. Just relax," and she went into the pantry. "So what did the doctor say?"

"I have to go in on Friday for a check-up, and I should take it easy; no heavy lifting and no work. What am I supposed to do for a whole week? I have to work!"

"Maybe you could just work from home. I know Connie would let you do that," my mom said just as Rosa walked in with my dogs and a tray of flan.

"Hello, boys! Mommy missed you," I squealed as I lay on the floor, and the three of us had a moment. I looked over at Rosa. "Thanks, Rosa, for everything."

"Oh, no problem, Mees Bailey. The boyz were good at Maria's. *Los niños* love them. Feeling *muy bien*?" Rosa asked.

"Sí, gracias," I said using the little Spanish that I knew. She smiled at my effort.

Rosa was short and squat with long salt and pepper hair she always kept braided in a coil on the top of her head. Her beautiful dark eyes reflected intelligence and her Indian heritage. She had a craggy worn face with prominent brows and chin that boasted character and toughness. No one messed with Rosa and got away with it.

"Here, Rosa, let me take that," Mom said as the two of them went into the butler's pantry to talk about the day's menu.

Being at my parents' house always gave me a sense of security. As a matter of fact, all of Riverside, where I grew up, felt comforting and familiar, a place I could always count on, where neighbor helped neighbor, and community meant everything. I roamed every street and every park. Living downtown, which I also appreciated, was much more interesting, exciting, and convenient for work. It was a place where I could be invisible and solitary if I chose to, yet I could make friends and meet people on my terms. Living in the city was freeing after being in a fish bowl in Riverside. Yet Riverside would always be home, and I looked forward to my weekly visits.

I also enjoyed my time in New York City, where I partied, shopped, and, oh yeah, went to college. I considered myself a city girl in every sense of the word–and one who had plenty of street smarts, and, I might add, a bit of savvy. I had never been afraid of my surroundings, and I'd been in some sketchy situations. Therefore, when I felt a sense of anxiety sitting in my parent's kitchen, it alarmed me. The small hairs on the back of my neck tingled and goose bumps popped up along both arms. I didn't know who or why, but I knew someone was out there watching, and it gave me the creeps.

I got up and paced from window to window, but didn't see a thing. I needed to get a grip. I took some deep breaths and tried to relax before I scared the wits out of myself. Suddenly my brother and his noisy brood banged through the door, followed by my sister and her boyfriend and my grandparents.

"Grandma, Grandpa!"

With all of the noise and commotion, I quickly forgot about the sensation of being watched. Several minutes later, after two fights and one broken vase, the kids were booted outside to play.

"Don't leave the yard, it's getting dark," Marny yelled as the back door slammed shut and the house instantly felt peaceful once again. The focus turned to my recent events. Everyone gathered around the table to listen to my tale, which I was truly tired of repeating. Appropriate questions were asked after my commentary, and anxious expressions were directed my way when I was done answering them.

"Don't worry," I exclaimed. "I'm fine."

"I've told you over and over again, a woman your age should be home with a good husband and taking care of children. I just don't understand you girls today. In my day–"

"Thanks, Grandma, but I'm okay." I had to cut her off before she went on one of her tangents. The crowd let out a collective breath of relief.

No one wanted to hear Grandma bemoan bygone days and how the world was going to hell in a hand-basket.

"Well, I think it's exciting. Especially the part where you were clinging onto a bone. How cool is that?" Kristen exclaimed as Jack nodded his head in agreement.

"Do you think you could get it back?" He said in all seriousness. "I could clean it up and lacquer it for your desk as a paperweight or something."

I saw Marny cut a disgusted sneer in Jack's direction.

"I think it's being held by the police," I said.

Marny's contempt only increased. She was appalled by my sister's current behavior and her choice for a boyfriend. My brother just sat mute, and dumfounded, which was his customary persona since his marriage to my sister-in-law.

"Why would you even go to that place after dark?" she asked in a patronizing tone. "I would have sent someone else to look."

My mom called us to help carry food to the table—*just in the nick of time*, I thought. *Before I said something I would regret.*

I offered to go hunt down the kids while the women brought out the food and the men took their seats. Yes, sexist. But that was just how it was in my family.

I went out to the backyard with the dogs, but found no one. *Where did those little brats go?* I wondered. I didn't hear anything, which was a bad sign. The niggling feeling of being watched again washed over me. I looked around but saw no movement and heard no unusual sounds. The dogs were just sniffing around and marking their territory as usual. I shrugged it off and walked over to the coach house. I heard giggling. *Oh crap, they got into my mother's office.* I dreaded going in there. I opened the door. *I should just go back in the house and let their father handle it*, I thought. But I wasn't a wimp, so I might as well get it over with.

The giggling turned into all-out laughter as I ascended the stairs. I approached my mother's conference/sex room and I heard voices coming from within. *Oh no, not this room!* I thought. My mother taught technique in that room. That room was off limits to everyone, even my father. It was sacrilege to enter that room! There was no way I was going in there. I was turning to head back downstairs when I heard a shriek, so instead I threw the door open.

"What the…" I froze! My two nephews, ages ten and twelve, were enjoying a sex DVD along with the youngest, my niece, who looked horrified. There were four other kids I didn't recognize: two boys and two girls whose ages ranged from about twelve to fifteen. But the worst offender much to my horror, was my eighty-year-old grandfather, who was clearly enjoying watching the writhing woman in ecstasy on the screen.

"Grandpa! What on earth are you doing?" I roared. The dogs started barking, then the rest of the family, probably wondering where we all were, ran up to see what all of the commotion was about. The crowd pushed into the room.

"Who are these children, and what are you all up to?" Marny hollered as she tried to be heard above the barks and commotion. Thankfully, the lights went on and the DVD stopped playing. The kids stood, and my niece ran to her dad for consolation. Interesting. The rest appeared to be hiding something behind their backs. My grandpa slowly rose and quietly edged his way out the door, where my grandma waited for him, grinning. I heard her whisper, "I hope you learned something at least," and I saw my grandpa give her a huge smile. Oh, god, I thought I was going to be sick. Meanwhile, Marny was not pleased.

"Give me what you are hiding. All of you!" She demanded.

They slowly handed over several vibrators, dildos—a couple of interesting looking ones—and various edible lubricants. I thought Marny was going to have a stroke; I could practically see steam coming out of her ears. I heard amused snickers from Kristen and Jack. Rosa looked about ready to faint, crossing herself and mumbling, but her eyes sparkled, and did I see a smirk? My father looked upset, and David, well, he just looked…clueless as usual.

Marny had just begun to launch into a long lecture and hand out punishments, when a couple of my mother's neighbors barged in, demanding to know where their kids were.

"Uh oh." The shit was about to hit the fan.

As if on cue, everything erupted, and the yelling and finger-pointing commenced. Much to my horror, Detective O'Connor strolled in, trying to stifle a laugh, probably wondering whether or not to go for his gun to control the rowdy bunch. Oh, man, he must have had heard everything my crazy family said, including my embarrassing grandparents. I managed to maneuver over to the doorway where he was leaning. But before I could say anything, my irate mother came storming in and ordered everyone out. She berated all of the kids, including my grandfather, who had the good sense to look ashamed. She made it clear to everyone that her office was completely off limits from now on, even to the adults, without her permission. Everybody promptly and quietly left the room. But before I could close and lock the door, I noticed Rosa had taken the DVD out of the player and slipped it into her pocket. Jeez.

Detective O'Connor waited for me to fiddle with the lock. Much to my annoyance, he looked as handsome as ever, wearing a linen jacket and black slacks. His cocky smile said it all. My family was nuts. Too bad I already knew that.

He held out his hand for me to shake, knowing that I held a huge double-sided dildo. I quickly put it down and we both left the coach house. He could barely contain his laughter.

"Nice office. What exactly does your mother do for a living?" he asked with a chuckle.

"She's a clinical sex therapist," I retorted a bit snappishly. "What are you doing here?"

He chose to ignore my question. "Nice family. A little strange, but nice."

We took the path to the kitchen door. It opened onto the smells and sounds of family life. The detective looked taken aback and a bit frightened.

"Come and join us for dinner, Detective?" my mother asked.

The detective seemed to snap out of it and entered the kitchen, extending a hand to my parents. "O'Connor. Please, just call me Declan."

He followed my parents into the dining room, where my family was piling large quantities of food onto their plates. Almost as if they've never eaten before.

"He was just leaving," I said at the same time that the detective sat in a chair at the table.

"Bailey, don't be rude. That's not like you," my mother admonished me with *that* tone. I immediately shut up. Jeez, I guess I had no choice in the matter; he was staying. *That's okay,* I thought. *Wait until he participates in a Davis family dinner. He'll run for the hills.*

The kids were unusually quiet sitting at the kitchen table while the adults ate in relative peace the dining room. They were probably worn out from their little movie premiere in the office. What wonderful creatures.

"Elvin, what were you thinking of? How could you watch those movies with the children?" Marny demanded of my grandfather. My brother just sat there with a mouthful of food oblivious to the question and his wife in general.

"What did you say?"

Grandpa always played up his hearing loss when he didn't want to answer a question. Marny was just about to ask it again when we heard a scream coming from the kitchen. We all ran in to see Greg pounding on his brother.

"Greg! Stop that this instant!" Marny ordered. "David, can't you do something?" David went over to Greg and lifted him off of his brother.

"Hey, Dad, put me down!" Greg demanded.

"They are just playing, Marny. It's perfectly normal," David made the mistake of stating.

"Not for *my* children, it's not!" she stammered back.

Oh boy; we all cleared out of the kitchen to let them fight it out.

"Makes you want to rush out and have kids, doesn't it?" Detective O'Connor said in my ear as we went back to our seats.

I couldn't help but smile at the remark. He was telling the hard truth. My brother's family was enough to turn anyone off from having kids.

"The ribs are wonderful, Mrs. Davis," he said, sucking up to my mom. She was thrilled at the compliment, as he probably figured she would be.

"Please call me Katherine, and my husband is Henry. And thank you. I use a smoker. It gives them a better flavor." The conversation turned to more mundane matters. We talked right over the yelling coming from the kitchen. I felt mortified that the detective was witnessing my family in such a way, but this was the reality of the Davis clan.

"So are you a Chicago or Oak Park cop?" my sister asked. I noticed Jack was unusually quiet tonight.

"I'm a Chicago Homicide Detective."

"Wow, I bet you see some really gross things," my grandma said with a broad smile on her face. Much to my dismay, I noticed she was missing her front tooth, and a greasy red spot was spreading on my grandpa's left shirt pocket. My sister must have also noticed because she asked, "What happened to your tooth, Grams?"

"Oh, your grandpa has it in his pocket." And she went back to gnawing on a rib.

"Isn't it kinda sexy?" my grandpa said.

Mom dropped her fork with a clatter, and Dad visibly blanched. Marny, finished with her tirade, stomped out the front door with a slam. David re-entered the room, visibly shaken, but calmly walked over to his place, sat and continued to eat.

Oh, god, was this embarrassing! I turned to the detective, who was trying not to choke on his food from laughing so hard. I was starting to get annoyed.

"Remember, you wanted to stay. I bet you'll be running back over next week for dinner," I stated matter-of-factly.

"Why, thank you for the invitation. I would be glad to join you next week. Is there anything I could contribute to the meal?" he managed to say with a straight face.

Mom was beaming, but Jack looked crestfallen. No one else paid much attention.

"No, of course not. Just bring yourself," said my mother apparently thrilled. But I couldn't believe my ears. Was he nuts?

"Very well. I'll look forward to it, and I thank you in advance. The food is delicious, and this has been very entertaining," he replied seriously. He *was* nuts. Certifiable even. And he spoke a little strangely too; *very formally*, hmm.

My mom kept eyeballing the two of us through dessert. I knew what that meant: trouble. David said nothing for the rest of the evening, and Marny never returned, but his cell phone rang and he ran upstairs to talk privately. The kids were unusually quiet and went straight down to the playroom in the basement for video game entertainment. I guessed they were tired from all of their earlier deviant behavior. My grandparents and Rosa, who had brought her own car, left as soon as the dishes were done. Rosa probably wanted to watch her new movie, and I didn't want to know why my grandparents wanted to leave early. Yuck. The rest of us went into the living room to settle with coffee, or in my case, tea.

We chatted about nothing in particular. Jack was unusually quiet, but I noticed my sister looked somewhat flushed.

"So, Declan, how long have you been a detective?" she asked with her gorgeous smile, batting her long eyelashes.

Oh, my god. Was she flirting with him? How annoying was that

"Oh, about fifteen years now. I started as a patrolman out of high school."

"How wonderful," she practically purred.

Kristen always had a way with men. She was almost six feet tall, with beautifully shiny auburn hair and big hazel eyes. She was stunning, and most men groveled at her feet. Jack was a complete change from her usual preppy rich guy who ended up treating her poorly. He was a big, kind teddy bear. I started to wonder if Kristen was getting itchy for something new. Why did the thought bother me?

That was it. I'd had enough of this. Besides, I needed to go home, take a pain killer, soak in a hot bath, and crawl into my comfy bed for a long uninterrupted night's sleep. I stood up and stretched.

"I think I'm going to take the boys and head on home. I'm getting tired."

"Oh, my. I'm so sorry, honey. Of course you need to get home. Henry, maybe you should take her. She looks exhausted."

"That's not"–I was about to protest but was abruptly cut off.

"I'll make sure she makes it home safely, Katherine. I'll follow her closely." The detective cut his baby blues to me, and my stomach did flips again. Damn. My mother noticed every nuance. Double damn.

We said our goodbyes, grabbed the packages of leftovers my mom made up for us to take home, and made our way to our cars.

"I need to speak with you again about what happened. Do you remember anything else?"

I shook my head. "Sorry. Besides, my head is starting to hurt again. I just need to sleep." I opened my car door.

"How come your head always hurts when I want to talk to you?" He sounded rather pissed off.

I shrugged. "If you want to follow me home, you're welcome to, but I still can't tell you anything more."

"We'll see."

I couldn't believe he was actually going to follow me home. I found it interesting and a bit odd that he would be working on this case, and at such peculiar hours too. I guess investigating homicides was not a nine-to-five job.

He managed to stay behind me most of the way home but eventually got stuck at a red light. I never saw him again, so I assumed he'd gone on to bother someone else. I was feeling disappointed and hating myself for it. Was I actually looking forward to bantering with this man? Hmm. I contemplated this as I entered Cedar Street, turned right into my alley, and finally made it into my garage. I let the dogs out to do their business in the backyard, and then we took the elevator up to the main level.

I looked around, let out a breath I didn't realize I'd been holding, and felt a million times better. I loved being home. I'd bought the Romanesque Revival greystone on a fluke. One of my clients suddenly got transferred to San Francisco before we could start the planned renovation on the house, and he was in desperate need to sell it fast. He had purchased it from an estate liquidation a year prior and knew it was in dreadful shape, no condition to put on the market. He didn't want to put any money into it because he needed the funds to buy another house in San Francisco. He sold it to me for what he paid for it, dirt cheap for the neighborhood, and we were both happy. It had taken me two years and lots of elbow grease, not to mention money, to get it to my liking. But it finally was.

The four-story house had been built in 1892 and was in a perfect location, two houses over from Lake Shore Drive and around the corner from the Magnificent Mile. My neighborhood was in a trendy section of the Gold Coast but it was still fairly quiet, which I liked.

Four stories sounded huge, but actually, the house was only twenty-five feet wide by about seventy-five feet deep. Each level was just big enough to accommodate two large rooms with a couple of closets or smaller areas. Almost all of the houses were identical in size and shape on my block, butted up against one another with differing facades to add some interest.

I had redesigned some of the spaces to accommodate my lifestyle. I added a large office in the English basement level, along with a guest suite and bath. On the main level I created my dream kitchen and added a small media area within it. There was also a great room on this floor, along with a small library. I used one of the spare bedroom spaces on the third level as a recreation room, adding a wet bar and pool table. I had another guest room and bath on that level as well. My sanctuary was on the on the fourth and final level. I used the other spare bedroom on that floor to enlarge the master closet and bath. I also added an elevator that ran from the basement to the roof, where I had installed an elaborate rooftop garden and party area with wet bar and small kitchen. The views of the lake were fantastic up there, so it was where I entertained my friends in the warmer months. Finally, I added an apartment over the existing coach house with a large rooftop deck. It was the perfect place for Rosa to live. Unfortunately, she stood in front of me now with a concerned look on her face.

"You go sleep!" She pointed to the stairs. "I take care to boyz."

We both turned when the doorbell rang.

Crap, I thought. He was tenacious. I stomped to the door, beating Rosa, and threw it open to find no one there. I looked down to see a large manila envelope lying on my stoop. I scanned the area but saw nothing unusual. I studied the envelope closely.

"That's funny, no return address or postage. Strange." *What the heck could this possibly be,* I wondered as I went into the library, Rosa at my heels, to take a better look. I ripped open the envelope and carefully drew out its contents: a picture of me leaving the hospital with a large slash across my neck and blood and gore dripping down my body. The hairs on my arms stood on end as I read the message:

KEEP YOUR MOUTH SHUT OR ELSE!

It was written in giant red lettering, and dripping in what appeared to be blood. I heard Rosa's sharp intake of breath as she ogled the image, shook her head, and then proceeded to go upstairs without a single word. She came back down holding a large baseball bat and mumbling expletives in Spanish. Scary. Rosa was small to be sure, but when she was mad, everyone scattered.

I felt a little queasy and was about to tell her to put the bat away when the doorbell rang for the second time that night. I was getting up to answer it when Rosa ordered me to sit. I automatically sat my ass down, as she instructed. I did take my phone out, and dialed 911, and held my finger over the *send* button.

Rosa pounded to the door with the bat held high, and I could no longer just sit. I sneaked up behind her. We both let out a collective breath when we saw it was Detective O'Connor.

"Mees Bailey. Deetective for you. Come in, Deetective." She unlocked and opened the outer door to let him in.

"What happened?" he demanded as he eyed the bat Rosa held, and our frightened faces.

I led him to the library. "I'm actually a little relived to see you here," I said as I handed him the envelope. He looked it over and a small sliver of white sparked in his eyes, along with a menacing scowl.

"How did you get this?"

"Please sit." I had to gather my wits. "Rosa, can you please make some tea? Or would you prefer coffee, Detective?"

"Tea is fine."

I could tell that he was mad and a little...worried? "I came home and the doorbell rang," I told him "I went out, but no one was there except that, lying on the stoop." I pointed to the envelope. He jumped up and flew out the door. I was beginning to wonder whether he would return, when about fifteen minutes later he reappeared and followed me back to the library, where we sat back down.

"Here, your tea is getting cold." I gave him his cup and our fingers touched. A tingling sensation went up my arm and settled in my stomach. Oh boy. I had to get it together!

"Is it safe...take *perros* out?" Rosa asked.

"Yes, whoever left the envelope is long gone," the Detective answered. "But stay in the yard, please."

"Just go to bed after the boys are finished," I said. "We'll be fine." She narrowed her eyes at me. "Really. Make sure everything is locked up tight. Thank you, Rosa. Good night." She turned and huffed off with the dogs.

"She's very protective of me." I glanced his way, but he didn't seem impressed by Rosa's security skills.

"Good. You need protection." He said "I will stay tonight so you can get some sleep." He continued to sip his tea while studying the gruesome image.

"Oh, really?" *The nerve of this guy!*

"Yes, really. Something is going on here, and you should be taking it more seriously. I talked to my superiors, and we all agree that you need protection. This threat may be quite serious. It does not seem as if you just spooked a burglar."

"Oh really?" was all I could think of to say. What a dope. He only stared. "Well, you can't possibly stay."

"Why on earth not?" He looked positively shocked by my reluctance.

"Well, for starters, I don't even know you, and secondly, I think I can manage just fine on my own, and thirdly, I have the dogs and Rosa—"

"Humf, those dogs of yours are not exactly the vicious guard dogs you need, and Rosa? Don't get me started with that idea. You're certainly stubborn, Ms. Davis, and a little too brave for your own good. You have no idea of what you are dealing with here."

"And you do? If so, please enlighten me." I was getting angrier by the second. I took a deep breath to try to calm my nerves and tamp down my annoyance.

"Detective O'Connor, I am tired and a bit sore still," I lied. "All I want to do is fall into my own tub and soak for a good hour before I dive onto my pillow-topped mattress and five-hundred-thread count sheets for a full eight hours of sleep. I'm sure this is just a prank and not to be taken seriously. The bur...person who attacked me could have done much worse, but didn't. I don't remember much anyway. So you see, I'm no threat to him." I was proud of myself. I had said it like I meant it.

"Bailey." He gazed at me with those eyes. Those incredibly gorgeous eyes that spread liquid fire through my veins. "You must heed my warning. It's not safe for you to be alone."

Heed? Did he actually say heed? He looked sincere and I was beginning to feel sorry for him. After all, he was just trying to help.

"I understand your concern, Detective, and I appreciate it. Really. But I will turn on the security system and make sure everything is locked up tight. I'll even go to bed holding my phone. I promise. I do not need, or want, a babysitter. Now if you will excuse me, I have a bathtub calling my name." I showed him the door, to his utter astonishment.

He hesitated, perhaps hoping I would change my mind. "Well, if you insist. Please call me immediately if anything, and I mean anything, happens, no matter how insignificant. Please promise me that much."

Wow, he was really laying it on thick. "I promise. But really, I'm not concerned about this. They are just trying to scare me. Besides, I can't tell anyone anything because I honestly don't remember. But if you keep this up, you *will* start to scare me."

He just stared and nodded once. As he left I thought I heard him mumble "Good."

After my bath, sleep did not come easily. I lay in bed tossing and turning, even though I had taken a low-dose sleeping pill. I kept thinking of the detective and those hypnotic eyes. There was something about him, something almost familiar about him. Eventually, I finally fell into a fitful sleep.

I was a small child, not more than four, running from the monster. It was always the same monster. He was huge, with claws for fingers, ruby lips, and long sharp fangs. But the most frightening were his bluish-white eyes that glowed pure white when he saw me. He growled as I sped past him, dodging his attempts to catch me. I was fast, almost as fast as he was. I ran down what seemed like an endless staircase, lower and lower, to conceal myself in my favorite hiding place in the subterranean spaces of the cellar. "Mother!" I cried to myself. "Mother, where are you?"

Just as I rounded a corner to get to my hidey-hole, the monster grabbed me from behind and threw me across the room. It hurt, but not as much as I thought it would. I managed to get back on my feet as the monster pulled out a knife. A huge old-fashioned-looking knife. I began to scream as he drew nearer, showing me his fangs, which were dripping with blood and saliva. He was hungry and he was going to eat me. I ran to my hidey-hole and dove in deep. The monster roared out of frustration as he tried to go in after me. He seized my leg and I thought it was going to rip off. His claws dug in deep, and the pain was excruciating. Suddenly he let go of me and was gone. I heard a loud piercing scream and then a popping, slurping sound....

I was startled awake by the whining of the dogs. I was drenched in sweat and shaking. My god, I hadn't had that dream in years. I looked at the bedside clock. Only 11:46, I got out of bed, went to the French doors, and opened them to let the chilly night air cool my damp skin. I noticed no headache, no aches and pains from my incident. In fact, I felt strong and invigorated.

So why was I suddenly having this dream once again after all these years? I tried to remember the last time…hmm, maybe as far back as my late teens. It was always the same, and I always awoke at that terrifying sound. I thought about the awful nightmare from the other night. The two had one similarity: the same monsters. The result of which was always constant—waking up drench in sweat, heart racing, and tremendous horror clutching my psyche. What could it possibly mean?

Suddenly, I felt the now-familiar sensation of being watched. I scanned the street below my window and spotted a man sitting in an undistinguished sedan, staring at me. It was the familiar shape of O'Connor. I should have felt reassured by his insistence on protecting me, but I didn't. I no longer wanted to think about what had happened, and the foreboding that I was experiencing. I was tired of it all. I wanted to think of nothing, and after what seemed like an eternity, I fell into a deep and uneventful sleep.

CR80

Declan watched, entranced by the vision in ghostly white that came out onto the balcony. She was the most infuriating woman he had ever met. She had no idea what danger she had stumbled onto, but he couldn't help but be impressed with her fortitude. She was definitely not the typical human woman that he was so accustomed to. On the contrary, she had many qualities that he himself possessed.

Declan was a Centurion, an honor bestowed upon very few select members of his kind, and even more rare for someone a mere four hundred years old. He led a contingent of warriors—a military elite team similar to today's SEALS. Only his SEAL team needed very few weapons. They all had special powers, some innate, others sharpened through decades of vigorous training. Declan himself possessed great power for someone so young. He fingered the butt of his custom-made Sig at his side. Just because he didn't particularly need weapons didn't mean he didn't have any. On the contrary, the Centurion Brigades used some of the most sophisticated weaponry and surveillance equipment in the world, not to mention special devices made specifically for interrogation. In that aspect, they had not evolved much since the Middle Ages. If the American armed forces could see their hidden weapons labs, bunkers, and torture caves, they would piss in their collective pants.

His team and others like them, from all over the world, were the protectors of their kind. In a sense, they were also protectors of humankind, from the darker side of the Vampire Nation and others that may threaten the status quo. Vampires had roamed this planet for thousands of years virtually undetected. If the human race knew of their existence, the wars that were sure to ensue would be horrific. So the Vampire Nation Council secured and financed elite forces, such as Declan's warriors, to eliminate rogue vampires, clans, and other species that would threaten to expose them, and also harm the human race.

So Declan, Centurion Guard and leader of one of the best fighting forces in America and possibly the world, sat. Sat and stared at a human woman whose life was in certain danger from what he hoped was a Russian rogue vampire named Mikel, one he had been hunting for over fifty years. A blink of an eye, really, but not finding him was certainly starting to piss him off.

He watched as Bailey locked eyes with his, sighed, and went inside. He could smell a hint of lavender that was probably remnants of her earlier bath. He also smelled fear. This surprised him, because he hadn't smelled it on her when he should have: when she was attacked and almost killed, and when she received the gruesome image. She'd been shocked and mad, but not scared. This was strange behavior; but it was not his concern. His focus was on the vampire out to kill her.

So far there was no trace of Mikel. But he knew his scent well, the same scent that lingered around Bailey's house and the place where she was attacked. This rogue vampire had been killing humans around the globe. Declan believed he was also connected to a large rogue clan that had proven extremely difficult to pin down—a clan, he believed, that had been globally recruiting rogues to do its dirty work. He had tracked the clan to France, where he thought their headquarters was located, and had linked them to money laundering, kidnapping, extortion, illegal flesh trafficking, and slavery— and of course murder of vampires as well as humans. A big no-no. The Council had given all Centurion leaders orders to find this clan, and to make it their top priority.

His mind would not turn off the image of Bailey Davis. Her reddish-blonde tresses cascaded around her slender shoulders, their strands fluttering slowly in the night breeze. Her defiant stature was an honorable trait, yet it was her sense of humor that seemed to better define her. He shook his head, remembering her crazy family and her obvious chagrin at their antics, but loving them all the same. But truth be told, Declan reveled in those startling green eyes. He had never seen such beauty in eyes before. Her voluptuous body, tough bravado, and defiant independence were only a precursor to the rich depths and intriguing clarity of those magnificent emerald pools.

"Jesus, Declan, snap out of it!" he demanded, shaking his head. There was no way on earth he would get mixed up with a human. Especially a human with some sort of abilities. He'd been shocked to find that his aura did not work on her. He had never before touched a human and not known exactly what they were thinking. Adding to his confusion was the fact that she defied his energies by not obeying his wishes. Declan held special powers of persuasion that humans could not fight. He had never before failed to bend one to his will like putty. Not that he tried often, of course. But when she'd unwittingly obstructed his aura, he'd been astonished, and he knew this revelation needed to be further explored. But not now. Now, he had other things to worry about.

Declan knew he should immediately report his findings to the Council, but hesitated to do so. Why? he silently asked himself. It was a question he had yet to fully grasp. A few more days of surveillance and he hoped to have more answers. Yes, even just a few more hours and he should have much more information on Miss Bailey Davis, and her relationship to the rogue, to report back to his superiors.

6

RUNNING CAN BE DANGEROUS
TO YOUR HEALTH

"**C**rap! Is it morning already?" I got no response from the dogs. Just a steady, beady-eyed gaze, a sniff, and a smacking of two pairs of lips. Damn.

"Where is Rosa?" They just continued to ogle. "Come on, guys, you know I'm not a morning person. Why can't you take yourselves for a walk like civilized people do?" I got nothing. "All right, I'm getting up." I checked my clock. 10:20 AM. *Oops, I guess I slept in a bit,* I thought, just as Rosa made an appearance carrying towels.

"*Buenos dias*, Meez Bailey. How are you feeeling today?"

"I'm feeling fine, as a matter of fact. I think I'll take the dogs for a run in the park. I assume that is what they've been staring me down for this morning." They hadn't moved. I knew the doctors and my parents would have a fit if they knew what I was about to do, but they didn't know about my strength. And what they didn't know wouldn't hurt them.

Rosa just shrugged and walked into my bathroom. "I feed them hours ago and they pee," she mumbled as she put away the towels and proceeded to clean the bathroom.

I hopped out of bed and opened the French doors. It irked me that I felt a little twinge of disappointment at not seeing Detective O'Connor at the curb. "It's another gorgeous day, everyone!" The dogs whimpered impatiently. "All right, all right, keep your knickers on."

I quickly brushed my teeth, put my hair up in a ponytail, threw water on my face, changed into my running gear, and headed downstairs. I was a bit annoyed that I had yet to hear from the office, so I quickly dialed Ron's direct line and was told he was in conference with my CAD techs. Hmmph. I'd try again later. I hated being left out of the loop. I had some work I could do from home, and that thought settled my restless urge to go into the office. But still...my thoughts were suddenly interrupted by the whining of Jerry who was practically jumping out of his skin to get outside.

"Oh, all right. Come on then."

It was one of those rare days when the air was crisp, clean, and held just a hint of autumn. The boys led me to the park, where we were left in solitude since everyone else was either at work or still asleep. Every so often a nanny pushing a baby carriage gave the boys a fun distraction. I was just working up a good pace, my hairline damp with sweat, my muscles working at ironing out the kinks from the past few days, when Tom stopped dead in his tracks and started growling.

"What on earth is wrong with you? Come on, boy," I cooed as I nudged him along. "You're about to ruin my workout." We were just coming to the area of the park, about three miles from the brownstone, that had a thicket of trees off to my left and a pond to the right, with more trees beyond, obscuring Lake Shore Drive. I stopped to listen, but all was quiet and I had no indication that anything was amiss, except for the hairs rising on the back of my arms.

I, along with both dogs, began to sense a presence. I looked around but no one was there. I quickly realized that I had nothing to use to protect us. I'd even left my cell phone on the kitchen counter. Stupid!

The dogs were growling, and Jerry began to shake. I bent down to console them and listened for anything out of the ordinary. I had always possessed keen senses. Or so my mother said. I heard birds darting in and out of trees, squirrels gathering for the upcoming winter months, the distant sound of a siren, and the hum of traffic along LSD. But no other sounds were clear. Just as I was about to resume my run, I heard it. It sounded like a gentle sucking, along with a very low and dangerous growl.

"What on earth?" I murmured as I whipped around, trying to pinpoint the sound. I concentrated on the reverberations, blocking out all other noise and distractions. The boys were shaking so badly it scared the hell out of me. They both had a line of fur standing on end and running along their spines.

"It's okay, boys," I said, trying to reassure them, or maybe myself. Suddenly I heard the noise again. I stood up. "There!" I pointed to the line of trees furthest away from us, wanting the dogs to understand me. I easily spotted the lone figure standing, impossibly, on a huge branch at the top of what had to be a thirty-five-foot tree, at least a half a mile from where we stood. He was too far for me to distinguish his features, but I sensed danger, anger, and—hunger?

"What the hell is that?" I couldn't believe my eyes. "Come on, boys." I dragged them back the way we came. They were more than happy to comply. We'd never run so fast, and I was surprised that the dogs kept the pace—obviously having the same feeling as I did. Suddenly, I felt as if someone was a hairs-breadth away from me. I heard the insatiable thirst of a hunters yearning for the kill as warm and fetid breath brushed against the nape of my neck. An insane urge to stop and fight overwhelmed me, but I pushed it back, and we didn't let up our pace until we passed North Avenue. Now the dogs labored to catch up as I all but flew out of the park and onto Inner LSD.

I finally relaxed enough to slow to a normal run as I passed several people that were out enjoying the day. I noticed a number of them look our way, a few stopped to outright ogle. Did I look as crazy as I felt? What in God's name had I seen, and why did he remind me of my nightmares? What the hell was happening? I felt as if I was about to lose my sanity.

The dogs were spent; their tongues practically dragged on the ground. I realized that they needed to stop for a rest, then walk the rest of the way home. Thankfully, it was just two more blocks. Poor babies. I bent to pet them as I scanned the area where we came out of the park. I couldn't see anything but I knew he was there, watching.

"Sorry boys. Don't worry, we're going home." They seemed to understand and led the way. As we rounded the corner, Detective O'Connor hopped down from my front stoop and came running towards us. I must have appeared distressed, because he drew close and started yelling.

"What the hell happened, and where have you been? Why does it look like you've just been through a squall, and why are your eyes the color of the sun? And look at your dogs. Did you try to kill them?"

I gaped at him, astonished by his perception. But even mute from shock, I found him unbearably annoyingly sexy. "Please let me pass. I need to get the dogs in the house and watered, and then I will try to explain what just happened."

He scowled, then gave me a curt nod. I watched as he went to the corner and stared in the direction we'd come from. I shrugged, then went in to take care of the dogs. Eventually, he followed me into the house.

After the boys settled on their beds in the kitchen, I retrieved a bottle of water for me and one for the detective, and I asked him to follow me upstairs. Rosa had left a note on the white board that she was out at the grocery store. Good, we had some privacy for a while. I led him into my sitting room off my bedroom. I don't know why I felt comfortable enough to take him up to my private sanctuary, but I did.

"Please sit while I shower and change." I punched in some soothing music and left him to *Architectural Digest*. He looked incredulous. *Too bad*, I thought, and walked away.

The cascading hot water loosened my tense muscles and gave me back my sense of peace, at least somewhat. I went to my mirror to wipe off the condensation so I could take a better look at myself. Damn, all the years I'd spent hiding my problems. Ever since I could remember, my eyes changed from green to a translucent yellowish flame when I was very upset or angry. I often felt more aware during these spells. I could hear and see things differently. Sometimes I could even sense what others were doing, thinking, and even feeling. Even from afar. But what frightened me the most was the fact that I was so much stronger during these episodes. One time, after a particularly ugly fight with John, I went for a run. Not just any run. I ran all the way to the Indiana border before I realized it. I remember walking the last couple of miles home in a daze, still astonished that I'd reached the "Welcome to Indiana" sign. I never told anyone, never dared to. But now, after only a couple of encounters, I'd let Detective O'Connor see my defect. God, how stupid I was! No wonder people were staring at me! I needed to get myself under control.

Once I threw on some makeup, gathered my curls into a knot at the top of my head, put on a cute top and my favorite jeans, and stepped into a well-worn pair of Prada loafers, I felt almost human again. I was even ready to face the inquisition that was sure to commence in my sitting room.

"Okay, I'm ready to divulge all," I announced to an empty room. "Where on earth did he go?" I glanced around but saw no one. And then I heard the distinct mumble of male voices down in the kitchen. What was going on?

"I don't know why you have any say in what Bailey does. She and I have a long history, and I am a good friend of hers," I overheard coming from the kitchen.

I knew that voice! John was here. Both men abruptly stopped their argument when I entered the room. Rosa was putting away groceries, pretending she wasn't listening, but I knew otherwise. She didn't miss a trick.

"John, what are you doing here? Is there a question about the Conrad project?"

"No–no, not at all, Bailey," he said in a frosty voice. "I am very upset that you never called me about your attack and that I had to hear it through the grapevine. Damn it, Bailey, you could have been killed!" He grabbed me and held me tight. What was with everybody invading my space today?

"I'm fine, John, look." I shoved him away and twirled around. "No worse for the wear."

He appraised me critically, and I guess decided I wasn't a damsel in distress. He nodded, wrapped a possessive arm around my waist, and turned to the detective. "So how do you know my Bailey?"

"What?" I almost choked. As I detangled myself from his clutches, I dared to glance the detective's way. He was smiling. The bastard.

"Shall I leave you two alone?"

"*Yes! No!*" John and I said in unison. "No, John was just leaving." I glanced towards his disappointed and annoyed look. "Detective O'Connor and I have some things to discuss." His eyebrows rose.

"Oh, I didn't know he was a cop," John said with surprise.

"Detective," O'Connor added in a somewhat menacing tone.

"Whatever. Maybe I should stay for support–wait just a minute. You are the one who shut down our project."

The detective just nodded.

"When can we get back to work? We have schedules to keep and clients that will be disappointed," John griped.

"When we finish our investigation." O'Connor sniffed.

I got the distinct impression that the detective was getting irritated.

"John, I promise to call when we can get back in," I said as I steered him to the front door. He suddenly turned, took my face in his hands and laid one of his better kisses on me. Shit, I couldn't help but respond just a little, but quickly came to my senses.

"Stop that!"

"What?"

"You know what. This is not happening, John. Not now, and probably not ever," I whispered so the detective couldn't hear the embarrassing exchange.

His face fell. "I'm not going away, Bailey. I made a huge mistake leaving you, and I'm not going to make that mistake again. Ever. I want you, and I will do anything to get you back. Even if it takes years to do it." He walked out the door before I had a chance to react.

"Damn," I mumbled as I watched the detective for his reaction. His expression was much more somber. "Nice boyfriend."

"He's not my boyfriend."

"Well, he certainly acts as if he is intimately familiar with you."

"Yeah, well, that was a long time ago and I'm over it," I said it with a lot more certainty than I felt. "Let's get comfortable in the kitchen; I'm starved. We can talk while I try to make something to eat." I was taking the frying pan out of the cupboard with the detective looking on from the island when Rosa came running up, thankfully taking over.

We walked back to the library after being shooed from the kitchen. "So you can't make your own lunch?" he said incredulously.

"Of course I can!" Even though I hated cooking. "It's just that Rosa gets mad if I do. She believes the kitchen to be her territory and I'm just in the way." I paused. "Well, honestly, I am kind of a disaster in the kitchen."

He smiled that big beautiful smile of his. "Then Rosa rescued me from certain death?"

"Ha, ha, very funny. I'm good at other things." *Did I just say that?* He graciously pretended not to have heard. "Okay, well I guess we should get started. I do have some drawings to get to and a few phone calls to make." I was quickly becoming a blithering idiot.

"Yes, please sit down here by me and relax, and explain what happened this morning." He patted the sofa right next to him.

"Okey dokey." *Okey dokey? What a moron!* I sat in the chair across from him and recounted my story. I was seriously worried that he would commit me to a mental hospital after I told him about the thing in the tree, but he didn't flinch. He just sat there, taking it all in.

"Okay, now close your eyes and tell me what you felt."

I glared at him like he was nuts.

"Go ahead. Close them and just relax. You would be amazed at the things you can remember when you just relax."

I did as he instructed. "Now take some deep breaths and think about running with the dogs. What did you hear? What did you smell? What did you feel?"

After a few minutes I answered. "I smelled the lake, and a hint of rain in the air. I smelled the beginning of the leaves changing and the faint scent of exhaust from the cars on LSD." After a long pause, "I smelled– hmm." I could tell that the detective went still. "Something like rancid meat…and….anger? I felt worried and I know the dogs were terrified." I opened my eyes. "You're right, I did remember more."

He looked very intent. "So this thing you saw in the tree. Could it have been a large bird?"

I shrugged. "I guess it could have been a crow. I just got the impression that it was staring right at me. The dogs sensed it too. You should have seen them. They were so scared, poor babies." There was no mistaking the sense that someone was angry and wanted to harm me, even followed right behind me as we were running full out, back to the house. But I wasn't about to admit that to the detective. He would certainly think I was crazy and may even decide to lock me up after all.

"It was probably nothing. I guess I'm still a little out of sorts from the attack."

"Hmmp." He paused, thinking intently. "Bailey, this is what I'm going to do, and I want no arguments. I'm going to stay in your guest room until we can catch whoever is doing this. You may work from home, for now. I will accompany you to work if it needs to come to that. I will arrange for Rosa and the dogs to stay somewhere safe until this is over." He stopped, and my face must have shown my feelings, because his expression hardened for a fight.

"Who the hell do you think you are?" I demanded. "I should kick your ass all the way out of my house right now. What century are you living in?" He reared back at that.

"What do you mean?"

"I mean this is the twenty-first century, and I don't need a man to keep me safe. And I especially do not need anyone telling me what to do. So you listen to me and listen good! I will not have you, or anyone else stay here to protect me! I will go to work tomorrow and—"

"No you won't!"

"Just watch me!" I was not going to be a prototypical weak female. He needed to understand that being worried about and coddled was not in my genetic makeup. It was never going to happen as long as I stood on my own two feet. I met his eyes, and he seemed taken aback. *Oh crap, my eyes.* I got up and turned my head away from him.

"Let me see," he demanded.

"No. Now get out." I knew I was being unreasonable and just plain rude, but I couldn't help it. I was taking my life back starting now. We both spun around as Rosa came through the doorway with lunch.

"Hola."

"Hola, Rosa. Detective O'Connor was just leaving," I said, as I ran up the stairs to my refuge and away from him.

Later, after I had eaten a delicious lunch of black beans and rice prepared by Rosa, I stewed about what I'd said to the detective. I was mean. I knew it. And he saw my eyes again. What was happening to me? It seemed as if my episodes were becoming more frequent. Or maybe I was getting angry more often. I turned to look at the boys, who were still soundly asleep on their beds in the kitchen.

"We had a rough morning, didn't we?"

Not even a flutter of an eyelid. *I bet they will sleep well into the afternoon,* I thought, as the phone rang.

"Ms. Davis? This is Detective Haines from the Oak Park Police."

"Oh, hi." I was not enthusiastic. "What can I do for you?"

"I just wanted to ask you to come to the station and sign a statement. The case has been turned over to Chicago Special Investigations, but we need to just finish up some paperwork."

"Oh, yes. I've met with Detective O'Connor a few times."

"That would be him," he grunted. "So can you come in sometime today or tomorrow? The paperwork will be here for you to look over and sign."

"Okay, sure. I'll try to come over tomorrow morning."

"Great. How are you feeling?"

"I'm back to my old self."

"Good, well, see you in the morning then."

Crap. I didn't want to deal with this anymore. I had just put the phone on the cradle when it rang once again. Ron's name showed on my caller ID.

"Hey, boss, just checking in. How are you feeling?"

"I'm fine. So fine, in fact, that I'll see you in a bit. Please have some prelims on the Trent job on my desk, Carl and Cathy's contracts for me to sign, and the revision of the windows in the Conklin's master suite. I need to work on the millwork in that area. Can you also set up an appointment for us to meet with the conservatory guy—what's his name?—on Friday so we can go over what it will take to keep the glazing intact while work commences?"

"Whoa, should you be doing this so soon?"

"I'm fine. So the answer is yes."

"Dragon Lady will have your hide and mine too. And I happen to like my hide."

"Are you working for me or not?"

"Okay, okay. Anything else?"

"That's all that I can think of right now. Thank you."

"Don't forget I have the test on Friday and Saturday."

"Oh, right. Make the meeting for Thursday morning if possible. That way you can take the rest of the day off afterwards. Thanks, Ron."

"That's my job and oh, how I love my job."

"All right, smartass. See you in thirty."

As I got dressed, I knew I'd made the right decision. I needed to get out of my bedroom and focused on work. I was tired of the sick and scared routine. I've never had to experience it before, and I didn't like one bit. Rosa complained about me leaving, but I just ignored her ravings, gave her a kiss on the forehead, grabbed my briefcase, and left the house.

7

THE MONSTER MASH

I made it to work with no further incidents, but I still couldn't shake the feeling of being watched. It was probably only Detective O'Connor. I mulled over my future apology for my earlier outburst, so I kept my eye out for him as I made my way to the subway, but to my disappointment I saw no sign of him. I checked in with my parents from the train and reiterated my fine health.

At this time of day, the commute was easy. No jostling crowds, no pushing, and plenty of seats. What a treat. The short ride into the Loop gave me a good opportunity to settle down and relax. I tried to concentrate on work, but my mind kept bringing me back to the park. To the crazy thing I'd witnessed. I was so lost in thought that I almost missed my stop at Adams. *Jeez, Bailey. Get a hold of yourself.*

I was bombarded with questions and condolences when I entered the office. Sammy was even less obnoxious than normal. Miracles do happen.

Connie came at me with real concern etched on her face. "Damn it, Davis, can't you take directions from anybody? I told you to stay at home this week." I noticed everyone had scattered, expecting a fight.

"I'm feeling fine, and I have a lot of work to do." I made my way to my office with Connie on my heels. Of course, Ron had everything I asked for on my desk. "Now if you will please excuse me, I really need to go over these things." With a frustrated humph, Connie left. *Boy, I'm making everyone happy today*, I thought as I skimmed over the drawings left for me.

I worked industriously throughout the day, getting a lot of things accomplished. I met with Carl and Kathy to go over the Trent job and to sign contracts. I ran Ron, Adam, Carrie and Stacy ragged with programming, revisions, and scheduling. It wasn't until I realized I was all alone in the office that I glanced over at the clock. I was shocked that it read 7:30. I clearly remembered people coming and going, the phone ringing, and talking to clients, and co-workers, but I was surprised that hours had gone by so fast. Good. Work kept me from thinking about what had transpired in the last few days. My eyes were tired and my body stiff from sitting so long. Getting up to stretch, I realized that my stomach was growling from lack of food. I looked out my window as the city settled into darkness. Thousands of beautiful twinkling lights dotted the landscape. *This was the prettiest time of the day,* I thought.

I had fielded several "How are you" phone calls throughout the afternoon, including one from John, who needed to talk about the delay on the Conrad project. Of course, our conversation steered towards personal matters, and I hung up feeling conflicted and confused. He was certainly laying it all on the line, and he was relentless. "This is crazy," I mumbled to the Chicago skyline. "I don't hear a word from him in two years and now he expects me to just swoon at his attentions? Screw that!"

I packed up some things I wanted to take a look at tonight and put several drawings in my tube. I could vaguely remember Ron and Stacy coming in to say goodnight. I guessed that must have been a while ago. It was strange that Rosa hadn't called to ask about dinner. I dialed my home number, but just got my answering machine. Hmm. I called her phone, and again there was no answer. Well, maybe she had to run out for a while; but my stomach clenched and my heart skipped a couple of beats worrying about it. I couldn't call her cell phone because she didn't have one. That was always going to be a fight between us. She just flat-out refused to get one.

I left my office to the evening cleaning staff. No one was around but I thought I would peek in to see if the big boss, Robert, was in. And sure enough, he was. He was concentrating on a set of drawings, so it gave me an opportunity to study him more closely. Robert Conklin was in his early sixties, tall and lean. I knew he was an avid racquetball player, and it showed. He also schmoozed on the golf course. He had been married for over thirty-five years to Marcia, a lovely woman whose sole purpose in life, now that their three kids were grown, was to raise money for various charities. The Conklins gave generously, and her good works made the couple one of the most highly praised philanthropists in the city. He was dressed in a tux now, no doubt waiting to go to yet another black-tie event. I wouldn't call him handsome, but he possessed strong features with kind eyes and a very generous mouth. He was a shrewd businessman, an excellent designer, and from what I'd heard, a good cook.

"Knock, knock."

"Bailey, I meant to stop in. I heard you were here today. How are you feeling?" He ushered me to his sitting area and pointed to a suede club chair.

"I'm fine; it was really just a bump on the head."

"Do the police have any leads? I mean, what do they think?"

"I have no clue. The Oak Park police came and talked to me once, and the case was handed over the Chicago Special Investigations."

His left eyebrow rose. "Who are they?"

"I guess they investigate the Chicago Mafia."

"What? Why on earth are they interested in your case?"

"The bone I found was human. One of their detectives has interviewed me several times, but I'm not getting much information out of anyone." I got up and started to pace.

"That's interesting. Do they think you are in any kind of danger still?" He looked concerned.

"No, I don't think so." I was crossing my fingers behind my back. There was no need to worry the man. And maybe Detective O'Connor was being overly cautious. At least I hoped so. Robert studied my face to determine if I was fit to be at the office. I guess I passed the scrutiny, because he offered me his hand and walked me to his door.

"I'm hoping this is all settled soon, and we can get on with the Conrad job. I know they are concerned and are on their way home."

"I wasn't aware of that." I wondered why Connie hadn't mentioned it.

"Well, what's important is that you appear to be fine. Marcia sends her love and promises to make you one of her cheesecakes."

"Tell her she doesn't need to do any such thing, but it is always appreciated," I said with an excited smile. He knew how much I loved her cheesecake.

We said our goodbyes and I left the building.

At this time of night the subway was nearly empty. A few people were going home after late day at the office, others to their night jobs, and a couple of students just finished with night school sat on a bench waiting for their train.

A flicker of unease suddenly scuttled over my senses as I boarded the train. I flipped my cell phone open. Damn, low on juice. With all that had been happening, I had totally forgotten to charge the battery. I tried Rosa again, but got sporadic service. I tried until I reached my answering machine. Crap. My stomach clenched. I needed to relax, I'd be home in about twenty minutes. I thought about calling Detective O'Connor to just check it out. I found his card in my purse and punched in the number. "Shit." No service at all now. I was striking out tonight. I decided to turn my phone off to save on juice until I got off the train and up on the street.

The fifteen-minute ride was uneventful, except for the niggling feeling that something was off. I looked around to find no one of interest—no one who looked threatening, and no one resembling the monster in my nightmares.

I got off the train, ran up the stairs, and immediately turned on my phone. There was a message from the detective. I punched in voicemail, but my battery had finally died. "Shit, shit, shit!" It was about four blocks to my house from the train, and I usually could make it in about five minutes, walking at a good clip. So I walked even faster than that. I felt like running but my three-inch Stewart Weitzmans would likely not cooperate. The streets were quiet and dark. Monday was not exactly a party night, except in my boss's case. I met a couple walking their dog, and Vince, the local homeless man, who I stopped and gave my usual five dollars. I knew it probably went towards booze, but you never knew. He had to eat at some point.

I was about halfway home when I felt it again: the same sensation I'd experienced in the park. I sped up some and glanced around. No one was out to help if I needed it. Great. I had started to jog when I felt him behind me, silently stalking his prey. I didn't want to stop and turn around, but I had to. And what I saw would haunt me for years to come. It was the terrifying thing in my dreams.

I tried to scream but it only came out a whimper. I attempted to run, but he grabbed me by the throat and lifted me off the ground. His eyes, my god, his eyes were almost white, and his teeth were fangs. This could not be happening. It had to be a dream.

And then the monster spoke. "Who are you?"

I almost gagged from his rancid breath and foul stench. Maybe I was crazy, but he almost looked frightened. Suddenly I got angry and kicked out with all of my might. I hit him hard in the abdomen. Damn, I missed his balls by about three inches. If he even had balls. It startled him enough to loosen his grip on me for an instant, and I fell back onto the sidewalk with a thud. I scrambled to my feet fast. I would think about my ass in the morning. I ran, but once again he was too fast, and he managed to grab my arm. He was not expecting me to be strong, not nearly as strong as I was. I twisted until he lost his grip, but not before he formed deep claw marks down my arm. The pain was immediate and excruciating, but I'd worry about that later, along with my ruined blouse, and–damn– another pair of good shoes. For now, I was really pissed off. I was getting tired of being stalked by this–creature? He screamed, a horrible, piercing scream of pure hatred and frustration.

"Leave me alone or I'll kill you!" I shrieked back at him. My vision sharpened and my sense of smell grew more acute. I heard someone open a window to see what was happening as I began to attack back. Now the neighborhood was starting to take notice. People stopped what they were doing and came to their windows and opened their doors. The monster noticed too. He tried one last attempt for my arm, but I was quicker and slugged him in the face, knocking him to the ground. I was startled, but not as startled as my pursuer was. He gave one last roar of frustration and fled into the night.

"Whoa." The world spun, and the next thing I knew, I was on the ground with the pissed-off face of Detective O'Connor hovering over me. Before either of us could say a word, he gathered me in his arms like I was a broken doll and ran back to my house. Did I hear sirens in the distance?

By the time we were inside, he had worked up a good head of steam and could only glare at me. I don't think he could trust himself to speak. He gently put me down on my sofa and went into my powder room. I heard cursing and a lot of banging before he came back with a wet towel and wiped the blood off my arm.

"You are starting to heal already." He didn't seem happy as he tended to my wound. "I took you away because I think this would be a little hard to explain to the police," he remarked as he checked my body for other damage.

"But aren't you the police?"

"I don't understand, I thought this wound was much more severe." He totally avoided my question.

I gave him a break because my headache was starting to return and I didn't feel like arguing. Besides, he was right. I wasn't even sure about what had just happened, let alone able to explain it to the cops. They would probably throw me in the loony bin. Then I realized the dogs were not on my lap.

"Where are Rosa and the boys?" I asked in a panic. "Rosa!"

"She and your dogs are safe. I put them in a safe place. So everything is in order. You *will* be joining them soon," he said. "I tried calling you several times but only got your voice mail, and you had asked your secretary not to disturb you."

I vaguely remembered asking Donna not to put through any more calls so I could get some actual work done after the upsetting conversation with John.

He pressed the cloth to my gash. It was still oozing a bit of blood.

"Ouch! That hurts."

"Quit being such a baby. I'll fix you up in no time."

"How did you ever get Rosa to leave? I can't believe it."

"I have good persuasion skills." His smile was beautiful.

We sat quietly for some time while he concentrated on cleaning my wounds. He worked fast and efficiently, as if he had done this a lot.

"So what was that?" I said, more to myself than him. I think it was all just starting to hit me. "I must be going nuts. My, god, it was the monster in my dreams. He's real. How could this be happening?"

He suddenly stopped what he was doing. "You've dreamed about this?"

"Detective O'Connor—"

"Declan."

"Okay, Declan. Please tell me you saw that. Please tell me I'm not going crazy!" I was now shaking so hard I could barely speak. I guess I was having a delayed reaction. Funny—I wasn't scared, so why was I trembling.

He stopped tending to me and took my hands in his. "You're not going crazy, but no, I didn't see it. I heard it though. We all did." He glanced towards my kitchen where three brawny men and one gorgeous raven-haired woman stood, all clad in skin-tight black leather. They carried a multitude of futuristic looking weapons and had grim written all over their faces.

"Whoa—what?" I jumped up and stormed towards them. "Who the hell are you people, and why are you in my house?"

One of the men stepped to meet me halfway, wearing a cocky grin.

"You were right about her, sir." They all glanced at me with smirks, except for the woman. She only scowled.

"What is that supposed to mean? What is going on here?" I swiveled towards O'Connor.

"Bailey, you must come with us now, and I will explain everything to you. Do not be afraid. I will not let any harm come to you." He looked dead serious and a little bit worried for me.

"Are you really a detective?" He nodded. "Are they policemen too?" I jerked my chin toward the leather soldiers standing in my kitchen.

"In a sense. Come with us, and all will be revealed." He walked me towards the stairs. "Please hurry, and pack for a couple of weeks."

"All will be revealed? For a couple of weeks? Who the hell are you? I want some answers right now, buddy! I can't just take off for a couple of weeks. Are you insane?" I wrestled away from his grasp, put my hands on my hips, and glared. He sucked in a breath, but didn't speak.

"I mean it, Detective. I'm not going anywhere with the likes of you and your brethren here."

I felt a slight prick on the back of my neck, and that was the last thing I remembered saying. As I fell into his arms, I remembered having the distinct impression that my life as I knew it had just ended.

8

REVELATIONS

"Go now. You have your orders. We will reconvene back at the cave at sunrise. We have his scent all over Ms. Davis. He will try to block it, but you know what to do. The trail is fresh so I expect him found tonight, preferably alive, but if you have to kill him, do so."

Declan's team nodded and left. He knew they would find the vampire that had been threatening Bailey. It was just a matter of time. He had treaded lightly for years so he could track him to his clan, but he could do so no longer. The rogue was a threat to Bailey, thus needed to be taken straightaway. He hungered to get his hands on him, to hurt him in ways that would be unimaginable to most humans.

He had decided that afternoon to reveal his discovery of Bailey Davis to his team. He knew he couldn't handle this alone, especially given he wasn't sure what he was dealing with. At first he had assumed she was just another victim of a rogue vampire attack. There were hundreds still out there who hunted on innocent prey of the human variety. But he'd known he was wrong the minute he saw her eyes and felt her aura.

After this morning's attack in broad daylight, he understood he had stumbled onto something big. It was almost unheard of that a vampire hunted during the daylight. Something much more sinister was at work here, and he was going to get to the bottom of it. He had given the kill order, but hoped it wouldn't come to that unless totally necessary.

Yet he still hesitated to inform the Council. He needed further information about Ms. Davis before he'd feel comfortable doing so.

Something in his gut was telling him to lie low. So he and his team were going to find out everything there was to know about Bailey Davis. About who was behind these attacks, and about why she was so powerful. But first he needed to secure the victim. Something he thought would be simple. Yeah, right.

He gazed down at the slumbering beauty before him. She was so delicate in stature, yet so prideful and bold. She was frightened by what was happening, whether she wanted to admit it or not, but she had not hesitated to fight back. He couldn't read her, but he knew. It was instinct–interesting.

While he was running, then flying to help her, he'd felt total panic. He couldn't think of the last time he felt so incompetent. God forgive him, he hadn't been there protecting her like he should have been. Damn it, he'd known he was supposed to have been shadowing her, but he had to admit, her rebuff had wounded his pride, and he was upset by her dreadful attitude. So he was forced to watch most of the confrontation from a distance. He'd been surprised by her attempts to get away from the rogue, but mostly astonished by her tenacity and strength. Most humans would be dead from such an attack. He corrected himself. All humans. So what was she?

He'd immediately gone to her when she was down, choosing not to follow the rogue. That act made him very uncomfortable, yet as he looked back on it, he would not have changed a thing. Shit.

He couldn't help but smile as he recalled how she'd reacted when she saw his team in her kitchen. She'd instantly jumped up to protect her surroundings when she realized strangers were in her domain. He shook his head. Very big and lethal strangers too. She didn't hesitate and clearly wasn't scared of him or his team one bit. That, and her relentless stubborn refusal to accompany him, made him believe she was either very brave or very stupid. He frowned even as he admired her beauty.

"You are very special, Bailey Davis. You have no idea just how special," he murmured in her ear as he carried her out into the late summer night.

⚜

I woke to a pounding headache. Again. "Ow," I complained. "This was getting old. Then I remembered and bolted up. "What the hell?" A steady hand on my shoulder pushed me back down.

"You'll be fine; we had to give you a good dose to knock you out. You'll feel its effects for a couple of hours still."

The speaker was one of the men who had been standing in my kitchen. He gently took my pulse.

"My name is Ohitekah, but you may call me Thomas, since my birth name is a challenge for most." He smiled. "Sir Declan will be here shortly."

Sir Declan? "Where am I?" My head was starting to clear. I remembered arguing with the detective, if he really was a detective, which I was starting to doubt. And then nothing. I looked around in anger and a bit of panic.

"Don't worry, you are safe. No harm would dare come to you here."

I studied my captor. He was a beautiful man, Native American ancestry, I guessed. He had long black hair that fell into a braid down his back, a very strong nose, full mouth and mocha eyes. He stood at six foot plus, and had sculpted muscles that rippled under his tight tee. I also noticed incredibly intricate tattoos running up both arms. He smelled like wood smoke and spice. Interesting. I snapped out of my stupor to see a stunned expression on his face.

"What?" I demanded, as the detective walked into the room. He nodded to Thomas, who quickly left.

"You bastard! How dare you drug me and bring me here!" I shouted. He just stood there, crossed his arms, and sighed. "What day is it? I have to go to work." He continued to stare. "Well, what the hell do you have to say for yourself? Don't just stand there and look at me like that. Where am I? I'm going to the real cops. Obviously you aren't what you said you were." I jumped out of bed. The room swam, but I held my composure until I saw I was only clad in my panties and bra. Thank goodness they matched.

"Whoa—who the hell took my clothes?"

"I did."

I flushed, more with fury than embarrassment. "Why?"

"I didn't think you wanted to sleep in them."

"Oh." I couldn't think of a nasty reply.

"Your clothes are hanging in the bathroom. I also brought you a couple of suitcases filled with clothing and other necessities. I suggest you clean up and then we will talk." And he walked out.

"Shit. Damn it! Let me out of here!" I tried the door, but it was locked. I forced myself to relax. If Declan wanted to hurt me he already had plenty of opportunity to do so. But I searched for my purse anyway. It was sitting on the bedside table. Of course, minus the phone. Then I remembered that it was out of juice anyway. I looked around to find a landline, and for the first time noticed my surroundings. Lavish. That was the best word to adequately describe what I was looking at. The space had to be at least twenty-five feet wide, forty feet long, and had twelve-foot ceilings. I had been sleeping in a neoclassical-style full tester bed, draped in royal blue silks and golden chinoiserie. The center of the room held a suite of Duncan Phyfe styled furnishings with silk upholstery. An enormous oriental wool rug in rich blues and reds with a black border sat underneath. Across from the bed, a huge fireplace with an intricately carved marble mantel had been laid for a fire. The walls were painted in the Robert Adam color palate of pastel blues and grays, contrasted with intricate plaster moldings and medallions painted a crisp white. Lovely. The only clue to my location was the fact that there were no windows. I had to be in some sort of hideout where these thugs did their dirty deeds.

I walked into the attached bathroom, and I was suddenly back in the twenty-first century: marble flooring and shower stall complete with sauna and steam; His-and-her sinks with silver fixtures; and a separate water closet complete with toilet and bidet. The focal point of the room was an enormous spa in the center of the circular space. The ceiling held a beautiful dome in gilded silver.

"Wow!" I couldn't help but breathe. At least the creep had good taste. I also noticed my cosmetic case laid out, along with my blow dryer, toothbrush, deodorant, and everything else a girl could ask for. Jerk. I had to give him credit for organization. I walked to the shower and punched in my preferred water temperature. Nice; digital valves. As I stripped out of my underwear, I wondered, once again, where I was. Either a cushy prison or underground. Perhaps both, but what a prison cell. Jeez.

I soaked in 102-degree water that poured down from the shower ceiling in massive proportions. It was like being in a caught in a major rainstorm. I must have lost track of time, because as I punched the water off and turned to leave the steamy stall room, I found Declan standing there holding a towel.

"You were taking so long, I was getting worried; sorry," he said without any remorse.

"Oh really? I can't imagine where else I might have gone. Or did you think that I would harm myself?" I was still standing there totally naked and not caring. Declan noticed, too. His eyes appeared even bluer against a blushing face.

"Well—um—here, take this," and he threw the towel at me. "Please get dressed. I'll wait in the other room."

I quickly toweled off, brushed my teeth, got dressed, and walked into the bedroom while still trying to untangle my hair.

"Okay, I'm calm, decent, and clean. Now can you please tell me what is going on?" I sat on the settee while brushing my mane.

"I don't want to frighten you, so this is difficult for me. Just listen to what I'm about to say with an open mind. And remember, you are in no danger here." Declan, paced the room, wringing his hands. Nervous. Hmm. Interesting.

"Okay, let's just get on with it," I demanded. "I have people who are going to worry about my disappearance. Especially after what's been going on lately."

He stared at me with a worried frown, and that was starting to worry me too, so I shut my mouth and decided to listen. He looked me in the eyes and I nodded for him to begin.

"The monster that is after you is not human. He is a vampire. Most of the people in this building are vampires. And I am, as well. You are in what we call the cave. One of the safe-houses we have in the District."

I must have looked it as dumbfounded as I felt. "Yeah, okay, and I'm Cinderella. Come on Detective"–

"Declan," he interrupted.

I sighed. "Okay, Declan—you can do better than that."

He eyed me with resignation. "Do you think I am lying? I would never lie about something so important." He continued to pace, but then abruptly stopped and faced me. "Very well. Bailey, look at me."

I watched as Declan's eyes went from sparkling blue to icy white. His face became sharper, more angled. His mouth, oh god. His lips turned a deep red, and his teeth–they were the same teeth as in my dreams. I screamed and ran to the door.

"Oh please, someone please help me!" I pounded, but got no response. I turned around ready to fight.

"Bailey!" he yelled. I suddenly felt dizzy. Shit, I was having one of my spells. My vision heightened, my hearing sharpened, and my heartbeat slowed. I turned….

"Bailey, it's all right! I won't harm you!" But his next words stopped in his throat. I stalked towards him, no longer scared, but angry and curious.

"Bailey," he whispered, but I heard him clear as day. "Who are you?" His features had returned to normal. "Look at yourself." He led me to a large mirror that hung over the fireplace.

"I looked!" Then I fainted.

03&80

"Jesus, twice in one day?" I mumbled as I got up from the bed. Declan was immediately at my side.

"Was it a dream?" I hoped, but I already knew the answer.

He shook his head. "I'm very sorry."

"Holy shit, holy shit. I can't believe it. Monsters do exist. And am I one?"

"I don't know, but I'd like to find out. You are not exactly one of us. You have some similarities, yet you seem to get along just fine during the day and without blood. I just don't know yet."

I started giggling. I couldn't help it. The thought was so ridiculous, it was actually funny. The giggles turned into all-out belly laughter. Tears streamed down my face and I started hiccupping. After awhile I looked up to find the same people that were in my house staring at me.

"Hail, hail, the gang's all here," I sang and broke up again.

"Sir, is she insane?" I heard the beauty with the raven hair ask.

Suddenly sober, I asked, "Am I insane?" I got off the bed and stalked to her. "I don't know about insane, but I certainly am a monster like you." I spat. She stiffened and went for her weapon at her side.

"Leave us!" Declan demanded. "She will be fine." They all nodded, gave me a mixture of looks, and quickly left.

"It is morning, and you need to break your fast. I will order something for you to eat. Do you want coffee or tea?"

I wiped my nose, which was running. "Tea, please." I answered as I went into the bathroom to splash cool water on my face, and to relieve my bladder. I gave Declan some time to get breakfast together and set up. I needed the space, and a moment to think. This was crazy. I just wanted my dogs, Rosa, and my life back to normal. But I had a sinking feeling that nothing would ever be the same. I studied my face in the mirror. No fangs. My hair was a wild mess, but Declan had brought all of my products so I applied the gunk to tame the curls. My normally fair skin, which had been tan from the summer, including had a few freckles over the bridge of my nose, was now sallow. Naturally rosy cheeks were drained of color, and my emerald green eyes looked dull, with dark smudges below. I was still reeling from the image of my eyes and face changing like Declan's did. I'd always known my spells were unusual, but I'd just brushed it off, not wanting to really recognize my problem. I supposed now was the time to face my—differences. *I'm a monster and my life is a nightmare!*

After shedding several minutes' worth of tears, I quietly returned to the bedroom and sat on the settee. A young woman was there finishing laying out a beautiful spread. Declan smiled at me, then took a muffin. I realized how hungry I was as I saw eggs benedict, bacon, sausage, fresh fruit, fresh-baked muffins, and Earl Grey tea. Yum. I couldn't help it, no matter how upset I was, superb food was calling my name, and I started digging in.

After we finished, my stomach all but stuffed to the brim, Declan moved to the fireplace with his coffee, and I made a rational decision in this irrational situation.

"I need to call the office. Ron will be worried, and I have work to do. I can't just blow off clients and jobs in progress." It felt good thinking about more routine matters, like work.

"I already let them know that you are in seclusion, and that there was a little trouble at your place last night." He held up his hand at my startled expression. "Don't worry, I reassured them that you are indeed fine and that you will contact them soon. Let's talk a while longer and then you may call whomever you wish."

That sounded reasonable.

"Okay." I settled back with my tea, ready to listen, hoping it wouldn't get any worse than it already was. I had so many questions clattering around in my brain that I was beginning to feel the dull throb of yet another headache coming on.

"How shall I begin?" he muttered to himself as he paced in front of me. He suddenly stopped, and met my eyes. "I will start from the beginning."

I nodded my approval.

"Vampires, my ancestors, are as old as modern man. A genetic defect–mutation during the last Ice Age, roughly 10,000 years ago–left a small clan, in what is now the Czech Republic, in a quandary. A boy, Ales, who was born healthy and happy, became unruly when he matured. As the story goes, he craved the taste of blood and he killed small animals, in the beginning, to get this blood. Eventually he started slaughtering larger animals to assuage his hunger. The clan kept this secret from neighboring clans because Ales protected them from invaders. You see, he was much stronger than any other man in the clan. He was fast, he had night vision, and he did not appear to age normally.

The clan happily existed like this for years, even though they were fearful of Ales. Then, one awful day, the boy's mother was brutally raped and murdered while collecting water upstream. Ales was beside himself with grief and anger. He tracked down her murderers by following their scent and drained them until they were dead. After he was found covered in their blood, the clan slowly began to despise him. As some migrated to other clans, eventually the word spread about his peculiar habit. Ales was ostracized and went into hiding. Feeling rejected and hated, he retaliated by hunting humans for blood.

Years later, and after various experimentations, Ales realized that he could change humans into what he was when the moon was right, and he was careful. The ritual entailed completely draining the subject's blood, then replenishing it with their own."

"Jesus," I couldn't help but interject. He nodded, affirming my statement and continued.

"Thus, the first vampires were made. My ancestors were brutal, hunting in large numbers, killing everything in their wake. But only Ales was allowed to change a human. He was very discerning and changed only men. Refused to even kill women and would not allow any of the others to do so either."

"It's incredible. How come no one knows of this? Shouldn't it be in history books or something? I've only seen it in the movies." I got up to refill my hot water.

"This all happened long before written language," Declan explained. "It traveled through the generations by storytelling and drawings. Eventually it was all written down, organized, and translated only by special vampire historians. My maternal grandfather was such a historian. He would tell me the stories and show me some of the imagery when I was a child. So the full story is only known to a few today. Plus, I have access to a wonderful research library here in the cave, and I know how to use it."

"Makes sense. It just amazes me that your kind has been able to hide from...well, uh...humans for so long."

He smiled wryly. "Let me tell you the rest, and some of your questions will be answered."

I sat back down and relaxed, as best I could.

"Where was I?"

"You were telling me about the ruthlessness of the changed vampires."

"Right. The changed vampires were not as strong as Ales was, not as fast, and appeared to age, though slowly. They also were allergic to silver, which burned their skin, and they were very sensitive to sunlight. They could not even come out during the day, even on dreary, sunless days.

Decades later Ales found a girl, Yannah, who had startling blue eyes and blonde hair. He was so enthralled with her that he kept her, cherished her, but did not change her. He very slowly fed her his own blood when she ailed, and she became stronger but she was still aging at a normal rate. She bore him three children, all of whom died at a young age. Eventually, not wanting her to grow any older, they agreed that he should perform the ritual. So he turned her, but she was different; she became stronger than he was.

In due time, Yannah bore Ales a daughter, the first sired from vampire parents. The daughter was very healthy; she did not die in infancy like most did during that time. She appeared to be human, but as she aged she began showing signs that she held special powers. At about the time of her maturity, about age eleven, she began to get restless and became a bit wild, even craving blood. So her father performed a new ritual, the ritual of First Blood Rites. The First Blood Rite is given to all born vampires when they become of age. It is the first drinking of human blood. Back then, they performed human sacrifice and blood was taken while the victim was still alive."

He stopped his pacing and narrowed his eyes, as if to assess how I was reacting to his story. I guess he felt that I wasn't on the brink of another episode, so he continued.

"The ritual was successful, and the child, Alleah, became the first Full Blood vampire. Yannah eventually bore Ales another child, a boy, Tothe. But the boy was weaker than his older sister and almost died in infancy. He lived, however, and even went through the ritual. He grew stronger, but never showed the special powers that his sister Alleah possessed.

The other vampires were frightened by Alleah and Tothe. Soon infighting began, and it was not long before blood was shed. The most significant casualty was the death of Yannah, the mother. Ales was so angry and heartbroken that he hunted all the others involved in the revolt. It took him many years, but eventually he killed most of them. A few of the perpetrators escaped and fled to other continents. Some went to the Americas. Others fled east, to what is now known as Russia and China."

"Hmm," It was a fairytale, one hell of a frightening fairytale. "So vampires are not immortal—like in the movies?"

He laughed. "Hardly, but I will explain," he continued.

"Over hundreds of years, Ales and his children moved from place to place, being very careful who they changed and who they killed. They ended up in Africa, in what is now known as the Sudan, around 8,000 B.C.E. Ales was never the same after his loss, but he eventually found another mate, Sekhet. He performed the same ritual as before, and soon after, she bore him a son. The son, Perithomas, grew strong, and First Blood Rites were performed. Perithomas became a great warrior and ruled over most of the clans in the Sudan. Sekhet also bore him a second son, Aarrath, who was again not as strong as the firstborn, but nevertheless lived.

Ales took special care of Perithomas and Alleah, teaching them the art of fighting, defense, and ruling. They became very powerful, ruling most of Africa and southern Europe.

It was arranged that the two would mate, thus creating a special, powerful line of vampires known as the Centurions. Alleah eventually bore a daughter, Karah, and a son, Kas. The oldest child, Karah, had the greater powers of the two. However, they were both Centurion, so they both possessed gifts more powerful than any living creature on earth at that time. It was rumored that Karah could fly and Kas could de-materialize. At least that's what was written in the oldest manuscripts.

"Crazy." I shook my head.

He acknowledged my statement with a sympathetic nod.

"Knowing he needed to continue his vampire line, Ales took another two wives, Duna and Panhsja. They both bore him two children, and the Full Blood line continues to this day.

Declan paused, watching me as I fidgeted. "So there are changed vampires and born vampires?" I finally asked.

"Yes. Full Bloods, as they are called, are fewer in number but are the most powerful, and live a very long time. And they are hard to kill. They are also strongly encouraged to mate only with other Full Bloods, continuing the pure bloodlines. Unfortunately, Full Blood females can only produce two children. Turned females are infertile, except for the ones who were changed directly by Ales. No one really knows why this is, even to this day. But those are the only females ever reported to reproduce after having been changed."

"Which are you?" I got up to stretch.

"I am a Full Blood, a Centurion sired from a firstborn. Perithomas was my fourth great-grandfather. All Centurions are warriors and protectors of the race, throughout our history. And the firstborns are the more powerful of the Full Blood lines."

"Oh." Like I understood perfectly well. "How old are you?"

"I was born in West Meath, Ireland in 1552, I believe."

I blinked hard, shook my head, and sat back down. "My god. This is all too much." I rested my face in my hands for several beats. "So you had a great, great, great, great-grandfather who was over 8,000 years older than you?"

He sat next to me and touched my shoulder. "We are not immortal, but we live a long time. I know this is difficult for you."

"Difficult? It's ludicrous." I halfway smiled. "I have so many questions that my head is spinning." I jumped up to pace. "I guess the obvious is, what the hell does any of this have to do with me?"

Declan got up and led me back to the settee. "I'm still not completely sure, but I may have an idea. And I need to tell you more of the story for you to understand." He sat me down and went back to refresh his coffee. Hmm. Vampires drink coffee? He must have seen the question on my face.

"Yes, vampires like to drink coffee, wine, and even Kool-Aid. We also eat human food. I enjoy a good steak. Rare, of course."

"Of course," I shot back.

"We do not require food or drink often, only the ingestion of blood to sustain our bodies. But we like to partake in the eating ritual, at least once a day. Our metabolism is slower than humans, so we don't need as much, at least the older ones. But we have bodily functions like humans do, and have a very strong–um–sexual appetite."

He cut his eyes to me, which seemed to whiten briefly. At my look of alarm, he hurried on.

"We Full Bloods can tolerate sunlight, especially the elders, but we are weaker and not at our best during the day. We are not dead, nor do we change into bats, or sleep in coffins like you see in the movies; but our anatomy is different from humans. We have a specialized heart with six chambers, a much more advanced stomach that helps to break down blood proteins, and a very large liver."

He stopped and waved his hand in the air. "It is all a complex process that I couldn't even begin to explain. However, we can instantaneously repair wounds, depending on the wound, bloodline, and age of the vampire, and can even regenerate certain body parts if given ample time and a strong blood source."

I visibly gulped and he smirked, to my annoyance. "How do you get– do you–"

"Do we kill people to get blood?" He laughed at my discomfort. "No, no. Of course, we no longer take blood against a human's will. At least most do not. But there are evil vampires just like there are evil humans. There are synthetic blood banks and human blood that is paid for. And there are blood patrons and blood whores."

I raised my eyebrows to that.

"The patron is a human who lives with the vampire, taking care of their needs. Becoming a family member so to speak. They are very well taken care of and are protected and well respected. Most often it is a family tradition, passed down from generation to generation. Some are even eventually changed."

"And the whore?"

The blood whore goes from vampire club to club, offering their body for money. They are often abused, and occasionally drained completely if they are not careful. But the act is very intoxicating for a human, and many get addicted."

"Wow. Do you have a patron?"

"The cave has several who live here and serve us. I will introduce you to them later."

I nodded and he went back to his narrative.

"After many years the numbers of vampires steadily grew. They lived all over the globe. They hid from humans in plain sight. Full Bloods could function pretty well during the day, so most immersed themselves in the human population becoming blacksmiths, bakers, cobblers, whatever they chose. Most Full Bloods worked alongside humans, befriended them, played with them, even loved and married them. That was looked on with disapproval, though, and in the beginning, strictly forbidden. Of course, human women could not bear a child from a vampire. The genetics just didn't work."

"What about the changed vampires?" I inquired, starting to get into the story.

"It was harder for the changed to integrate with humans. They are, at the very best, lethargic during the day and most could not bear the sun at all. A few grew a tolerance to the daylight as they aged, but they needed more blood to sustain themselves, which is not as easy as you may think to obtain, especially back then. And the changed vampires are extremely allergic to silver."

"Now I thought that was a werewolf thing."

He only rolled his eyes and continued. "All vampires are somewhat allergic to silver, yet the changed are severely so, as well as some other metals, like nickel and zinc. The electrical conductivity in pure silver ore somehow agitates our electrical impulses; therefore, we have a harder time healing and literally burn under prolonged exposure. "In addition..."

He was speaking like a professor now. I suddenly realized he could have been one in the past. One hot professor–hmm.

"...changed vampires do not have the powers and certain gifts that Full Bloods have. Some changed vampires did integrate, finding jobs and industry during the nighttime hours. Others, the older ones, could even work during the day with humans, although their powers and strengths were diminished. A few even married humans, but not many.

Most changed vampires became angry and resentful of the Full Bloods. They were more dependent on each other and could not sustain themselves very well without human help, which was a problem, at times. Infighting between the clans became prevalent and wars ensued. At one point, Full Bloods and changed vampires killed each other on first sight, but that was many years ago. During the age of Constantine."

"Holy crap!" I couldn't help it. He acknowledged my outburst with a chuckle.

"But I'm getting ahead of myself." He paused to think. "It was around the time of Khufu, during the fourth dynasty in Egypt, that a Full Blood, a very powerful Full Blood, who was a direct descendant of Alleah, fell in love with a human woman. A very unusual human. A princess with golden red hair and emerald green eyes, who could see into the minds of others."

I visibly swallowed.

"They could not express their love because she was the niece of the Pharaoh, and heavily protected. Arabet, that was her name. One day her uncle informed her that she was to marry Menkaure, the Pharaoh's son by his chief wife Khameremebty. She was crestfallen. She only wanted her true love, Reneb the Centurion."

"Did she know who he really was?" I asked, thinking I needed some popcorn to go along with this tale.

"Yes, she knew, but it didn't matter to her." He looked at me, but I couldn't tell what he was thinking. His face was a mask.

"Oh, okay."

"When Reneb became aware of Arabet's betrothal he stole her away, not wanting anyone else to even touch her. Together they left Egypt and sailed out of the Mediterranean. They stayed in what is now known as Spain for several months, until Reneb could secure safe passage to the West, and the seas turned favorable. They left in late spring and sailed for almost six months until they hit land. It was a very long and treacherous journey. But Reneb was very powerful, and he sustained Arabet during the bleakest hours with his own blood. It worked, and they landed in moderately good health in what is now known as the Yucatan Peninsula.

Reneb did not care that Arabet could never bear him a child. He could get that elsewhere. She was his life, so they were bonded in ritual and lived a relatively peaceful existence for many years. He quickly challenged local tribesmen, eventually claiming his own large territory. He formed a class of warriors to protect his kingdom. He changed a few of the worthiest local natives and sought out others like himself.

Reneb was a born leader, fair and honest, and his area began to thrive. His people became successful farmers and goldsmiths. The mountains and valleys of the area contained some of the best minerals on earth."

"You can't be serious! Do you mean to tell me that these two were the founders of the Mayans?" I asked.

He only shrugged. "Who's to say for sure? I only know what has been written. Whether or not it's fact is anyone's guess. But I tend to believe it."

"This is just insane," I muttered under my breath, but I was surprised by my relative calm. "Go on."

He nodded and continued. "Reneb refused to change Arabet. He did not want her cursed like he thought his kind was. He wanted her pure and untainted by vampirism. So life continued for the couple. They were extremely happy, and their community continued to grow and prosper. Bound to his duty to keep the Full Blood line intact, Reneb fathered as many as five children by various Full Blood women. Some accounts say only three, some say as many as six. No one knows for sure. But one thing is for certain; he only loved Arabet. At least until she became pregnant.

I gasped. "But you said—"

"Yes, human women could not get pregnant by a vampire. That was the thought until then." Declan got up to pace.

"Reneb accused Arabet of being unfaithful and vowed to kill whomever had impregnated her. Devastated, he went seeking trouble, invading other territories and starting unprovoked attacks. He was gone more and more often, until one time he did not return for five years. Then, scarred from battle, tired, and emotionally spent, he sought out Arabet, only to find she had died in childbirth. He broke down and cursed himself for leaving her, sickened by the thought of everything she must have gone through without him.

He learned that the child, a girl, was born healthy, but no father had stepped forward to claim her. She was sold to a traveling group of explorers only the year before his return. He learned that the tribe had tried to raise her, but she was passed from family to family because they were scared of her. She was stronger than most boys her age, never got sick and always healed extremely fast. They were frightened of her fiery golden curls and translucent green eyes, which blazed gold when she was angry or upset."

I almost fell off of the couch. "That's like me! Oh my god, oh my god!"

"Yes. Please, I'm almost finished."

I managed to shut my mouth but I could no longer sit. I got up to pace alongside of Declan.

"Reneb immediately knew then that he was her father. But how could it be? He organized a group to find her, and he spent years, fruitlessly searching. He could never discover where they had taken her. He went into a depression, until one day about ten years later, she came back to the village.

She was extremely beautiful and very special. Her name was Ah Kin meaning Sun God. It was a heartfelt and emotional reunion. Reneb explained to her his past and the vampire kind. She understood and even agreed to partake in the First Blood Rites. He performed it at the next new moon, but it was not like the other Full Blood Rite ceremonies. Ah Kin did not sprout fangs or crave blood, but she still had the power of a Full Blood. She could walk in full sunlight and was not allergic to any known substance. Ah Kin also possessed something very dangerous. She could not only see into the minds of humans, like all Full Blood vampires could do, but she could read the minds of other vampires, all vampires. She also had the ability to manipulate fire and water. She could burn objects, even people, and she could move water in small amounts. Ah Kin was something totally different, therefore they were concerned about the reaction from others. So they decided to keep her powers a secret, and they lived happily for many centuries.

Ah Kin eventually married a Full Blood, Butz Chan, and had a daughter of her own. She looked identical to her mother. Ix even had her mother's powers. A few years after her First Rites ritual was performed, the Aztecs threatened their kingdom. The women's powers were revealed while defending their territory. The other vampires were frightened and angry so eventually they hunted them. They managed to capture Reneb and Butz Chan and brutally tortured them before they were killed, but Ah Kin and her child managed to escape.

They hid for decades, moving further and further north. They were crushed and angry over the loss of their father and grandfather, and vowed to avenge their deaths." He paused to face me.

"This is where the information, the written history is vague. There are only rumors about what happened next. The most plausible account says that Ix escaped to the north without her mother. She spent decades wandering until she met a human and fell in love. Ix produced eight children, and all survived but three."

"I thought vampire women could only produce two children?" I asked surprised.

"That's true, except for the Ahkin bloodline. They seemed to be different in many ways. Not only could they give birth to more than two children. They produced babies that survived when most perished."

We sat in silence for a couple of beats before Declan cleared his throat and commenced with his narrative.

"Ix's surviving five children had powers, but one was special, identical t o her mother in every way. When Ix realized this fact, she shaved the child's head, packed her up, and gave her away to a local nunnery. Meanwhile she pretended that the child was lost while bathing in the river. No one knows whatever happened to the child. Several vampires throughout the years claim to have seen a woman with similar features and powers, but nothing was ever confirmed. These sightings have been reported from various places all over the world." He finally stopped his narrative and went back to his coffee.

"Do you think I could be one of their descendents, I mean Ix and her husband?" I asked not thinking he would ever confirm my suspicions.

"I'm beginning to believe so, yes."

"Oh man, this is a crazy. I need some time to understand all of this." I sat back down.

"I understand."

"That would mean my parents–?"

"I don't know what it means yet," Declan said in a kind voice as he walked to me and touched my shoulder.

"But I still don't understand why they–or he, whatever. I mean, why me? Why now? Who are these vampires that are after me?"

"It is written that many of the changed vampires went after Ix and Ah Kin. They searched for many years but had no success. Maybe there are still some who are looking, although I've never heard of any such group."

"Why not the Full Bloods? I mean, why did they not pursue them?"

"I'm not sure. Maybe they felt no threat from the women. Or perhaps they considered them family because they are from the Full Blood line themselves.

I think when you stumbled onto a burial at the Conrad Estate that someone or some group wanted hidden, you became a threat. They didn't want anyone knowing about the bones. Obviously they are important to someone, but I still don't know why."

"Bones?"

"Yes. They found a whole body minus the head. The headless issue raised my interest."

"Why is that?"

"Because it is the only real way to kill a vampire, even a Full Blood. You detach the brain stem from the body, the rest dies. The head cannot regenerate."

We looked at each other for a long and uncomfortable moment.

He went back to pacing. "Preliminary investigation puts the body at about sixteen to twenty years of age, and female from the shape of the pelvis. Not much more is known at this time. We are checking into any missing persons that fit that description in the area."

"So you are a cop?"

"Yes, that was the truth. I have been a policeman in some way, shape, or form, for about one hundred and twenty five years now. Much longer if you count the years I've been a Centurion, which has been my entire life."

"Wow."

"I move around for obvious reasons, but I've been in Chicago for about fifteen years now, working special detail for the homicide division. Solving human crime is not difficult, and I move up the ladder fast. I am a full lieutenant on the force, specializing in Mafia crime. I do that in tandem with investigating vampire activities, which I spend most of my time on. So I was alerted to your attack and the unusual circumstances behind it."

"Who told you?"

"There are thousands of vampires, and many humans who know about our kind who work for police departments across the country. Even in the Oak Park department. But this came through normal channels because the Conrad house once belonged to the Frank Tandini family. He was a Mafia don whose whole family disappeared under mysterious circumstances about thirty years ago. No one knows what happened to the family to this day."

I felt like a bowling ball just landed on my chest. "Did you say Frank Tandini?"

He stopped in mid pace and raised his eyebrows. "Yes. Why?"

"Oh boy." My head landed in my hands, once again. "Nuts, nuts, nuts." I mumbled to myself.

"What's wrong?"

"I dreamed it. Or it was–a vision–or something. Jasmine Tandini–I saw her death." I described the whole nightmare to the best of my memory.

Declan was speechless for a couple of minutes "I have read about this. Very few have the gift of seeing the future, others the past from someone else's eyes. But I have never met anyone with the ability."

He sat down next to me. "Quite frankly, I'm astonished, and I don't know what it means, but I will see to it that we find out. I'll start by trying the get some DNA matching. If we are lucky enough that Jasmine Tandini ever had blood drawn."

"Okay. This is really creepy. I'm trying desperately to hold onto my sanity."

Declan slid his hand onto my shoulder. "Don't worry, we'll find out what's going on."

His eyes held such conviction that I immediately felt better. I let out a big breath of tension and nodded. I was ready to handle the next battle.

"Wow, and all of this goes on completely under human radar. It's truly amazing you have gotten away with it for so long."

Declan smirked with a shrug. Happy perhaps that I was changing the subject. "We've had millennia to practice. And we do have vampires integrated in every aspect of human society, including politics. So we work hard to keep our existence quiet. But it's getting harder and harder. It seems that technology may be our truest enemy. Everyone has cameras built into their phones. Even video capabilities are commonplace. Not to mention the aggressiveness of the media today. There have been noises about coming out of the closet, so to speak, but I can't imagine that actually ever happening. We are too much for most humans to comprehend. There have been so many negative stories told about our kind."

"Maybe you are underestimating humans," I suggested. "Maybe their reactions wouldn't be as bad as you think."

He looked at me like I had three heads. "Oh, right. Humans have slaughtered millions of their own kind because of race, sexual orientation, and religious beliefs. They are far more violent and less accepting than any other living being on earth. Vampires have nothing on humans."

I didn't want to think about what his last remark implied. But he was right. The human race had not been very altruistic in its behavior. In fact, we were downright scary.

"You're right. I've never really thought about it before," I said. "But I still have to believe that there are many who are unselfish and can rise above their prejudices to make logical assessments and rational decisions."

He grunted his amusement. "You are very young and naive."

I narrowed my eyes. "No need to be insulting, O'Connor."

He chose to ignore my comment. "So whoever found you with that bone must have panicked and probably tried to erase your memories."

"You can do that?"

"Some can, yes, even a few changed ones. It takes some training and strength. Usually older ones are better at it, but eventually most Full Bloods can read and manipulate human minds, as well as a few of the changed."

I could only gawk.

"I think I know who is behind your attacks, "Declan went on. "He is a rogue I've been tracking for some time."

"What's a rogue?"

"It's a vampire who hunts humans for food and is an all-around criminal. Usually they work on their own, but there have been a few instances when groups of these renegades unite and create havoc for humans, as well as vampires. We call them rogue clans."

"Damn. They sound scary."

"Yes–Anyway, he probably only wanted to erase your memories, but when he couldn't and saw that someone was coming, he knocked you out. He was probably thinking he would come back at a later point to either try again or kill you."

"Oh great!" I shuddered. He grabbed my hand and squeezed.

"Yes, well he or they, I don't know which yet, is certainly keeping track of you, and during the day too. It's very unusual that a vampire would hunt during the day, and it tells me that he is either very determined or very old. Or both."

I suddenly felt worn out. "I think I need some time to digest all of this. I can't quite fathom it right now."

"Of course. I need some shut-eye anyway." He gave me one last squeeze and aimed toward the door. "I'll leave you to rest for awhile. Maybe I could show you the rest of the cave when you're feeling up to it, and I have a surprise for later. I'll have someone bring you an untraceable cell phone to use. We have no landline in these rooms for security purposes. You'll be staying with us, where it's safe, for at least a few days. I'll have someone pickup whatever you may need for work. No need to worry. You are safe here."

"Okay." I couldn't believe I was agreeing to all of his orders. "That sounds good." I think he was shocked that I didn't put up a fight, because he raised his eyebrows and got a cocky grin on his face. I went along with it because I really had no other choice. I didn't want to put anyone else I cared for in danger. Plus, I couldn't imagine what his surprise might be–werewolves, witches, little trolls perhaps?

Declan suddenly came back, clasped my hands, and walked me toward the door. "There is no need to be frightened of me, Bailey."

"What?"

"I may not be able to look into your mind, but I can still smell it on you."

"Oh." I guess I was a little scared of him. But only a little.

He stared into my eyes with his hypnotic gaze.

"This place, my Guild, is of utmost importance to me. I have a large responsibility to guard this area of the country, and I will not let anything interfere with my job. I will do anything in my power to protect you. As long as I am alive, you have my vow."

Wowsy. "But why would you put your life at risk for me? You don't even know me. It seems—I mean it *is* a bit crazy. Don't you think?"

"I am a Centurion; therefore I am a bit crazy." He laughed. A big, beautiful riotous laugh that filled the room. "Plus, to be totally honest, my motives are somewhat selfish. I believe you are connected to Ix and her story, and I want to get to the bottom of it." He was gone before I could reply. Of course, the door locked behind him.

"Crap."

9

THE GUILDED LILY

slept fitfully. Dreams that wouldn't quite solidify kept me anxious, and I knew that the monster was lurking somewhere close. I awoke to a soft hand on my shoulder.

"Miss Davis, your lunch is here. Are you hungry?" A beautifully angelic face drew close to mine, framed by a cloud of white-blonde hair.

"Oh, hi. Yes, I'll eat a little something. Thank you."

"My name is Lily. I work here in the cave."

"Really?" I got up and headed to the bathroom.

"I apologize for waking you, but you've been sleeping for about three hours."

Great, did they have cameras in the room? "What exactly do you do besides serve food?" I asked her as I returned with my hair freshly fluffed.

She smiled. "Whatever Sir Declan wishes." She slid her eyes towards me.

"Oh." I really didn't need to hear about that. I considered the feast laid out before me. "Wow, look at all of this food. Please sit and help me eat this, Lily." She nodded and joined me at the table.

"So tell me, are you the only one working here? I haven't really seen anybody else. Except for Declan's other friends–I mean–"

"Warriors," she said, her wide blue eyes twinkling.

"Okay, warriors."

"There are several of us who keep the place running. Many more act as security for this site. I'm not allowed to disclose just how many; you know, safety reasons."

I couldn't imagine this little thing being security for a gerbil, let alone a whole bunch of vampires. The thought made me smile. I bit into my croissant.

"Yum, this is fantastic. What did you put in this?"

"It's an old family recipe from Sweden, but the main ingredient is fresh shrimp mixed with sour cream and Swedish cheeses. And lots of dill, of course."

"Wow. It's really great, thank you for making it."

"Oh, I didn't make it. We have two cooks on the premises at all times." She dapped at her lips with her napkin. "So are you well rested?"

I nodded with a mouthful. After I managed to swallow, I said, "I'm starting to get a little stir crazy, and I would really like to call my folks so they don't worry. I also should check in at work. I have some jobs I'm needed on. I can't stay here forever. I do have a life."

"Yes, I almost forgot. Sir Declan gave me this to give to you." She went for her pocket. "He said that he trusted you to do the right thing." She handed me a fancy new cell phone. "Here is the number, and he also programmed his cell number on speed dial, along with a couple of others. See here?" And she showed me how to work the futuristic thing. "Here are Thomas's and Daniel's numbers. Thomas is the head of our medical team and Daniel is head of security for the Chicago Guild."

"Guild?"

"Yes, didn't Sir Declan explain this all to you?"

I shook my head.

"Okay, I will try then. The entire country is sectioned off into what we call Provinces—for example, the Southeast, the Northwest, or the Western Province of the United States. Each province has roughly six Guilds, depending on the vampire population. We live in the Great Lakes Province of the United States, Guild of Chicago, which is one of the largest Provinces and Guilds. Our region encompasses Detroit, Buffalo, Chicago, Cleveland, and any other city and environs that are near the Great Lakes. Canada has its own Provinces, as does every country around the world. Each Guild has a Senator and several advisors and staff who work for him or her. The Senators make local laws, decide on disputes, and oversee the general welfare of their Guild. Each Senator answers to the Great Council, which is like the Supreme Court of the vampire nation. They meet twice a year at a secret location.

"Vampire politics. I don't know if I want to think about that." I shook my head.

She brightened. "Of course you don't, who does? It's all the same. Humans, vampires; some just want the power to control others."

"You got that right, sister." We both laughed, and I knew we were going to be friends.

"Enjoying lunch?" Declan asked from the doorway.

"Yes, immensely, but if that clock is correct, three P.M. is a little late for lunch."

"We didn't have the heart to wake you," Lily said as the two of them exchanged glances. Lily immediately cleared the dishes and turned to me. "I'll see you soon. Come to me for anything you may need."

"I will." I winked at her. She looked shocked, then she laughed.

"I'm so happy you are here to spice up this dreary place, Bailey Davis."

When Lily closed the door, I focused on Declan. "Does everybody around here jump on your command?"

He looked at me like I was nuts. "Of course they do."

"Oh boy." I was sorry I had asked.

"I see you got the phone. I hope you don't find it too presumptuous of me, but I knew you would be missing yours."

"Thank you. I really do need to make some calls; will you please excuse me? Oh. but first—when do you think I'll be able to get back to work? I have a lot scheduled and an important job I just started."

"What?" His eyes narrowed and his lips thinned. There was a little vein at his right temple that bulged and pounded to his heart rate. "Bloody hell, woman! You cannot possibly go back to work until we figure out who you really are, and the threat to your life is dealt with." His Irish lilt was prevalent now, and it was nice.

"But that could take days, weeks even!"

"Yes, it could." His jaw was set into a stubborn line that I was getting accustomed to.

"Well, I'm not sitting locked in this room for one more day. No way. I refuse to be jailed!" Little did he know that I could be even more obstinate than him.

"But–"

"No buts, pal. I will not be scared away from my life by some–blood-sucking vampire."

Declan's eyes blazed. I don't think he was used to the word, no. He started pacing and mumbling. "I've never had to deal with such insolence before in my four hundred-odd years of life!" He said much louder. "*A bhidse!* I will not toler–" He abruptly halted and pivoted towards me. I think he was speaking some other language under his breath.

"What were you about to say to me?" I glared with all of my might. He merely appraised me, no longer angry, but with a thoughtful expression.

"Okay, how about a deal?"

I could almost hear his wheels turning.

"Give me three days to find out what's going on. You can have free rein of the cave, but you must not leave, under any circumstances, unless you are with me or one of my men. Or speak to any of your human contacts about all of this, and of course, everything you have learned here. That you should never do, under any circumstances."

I thought about it for several seconds. "I need my computer and some of my disks for work. And I need to be able to call anyone I choose, at any time. And I need somewhere to workout. I can't take sitting here all day."

"Done." He begrudgingly smiled.

"Fine. Now please excuse me while I check in at work. Oh wait. Before you leave. Please tell me where the hell I am?"

He brightened. "You're on the south side; about ten miles from home. I'll be back in a half an hour to take you on a tour. You may be surprised at what you have here to utilize."

As we walked towards the door he shook his head. "You are one mulish woman, Bailey Davis. Almost as bad as Queen Elizabeth."

"Oh, you know the Queen of England?" I asked casually. *Name-dropper.*

"No, not this one, the last one."

10

CAVING IN

After countless fibs about my situation and words of reassurance about my fine health to Ron, Connie, and my parents, I was finally able to get off the phone. Declan had been waiting patiently, and seemed excited when I was finally ready to follow his lead.

I could not believe my eyes. The so-called cave was an elaborate, complex multi-leveled array of spaces that all met at a central axis point. The level Declan took me to, which was one up from where I was staying, contained the main entry, security, a commercial kitchen, dining room, and social spaces, including a French baroque-style ballroom. In the main security room, which we had to pass through in order to get into any other space or level, sat several men. I said hello to them all as Declan directed me towards the largest one, who had been in my kitchen the night before.

"Daniel, I want to introduce you to Bailey Davis."

He was huge. He had to be at least six foot six, with brown hair that curled and hung in his big blue eyes. He was neither lanky nor stocky, but somewhere in-between. Just right, I would say. I held out my hand.

"Pleased to finally meet you, Daniel." I dazzled him with my best smile.

He studied me with what looked like admiration, and met my smile with a great one of his own. "The feeling is mutual. I hope we didn't frighten you too much last night, *ma cher*? I do apologize if we did." His mitt-sized hand dwarfed my own.

"Not at all," I replied. "I was just a little taken off balance. You are from the south?"

"Why, yes ma'am, New Orleans originally," he beamed.

"I'm sure you knock the girls dead with a smile like that," I couldn't help but say.

"Why, yes *ma cher*." And he raised my hand to his warm lips. Wow.

"If you two are finished, I would like to continue to show Ms. Davis around." Declan shoved me out without as much as a goodbye.

"That was rude, Declan."

He just mumbled incoherently and continued with his tour.

"How many feet are we below ground?" I interjected during his spiel. Declan froze as if startled.

"How did you know we were below ground?"

"I don't know, just a gut feeling, and the fact that I haven't seen a window."

"Oh, of course. We are about one hundred feet below ground level," he said proudly.

I couldn't believe it. I had to jump through hoops with inspectors, permits, building departments, and preservation commissions. And they'd built this incredible underground structure without anyone knowing? It seemed impossible.

"That's about ten stories! How on earth did you ever get this built without someone finding out?"

"With a lot of ingenuity, and even more greased palms." He smiled. I just shook my head.

We ran into several people who said hello, but Declan did not stop for any formal introductions. I could only wave to Lily as we passed the kitchen and saw her talking with a chef. Declan kept me moving along at a good clip while continuing his monologue.

The cave featured six main wings, or spokes, so to speak, off of the central axis. Each one was a little different from the others. Some had stairs leading up or down to other spaces. The first corridor Declan led me to was the main research wing, which contained a computer lab with some two dozen computer stations. Two men were arguing about something on one of their monitors.

"Vampire geeks? Now I've seen it all." Declan laughed, and we continued on.

He led me to another security checkpoint. He nodded at the man in the office and put his eye to a scanner. A door hissed open, and we entered a magnificent library stocked full of books, manuscripts, and what looked like scrolls. The library was the only room in this wing to look historic. Someone had done a superb job designing the immense room that included two levels of stacks surrounding a large circular space that housed several library tables and comfortable-looking club chairs. The ceiling boasted a splendid fresco that Michelangelo himself could have painted. Niches at various points along the perimeter contained ancillary spaces, copiers, computers, scanners, and the whole ball of wax.

"How wonderful." I couldn't keep the admiration out of my voice. Declan looked pleased and nodded.

"Yes, we have been collecting for hundreds of years. This is one of our main research facilities. Only a select few have access to this space because it contains many rare artifacts and important documentation. Did you notice the heavier security?" I nodded. "This place has separate electrical and security systems." He walked around as he spoke. "It is completely airtight, and the correct proportions of humidity and oxygen are pumped in via these ducts here." He pointed to several small openings hidden behind draperies and under furniture. "All of it runs on its own system, in a different building off-site. And it's entirely fireproof; even the furnishings are made from fire-retardant materials." He grinned like a proud papa.

"Wow, you would never know, everything is so well hidden. I don't even see sprinkler heads."

"That's because there are none. We assumed if there was a fire, the water damage would be just as bad as the fire itself." I must have looked surprised because he snorted. "We installed heat and smoke sensors in various locations that would detect any problems and would automatically set off a trigger, that seals the room, cuts off all of the oxygen, and pumps out any remaining air in the space. A fire wouldn't get very far."

"I wouldn't want to be in here if that happened."

"No, I don't think anyone would. We do have a built-in timer that allows ninety seconds for anyone to get out. Plus, there are a few oxygen masks hidden about."

"I'm impressed, Declan." Did I see his chest puff out? "I feel honored to be allowed in to see this state-of-the-art space."

"You don't pose a threat, and because of my lineage and researching history, I have total access to all of the vampire nation archives. It's an honor that I am proud of."

Did I see a bit of a blush?

"Anyway, we will both be using this to further our research into your situation. I've reported to the Council, and you, my dear, are a top priority now."

"What about your other job?"

"I will still go to work, however, I don't have much pending right now that can't be put on the back burner."

"Good, I'm looking forward to getting to the bottom of all of this."

The next wing he led me to contained the medical facilities. Several people were milling around one bed in particular whose occupant was yelling such violent obscenities to the medical staff that my grandfather would have been impressed. I caught a peek at what was left of his right arm, and I almost lost my lunch. Blood was everywhere on the poor man and the lucky spectators.

"My god, he lost his arm. How horrible."

"Yes." He must have looked at my stricken face because he added. "Do not concern yourself. It will grow back. But it takes some time and it is a rather painful process."

"Ahhh, ya think?" I couldn't help but say. Just then, Thomas bustled in. We said our hellos, but he was obviously too busy to chitchat, so we moved along.

"We can talk to Thomas later. I would like him to explain to you a little bit about our anatomy. It's somewhat different than your–I mean to say, humans'."

"Because you're not sure I'm human, right?"

"Well, yes. I'm sorry."

I took a deep breath. "I still cannot accept the fact that I am one of–well–um, a vampire. It can't be. Sun doesn't affect me at all. Well, I do like to sleep in on occasion, but I can touch silver with no effect, see?" I showed him my necklace, which was a small, custom-made sterling Queen Anne house very intricately detailed with porch balusters and a diamond in one of the windows.

"Yes, it is quite unique, and beautiful. Where did you have it made?"

"It was a gift from my parents last Christmas." He nodded his approval. "So you see, I cannot possibly be a vampire."

Declan looked unconvinced. He came closer and looked into my eyes. He lightly touched my necklace where it hung on my chest, on my bare skin.

"Since I am a Full Blood, I am not as sensitive to the metal either. See?" And he held my necklace. "It feels warm to my touch, and if it were pure, it could burn just a bit, but it is not as harmful to my kind as it is to the changed vampires."

Whoa, he wasn't the only one feeling warm. My stomach clenched and my legs grew weak. Declan must have sensed my excitement because he produced a very sexy smile, but then abruptly put the necklace down and stepped away. Darn.

He cleared his throat. "Let's continue this way."

Our next stop was the activity area, which encompassed two full wings. I counted a couple of dozen people partaking in the various activities, which included a shooting range and weapons locker, full gym, equipped with the most state-of-the-art machinery I had ever seen, an aerobics room, a boxing ring, a martial arts room, and a quarter-mile track on the perimeter of a full basketball and one tennis court. Two couples having fun playing doubles waved as we walked by.

The south wing contained a large locker room, unisex of course, that had changing facilities, a steam-room, sauna, massage rooms, beauty salon, and elaborate showers. But the focal point of all of it was the swimming pool that joined the two wings together in the center. It was a magnificent pool, similar to the one at Hadrian's Villa, including the Roman statuary and fountains. But the most interesting aspect was the fact that someone had recreated sunlight and painted the high ceiling with blue skies and big puffy white clouds. Lush palm trees and planted flowerbeds decorated the space. They even had birds and other outdoor sounds piped in.

"Wow. This is just beyond belief. This whole place." I stood momentarily in awestruck silence. "Declan, you could live down here for years and never feel claustrophobic. It is amazing. I am extremely impressed."

"I'm very pleased you like it," his eyes shined. "The people who use this facility have no complaints."

"Do you have more just like this one?"

"Not exactly, no. They vary. Some have climbing walls and others have caves for spelunking. One even has a connection to the ocean, which is used for diving practice."

"It is truly astounding," I said, as I marveled at the artistry.

"Here, take this." He gave me a key card. "This will get you into these spaces and the computer lab. We have to have your eye scanned to get you into the library and the weapons locker. There are some areas I cannot show you—you understand?"

"I guess so. I don't really want to know about all the things that are too sensitive for me to see."

Just then, the dark-haired woman who had been at my house came strolling in with another woman, both wearing teensy weensy thong bikinis. *Jeepers, why bother to wear anything?* Declan didn't seem to pay much attention. It was probably nothing he hadn't seen before. Hmm, interesting. Maybe he had already seen it *all* before. And that thought made me uncomfortable. Crap.

"Bailey, I would like to introduce Shila and Lucissil."

"Just call me Lucy," the blonde said with a smile. "It's a pleasure to meet you."

"Thank you, likewise." I returned the smile. Shila just stared a hole into me. *I guess we wouldn't be friends,* I figured. *No big loss.* Declan must have noticed too, because he was frowning at her.

"Well, Declan, I'm getting a little tired. Can you please take me back now?" I said to break the tension. "It was nice to meet you, Lucy. Shila." I sniffed. And we left.

The last two wings were the multileveled personnel quarters. The larger suites were given to the more important vamps, like the Centurions, the Senator, and his staff.

"How many people—I mean, vampires live here?"

"There are thirty three of us here full-time. We often have many visitors stay; a few for the archival research, others to visit friends and loved ones. Not all are vampires. Some bring their human mates. We have about fifteen patrons and a few humans who just work here and go home after their shift."

I was surprised by this notion. "And you trust them with your secret here?"

"Oh, yes. They go through a very thorough security screening process and sign a blood oath as well. Remember, we can see into their minds. They would never betray us. We would know immediately."

"Blood oath? Oh, forget it, don't tell me." He only smiled and nodded. I didn't believe he was too eager to explain it to me either.

"I'll take you back to your room now. I had some more appropriate clothing brought to your room for dinner tonight, which is at seven thirty sharp. We dine more formally than what you are probably used to, and tonight especially there will be music and dancing. A lot of people want to meet you, including the Senator." He lowered his voice and shoved me into a niche. We are keeping your–um, abilities a secret for now. I told everyone you were my new girlfriend. I hope you're not offended, but we needed a reason for your visit, and since I am detached as of late, I thought it an adequate cover."

Detached as of late? "What? Well, okay–but what if–I mean, are you sleeping in my room then?" I was stammering like an idiot and my heart sped up. I couldn't imagine sleeping in the same bed as him. Or maybe I could imagine it all too well.

"Only if you want to make it look like we didn't lie." He smirked.

"But what if–I mean–uh, what if you get hungry?" *What a moron!*

He laughed out loud at that. "Well, I'll just eat, of course." He frowned for a second. "Bailey, do you honestly think I would feed from you without your approval?"

I sighed. "No, I guess not. But I don't think I'm up for a party. I really just want to figure this out and get back to my life." We continued to the door of my suite.

"Bailey, this *is* your life now. I'm so sorry, but your life is going to be different." He looked genuinely sad, and that made me angry.

"I don't think so," I snapped. "What this is…is a nightmare. A nightmare that will end, and then I will go back to my real life!" I could feel my temperature rising.

Now was Declan's turn to sigh. "I was going to tell you later. We caught the rogue who was threatening you. We are in the process of extracting information."

I didn't want to know how they were doing that. "Great, I want to interrogate the bastard. Where is he?" I said with force.

"You cannot possibly see him. I will not let you anywhere near him, and that is final!" He responded incensed. "We know this goes further than just Mikel."

"Mikel, is that the jerk's name?"

"Yes, and we have to be careful that we do not alert others to his capture."

"What others?"

"We don't know for sure yet."

"But, if you have this creep, then I can go home. I'm safe from him now, right?" I felt hopeful for the first time since I'd arrived.

"Absolutely not. I believe there are others involved, and I will not risk it."

"*You* will not risk it? Who the hell do you think you are?" I yelled. At that moment my door opened to the squeals of Rosa and the boys. Hugs and licks ensued.

"Surprise," Declan said and shrugged.

"Mees Bailey, I so worried." Rosa came in for a hug.

"It's okay, Rosa, we are all safe here."

"Who are they?" She pointed to Declan.

"They are friends and are going to keep us safe." I looked at Declan. He nodded and took Rosa's hands.

"*Nos mantendremos segura. No hay razón para ser asustado de nosotros.*"

Rosa's eyes widened. "*Muy bien, pero este lugar es aterrador.*"

"Yes, it is." And they both laughed.

"Okay, what's so funny?" I turned to Declan. "And since when do you speak Spanish?"

"You can't live as long as I have and not know a few languages. Rosa will be staying next door in a smaller apartment. You can see each other whenever you wish."

I took him aside and lowered my voice. "Do you think this is wise? What if she finds out about you?"

"It's okay. We'll worry about that when, and if, it comes. She thinks we are the police. Let's leave it at that for now. She knows she's safe here. But she doesn't know the specifics, and it's better left unsaid. Remember, I do have…" He tapped his head.

"Ah, will that hurt her?" I wasn't too sure about this mind-wiping stuff.

"No, of course not, and there is no permanent damage."

"Okay. So where do I walk the dogs?"

He stiffened. "Um–I can get someone to take them up a couple of times a day."

I giggled. "So you didn't think of everything, now did you?" I patted his hand. "This is a nice surprise. Thank you. But we will finish our other conversation later."

He walked over to the desk. "Here is your laptop all set up and your disks that you requested. Am I missing anything?"

I couldn't help it; I threw my arms around him and planted a kiss right on his mouth. *H e l l o.* It was like fire melting my insides, and I could feel my nipples harden. I broke contact. "Um–sorry. I didn't mean–"

"It was my pleasure." And he gave me a very sexy smile. I turned to Rosa, and she had a grin on her face while pretending to ignore us. I cleared my throat.

"Well, guys, I'm going to rest up and take a long hot bath before dinner."

"Si, Mees Bailey. I will take dogs."

"No, that's okay. I'd rather have them with me for now. Rosa, thanks for everything."

"Is okay." She smiled.

"I'll walk Rosa next door. She'll be fine." Declan pulled me aside. "I've arranged for Rosa to have dinner in her room." He whispered. "I thought it best she not see a whole room of vampires just yet."

I nodded. "Good idea."

"I'll pick you up for dinner."

"I can manage to get to the dining room on my own."

"I'm sure you can, but you are my girlfriend, so how would that look?"

"Okay, okay. You've made your point. I'll be ready by...?"

"Seven o'clock for cocktails. And Bailey, just so you are prepared, some of us prefer to, um–eat–um. Well, let's just say they bring their own willing hosts for dinner. You know, the patrons. Don't be frightened. You are in no danger."

"Oh, just great. I'm sooo looking forward to this. Yuck!" But he merely winked and left with Rosa.

"Wonderful," I murmured to the dogs, who only lifted their ears and tilted their heads.

CR80

After he dropped Rosa off at her door, Declan went to the tombs. This was one area he had not shown Bailey. He thought about her then. He was impressed with her continued strength, even sticking up for herself against Shila. He smiled, remembering the moment.

Yes, Bailey was a very intriguing woman. And her lips–he shook his head. Yes, he was certainly attracted to her, he begrudgingly admitted, but he was not about to get involved with a human. Well, at least part human. Her abilities had to be related to the story of Ix–though he knew it was all hearsay. Most of the written documentation he'd found on the subject had been shoved away under vampire folklore and long ago forgotten. No one seemed to be interested until Mikel's obsession with Bailey. If it were true, and Bailey was a descendant of Ix, she was probably the last of her kind, any others were sure to have been destroyed long ago. At least that was what he believed.

Of course Declan had known for awhile that Bailey was not who she thought she was. He also knew that it would break her heart when she found out for sure. Right now she was still in denial. And that was all right. Bailey needed to slowly realize who, and what, she was, and he had all the time in the world to wait for her to do so.

He rounded the corner, positioned his left eye in the scanner, and the steel door slid open with a hiss.

Charles met him at the outer door. "The prisoner is still not talking much. He's quite a tough subject. We've pretty much bled him dry." Declan nodded. "Very well, give me a couple of minutes, and then kill him." He didn't think he would get much information out of Mikel, if that was his real name.

He and Charles stepped up to another scanner. This one was a bio-reader. After their bodies were scanned a green light flashed, a door unlocked, and they entered the tombs. He could immediately hear screaming. Their methods were not pretty, but he did not regret it, because he needed to know whom Mikel was working for. He had to find the rogues and protect Bailey at all costs.

Charles led the way, passing a couple of other prisoners the Senator had yet to decide what to do with. Petty crimes mostly. The prisoner Declan was interested in was at the very end of the hall in a very special cell that was encased in pure silver, except the flooring. Mikel was shackled prostrate on the wall, burning slowly. The cuff, midriff, and ankle bracelets that held him also contained retractable spikes that pierced the skin on command. Puncturing the skin often enough, especially when the hollowed silver spikes contained anticoagulants specifically formulated for his kind, caused permanent blood loss and eventually a slow, painful death. Shila was manning the controls.

"I don't think he has much left, sir." She dropped the controls and ran her card through the card slot on the door. It opened to the burning stench of dying vampire.

"Retract and leave me for a couple of minutes." Charles and Shila stepped out and flanked the doorway. Declan closed the door behind them.

The silver made him uncomfortable, but it was tolerable as long as he wasn't touching it for a long period of time. A changed vampire would burn just setting foot in this room. But this space was not intended for them. It was meant for the special old changed vampires, like Mikel, or Full Bloods like himself. Yes, they had many very interesting surprises in this room.

"Mikel, this is your last chance to speak with me. You will certainly die either way, but at least you will die quickly if you tell me what I want to know." He walked toward the prisoner and lifted his head to meet his eyes.

"Who sent you to kill Bailey Davis? We know you are not working alone."

The only reaction was the drool glistening off Mikel's fangs. Then he suddenly reared up and mumbled incoherently. He fell silent once again, then opened his eyes and looked straight at Declan with clarity.

"They will kill her, you shall see. They will hunt her down like the witch she is and they will torture her for their pleasure." He closed his eyes, his energy spent.

"Who, you bastard?" But Mikel kept his silence. Declan let Mikel's head fall back and stalked to the door. Charles immediately opened it.

"Kill him—painfully."

☾☽

I rested with the dogs for over an hour, then went to soak in the most luxurious bathtub I had ever been in. The lavender bath salts not only smelled great, but soothed my skin. This was just what the doctor ordered. I shaved my legs, under my arms, and my bikini line creating a little strip right down the center.

"What am I doing?" I demanded of myself. "This is not a date!" The dogs raised their heads at my outburst.

"It's okay boys, Mama's just frustrated." I had yet to fully digest the crazy tale Declan had divulged. How could there be vampires? And how could I possibly be related to those vampires? The thought was just nuts. I had a perfectly normal–well, kind of normal–family. And I never saw any indication that they had any type of special abilities, but why, then, did I?

I refocused on getting ready for dinner because I couldn't investigate this any further at the moment. It was just too exhausting to comprehend. I took my time putting on my makeup and drying my curls, which seemed awfully shiny. The strawberry blonde almost glowed. I looked in the closet. Wow, Declan had left an array of beautiful dresses and none too conservative. I picked one the color of emeralds, which would look great with my hair and eyes. The satin clung to me like a glove. The front draped to the tops of my ample breasts, showing off my abundant cleavage. The straps, if that is what you wanted to call them, held tiny rhinestones that glistened when I moved. The back was all but nonexistent, and draped all the way to my lower spine, showing off my tribal tattoo. I also realized that the slit came to my, well–coochie. I was glad Rosa was staying in her room.

The five-inch emerald satin Jimmy Choo stiletto sandals were going to kill me, but hopefully I could manage to walk without breaking an ankle. I was just about to call the dogs when I heard a knock on my door. I opened it to Declan and a young slender man I did not recognize. They both stared with their mouths ajar.

"Well, are you coming in?" I asked, pleased by their reaction. They entered like zombies. "Is something wrong?" I started to get nervous.

Declan cleared his throat and croaked, "Bailey, you look stunning."

"Thank you, so do you." And he did, with his wavy dark hair and vivid blue eyes, in a black tux that fit him perfectly. I cleared my throat and nodded to our guest.

"Forgive me. Roran, this is Ms. Bailey Davis."

"Pleased to meet you, Roran," I said with my best smile.

"Roran assists me, and he has agreed to help with the dogs. He loves animals." And as if on cue, the dogs rushed to be greeted. Roran knelt on the ground and playtime commenced. I watched amused, as the brown-haired, fresh-faced young man enjoyed my dogs.

"He will feed them and then take them up for a long walk."

"I'll drop them in Miss Rosa's room when I'm finished," Roran said shyly with a surprisingly deep tenor.

"Thank you." I could see at least this aspect of my short stay in the cave would work. The dogs loved him. I handed over their leashes and showed him the food in the kitchen. Then Declan escorted me to dinner.

The dining room was decked out with royal blue and gold linens. People were milling about with drinks in their hands, talking and laughing. Servers rushed from group to group carrying trays of canapés and glasses of what looked like—oh boy, was that blood?

I noticed that most of the women were beautiful, and I was certainly not overdressed. I took Declan's arm as he led me from group to group, introducing me to many of his friends and coworkers. They were all warm and welcoming, and a few of the men openly gawked at my cleavage. Declan must have noticed too, because he did a lot of glaring.

Lily walked up to us with a very handsome man on her arm. "Good evening, Sir Declan, Bailey." And she winked at me. "This gentleman wishes to be introduced."

"Of course, allow me," Declan stated. "Bailey, this is our Senator, Clive Reardon. Senator Reardon, this is Bailey Davis."

"What a pleasure it is to meet you. I've heard how beautiful you are, and I was not lied to. Declan, she is a knockout." Declan looked irritated and gripped my arm, but I was secretly loving all of the attention. It had been so long since I'd felt pretty and even longer since I had been paid such compliments. Yes, vampires seemed very forward. But hell, it was going to be fun playing along.

"Why, thank you, and you are very handsome yourself." I gave the Senator my best smile. I was lathering it on thick, but I didn't have to fib. He was about six feet tall, of a medium build, and about forty-five in human years, with the beginnings of laugh lines and crow's feet. He had blond hair and sparkly hazel eyes.

"Declan tells me that you are a designer. How fascinating. What do you think of our facility here?" he said as he took my arm in his and turned me to gesture to the dining hall—forcing Declan to release his possessive grip.

"It is spectacular. I've never seen such beautifully created spaces. I am especially fond of the pool area."

His eyes sparkled. "Oh yes, it is quite something. Well, I hope to spend much more time with you, Bailey. I insist you sit by me at dinner. That would not be a problem, will it, Declan?" He looked over his shoulder to Declan, who had been boring a hole into the Senator's back.

"No sir."

I could tell that he wasn't happy. He was doing a lot of scowling and mumbling. The Senator kissed my hand and then he and Lily continued with their mingling, and I turned to find Daniel at my side with a glass of champagne.

"I thought you could use this, *ma cher*."

"You read my mind." We both laughed.

"Daniel." Declan greeted him curtly.

"Sir Declan, I must ask your permission for a dance later with the most beautiful woman here, *oui*." He turned to me, grasped my shoulders and kissed both cheeks. "Until later, *ma belle* Bailey." And he disappeared into the crowd. Wow.

"That was interesting," I remarked to Declan, who was visibly fuming.

"My god, all of these scoundrels are salivating over you. It's disgusting."

"Gee, thanks a lot. Besides, you picked the dress."

"You know I didn't mean it like that." Dinner was called which prevented me from saying anything I would regret.

I was seated to the left of the Senator, who was at the head of the table, and Declan was to my right, flanked by Mazva, a beautiful exotic-looking African woman. Across the table, Lily sat next to a gentleman I had not met.

The table was filled with glittering crystal, cobalt blue china, and gold-accented serving ware. Spectacular flowers in gilded vases ran down the entire length of the table, which sat at least fifty. Interesting, I noticed—no silver anywhere. Even the flatware was gold.

Waiters appeared out of nowhere with huge trays of whole fish, sliced roast beef, and whole legs of lamb. I piled my plate high with a little bit of everything; leg of lamb, beef roast, pork tenderloin, a variety of roasted vegetables and salads, and mashed potatoes galore. It was delicious. The conversation was no different than any other dinner party: fashion, architecture, politics, and gossip about people I had no clue about. Declan was attentive, including me in his conversations and even brushing against my leg on several occasions. Yikes, I was paying way too much attention to that.

After a delectable dessert of chocolate soufflé with clotted cream and berries, Declan escorted me to the ballroom, where the band was just beginning to play. We found seats close to the dance floor and enjoyed the music. Sitting close to one another, even holding hands to maintain the pretense of being a couple, was nice and I was happy, considering the circumstances. I knew that we were just keeping up appearances, but this was one of the better dates I'd had in awhile. Declan was easy to talk to, smart, attentive, fantastic to look at, polite, and liked to laugh. All around, he was just too good to be true. Oh, yeah, except that he was a VAMPIRE! Crap, way to burst my own bubble.

Declan excused himself to go see a man who had been trying to get his attention for some time. When he was gone, Daniel appeared, took my hand, and escorted me to the dance floor for some disco dancing. I loved to dance, so I readily accepted. We were bumping and grinding to the music, and having a great time, when I noticed the far doors open and about twenty people came in. The women wore very skimpy, very tight, shiny rubberized skirts with see-through halter-tops; the men were shirtless in tight black satin pants. All of them looked excited to be here.

"Who are they?" I yelled over the music, angling my chin toward the group.

"They are our patrons. Didn't Sir Declan tell you?"

I gaped at a woman who was sitting on the lap of a vampire. His eyes were the color of my monsters, and he had her neck in his mouth.

"Holy shit. Oh, crap! I need to stop and sit down."

Daniel looked startled, but he led me to the nearest empty couch. He took my hand and said something to me, but my ears were ringing, and I couldn't understand what he was saying. I took a good look around, awestruck. All of the patrons had hooked up with a vampire, literally. Not all vamps partook in the festivities, but the ones who did looked as though they were having a splendid time. And the patrons seemed to be enjoying it just as much. Some even had two vampires sucking on various body parts. I heard a lot of moans over the din of the music, and some couples looked to be close to having sex. A lot of clothes suddenly went missing. But what shook me most was that, instead of being sickened by the whole ordeal, I was fascinated. In fact, seeing all of these people in various forms of ecstasy was turning me on. Suddenly, Declan was in front of me, on his knees, shoving a glass of water at me.

"Come on, I'll take you back now." He looked worried.

"Oh–um–I'm okay. Really, I was just a little startled."

"Are you sure?" I nodded as I drained the glass.

"I'm sure. Please, let's stay a bit longer." I grabbed his hand and led him to the dance floor. He smiled as I guided him into the mass of writhing people. Damned if he wasn't a good dancer too. Was there anything he couldn't do?

"Are you having a good time?" he yelled over the music. I grinned and spun to shake my bootie in his direction. He laughed and seized my hips, swaying with my motion. I felt the beginnings of sweat forming on my forehead and between my breasts as we rocked to the bass. I was oblivious to anyone else in the room while I concentrated on my warmed muscles contracting, stretching, and grinding in sync to Declan's every move. I could feel his heartbeat, smelled his pleasure, and it made me that much more excited. Did I just think…*smelled*? Oh boy.

He held me tightly as he closed his eyes and enjoyed the feel of my slickened skin on his. He was into the music now; the sensation of me so close, my aroma was intoxicating to his senses. Holy crap. I knew what he was thinking. That realization stopped me in my tracks.

"What's wrong?"

"Um, nothing." But he didn't believe me and narrowed his eyes. I began to grind to the music once again.

"Please don't stop," I said. "I'm having a wonderful time."

My smile must have assured him. He twisted me so my back was against him. The feel of his arousal all but knocked me to my knees. We rocked to the music and to each other until a stranger tapped Declan on his shoulder.

"May I cut in?"

An incredibly gorgeous man with eyes like the Caribbean stood at my side. Hmm, green–no blue–yet aqua? Wow, I could feel my heart begin to race. I'm sure Declan felt it too, because he stared at me with an intense frown.

Slowly and reluctantly, Declan moved aside. "I will be right here, Bailey." He gave the stranger a menacing scowl and said something I couldn't quite hear over the music, but it was not nice, I was sure of that. The stranger dragged me to a different area of the dance floor, away from Declan.

"Hey, what are you doing? Let go of me." I pulled my hand out of his. How dare he? Who the hell did he think he was?

"I do apologize," he yelled over the din. "Let me introduce myself. My name is Gregory. I am Declan's brother." His smile lit up the room.

I must have looked dazed, dim-witted or, to my utter horror, a combination of both, because he began to laugh.

"Priceless. I can assume that he didn't tell you about me." I could only shake my head like a dork. "I'm just visiting for a few weeks. I live in Rome."

When I could finally find my voice, I said, "Wow, that sounds wonderful." *What a big dummy.* I turned to show him my moves because I had nothing of importance to say. *Dope, dope, dope. Come on, Bailey.* I'd seen unbelievably gorgeous, hunky men before. Well, at least in the movies. I couldn't believe I was actually tongue-tied like a teenager.

He clasped my waist and began to move. He was not a good as his brother, but he was convincing. It gave me the opportunity to thoroughly look him over. His dark curls were cut short over a pair of perfectly sculpted ears. His face looked angelic, even feminine in a way. He had Declan's chin and coloring, but other than that, little resemblance. Gregory was of average height and lanky, almost skinny, to Declan's tall, sturdy frame. He was beautiful in stature and grace to Declan's manly gorgeousness. He was more of a free spirit to Declan's seriousness. Don't ask me how I knew that, I just did. Here were two completely contradictory personalities born out of the same womb. I could relate to that.

"So, how do you like Chicago?" *Lame, Bailey, lame!*

"Oh, I like it fine. It is quite a beautiful city–even more so now."

Oh boy, I felt faint. *Pull yourself together, Bailey!*

"I'm sorry, I haven't introduced myself." I yelled over the music. "I'm Bailey Davis." And I threw out my hand for him to shake.

"I know. My brother's new girlfriend. He was always the lucky one." And he pulled my hand to his lips. Wowsy.

The moment was broken by the end of the song and Declan's sudden arrival. He stepped very close to his brother and whispered something in his ear. Gregory regarded me with a poignant look upon his beautiful face.

"Unfortunately, I am called to my duty. I do hope to see much of you, *mia bella,* before my return to Italy. *Ciao.*" He scowled at Declan and left.

"Wow." Oops, did that come out of my mouth? Declan was giving me the evil eye. "Um, you didn't tell me you had a brother?"

"Yes, well. I didn't have the time, yet."

"Don't you two get along?"

"Oh, we get along just fine. I haven't seen too much of him over the last few decades now that he is the Senator of the Roman Guild. I don't get to Rome often, and this is his first visit to Chicago."

We strolled to the couches to sit for a while. I noticed that many of the vampires had left and others were still engaged with their patron. One couple was even openly having sex. Crazy. I felt like I was on another planet, or back in college.

"I'm getting tired. Do you mind taking me back now?"

"Of course not." He stood up to take my hand. The Senator met us halfway across the ballroom.

"Are you leaving us so early, Ms. Davis?"

"Yes, I apologize, but it's been a long day. It was so nice to meet you, and I hope to see you again soon." I gave him my best smile.

"It was my pleasure. You have a good evening." He bowed slightly, then walked towards a group that was sharing in a meal of one of the human men.

Declan escorted me to my door.

"Well, thank you for a very interesting evening," I said.

He used his key card to unlock my door, opened it for me to walk in, then followed right behind me.

"Oh! I thought you were just teasing about staying here with me." I fidgeted with my necklace.

"Does it look like I am teasing you, Bailey?"

"Um, well–I guess not," I said as I staggered to the settee. "My feet are killing me in these things." I bent down but Declan was there. I swear, I blinked, and he was on his knees, once again, in front of me.

"Let me help you."

He gingerly traced my calf down to my heel. Whoa, holy hell, just his touch was making my dizzy. He gently unhooked my strap, and very slowly lifted my foot from the shoe. He threw the shoe aside, grasped my foot in both hands, and started massaging it in tenderly. Heat shot up my leg and landed in the right spot. He then went for the next. Oh, it was getting really hot in this room. I was experiencing was the most erotic moment of my life. And it was shoes!

I jumped up. "Um, I, ah better get out of these clothes. I mean get ready for bed–crap. You know what I mean." He only smiled wickedly. I managed to make it to the bathroom without running into any walls or stubbing my toe. I tried not to think about what was about to happen.

"Is Lily dating the Senator?" I called from the bathroom. I couldn't find any old tees and pajama bottoms in the bag that Declan packed. Damn.

"They have been dating on and off for over twenty years, I believe."

"Oh, wow. That's a long time." I heard him snicker from the bedroom.

I was so nervous that I could hardly brush my teeth. I carefully removed all of my makeup, and washed my face. I felt better already. I looked in the mirror. A gorgeous man was waiting for me on my bed. Oh my, I felt faint. I'd better freshen up just in case something transpired. *This is so crazy.*

After I sat on the bidet, which was an experience, I toweled off and searched for an old lady nightgown. Damn, nothing. Why was I so afraid? Well for one, he was a goddamn vampire! I finally found some gorgeous silk nighties in a drawer, wrapped in scented paper. Hmm, Jessamine. And in my colors too. How convenient. He'd thought of everything.

I chose the pale pink one. It looked great with my skin, which was still silky smooth from the bath. It fell to mid thigh and scooped low in the front. Oh boy, here goes nothing.

I flung open the door and looked around. No Declan. "Declan?" I called. I went to the door and peeked out. No one. I couldn't believe it. I'd been stood up. I started to laugh. I didn't even have any luck with a different species. Figures!

I crawled into bed thinking it was just as well. It had been one hell of a day. Then I saw a note lying on the bedside table.

I had an emergency I need to see to.
Sorry, Declan

No "love," no "I'll miss you desperately". No nothing. Oh well. I fell asleep quickly and did not dream at all.

∞

He had nearly passed out when he saw her beauty. My god, he had never seen anything like her before. And it was quite obvious that Roran felt the same. Declan had never seen him so shy around a woman. He was usually very smooth with the opposite sex, human and otherwise. But he couldn't blame Roran for his shyness. He closed his eyes and envisioned her again. He remembered that dress, which clung to her in all the right places, and the color against her fiery hair and peaches and cream skin, and those incredible eyes–he couldn't even think straight around her. And his body was responding yet again.

She hadn't even noticed the stares and ogles by all of the men in that room last night. It infuriated him just thinking about it. She had no clue what kind of danger she was in, just from her looks. Vampires were a horny bunch, that was for certain. And that damn Gregory was the worst of the lot. Everything was a game to him. He was always in competition with his older brother. Well, Bailey was certainly not going to be any man's prize, if he had anything to say about it. That was one of the reasons he'd sneaked out of her room last night. There was no way he could just casually have sex with Bailey

Davis. And he was not about to become attached, that was for sure. He had only been married once in his long life, and he had sworn off love ever since. Good riddance.

But he did feel gutless. He should have never left her that way, and with that pathetic note too. She would probably never speak to him again, and he wouldn't blame her. He had to get his act together and straighten out around her. He was behaving like a lovesick child.

After leaving her he had gone right to his rooms to change his clothes. He put on his working attire and paid a visit to the tombs. The body of Mikel had already been removed, but the scent of him still lingered. Declan stayed in the cell for hours, thinking about this puzzle. He then went to the research library and started digging some more. He needed to find out who Mikel's master was and then maybe he could get some answers. Yes, that was what he needed to think about instead of Bailey Davis in the nude.

He was startled to look at the clock on the wall and realize that it was 6:30 in the morning. He got up and stretched. He'd come up with a few possibilities he wanted to check out later. Some interesting ideas started to form in his head. And then he thought about her again. Damn. His body was not happy with last night's outcome either. Well, he had a remedy for that.

 conclusion

I was up early feeling restless and disappointed that Declan had never made an appearance the previous night after his emergency. Why, I didn't know, but I did. The best course would be to get away from him. But I needed to try to figure out why I seemed to have these abilities and what it had to do with Declan's story of vampire history so I could get back to my life, and the sooner, the better.

I would visit with Rosa and the boys after my run. I changed into workout clothes, put my curls up in a ponytail, and headed to the gym. I brought the only bathing suit I could find in case I wanted to swim laps later. The skimpy two-piece was completely inappropriate, but I figured no one would be there this early anyway, certainly not after the party the night before.

I thought about all of the humans in various states of bliss while being eaten by a vampire or multiple vampires. It surprised me that I wasn't frightened by it. It was crazy to think that a whole other world lay hidden, right in front of everyone. An entirely alien culture, with a history of its own, living with humans since the beginning. Incredible. I couldn't blame them for wanting to stay under the radar, though. Just envisioning the mayhem that would ensue if the vampires came out of the closet was enough to make me ill.

So last night had not alarmed me. Why? Was it because I could sense that no one wished me any harm? Well, except for Shila, of course. She definitely would not mind seeing me gone, because she thought Declan was interested. Well, Shila had nothing to worry about. After last night, Declan had made his intentions perfectly clear.

I swiped my card, and the door to the activity wing hissed open. Just as I expected, no one else was around. They were probably all sleeping off last night's orgy. I wondered if Declan went back and had a little snack of his own. The thought really pissed me off. *Okay, Bailey, time to act.*

After ten miles around the track as fast as I could run, I really had worked up a decent sweat. My muscles relaxed, and the tension from the last few days vanished. I slowed to a fast walk to cool off before I hit the gym.

I did a round on the circuit and still felt the energy coming off me in waves. I was far from tired so I decided to hit the punching and kick bags. I'd taken three years of jujitsu for self-defense. The movements were quick strikes so your opponent wouldn't know what hit him before you slit his throat. It worked especially well for women, because it used the opponent's own strength against him.

I found some gloves and footgear in a cubby and began my reps. I started with front jabs followed by back kicks and finally roundhouse kicks. I sensed–and turned to find Declan staring intently at me. He was dripping in sweat. I pasted a smile on my face and moved to the mat beckoning him to follow. I'd reached a point that being pissed off was an understatement. I was hurt and tired of the mind games that the men in my life seemed to enjoy playing.

"Want to see some of my moves?"

He laughed, but abruptly stopped when I didn't respond in kind.

"Ohhh, don't tell me you're scared of little ole me?"

This time he didn't laugh, but instead joined me on the mat. By the look of him, apparently he had been in the gym for quite some time. Funny, I never saw or sensed his presence.

"So I see vamps can sweat. Nice to know." *Now why did I say that?* He wasn't speaking, only staring, looking bewildered and embarrassed. *Good.*

"What's the matter, cat got your tongue?"

"What is that supposed to mean?" He looked at his feet. "Um–about last night–I."

"You what? You suddenly got busy? Something that just couldn't wait? Or maybe you just don't like me. But then why be so nice–why act interested?" I flushed, horrified at my outburst. I was whining like a lovesick schoolgirl.

"Oh forget it!" and I kicked him right in the chest. He was so startled that he fell back onto the mat. He got up rubbing his ribs.

"Not bad for a–um–human. Want to try that again?"

"It would be my pleasure!" This time when I kicked, he grabbed my foot and threw me to the ground. His eyes popped when I sprang right back up. I answered with a jab to the left cheek, then a roundhouse to the kidney. If he had any. He stumbled and returned with kick to my midsection, which threw me all the way to the wall. Ouch, I was really getting mad now.

"Maybe I should have taken Gregory up on his offer."

I couldn't believe I'd just said that. *Why was I stooping to this level?* The fury in his eyes made my heart race. I ran back to the mat and scissors-kicked him, but he moved out of the way so fast, he was a blur, and I missed by a mile. I landed on my backside, and he was on me in an instant. I wrapped my legs around his middle and squeezed with all of my might. He let go, broke my hold and stood up fast, peering at me strangely.

"Your eyes are changing to gold."

"Good!" I hit him so hard his head flew back. I hopped up and round-housed him again, but he was too fast and grabbed my leg. My heart was pounding and then suddenly it slowed; my vision sharpened and my hearing grew more acute. I could smell arousal on him and just a bit of fear.

He spun me around in a chokehold. My god, he was so strong, but I managed to use my jujitsu knowledge to my advantage. I struck fast, hitting his ears with my palms. It worked, because he was holding them as I twisted and lunged for a reverse wrist throw. He came off the mat and into the air, but never came back down.

"What the hell?" I screamed. "Where are you, vampire? I was just getting started!"

Suddenly I felt the hairs on the back of my neck rise, and I was grabbed from the back and thrown to the floor.

"Enough!" He stood over me and demanded.

But I couldn't stop. I wanted to hurt him for everything that had happened in my life in the last seventy-two hours. It wasn't fair; he'd been the only one trying to help me. But he had bruised my ego more than I was willing to admit, and I wasn't thinking rationally. I jumped back up and punched him, hard in the stomach, and he wasn't expecting it. He went down hard and I jumped on him and started pummeling his whole body. He put his hands up to block, but I was very quick and got in a few good shots. He finally had enough, and he threw me across the room, breaking the mirror on the far wall. I slid to the floor in shock. My anger spiked. I couldn't think straight as I began to get up again, but he was on me before I could. He held me down as I tried over and over again to punish him. I bit, scratched, raged, and screamed until all the fight drained out of me and left my tattered body in total exhaustion. I couldn't speak as he slowly let go of my bruised arms.

"I apologize, Bailey. I would have never done that but you were almost, um, out of control."

I looked into his eyes, and I knew he was scared and sorry. Sorry that he may have hurt me, but mostly terrified about what I could do.

"Let go of me!" I jumped up. Well, okay, slowly edged my way up. "I'm taking a shower."

I staggered to the locker room with as much dignity as I could muster. It was empty, no surprise there. I looked in the mirror: bloody nose, a big welt on my left cheek, and a puffy left eye. Pretty. I grabbed some tissue and shoved it up my left nostril to stop the bleeding. I stripped out of my soaked clothing and limped to a shower stall. The steaming water felt great on my tightening muscles. I shampooed my hair and turned to rinse and there was Declan, standing in all of his natural glory. He gently pushed me under the water to rinse. Without saying a word, he lathered his hands with lavender body gel and proceeded to wash me everywhere. Oh my. He turned me around and started with my back, kneading as he went up to my neck, which he lightly caressed with his lips. Jesus, I was already hot. I tried to resist.

"What the hell do you think you are doing?"

"I'm washing your back."

He said it so matter-of-factly that I burst out laughing.

"Well, in the human culture in which I was raised, it is highly presumptuous and a bit rude to just walk in on someone taking a shower." I twisted to face him. His eyes were a sparkling blue the color of the deepest of oceans. They sucked me right in. Crap.

"I have to be honest. I do not wish to become entangled in a relationship right now."

"But what—"

"Let me finish." He put his finger on my lips. "I do not know what the future could possibly hold for us, Bailey, but I do like you. Very much. I find myself thinking about you—um, sometimes I feel like an utter imbecile around you." And he began to pout.

I couldn't help myself. He was so cute and sexy. I threw caution to the wind. I mean really, what did I have to lose? Well, except some of my blood, of course. I wriggled like a snake and pointed. "You missed a spot." *Oh boy, this was going to be scary.*

He hesitated, and then I heard an intake of breath. "Jesus, woman. You are beyond beautiful."

I smiled and felt warm all over. He continued to wash my back, then moved on to my rear, where he spent a lot of time, making sure it was thoroughly clean. I was practically shaking after that. Each leg was carefully washed and massaged. I was certainly feeling no pain by now. He finally spun me around to face him, but I couldn't look into his eyes. I felt awful for what I'd done to him. He had been nothing but open and honest. He tried to protect me and this was how I had repaid him. By attempting to beat him up? What was the matter with me? Plus, I was sure I looked a mess, all bruised and bloodied.

"Look at me." I managed to glance at him briefly.

"I am truly sorry for all of this." He kissed me, the most amazing kiss of my life. I was practically panting by the time he had finished to resume washing my body. I could see that he was enjoying it just as much as I was. He stroked my breasts with a very light touch, cupping them in his large hands. He moved to my stomach, where he massaged me until I groaned. He lowered his hands until they lightly brushed my mound, and I thought I would pass out. I was dripping wet, and it wasn't from the shower.

He took my legs in his hands and spent several minutes on each, massaging and rubbing them, and my feet, until they were rubbery and I could hardly stand. I couldn't take it anymore and lunged for him, devouring his lips. He moaned with pleasure, and a bit of surprise. I squeezed the tube of gel and used it to wash every part of his hard body. And what a body it was. All Greek god, I would say. There was not a flaw anywhere on this gorgeous creature. As I cleaned every square inch of him, he began to groan louder. I fell to my knees and took him in my mouth.

"Oh, Bailey, my god, Bailey," he whispered, while I sucked and played with his foreskin. Several times I brought him to the brink, only to pull away at the very last second.

"Are you trying to kill me?" he growled in a voice that I was not familiar with. I looked up to see that his eyes had changed to an icy blue and his fangs were extended. I hesitated.

"I won't harm you—ever."

I believed him.

He lifted me up and proceeded to take each breast in his mouth. He suckled my nipples until I was whimpering with delight. He lifted me up by my hips so my back was against the glass and got a better hold under my butt. I opened my legs to him, and he ravaged my dripping center. I had the most earth-shattering orgasm of my life almost immediately. But he didn't stop until another was threatening to unleash and bring me to my knees. Another spell must have been upon me; all of my senses were heightened.

He finally stopped and lowered me just enough to enter me in one fluid thrust. We both gave a throaty roar at the pure pleasure of our joining that echoed in the shower stall. Every sense in me was on alert, every cell in my body reacting to his touch. I could die from this bliss. He hammered away, not letting up for a second until I cried out from yet another orgasm, which was just as strong as the first. I felt light-headed, close to losing consciousness from the intensity of it all.

He suddenly stopped, turned off the shower, picked me up, and carried me out the door. I was whimpering for more as he led me to the steam room, where he slammed the door behind us. It was probably 110 degrees, but I wasn't paying any attention. He gently placed me on a bench and kissed me again and again, his tongue memorizing every element of my mouth. His cock was so hard I could see it throbbing as he sat on the bench and lifted me onto his lap. I plunged deep. He moaned with desire as I began my frenzied riding. We were slick with sweat as our bodies slapped against one another over and over again. He grabbed my breasts, rubbing the nipples until I could stand it no longer. I felt him on the brink of his release, only to realize that mine was not far behind, and we both succumbed to the ecstasy together at last.

After several minutes, I finally got my breath under control. I stood up and wobbled to the shower without a backwards glance. I felt humiliated. Mortified. I'd acted like a hussy. I showered and changed into a low-rise pair of jeans and v-neck tee shirt that barely covered my midriff, feeling like a total slut. I looked in the mirror. My cut cheek was just a slight welt now, and my eye was no longer swollen. I played with my wild curls until I was satisfied and put on a pair of wedged sandals.

I walked out of the shower area to a sight that made my heart stop: Declan had showered too, and changed into jeans and a black polo shirt. Damn, he looked good. He was leaning against the wall with his arms crossed. I was kind of hoping he would be gone, so I didn't have to face him so soon. Crap.

"Why did you leave like that?" he asked, with a look of total confusion.

"Well, um–hell–I shouldn't have. Oh, forget it. I'm sorry."

He shoved off of the wall and gave me the sweetest kiss. And then he smiled and lifted my chin to meet his azure depths.

"Don't be embarrassed. It was just you and me here this morning, and I do not regret it in the least, and I never will." He hugged me and left.

Which was good because I was just about ready to suggest another shower.

11

AHKIN IS THY NAME

I made us a good breakfast in the kitchen, then spent some time with Rosa and the boys. It took awhile to find everything needed to make veggie omelets, but I was famished after my workout and subsequent activities. Besides, I owed Rosa some attention. I stayed and talked to her without being bombarded with too many questions, and played with the dogs for a couple of hours, but I was anxious to get some work done. Besides, the boys were going up with Roran for the afternoon, and Rosa was going to the kitchen to talk to the head chef about some suggestions she had on a Mexican menu. *Good luck to the head chef,* I thought. So I sat at my laptop for a couple of more hours and talked to the office several times. Ron was horrified that I had to go into hiding but he promised not to breathe a word and to go along with my cover that I was still recuperating and working from home for a while.

Declan had said that he'd cleared the way for me to get an eye-scan to enter the archives library. All I had to do was see the security officer at the desk. So after I was all caught up at work, I gathered several sharpened pencils and a notebook and headed up to the research wing.

I saw a few people along the way but no one stopped to talk. I had seen no sign of Declan. He'd probably run for the hills after our interlude. Could I blame him? I'd been acting like a total jerk. But then I thought about the most spectacular sex I'd ever experienced, and I was getting myself all worked up again. Wow, I could stay in bed with him all day and night, and I would never get anything done. I shook myself to get his image out of my head. Well, I tried anyway.

I used my card to get into the research wing, then approached the security man, Scott, who took scanning imagery of my left eye so I could have access to the library. And then I was in the beautiful space all alone. I found the shelf where Declan said the acid–and fiber–free gloves were stored and put a pair on. Last thing I wanted to do was harm anything.

Where to start? I had to familiarize myself with the layout and organization of the stacks. I walked the space for about an hour, just taking in the plan. Eventually I figured out that it was primarily organized by country or region, then date or era, such as Rome, Egypt conquest; Constantinople, Byzantine; France, Middle Ages; England, Restoration; etc. I followed the rows of stacks until I found Mexico/Central America, Mayan Era section, specifically, the Yucatan area.

The shelves held dozens of books and manuscripts on Mexican lore and vampirism. I selected a few at a time and brought them over to my table. I collected a substantial pile to go through by the time I was done. I scanned for the names of Reneb, Arabet, Ah Kin, or Ix. I found several stories on Reneb. Unfortunately, most were written in languages I could not decipher. I concentrated on the few that were translated into English, but only garnered information on his strategic planning and military conquests. No mention of his wife, daughter, or granddaughter. I came across a very faded sketch of him made by a primitive hand. It was very hard to ascertain his features, but he looked formidable in his Mayan garb, holding what looked like a very elaborate bow. I put that aside for scanning later. I wrote down each book and manuscript I couldn't understand to ask Declan about later. Maybe he could translate them or knew of someone who could.

I decided to go to the computer and do a search. The archives internal search engine made seven hits when I typed in Arabet. I wasn't expecting anything to be decipherable, so I was astounded by all of the information that had been translated into modern English. Someone had obviously been working on transcribing the vast holdings in the library. All seven hits were references to the same article, which detailed her voyage to the New World, but unfortunately it concentrated mostly on Reneb. There was no imagery, of course. I typed in Ah Kin and the computer hummed and clicked, eventually coming back with one hit. It contained only a series of numbers. 12.3.8501. Hmm. I typed in the numbers for a new search. Nada. I copied the numbers down and typed in Ix. Nothing. There were twenty-six hits on Reneb but most of the information I already knew, and again, it concentrated on his conquests and political planning. Crap.

I checked my watch and I stood up to stretch. I had been at it for over four hours already. I found the bathroom, and on my way back I spotted several cubbies tucked away behind the last stack that contained what appeared to be rolled documents of some sort. I walked over and was astonished to find what appeared to be a large collection of ancient scrolls. As I gently began pulling them out, I heard someone come in. I turned to look but saw no one, so I went back to my task.

It was obvious that no one had bothered with these old scrolls in years. Dust and dirt flew into the air at the slightest contact; the parchment was old, torn, and brittle to the touch. I was very cautious not to crack any documentation. The several I unrolled were all written in a language that was completely foreign to me. All contained numbers written on the upper left hand corner of the scripts in what appeared to be newer ink and created by a different hand. Hmm. Some were so worn that the numbers were no longer decipherable; others looked almost new. None contained periods, dashes, or any other symbols, just seven to nine numbers in no particular order that I could see. I found the numbers that I had written down: 12.3.8501, no matches.

I heard the door open again but I was too engrossed to bother checking who had come in or left. I dug out all of the scrolls, dragged them over to another table, and lined them up. Then I very carefully unrolled each one starting from the beginning, writing down each number as I went along. After an hour and a half, I had still found nothing close to the Ix number or any text containing the three names—at least what I could make any sense of. Many of the scrolls seemed as though they hadn't been unrolled since they were written, their parchment sealed in a permanent spiraled position with their leather and reed ties intact. Others were so dry and brittle that I could scarcely take a peek. Opening them proved to be time-consuming and difficult, since I was determined to prevent any damage.

Several of the scrolls contained engravings, or sketches of various people, animals, or buildings, and some still held a hint of color. I ran my gloved fingers over a particularly beautiful sketch of a mother and a figure I believed to be her daughter in an embrace. They were wearing what looked to be Roman dress. They appeared happy and content. I wondered about their lives and how it must have been to live in those scary yet extraordinary times. I marveled that I was examining evidence of beings of a different species in ancient societies that had been a part of the human culture all along. No wonder this archive was behind lock and key. The scrolls should have been behind glass in a museum, but I knew that was impossible, at least for now.

I was getting close to the end and more frustrated with every parchment that gave me no clues. I scanned each one for any name of significance, but I knew the odds of recognizing them written in any of these ancient languages were slim at best.

I was about ready to hang it up for the day when I came across a smaller scroll that had fallen out of a larger one. It must have been tucked inside where it laid hidden; the leather tie so brittle it looked as if it hadn't been opened in decades, possibly centuries. I opened it slowly, found the number in the upper left-hand corner, and blinked several times in disbelief: 1238501. My heart started racing as I scanned the document, which was just another I couldn't translate, but what caught my breath was the stunning representation of a woman. The vivid coloring was still intact, as if painted only yesterday. She had vibrant green eyes, a pert nose, and a cascading mane of golden red hair. It was me. Oh, god. I reeled, close to throwing up right there on the priceless manuscript.

After I got my breath and heart rate under control, I studied the image further. It was a two-dimensional rendering; no volume, or form. It was apparently painted before the idea of perspective was commonly used, which meant it could have been created anytime before the Italian Renaissance–the fourteenth century. I studied her clothing but I couldn't make out much because the artist had concentrated on her face. All I could see were a set of half bared shoulders, a slender neck sans jewelry, and a partial chest with ample cleavage. A golden wrap appeared right below her collarbone and slid around her upper arms. She wore her hair down with no noticeable ornaments and her ears were well hidden.

That was all there was. But how could this be? She had the same wild mane of strawberry hair, the same green eyes; the same skin, nose, and chin.

In a daze, I carefully replaced the rest of the scrolls. The door opened to an unfamiliar face. He nodded to me and moved to another section of the library. I returned my attention to the scroll. *My god. Am I really part of all of this?*

More people came and went until I was once again all alone. Tears streaked down my face and threatened to land on the precious parchment. Using the back of my hand to quickly flit them away, I couldn't bear to take my eyes off of her. I felt afraid and alone. But I knew who my parents were, didn't I?

I smelled something like smoke drift down from the upper level. Some jerk probably smoking. As if on cue, I heard a piercing scream fill the air, at the same time the lights shut off throwing the library into complete darkness. I had to cover my ears from the deafening onslaught, as my keen sense of vision wakened and enabled me to distinguish certain shapes. I looked around, but saw no one–then I remembered. This place had a special fire suppression system separate from the rest of the building. I only had ninety seconds to escape before all of the air in the space was expelled. Shit. I shot out of my seat, grabbing the scroll. There was no way I was leaving my only connection to Ah Kin to burn. I ran for the door but it was locked. I began to panic and kicked at the door while screaming for help. Precious seconds ticked by as I fumbled for some way to breakout. The smoke was starting to sting my eyes and throat, making me cough and gag. I felt light-headed as I searched through the darkness to find the oxygen masks Declan had talked about. I ran to the first computer niche and looked in the desk. Nothing. I ran to the next and then the next. All of the drawers were empty of any breathing apparatus. I ran from room to room but I couldn't see clearly through the smoky darkness.

The library began to spin and my head pounded. I fell to my knees and crawled over to one of the niches to try to get away from the blinding smoke. My sight was fading and then I knew I would die if I didn't do something. With the last of my strength, I rounded the corner to the bathroom and bumped into a knob for a door. A closet. It was locked. I pounded in frustration, and something hit me on the head. It was a key that had fallen from the trim around the door. Shaking, I tried to pick it up, but realized I still had my gloves on. Shucking them, I found the key and struggled to put it in the lock, but I could barely see and I was losing the battle to stay conscious. Somehow I managed to insert it and release the lock to the closet. Inside was pitch black, but I crawled in anyway and closed the door behind me in hopes that they hadn't included intake vents in ancillary spaces. I scrambled to the open shelving and felt for something, anything, to help me. I hit something cylindrical and heavy that rolled off a shelf and fell on my foot, making a sickening crunch. But I barely had enough breath to howl in pain. My time had run out, and I fell to the ground. I knew I only had seconds before the air was gone. My heart was pounding in my chest. I reached out in a final desperate attempt to find salvation and my hand landed on the tank. It had to be oxygen. I blindly groped until my hand hit a handle. I used all of my remaining strength to twist it open, and I heard a hiss. I felt for the plastic tubing that led to a life-saving mask. I lifted my hand to put the mask on just before everything went black.

ᏨᏂᎬᎧ

Still huddled on the hard floor, I awoke in the main library not knowing how I'd gotten there. My eyes stung from the smoke, which I could no longer detect, just a lingering acidic scent. A fit of coughing so fierce erupted from me that I though I would damage a lung. Large and steady hands held me, and I felt the presence of Declan supporting me from behind. I turned to a worried smile.

"That's better. She'll be fine now. Her foot is healing nicely. Good thing she had enough sense to get into the closet where there is no venting. The extra time saved her life." Thomas looked at Declan as he spoke and then turned back to me. "You're sure to cough up some mucus for the next day or two, and that foot will be sore for a couple of more hours, but you'll be fine." He patted my arm and left.

Another episode of coughing caught me by surprise, but Declan was there to hand me a glass of water. "It's okay, you're safe now." His face flickered from relief to fury and back again.

He helped me to stand up. A wave of pain and dizziness threatened to topple me over, but Declan was there to catch me and I felt secure in his arms.

"What the hell happened? Where is the fire damage?" I croaked. I couldn't see any damage to the library at all.

"There was no fire. It was a smoke bomb that someone set off upstairs and then cleverly took all of the oxygen masks. Luckily you found a spare tank and mask in the janitor's closet." He let go of me and walked over to a niche to show me a panel that was clearly marked with a picture of a mask. He opened the panel and pointed to a hole in the wall where it was supposed to be hanging, connected to a hidden tank on the other side. There was a red button on the side to activate the airflow. He gestured around the room. "All of them are gone." He slammed the panel closed so hard that it splintered into pieces.

"What? Why–who would do such a thing?" My legs began to tremble and my foot ached, so I hobbled to a library chair and sat down hard. Another coughing fit commenced. Declan handed me the water, while rubbing my back.

"I don't know yet. But I will find out, and soon." His eyes narrowed and his breathing hitched.

"The door was locked. I couldn't get out. How could that happen?" I felt my voice getting back to normal, but it was still raw and scratchy.

"Someone set the power to immediately shut down when the alarm sounded. All the lights and the doors were inoperable. Whoever it was, we will find them soon enough." Declan's eyes flared, his voice icy. "I will not tolerate a traitor in my own home."

Daniel and Shila came through the door.

"Charles is working on tracing the codes for the lock," said Daniel. "Here is the list of people who have entered this facility within the last three days."

I rose to look over Declan's shoulder at the list. The only people I recognized were Lily and Shila. I glanced at Shila, who merely sneered.

"I may not like you, but I would never betray Sir Declan." And she glared. The tension in the room was thick, but was broken by Charles's entrance.

"I have it traced to within this very wing. I will have the exact computer within the hour."

"Good. Daniel, I want everyone who is on this list thoroughly searched, his or her rooms here and off-site. Bring them all to the tombs. You know what to do. I want this traitor tonight. I'm going to see Bailey to her room now." They all nodded and left.

Declan held me tight. "I'm so sorry, Bailey. I brought you here for your own protection and look what has happened. It never occurred to me that this place would be a danger to you. I will not leave you alone until I secure you somewhere I can better protect you."

I could see that he was disgusted with himself.

"I'm almost back to normal. Don't fret. Everything worked out. See?" I twirled around. "I'm as good as new." I fell against his chest and coughed. "Well, maybe not quite as good as new." I laughed. Declan frowned.

"It's not funny. You could have been killed."

"Yeah, well, I'm not dead and you will catch whoever did this, just like you did Mikel. I have faith in you and your Centurions. I'm certainly not scared here." I said it with a lot more confidence than I felt, but he couldn't read my mind so he would never know.

"You are certainly right about one thing; I will catch the perpetrator." His eyes suddenly turned white and his fangs extended for a split second. Then, just as quickly, he snapped out of it and he was back to normal.

I straightened up and looked around.

"What? What is it, Bailey?"

"I completely forgot with all that has happened. Now where did it go?" I got down on my hands and knees to search the floor.

"What is it Bailey? What are you looking for?" He followed behind me closely.

"I had it over here, then I ran over here, then I crawled to the closet there." I limped to the closet and opened the life-saving door. The electricity was restored, so I could see inside. The tank and mask still lay on the floor, and next to them sat the scroll.

"Here it is." I picked it up carefully and handed it to Declan. I hobbled back to the doorway where the gloves laid, and put them back on. He handed over the precious document. We sat at a table, and I unrolled it very carefully, even thought I wanted to rip it open, I was so anxious to share my discovery with him. His look of astonishment was priceless.

"But I searched high and low for information on all of this, and I could only find bits and pieces to put together," he sputtered. "I never thought we would discover anything else here. Where did you get it?"

"Over there." I pointed to the scrolls.

He walked over to them. "But I went through all of these."

"It was nicely hidden at the bottom of the pile and wound with another, larger map."

He came back and concentrated on the scroll. "I don't recognize the language. It could be an obscure native dialect. There were hundreds of tribes that spoke dozens of different languages back then. The resemblance is astounding. She is you. I really only had a theory, but this proves it." He gripped my hands. "Bailey, you must be a descendant of Arabet."

I jumped up and paced before I realized that my foot was throbbing and sat back down. "But how could it possibly be, Declan? My fam—my parents? This can't be right. It can't!" I started to get loud and my voice cracked from the strain.

"Hold on." He went out into the entry, where I heard him speak with the guards, and then the door opened and closed. He came back to the table and sat down. "I asked them to wait outside and let no one enter except my team so we could have some privacy." He met my eyes.

"I have thought for a while now that you were of the same blood, but I had not truly believed it until this." He indicated the drawing. "How do you explain your abilities? And the way your eyes turn golden when you are upset or excited? Vampires' eyes turn white before they feed or when they feel threatened—not gold. And what about your strength? I could barely keep up with you in the gym, and you've had no formal warrior training. Good god, Bailey, I have never before witnessed any human with your strength. Even most vampires could not do what you did to me. Especially the changed ones. Also, look at your healing abilities. How would you explain your speedy recovery?"

I was speechless. He had made all good points. "Oh, man. I think I'm going to be sick," and I ran to the bathroom. After heaving up my insides, I turned to find Declan in the bathroom with me, concern etched on his beautiful face.

"Are you all right?" He held me tightly while pressing a cold cloth to my face.

"No, I'm not all right! My whole life is in the toilet. What about my family? My job? Everything I know is a lie, a sham. I can't stand it!"

This time I couldn't help it, the tears came gushing. I blubbered for what seemed like hours, while Declan gingerly rubbed my back and made soothing noises.

"Don't worry, I will be with you. I'll make sure you are safe. And I will help you to get to the bottom of this. Please let me help you."

He said it so gently that I could not refuse. "All right," I said as I moved to blow my nose. "I would love to have your support. Of course, thank you."

"You never need to thank me."

But oh, how I did.

As we left the library he whispered close to me. "We kept the incident quiet so as not to raise a panic. Also, we want to let the perp think he got away with it. So mum's the word if you please."

"What about the alarm. Didn't others hear it?"

"Only the guard stationed at the entrance, and of course we were immediately alerted, along with all of security. The library is soundproof, for obvious reasons. Even the alarm cannot penetrate those walls. And of course the smoke was purged within minutes, via the venting." I could deduce from his distressed expression that he was thinking back on what had happened.

"Oh, all right then," and I nodded in support.

His internal struggle was disrupted. "Good. The first thing to do," he was informing me on the way back to my room, "is to try and get this translated." He patted the scroll, which he had hidden under his shirt and smuggled out of the library. "We may have to take a trip to Boston, where I know a prof—"

We heard a crash, followed by yelling in—was that French?

"*Obtenez l'enfer de ma cuisine, femme folie. Je ne dira quoi faire!*" We hurried to the noise, and of course, Rosa was at the center of a small riot.

"*Yo loco!*"

I could tell Rosa was just getting started. Various people came running, eyes blazing white and fangs extended. Realizing there was no threat everyone retracted but kept a vigil. A few stayed because they were quite amused. Luckily Rosa never seemed to notice.

"Rosa!" I yelled over the noise. "What are you doing?"

"Oh, Mees Bailey. This man is mean to Rosa. Won't cook Mexican!" She jerked her chin and crossed her arms as if completely insulted. I wouldn't have been surprised to catch her stomping her foot for good measure. The chef had thrown several pots and various utensils, and it looked like Rosa had heaved a few herself. The kitchen was a mess.

"It's okay, Rosa, let him continue his cooking. Come with me, let's go see the boys." She pouted and gave one last glare to the chef, spun on her heel, and left with me. I mouthed my apologies as I shoved her out the door. Declan sported a grin I could see he was trying to hide, without much success.

"Stop smiling. It will only encourage her," I whispered to him.

He straightened and lost his grin, but I could tell he was having a hard time of it.

Rosa pouted all the way to her room. Declan slid her card in the door slot and opened it for us to follow. The boys greeted us with exuberance. After the proper scratching and licking, Declan and I went to my room.

"We need to do something with Rosa. If someone wants to harm me, they could get to her to do it. Plus, she will discover what you people are very soon, not to mention the havoc she is sure to cause just being around here. It's too dangerous."

"I agree. I'll find a better place for them to stay." Declan shoved me through the door and pushed me against the wall. "First things first, Davis." He ravaged my lips. My knees went weak, and I realized that I was no longer embarrassed about my earlier actions during our lovemaking. He took a breath, leaving my lips momentarily.

"I–I–was so frightened for you. It makes me sick to think that someone within my own house wants to harm you," He whispered. He leaned down and kissed me again. His arousal was intense and mine was about to match his, until I managed to remember the problems at hand. Don't ask me how or why, but I pushed him away. I must have been nuts.

"Declan, not now. Please, we must take care of this first." But I gave him a quick kiss and a smile. "It's not like, I don't want to–you know."

He smiled. "Really, Davis. Do you actually think there is proper time now for what you have in mind? We have work to do." We both laughed.

"Okay, I will arrange an extended vacation for Rosa and her granddaughter, and the children. Do you think the kids could be excused from school for a couple of weeks?" I nodded. "Very well. Do you think they would like Disney World?"

"Could you really do that? It would cost a fortune for all of those people."

He rolled his eyes. "I've been working for over three hundred and seventy five years. And I've made some good investments on top of that. Yes, I think I can swing it. I will work on it immediately."

"Great; now what about my dogs? I hate to be without them. But I guess I can drop them at my parents' house. Oh my god. My parents. I haven't even talked to them." I slid to the floor with my head in my hands. I didn't know if I could bear not having them as my family. Just the thought of it made me sick. Tears slid down my face, once again, and I began to cough.

Declan was already on the phone, but saw me in distress and immediately finished his conversation and came to me. He lifted me tenderly, and laid me down the bed as he slid in beside me. "Don't worry, Bailey. Things will work out. I will make sure they do." He very gently kissed my head, cheeks, and neck, adding comfort along the way. He played with my hair, running his fingers through it, calming himself as much as me. I could feel his worry for me, terrible worry.

I eventually managed to show him a smile. I started massaging his back and before I knew it, our clothes were discarded and I was riding him until we were both drenched in sweat and causing quite a ruckus.

"Bailey, may I take a bit of your blood?" He panted.

"Oh god, yes!" I couldn't believe that I wanted him to do it, but somewhere deep inside I knew it would only bring us closer. I craved for him to ravage me and anticipated the act with pure pleasure. I almost had an orgasm just thinking about it. "Please, Declan, yes."

He abruptly flipped me over so I was on my back. He grabbed me from behind my knees and lifted my legs up so they were practically touching my ears. He entered me in one fluid thrust. I climaxed immediately and I could tell that he was getting close. He bent down to suckle my breast while wildly thrusting. Suddenly, I felt a slight prick and warmth spread throughout my entire body. I had never felt such clarity, every cell in my body reacting to each nerve ending. I could feel Declan's release, every ounce of fluid being pumped into me. I could hear each and every one of his heartbeats and see his blood coursing through his veins. I felt his screams even though he was just moaning as he suckled my breast. I knew every inch of him. I could smell his lust, his dreams, his anger and his desires. All of these senses flooded me at once and overloaded my brain, triggering the most intense orgasm I could ever possibly feel. I almost forgot to breathe. I felt as if we had reached some sort of spiritual plateau, and Declan and I were together understanding and experiencing a complete body and mind union. And it ended all too soon.

Declan retracted his fangs and licked my skin until I stopped bleeding. I studied him closely enraptured by the action.

After I could catch my breath and speak again, I asked. "Are you all right? You look startled and a bit scared."

"I should be asking you the same." He regarded me soberly as his eyes changed back to his sparkly blue. "You are special, Bailey. Um–I have never–" He abruptly rolled off of me and onto his side. He ran his fingers through my hair, inspecting it as if he was seeing and feeling it for the first time.

I felt cold and alone without him on top of me. I gazed into his depths.

"That was amazing. I never could have imagined something so intense. I can see why there are blood whores." I kissed him thoroughly.

"That was not typical, Bailey." I felt fear drifting off of him in waves.

"Oh, really?" I was dumbfounded by his reaction.

"Yes, you can trust me on that." And he smiled, which melted my insides.

I forgot all about his dread because I suddenly had a ton of energy. In fact, I felt great. I got up and started pacing. "Okay, where were we before–um." I stammered as I walked into the bathroom to clean up. "First off, I drop the dogs at my parents' house, and I need to talk with them–tell them, uh–I guess tell them who I am?" I peeked out of the doorway to see his response.

He paused for sometime. "Yes, all right tell your parents only. I will come with you. I don't want you alone for an instant." Mikel is dead, but whomever he worked for is still around, and we have an internal problem as well. Until we find out what's going on here, you are not safe." He knitted his brows with worry again.

"Mikel is dead?" I eyed him, but let it go and went back to my task.

"Yes, and unfortunately we didn't get anything out of him that was of much use, except that they are still after you."

"But why? What the hell did I ever do to them?" I asked as I walked out of the bathroom stark naked to retrieve my discarded clothing from the floor. I guess I'd lost my shyness. He gave me an appreciative once-over with one corner of his mouth twitched into a grin. He cleared his throat.

"You pose a threat somehow, I suppose. Just like Ah Kin and Ix did."

"But—well, am I truly like her?"

"There is only one way to find out." He bounced off the bed and took my hands in his. "I've been thinking about this a lot. I believe the only way to know for sure if you are like Ix and her mother Ah Kin is if you partake in First Blood Rites."

"Are you crazy?" I withdrew my hands from his grasp so I could fling them into the air. "I'm not a vampire; I don't crave blood or have fangs, and I like the sun!"

"Neither did Ah Kin or Ix, and they both could walk in the daylight. And remember, I can tolerate sunlight as well. I'm not at my best during it, and you won't catch me on a beach sunning myself, but I can function well enough."

He was serious and I was wavering. "But—" I sputtered losing my resolve. "Shit, what exactly is involved?"

"An ancient ritual that must be carried out by a Full Blood. It can be anyone who is familiar with the ceremony. It has to be performed during the new moon cycle, which, I believe, is four days from now. I've already checked into it. And you must receive the Full Blood's blood."

"You mean I have to drink blood?" Yuck. "How do I do that if I don't have fangs?"

"Your teeth can puncture our skin, trust me; it can be done."

"Oh, great. And I suppose you know from experience?"

"The exchanging of blood during intercourse heightens sensitivity, thereby creating a superior sexual interaction."

He'd spoken so straight-faced he could have been lecturing to a class. *Wow, how could it get any better*, I thought?

"Well, I guess that would put me straight into intensive care, thank you. I can see it now: Interior designer dies of stroke during vampire sex!" We laughed. "But seriously, Declan, what can I expect if I go through with this?"

He paused as if in deep thought. "Your full powers will come to light. With practice and proper training, you will become stronger and all of your senses sharpened. And your ability to heal will be almost instantaneous, depending on the injury. From what I've researched, you may experience powers unknown, such as manipulation of fire, water, and who knows what else. The point is, Bailey, you could hold abilities we cannot fathom. It is the only way to know for sure."

"Holy crap. All of this is a bit intimidating. But if it is true and I do—um—evolve, so to speak, does that mean my mom and dad are not my biological parents?"

"I don't know. I guess your mother would have to possess the same powers as you. So my best guess is that they are not your biological parents."

I deflated at his response. I couldn't think about that right now.

"There is another thing you need to be aware of. In one text that I uncovered, which was very difficult to have translated, there was a recounting of the battle when Reneb was captured, from a villager's perspective. He stated that Ah Kin tried desperately to save her father and son-in-law. She walked right up to this man and put her hand on his head, and asked where they'd taken the prisoners. He said that he didn't know, but she left in the direction that they had gone."

"What does that mean?"

"The villager believed that Ah Kin had read his mind, because he did know where they had taken the prisoners, and she nodded and left in the same direction. This is very dangerous information, which I believe very few know."

"Why is this so significant? I mean, you can read the minds of humans. Why should this matter?"

"Because, Bailey, he was a vampire, and if you could read and manipulate the mind of a vampire, then you become the biggest threat of all."

"Oh." I was starting to see his point. I had a sinking feeling in my stomach.

"It is this ability that poses the largest threat to your safety. So if you ever gain that capability, you must never tell a soul about it, because it could mean that you would become the enemy of the Vampire Nation."

I visibly gulped. What he didn't know, and I wasn't about to tell him, was that I had already experienced this skill last night. "Okay, no problem, my lips are sealed." I quickly changed the subject.

"How about the blood? Will I constantly crave blood?"

"From what I've read, no. No blood cravings, and you will not require blood to sustain yourself. But the drinking of Full Blood's blood will strengthen your abilities. There is one last thing. While performing the First

Blood Rites, you will receive blood from a Full Blood, and he will also take your blood, bonding with you forever."

"What is that supposed to mean? Like in married?"

"No, just a mental and physical connection, until one is dead. For instance, you will be able to sense when that person is around, sense if they are happy, angry, in pain, and so on. You will feel a strong sexual connection as well."

"Oh, great! With my luck I'll draw the creepy old man for my vampire."

He grinned. "Don't fret over it. I will be performing the ceremony."

"Really, you can do that?"

"Yes." He seized my half naked form. "Do you really think I would let anyone else perform the ritual on you?" He laughed. "Over my dead body!"

Oh, boy. And what a body. But I was hoping it wouldn't come to that.

12

THE CHANGE IN ME

Declan left me for a couple of hours to take care of some business. From what I'd overheard, the tombs were going to be very busy tonight. He was also arranging for Rosa's departure, which couldn't come soon enough. I was constantly anxious for her safety.

I'd promised Declan I would not open the door for anyone, and that included Rosa. So the boys and I rested and then I tried to work further on some drawings, but couldn't concentrate. I kept examining the scroll, willing it to magically transcribe so I could read the text. The solitude also gave me a chance to figure out what I was going to say to my parents. How was I going to even approach the subject? I was thinking about this dilemma when Declan knocked on my door. He had Roran and his brother with him. Gregory sat on the settee, legs crossed scowling. Oh boy.

"Roran will feed and take the dogs up for a long walk." Declan nodded to Roran, who took the hint, fetched the leashes, and led the dogs scampering out the door. I turned to Declan as soon as the door shut.

"So what have you found?"

"We have it narrowed down to two people who are mysteriously missing, but we will find them. I have my best people working on it."

"Who are these two and why would they want to hurt me?"

"One is a vampire who goes by the name of Duric. He has never liked me much and might want to hurt you to get at me. It's a long shot. Vampires usually are not so vindictive and petty."

"Why? What happened between the two of you that he would take such a chance?"

Declan slid his eyes to Gregory, and I narrowed mine. I wasn't too sure I wanted to hear about this.

"He trained as a Centurion but I rejected him as a warrior here because of a family issue." And he left it at that.

"Okay, So who is the second person?"

He looked at me and sighed. "Lily."

"What? No way. She's so sweet–and–little." I realized that was a totally lame reason not to believe it.

"We don't want to believe it either, but she was in the library today and was also spotted on the computer that was traced to the hacking of the electrical components in the archives. And now she is suddenly missing. She's not answering her cell phone and no one has seen any sign of her for hours."

I shrugged. "It does sound suspicious, but maybe she's just shopping or something."

Declan and Gregory just rolled their eyes at my obvious naivety.

"Well, I don't want to believe it." I sat heavily on the wing chair.

"Be that as it may, if you see her just play dumb and alert one of us immediately–and don't go anywhere with her alone or with one of her friends. I'm not too worried because we are certain neither one is in the cave, so you should be safe. But, I'm not taking any chances, so you will not be left alone. Gregory is going to watch over you while I get Rosa and her family settled." I looked to Gregory and he smiled. The smile of a predatory shark.

"I'm glad you're taking Rosa yourself," I said. "She trusts you and she should behave for the trip if you are in charge."

Declan raised his eyebrows in surprise.

"Well, you do piss me off when you make up *my* mind on things," I added. "But you are the expert. Plus I'm starting to get tired of being attacked. So you won't hear any complaints–but don't push me, O'Connor." I poked a finger to his chest, causing Gregory to break out in laughter.

"I love her spunk, brother," he said. "She's certainly too good for you."

Declan grunted at his brother but I could see the affection in both of their eyes.

He turned to me. "Charles and I will be flying the private jet, so I should be back around midnight if all goes well. Gregory will escort you to dinner, and Daniel and Shila are on high alert tonight. We have extra people walking the perimeter, but we have to tread lightly so no one is the wiser. Remember to act normal. We're hoping whoever is threatening you will get over confident and make a mistake."

We said our goodbyes, not properly as far as I was concerned, but more importantly, Rosa happily let Declan escort her out of the building. I assumed he would have to do a little mind-bending thingy so she would forget where she had been.

Dinner was to be lower key that night, to my relief. No patrons and no band. I guessed the real party only happened once a week. As I chose my outfit for the evening, I thought about the course of action we had settled on earlier. It felt good to have a direction. As it turned out, Declan had a small villa in Orlando. He liked Disney World, especially Universal Studios. I smiled at the thought of him on the Dumbo ride.

We'd decided to pay my parents a visit in the morning, when it was safer to be out of the cave. I knew, however, if Mikel was any indication, my pursuers wouldn't stop just because of a little sunlight. And I was dreading facing my parents. How was I going to explain any of this?

I'd given Daniel my list of information that I had compiled on Reneb, Arabet, Ah Kin and Ix. His task was to go back to the archives gather it all in one spot for later retrieval. He'd place it all in a safety deposit box off site for safekeeping. Charles would hack into the archives computer and permanently erase all of the information. It went against my preservation ideology to erase anything, but the less information about—well, what might be about—my biological family and me, the better.

I perused the choice of dinner dresses Declan had left me to wear. What was with these people and the formal dining? I threw on a short silver silk dress, with a tight bodice and a loose, flouncy skirt cut on the bias. Of course, it came only to mid-thigh. Silver Borgo degli Ulivi strappy sandals with three-inch heels completed the ensemble. I would actually be able to walk tonight—yipee! I was just applying my last bit of lipstick when I heard a knock on the door. I opened it to the angelic face of Gregory.

"I heard my brother had to go out of town tonight. May I escort you to dinner in his absence?"

He looked positively stunning in his perfectly fitted black suit and deep purple shirt, which was open at the neck. He was playing his role flawlessly.

"Why certainly. I was just about to leave."

I was dying to ask him how things were going, but I knew that vampire hearing was superb so I stifled my curiosity and just played my part. To my surprise, I had a lovely evening with Gregory. Reminiscing about his childhood with Declan, whom he seemed to admire and respect, had me beaming with mirth. He regaled me with stories about Ireland, England, and France during the Gothic, Neoclassical, and Georgian periods. Gregory was a walking history book, and I was hooked. I'd never realized just how much he and his brother had gone through. From Queen Elizabeth I to the American and French Revolutions, they had lived through it all. By midnight, however, I could barely keep my eyes open and I was longing to see Declan's face.

"Gregory, I'm so sorry, but I am going to have to continue this at another time. I'm exhausted."

"Oh, no worries. I shall walk you back to your room."

"No, that's okay. I'll be fine."

"Declan would have my head if I let you go alone. Sorry." He got up to escort me. We made small talk until we reached my door.

"So how did everything go?" I whispered.

"Smoothly. Daniel found everything you had researched, and has already secured it with no one the wiser. Charles was also successful."

"Excellent." I was turning to go inside when Gregory grabbed my head in his hands and leaned in for a kiss. Despite my shock, I managed to pop him a good one right in the eye.

"What the hell? What are you trying to do?" I snapped.

"Ow. Why did you hit me?"

"Why? Are you insane? I'm with your brother; well, kind of. Actually I don't know what our relationship is, but you have the nerve to make a pass? What kind of lousy brother are you? Don't just stand there and smile at me." I was aghast that he had the gall to deliver me an obtuse grin.

"Can I come in to get some ice for my face?"

I narrowed my eyes. Should I trust him?

"If this is some ploy to just get in my room—"

He raised his hands in surrender. "Honest."

"Well, okay. But make it quick."

I opened the door, and he went straight to my ice bucket. I noticed the boys already asleep in bed. They didn't even twitch. *Some watch dogs.* I turned back to Gregory. "I mean really. What a baby you are. You're a vampire, for crying out loud. You heal in no time and you're worried about a swollen eye? I mean, I'm sooo sorry I may have marred that beautiful face of yours for all of ten minutes."

He roared with laughter.

"What's so damn funny?" I gave him my scariest glare. It didn't have the desired effect.

He wiped the tears from his eyes. "I was just thinking how unbelievably lucky my brother is to have this beautifully delightful and faithful woman by his side. You are a true breath of fresh air, Bailey Davis. I sincerely hope Declan intends to introduce you to the rest of the family. It should be very interesting and quite entertaining!" He gave me a quick peck on the cheek as he passed me on the way out the door. "Good evening, *mia bella*. And remember, do not open the door for anyone."

"Well, that was interesting," I mumbled to myself as I closed the door behind him. These vamps were a lively bunch, that's for sure. I surely wouldn't be bored from now on.

I sat on the couch and tried Declan's cell. No answer. He was probably still in the air. I'd try again later. Funny, I'd just had a good time with his brother, but I missed him. It was as if part of me was absent. I didn't feel quite whole. Oh boy, I was in deep, and I had a bad feeling that I was going to get hurt again. Why couldn't anything be simple? I went into the bathroom to change. I was exhausted from the day's events and couldn't wait for my head to hit the pillow. I was hoping that Declan would snuggle in beside me when he returned from Florida.

I was heading for that pillow, thinking nice thoughts about different parts of Declan's anatomy when I noticed an envelope sitting on the floor by the door. I went to check it out, even opening the door a crack to see if anyone was loitering in the hallway, but nobody was around. Hmm–It must have arrived while I was washing up for bed. The white standard business envelope had my name scratched on it, so I opened it.

Bailey,

Your father has been in a car accident and is in intensive care at Northwestern Memorial Hospital. Please hurry....Mom

"Oh my god!" I yelled. But I immediately felt suspicious. Who had left the note, and how did they know where to find me? It had to be a trap, but how could I be sure? I tried Declan's cell phone again. Nothing, damn. I left a message telling him about the note, and that I would be at the hospital. I didn't have my contacts, and I hadn't memorized my parents' new cell phone number. Crap. I tried my brother but it clicked right over to an answering machine. Marny always turned the phone off before bed so they wouldn't be disturbed. And I didn't have his cell phone number memorized either. Why didn't I have anyone's cell phone number memorized? But, I had no choice, and I was wasting time sitting here debating.

I tried not to cry, but the tears came anyway. I studied the note more closely. It was my mother's writing, all right. I ran into the bathroom and threw back on my dress that was hanging over a chair, slid on the shoes, grabbed my purse, and ran down to security.

"Is Daniel here?"

"No ma'am, he went up for his rounds."

"Okay I'll call him." And I punched the number that was programmed into my phone.

"Daniel?"

"Yes."

"This is Bailey. I need your help. My father's been hurt in a car accident and I need to get to the hospital, and Declan is not around."

"Okay, I'll pick you up at the entry to the cave in fifteen minutes."

"Great, thank you Daniel." But he didn't hear me because he had abruptly hung up. Weird.

"Can you please have Roran take care of my dogs? Here's my key," and I slid my door key to the bulky security guy. He nodded and called Roran for me. He also called for someone to escort me up.

I fiddled and paced trying to patiently wait, but I was so wired that I was ready to jump out of my skin.

"I can see myself up." But as I waited by the elevators, a tall blond arrived and smiled for me to join him. I didn't remember coming down, so going up was a new experience. He swiped his card and we rode up for a couple of minutes and got off, but we were still not at ground level. *This place must be better secured than the Pentagon*, I thought as we passed another security checkpoint. He led me to further to entry area with rooms all around and a bank of elevators off to the left. He swiped for a second time and we went up again, where we finally hit the surface. We emerged into a vast warehouse that looked about ready to collapse. After passing through another checkpoint, my escort and I headed to the entrance.

"Daniel said he would meet me right outside of the building." The blond simply nodded while we continued through the dilapidated structure. I'd guessed he wasn't a talker. Just as well; the last thing I wanted was to have to make small talk.

We emerged to a waxing moon and a chilly late summer evening. The place was deserted. Hmm. I had no idea where we were, but it felt like the far south side. Perhaps the Roseland area by Lake Calumet, in the industrial part of Chicago. Even the security personnel were nowhere to be found, or they were well concealed. *They must have hidden cameras around here somewhere*, I thought as I scanned the dark landscape. What a great place for a hideout. I was betting they owned all of this property, and then some to keep the trespassing to a minimum.

I was starting to get impatient. "Where is he?" I mumbled to myself, and then a car rolled up. I couldn't see through the tinted windows, but a stranger emerged. I don't know how or why, but I felt threatened. This definitely wasn't right.

"Where's Daniel?" I shouted, while looking around. Now I could see several hulking vamps, along with a driver that I didn't recognize. My escort hadn't moved a muscle. But he met my eyes, and I knew.

A large black man got out of the car and answered my question. "Daniel told me to pick you up and bring you to the hospital because he had an emergency he needed to attend to."

He was lying of course. My phone rang. Then everything slowed down in an instant. I saw commotion up ahead, where the car had come from, as my phone continued to squeal. The stranger and I looked down at its glow in my hand for several seconds, neither of us wanting to make the first move. Finally I moved my fingers to flip it open, which seemed to take hours. My hand was bringing it up to my ear when the vampire decided it was a good time to pounce. Therefore, my scream was cut off rather abruptly, and the phone went flying from my grasp. I felt a prick at my neck; then blackness blurred the edges of my vision as I struggled to stay awake. I heard a laugh as I fell to the ground. I groped on my hands and knees as the whole world spun, but I managed to peer up through the fog, to see that I was surrounded by vampires. I should have been scared, but all I could think of was how furious Declan would be with me.

"I've been searching for you for a very long time, Bailey Davis," I heard someone whisper in my ear, as I finally succumbed to the blackness.

CHARLES

"Bailey!" he yelled. "God damn it, Charles. Get this bloody plane down now!" He'd felt edgy leaving Bailey for so long; his cell reception was sometimes spotty in the air, but usually he had very few problems. Now he knew he should have let Daniel take over transporting Rosa so he could have stayed with Bailey. But who would have thought she could be in any danger in the cave now that Lily and Duric were gone? Someone else must have betrayed them, but he couldn't think about that now. And where the hell was Gregory? He was supposed to be watching her!

He finally got a signal. "Daniel, where the hell were you? You should have been guarding her!"

"Yes, sir. I'm sorry but I went up for my usual rounds. Last I heard was that Ms. Davis was secure in her room. Gregory escorted her to dinner and after they came back to her room, he quickly left. Paul reports that she came to him at around 12:40. She had been crying and was very agitated. He says she called and talked to me from her cell phone right in front of him, but I received no such call. She told Paul that her father had been hurt and she had to get to the hospital. Paul then had Marcus escort her up and out, thinking that she was meeting me."

"Marcus should have stayed with her until you arrived! He will answer to me, I assure you." He wondered if Marcus had been in on it. Well, he would find out soon enough.

"Both Marcus and Gregory are missing at the moment," Daniel continued. "We are searching for them. And sir, I found the note in her room. Whoever set this up has total access to the cave."

Shit, a set-up. He thought for a moment. *How did they get past our outer security?* "Daniel, I want the place torn apart. We need to find out who is betraying us in our own house. Alert everyone now. Wake everyone up if you have to. I want no one in or out. Even detain the fucking Senator if need be! I want Shila on point for a sweep of the whole goddamn area, now! And I want noses to the ground on this. No fuck-ups! Daniel, I want her back in one piece tonight! And someone find my bleeding brother! I'll be on the ground in fifteen."

Declan roared, about ready to blow a gasket. If he could get out of this plane right now without crashing it, he would. He smashed his fist against the wall and flung around some of the seats.

"Try not to kill us all, Sir Declan." Charles looked over at the mess. "We will be landing any minute. We'll find her. Don't worry."

"I will personally filet anyone who touches her, Charles. As God is my witness, I will make them sorry they were ever born."

ಇಂಬ

I laid on a strange bed in a stranger bedroom. The world was fuzzy and my neck hurt. I was getting sick and tired of being knocked out and dragged around. A lot of good my "powers" had done me thus far. My mouth was dry, and the red walls were giving me a headache. After a bit, when I could focus more clearly, I noticed a man sitting in a wing chair by the far wall.

"Who the hell are you and why did you take me?" I demanded.

"Ah, Bailey. It's nice to see you awake. I was beginning to think you were going to sleep the night away."

"Answer the fucking question!" I yelled, my head pounding at every syllable.

"My, my Bailey. Such language." He shook his head. "It is not called for. You are safe, for now. As long as you do as I say."

When the next wave of dizziness subsided, I was able to ascertain that he was about forty-five in human years. He rose and approached me; his black slacks and black silk tee fit him like a glove. He looked as if he had just walked out of a pyramid, with olive skin, a chiseled, angular face, and dark hair sprinkled lightly with silver. But most startling were his eyes: deep dark pools filled with evil.

"My name is Sethe."

"Well, I can't say it's a pleasure." He smiled at that, the smile of a tiger ready to play with his prey. "Was this all a setup? Is my father okay?"

"Yes. I apologize for frightening you, but it was the only way to have you come to me quietly. I didn't want you hurt in the fighting."

I let out a breath that I had been holding and stood to face him. "Did you say fighting? What fighting?" Then I got a sinking feeling in my gut. "What are you going to do? What do you want?"

"I want you, Bailey." He must have seen my look of incredulity, because he smirked. "I know who you are and what you will become. I intend to be by your side when you do."

I repressed a scream. "Why would you want that?"

"I have my reasons. There is no need for you to worry about it now. I will not let anything happen to you. Come sit here." He led me to a small dining table in an adjoining room. "You must be starving."

"Let go of me." I pulled free of him and ran to the door. Of course, it was locked.

He just shook his head. "I was hoping you would be more reasonable." He came for me then, and slapped me so hard that I flew across the room. I was so dazed that I just sat on the floor and did nothing, letting the blood from my split lip drip in a small pool on the floorboards. It must have been the drug I was given, because I didn't have the strength or inclination to fight back. When I finally looked up, he was gone.

"Son of a bitch," I said to myself. I staggered to my feet and tried the door again. Locked as expected. I looked for a phone, nothing. A makeshift weapon? Not much, a lamp, a furniture leg. Crap. No a window either. Declan was going to kill me for leaving.

I climbed into bed, my mind churning. I had no recourse; I had nothing but the hope that someone would find me soon. It was hard to imagine that my life had been normal only the week before. I went to work, had drinks with friends, worked out, shopped, and now I could only dream of doing those things I thought mundane just a matter of days earlier. I closed my eyes, but sleep wouldn't come, just the tears. Lots and lots of tears.

Several hours later a woman came in and placed a tray of food on the table in the next room. I got up and went to her.

"Please help me," I pleaded. She showed me her fangs, growled, and left. Shit! Next time I would attack, even though I knew that I was no match for a vampire–unless I changed. But I didn't know how to trigger a spell; they seemed uncontrollable. I needed to work on that.

I recoiled at the bacon and eggs, but I knew that I needed to keep up my strength, so I made myself choke it down. I didn't have any idea whether it was day or night, or whether it had been ten hours or thirty-six, since my kidnapping. After I ate, I went back to lie down. I felt so dizzy I wondered if they drugged my food. I wanted to sleep and then awake from this nightmare. Eventually, I did. Sleep, that is.

I was awakened by a different woman who brought me a gown, shoes, and some makeup.

"You are to bathe and get dressed for the master. I will pick you up in an hour to take you to him."

Before I could say or do anything, she was gone. Damn. I'd had an opportunity, and I blew it. But I couldn't seem to muster the energy to even care. They must be drugging me.

I dragged myself into the adjacent bathroom and climbed into a hot bathtub, washed and rinsed my hair, and then soaked. I had to figure a way out. And how had this even happened? I realized that I hadn't spoken with Daniel, but with someone pretending to be him. I'd thought the voice was a bit different from his native French Cajun, but I'd been so distraught that I just shrugged it off. So that number in the phone–it was not his–or he lost his phone. Or someone took it. Somehow, I doubted that scenario. Okay, then it had to be the person who programmed the numbers. Declan? No way, not in a million years. Okay, Lily, then? I hated to think Lily was involved, but who else could have programmed the wrong phone number in my phone? It was just too much of a coincidence, but what a huge risk she'd taken took to do that. Didn't Lily know that Declan would be sure to figure it out? And to think, I wanted to be friends with her. I was a bad judge of character, that was for sure. And what about Marcus, why didn't he help me? And where was Gregory? Why wasn't he stationed out in the hallway where he was supposed to be? Were they in on it with Lily?

I got up after the water cooled and managed to get myself dressed when all I wanted to do was crawl back into bed. I had lost weight in the last few days. I could just make out my ribs as I looked at myself in the mirror. Great way to diet. I put on the slinky red dress and red stilettos that were left for me. What was with the slut wear that these vamps were obsessed with? I towel-dried my curls and put on a bit of makeup to pretend I cared. I decided I would not give up. I would play along until I got my opportunity, and then I would fight them tooth and nail, and I would win. At least I hoped I would win.

The woman came back and gathered me for a walk through a huge mansion. It looked to be built around the 1880's with elaborate woodworking, tall ceilings, and meandering spaces. The decor was a little over the top for my tastes, but maybe it was the latest vampire look. It was certainly the opposite of the cave, which was decorated tastefully. We went down several flights of stairs and into a very formal dining room, which had to be fifty feet long. Sethe was sitting at the end of an enormous table by himself. Two vampires stood guard at the doorway into the space. He stood when I entered.

"Welcome, Bailey. Come and sit for dinner." He acted as if nothing had transpired between us. I had no choice but to sit. Yes, I would play the good little girl, for now.

"I hope you are comfortable in your room?"

I just nodded and picked at the food on my plate. I noticed he did not eat at all. I pretended to listen to his incessant babbling about his beautiful house, and what did I think as a designer, blah, blah, blah. I was almost through the ghastly meal when a beautiful blond came in, totally naked. She went to Sethe and sat on his lap. He started kissing her. I felt it was time to go, so I got up to leave.

"Stay." Ordered one of the vampires at the door.

"It looks like he wants some privacy, so I'll just go back to my room now." The guard didn't budge. "Okay, fine, I'm not into watching, but okay, if you insist." I took my seat once again.

I tried not to watch him ravage her mouth and suck on her breasts. I tried to block out her moans of delight, but I couldn't. He slowly removed his own clothing showing off a magnificent body that was covered in very intricate tattooing, which seemed to change and glimmer before my very eyes. I glanced at the doorway where the two guards stood, but they were facing the other direction, not paying any attention at all.

I stood and turned around. One of the guards came and turned me back to face the writhing pair at the end of the table.

"What kind of game are you playing here, Sethe?" He stopped what he was doing between her legs.

"I am simply showing you your future. Well, not exactly, but close." And he went back to his ministrations.

I froze with fear. He looked up and smiled. Shit, he could smell it on me. Relax, Bailey, take a deep breath. So he planned on trying to seduce me. It would have to be rape, because I would never let him touch me. Ever. And I thought of Declan.

"So what. Am I supposed to be impressed now?" I crossed my arms. *Dumb Bailey, dumb.* Before I knew it he had me on the table, knocking dishes out of the way. His fangs were glistening as he stood glaring down at me.

"My silly Bailey." And he ripped my gown apart. He tried to kiss me, but I moved fast, and he missed my lips. I managed to punch him in the face, and I heard bones crack. The two guards had a good hold of me now. My naked breasts heaved as my anger spiked. Sethe got up very slowly. He took one look at me and suddenly stopped and started laughing.

"I know you are special, Bailey. However, I could do anything I want to you, and you could do nothing. Nothing at all. So if I were you, I would be nice. You will learn to love what I do to you. Yes, you will enjoy it immensely."

I scrambled away from his thugs as he gave the okay to release me. I tried, without success, to put my dress back together. He chuckled as he went back to his woman, who was sitting at the end of the table. I sat numbly through his rough foreplay, and rougher sex, with the woman, who seemed to enjoy it. As he was about to climax, he bit her on the back and drank her blood. She was moaning with delight. I was shaking badly and close to vomiting.

I was eventually shown back to my room, where I went to the corner and curled up into a ball, waiting for my turn.

⋘⋙

"Where the hell could she have gone? She can't just disappear off the face of the planet!" Declan was screaming, his fangs showing. "It's been two bloody days and time is running out!"

He had quickly figured out that both Lily and Marcus were in on the scheme. They had found the four guards who were on duty, murdered and thrown into the Cal Sag River. Lily and Marcus had replaced the two guards on top at the cave's entrance with two of their own. Gregory had fared much better; he had been drugged and shoved into a locked closet in the buttery. He was still feeling the effects of the vampire narcotic they'd injected into his system. He still didn't know if Duric was involved because he had yet to be located. Shit. They were organized and smart. Who were they working for? Declan himself had interrogated everyone in the cave, including the Senator, who was horrified to know his Lily could be so devious.

"Sir, we have all of our people on the streets. We will find something." Shila spoke reassuringly, but Declan could smell the worry she felt.

He tried to use his blood connection but it was of no use. He could not sense her, which only added to his frustration. It meant that she was either far away, unconscious, or god forbid, dead. He couldn't even entertain that theory.

"Don't fret, my brother. We will find her and the scoundrel who has her. We'll make him pay." Gregory grabbed Declan's shoulder and squeezed. For once, Declan was glad his brother was here and that he hadn't been seriously hurt. He appreciated his advice and help in the search. Gregory was also reporting to the Council members so Declan had one less thing to worry about.

Daniel hastened in with his head lowered; still smarting from the tongue-lashing he had received earlier. Declan was beginning to feel guilty about that. Daniel was sure to believe the full blame lay on his shoulders in Bailey's disappearance without being chastised further.

"Sir Declan, we have someone who spotted Lily last night at a club on Halsted."

"Bring him in," he ordered.

A kid in his early twenties ambled through the door. Declan could smell the fear on him, but he didn't care. He had to find Bailey at any cost. The kid would remember none of this when they were through with him anyway. He put his hands on the boy's head and looked into his mind. He had seen Lily.

"Okay, ah?"

"Tony."

"Okay, Tony. Can you please tell us about seeing this woman?" He held out the picture of Lily his team had been circulating for two days.

Tony told Declan that he and a friend had been standing outside of Tuba, a club on Halsted, at about three that morning, and this woman strolled by them. He would never have even noticed, except that she had blood on her face, so he went to see if she needed help. She laughed at them and then took off so fast that they almost thought they had imagined the whole episode, and chalked it up to an overindulgence of partying. Tony hadn't thought of it again until someone came around where he worked today with her picture, and he recognized her immediately.

"Can you show us exactly where this happened?"

"Sure."

"Let's go. Daniel, call Shila in on this. Tell her to meet us upstairs. Charles is still canvassing. Let him continue with what he's doing but report to him on our findings." He nodded and got his phone out.

"Okay Tony, lead the way."

ೞೞ

"This just doesn't feel right. Why come out in the open? Why, when she must know we are tearing the city apart looking for her?" Declan scrutinized the spot in front of the nightclub.

"I don't like this." Shila stated the obvious. Gregory nodded in agreement.

Declan thought about it for a couple of minutes. "Okay, this is what we are going to do. We will follow this trail to where it ends, but we do not go any further. We put up surveillance, and watch her as she comes and goes. It's a trap. She's trying to lure us somewhere, but we'll stay at a distance, and we will be silent. Do not approach her, and we'll continue our search elsewhere. If Lily thinks we're still looking in other areas, she may get bolder."

Declan left to follow Lily's trail in an obscure way, as not to be seen. It led to a boarded-up house on the west side. He could still smell her, but nothing else, no other vampires. What was she up to? Lily was a Full Blood but was not very old, and was certainly not a Centurion, so she had limited powers. But she could set a trap. Yes, she had already proven that.

Declan phoned in his instructions after finding a building on the next block whose roof was at a perfect angle for surveillance, yet far enough away that no one would think to check. He had Shila set up in a flanking location with Thomas and Daniel perpendicular. He sent Gregory back to the cave to further question any witnesses and deal with the Council. The whole area was covered, and as Centurions, they could sit for days and not move an inch. They could also mask their scent. No other vampires would ever know that they were there. Declan also saw to it that they were all well fed so no one would require blood for several days. So now the hard part: sitting on their hands and waiting. An aspect Declan found agonizing, knowing Bailey was out there hurt, or worse.

"Bloody hell," he grumbled to himself.

ರಞ

I don't know how long I was curled in a ball in the corner, but I was awakened by another girl I didn't recognize. My god, she couldn't have been older than twelve. She was carrying a tray of food in her wobbly hands that she left on the table in the next room. *I should attack, and make my escape now*, I thought, but in the end, I didn't want to hurt an innocent girl, a child. There was no way I could do something like that. She probably didn't know what was going on anyway. She swiftly left without a word or even a glance my way.

It must be breakfast so maybe its morning and the creeps are in bed, I thought. At least, I hoped so. But to my surprise, it was dinner. Had I slept for over twenty-four hours? I unrolled and stood up. My dress fell apart but I no longer cared. I was tired of being the victim. I want to be on offense for a change. I ate heartily to gather my strength, which I was sure I would need. I still felt a bit dizzy, but better than the day before. I showered and changed back into the silver dress that I was kidnapped in. I preferred bare feet to the strappy silver heels because I could run faster if need be. I rooted through the makeup and everything that was left for me. No hangers, no nail file, and no scissors. Crap. Then I stood considering those Brunomagli sandals that were strewn on the floor. Hmm. It'd be sacrilege to ruin such beautiful Italian shoes, but the heels would make nice little stakes. But how to get them off and hide the rest?

I started to put my hair back up and out of the way, as another idea began to form. I inspected the hairpins that I had in my hair from the previous night, which were lying on the counter. But no way, this wasn't the movies. I had no idea how to pick a lock, but that wasn't about to stop me from trying.

I inspected the door. I had no idea whether or not someone was posted outside, but I hadn't sensed anyone around. They seemed confident in my submissiveness. The lock appeared to be an old-fashioned skeleton key mechanism. Could it possibly be that easy? No way. There had to be something else. And then the hair on the back of my neck rose, and I realized that I was being watched. Of course, I felt certain I was being observed this entire time. How I knew was anyone's guess, I just did.

Now to find the source, and I had to be fast. I had to disconnect the feed and pick the lock almost simultaneously in order to get out, before they were alerted. I walked to the bed and lay down, pretending to rest. I had to relax. My heart rate was skyrocketing and my palms were sweating. I realized that I was petrified of getting caught. But what choice did I have? I wasn't going to just sit and wait to be that monster's next meal. *Okay, breathe. Easy in and easy out—good, just relax. Sure, easier said than done*, I thought. But as I concentrated on my breathing, I scanned around the ceiling and cornice lines for any type of holes for cameras or hidden spots. But there was not even a pinhole. Nothing. I slowly felt around the bed frame at my head. Nothing.

Once I thought I wouldn't faint from fright, I got up and casually strolled around the bedroom. I picked up a book and leafed through it, and did the same, until I exhausted all of the books on the shelves. I had scoured the shelving and fireplace and found nothing. I moved, very casually, checking moldings, commenting aloud as if assessing the historic integrity and appropriateness of the décor. I sat on all of the furniture, running my hand underneath, and still nothing. In the bathroom I looked everywhere while pretending to spruce myself up and using the facilities. Nada, crap. They were probably getting suspicious by this point, so I decided to quit my search for the time being and lie down with a book. Then I saw it.

Yes, it had to be it. This was a house built in the latter part of the nineteenth century, well before central forced-air, heating and air conditioning were standard issue in new homes. This house still had functioning radiators because they were pinging this very minute—but I did not see or feel any forced air out of the small duct on the wall in front of me. Bingo. Now, to ignore it and figure out how to cover it up. I searched the space. The William and Mary wing chair would be perfect. Great. Now the lock. I thought about the lock as I lay back on the bed pretending to read.

I wished I knew what the hell I was doing. I took a pin out of my hair, as if scratching my head, then flopped on my stomach with the book, so my hands would be concealed from the heat duct. Carefully, I straightened the pin. Okay, now what? I knew I'd seen this in the movies, at least once. Yeah, a lot of good that would do me now. It wasn't much of a plan, and I hoped it wouldn't get me killed.

In the end it didn't matter, because my time was up. A bruising hulk of a vampire came to give me two gift-wrapped boxes. "I will be back in ten minutes. Be dressed."

I looked the boxes over. The hatbox was wrapped in a beautiful purple jacard fabric, fastened with a pink satin bow. The second, in the same fabric, but with a white satin ribbon, was a large dress box.

I opened the dress box first and sure enough, inside lay a gown of black transparent gauze that was extremely low cut in the front as well as the back. The inner layer was an iridescent emerald color that shimmered in the light.

The strapless gown had sparkly deep green rhinestones sewn along the top, all the way down the plunging neckline, and around the hemline. The box also contained cheap, but matching deep green stilettos, and an emerald dropped earrings and bracelet set. No necklace, the neckline needed no further decoration. But the box did contain an emerald headdress, a prom queen crown. He couldn't be serious.

I opened the hatbox, thinking it was part of the outfit, but I couldn't have been more wrong. Inside lay the head of the blonde woman Sethe had had sex with the night before in front of my very eyes.

CRBO

He was getting restless. It had only been about nine hours, and already he was about to scream. Tonight was the new moon and he knew that she was in serious trouble. It made him sick to even think about it.

Just as he was about to call and check on his team, a lone figure moved to the dilapidated building. It was about four A.M. and still pitch black out. Most of the streetlights had been broken or burned out long ago, and the city neglected to replace them. No one cared in this part of town. He didn't care either, considering he could see in the darkness just as well as in the light. He pointed to his eyes, knowing that his team would see him do it. They watched as several more vampires gathered, eight in all, all changed ones, some old, and some new. *Amateurs*, Declan thought; they were completely unaware of his team's presence. They talked very quietly, but he could pick up some of the conversation anyway.

"He…wanted it done."

"But they are looking…wrong place."

"We…make them come. Take…places and make sure…guns are on…"

Six of them found places to wait for the ambush that would never come.

Declan signaled for Shila and Thomas to stay put and watch the morons just in case they made a move on someone innocent. He and Daniel would follow the other two to see where they would go. He craved to see Lily; he knew she was the key.

After meandering through the ghetto and finally emerging in the west loop, the two vampires split up. Declan gestured for Daniel to stick with the blond man, while he stayed with a brunette amazon of a woman. She led him through the loop, coming closer to the lake. He spotted several of her team members posted on buildings and discretely on the street along the way. She had made eye contact, but no words were spoken.

She moved fast now, a destination in mind. She passed through alleys and over buildings, but Declan had no problem staying with her and keeping out of sight. He had the gift of shadowing, and these incompetents would never see or smell him.

The amazon eventually emerged at Stateway Park on South State Street, by Cellular Field. The park had seen better days, if the broken equipment and missing basketball nets were any indication. Suddenly he saw her; she moved slowly out of the shadows. Lily. He longed to rip her head right off of her neck with his bare hands. But that would do him no good. He knew that Lily could lead him straight to Bailey. He just had to have a little more patience to find out exactly where that was. He clenched his hands at his sides; it took all of his will power not to kill her immediately.

"He wants him!" Lily shrieked at the amazon. "And if we don't come through, you know what will happen. Make sure he follows you this time, but don't make it too obvious. Sir Declan is not stupid, just impulsive when it comes to this–human." She spoke of Bailey with such venom that Declan had to suppress a hiss.

They parted, and he stuck to Lily like glue. She was smarter than the amazon, so he was very careful not to alert her to his shadowing. Dawn was approaching quickly, so most of the vampires needed to seek shelter, but not his team. And unfortunately, not Lily. She was a Full Blood, so even at her young age of a little over one-hundred, she could tolerate the sunlight. She would be slow, uncomfortable, and would lose some of her abilities, but overall could manage if she had to. And it was obvious that she had a job to do, so they would be busy for some time.

She stopped in an alley at North Avenue to talk to another of her gang. Most of her team of vampires were young and changed, because all but one took off to seek shelter until the evening. Lily appeared livid, pacing and cursing, but could do nothing about it. She had to wait until night.

Declan trailed her to an older nondescript brick house in Rogers Park, where she unlocked a series of locks and went inside. He watched as lights turned on in various rooms. He called his team from the roof of the apartment building across the street.

"I'm shadowing Lily." And he relayed his location. "Meet me here for a briefing."

An image of Lily pacing while talking on the phone came into view through the shabby sheered draperies in what seemed to be a living room. He couldn't hear her words, but he could see her heated discussion and furious expressions. She threw her phone against the wall and hung her head. Good. Her stress would likely cause her to make mistakes.

The lack of Bailey's scent anywhere in the area led Declan to believe she was not here, nor ever had been. Damn it. He needed a break, he thought, as he felt a light stirring of the air around him and knew his team had arrived.

⊂⊃⊃

The sight of a severed head left me horrified and sickened, but I refused to let them see me fall apart. I calmly replaced the lid and put the box on the tray with the leftover food for them to pick up later. I tried not to vomit by swallowing the bile that was threatening. Now they had really pissed me off.

"Is that the best you can do?" I yelled to no one in particular, but I knew they were listening. Five minutes later the same girl came to the door, took the tray, and left. I tried to make eye contact with her, but she was having none of it. She was human; I could tell from the bruising along her neck and arms. I wanted to tell her she wasn't alone, but I knew they would just punish her because of me and my big mouth.

The big vampire came for me like he'd said he would. I left with him, having little choice. I had no time, no weapons, no ideas, and I couldn't make one of my abilities just appear. If I could only get to a phone, I would need only seconds to send a text message to Declan—and then say what? I had no clue where I was.

We marched along a series of corridors, then down a set of stairs I'd never seen before. We descended at least three levels, to a basement that was completely furnished with rooms off of a main hallway. This part of the house was new, complete with state-of-the-art security.

We passed a checkpoint and entered a large room, where at least a dozen vampires stood around in white robes. The hulk led me toward a giant throne in the center of the room and told me to sit. The vampires took their seats in tall-backed chairs that lined the perimeter of the room. They began to chant in a language that was completely unfamiliar to me. I began to think about getting up just as elaborately carved leg and arm braces sprang out of the chair and restrained me. Did I see dried blood on them? Great, now I was getting nervous. I strained against the shackles, but only managed to hurt my arms and legs. I felt my heart race...

Sethe swept through a door to my left, wearing a black satin robe with complex script embroidered along the arms. I had no idea what the writing meant; once again, the language was alien to me. However, it did remind me of some of the writing I'd seen on a couple of the scrolls from the library. Interesting—and frightening. *He must know. Oh my god.*

"What do you want with me?" I demanded. "These games are getting tiring."

He smiled the most vicious smile I have ever seen. "The time has come, my precious Bailey." He flicked his wrist to one of his underlings, who pressed a button on the wall. A loud popping noise surrounded us as the floor and walls vibrated. They started to shift, and my heart began pounding–my vision cleared, and my hearing became acute. I was having an episode. I glanced up to see that the entire ceiling had retracted into the walls, and fifty feet above me was the night sky.

"Why not just go outside if you wanted fresh air?" I said with a sneer. He eyed me with a puzzled frown, my growl giving me away. I fought the restraints and managed to break one arm free. Sethe ordered the hulk and another to come forward and restrain my arms. Sethe was on me in two strides, inflicting a vicious slap, which only pissed me off more. He mistook it for shock–stupid move. I heard gasps from the others, as I was up and off of the chair in a flash. I attacked Sethe with all of my might and landed a few great punches–even managed to get a shot to the balls–before I was overwhelmed by several of his goons.

I awoke to chanting, or maybe it was just a nightmare, but no such luck. I had been restrained this time by silver manacles attached to the concrete floor. I had no idea how long I'd been unconscious, but the sky was still dark, so probably not long. My head throbbed. I tried to move, but let out a yelp as I jostled my right leg. Splinters of pain shot through me, seizing my breath and causing tears to well. Broken. Shit. I took a series of short controlled gasps until the pain finally ebbed to just a dull ache.

Sethe began chanting along with the others. He rose and circled around me. I tried to concentrate on how chilly it had gotten now that we had the roof open. I could see thousands of twinkling stars, so I knew we were far beyond the city limits. But there was no moon, therefore very dark. No moon–no–what day was this? Could it be that Sethe was trying to perform the First Blood Rites ritual on me? Oh no! I had to get out of here. "Declan!" I screamed over and over again.

Suddenly the chanting stopped and Sethe came to me. Without warning he exposed his fangs and sank them into my neck by my shoulder. Once again my body was teeming in excruciating pain. I felt no sexual excitement whatsoever. I heard his gulping as I tried not to throw up from the closeness of his face next to mine. I started to feel faint and began gagging, as the thought of him on me was just too much to bear. I closed my eyes and thought of Declan, his wonderful face, his sexy scent, and his beautiful eyes. The next thing I knew, I was being slapped awake with a bloody knife held above my face. He had cut himself and expected me to drink it. He held his arm to my lips, but I turned away.

"No, never!" I screamed. There was no way I was opening my mouth to him. My heart suddenly began to beat fast and my eyes sharpened. I was going to have another spell, I could feel it.

As Sethe tried desperately to get me to drink, another vampire came over to help, and eventually several were on me. I was punched, my leg tugged on, and my nose held shut, but I would not sway. I struggled against my restraints and eventually broke loose, but they were too powerful for me. I was desperate to open my mouth and take in air. I began feeling dizzy, and I knew I would die soon if I didn't breathe. But, I didn't care to live anymore, especially with his blood in me. My body betrayed me however, and my mouth opened for just an instant to breathe. Too late–his blood trickled down my throat, searing it along the way. I gagged at the coppery metallic taste of it and tried to vomit, but couldn't do it. I managed to spit most of it back out and onto him. But it was too late. Enough had managed to go down, because I could feel his strength, his raw essence within me. The thought made me want to die. Anger sliced through me as my helplessness was evident.

I closed my eyes and I saw Sethe in his native land of France, screwing a young girl who was frightened and in pain. They were covered in white gauze, or maybe it was just my vision. He was brutal, and she was not enjoying it. Then I saw him in battle with a huge man with skin as dark as the night. He cut the dark man's throat. I flinched as a giant bird dove towards me and missed by mere inches as it landed on a Romanesque structure, St. George's Basilica in Prague, where many other birds were perched. Sethe was there talking to a man in breeches and hose, and then he transformed into a savagely bloodthirsty warrior, cutting down hundreds of men in a single battle.

I closed my eyes against the carnage, and opened them to the sensation of cool water. Sethe was bathing in a picturesque crystalline lake, surrounded by a beautiful meadow and edged by a rich green forest. I could hear the birds singing and see and smell the slight fragrant breeze blow through his long dark hair as the water cooled his heated skin. He was happy; he looked–beautiful and content, as a stunning red-headed woman, who could have been my twin, splashed by his side, helping him bathe. Then the woman was laid out in a stone coffin, dead. Sethe was there on his knees, being restrained by other vampires, crying and cursing. I could feel his anger radiate through me. He was dragged out of the church and thrown into a stone cell.

Suddenly I was in a clearing in what looked like the English countryside. Sethe was hidden and watching a red-headed girl of about ten, who was playing by a stone cottage. He cursed and strode off. My vision blurred, then cleared to witness Sethe in a dark place, his eyes glowing a bluish white. He was excited about what was to come as he stepped into a room with high ceilings, stone walls and a huge bed draped in deep blue velvet. He undressed a woman, while three others, all naked, watched. In what felt like slow motion, he drank from the thigh of the woman, as the others writhed around him. He entered one as the others enjoyed each other. After he was completely satiated sexually and physically, he stood, grabbed his sword, and killed them all. He stabbed them over and over again, immune to their pleas and screams, eventually cutting off all of their heads and throwing them aside. He felt nothing; no love, no hate, no pity. He was empty, heart and soul. He turned to me and smiled with a face smeared in blood and eyes flashing white.

I screamed and opened my eyes to him, standing in his black robe in front of me. I was panting and holding a large machete. I heard whimpers and moans, as most of the other vampires lay strewn on the floor in various stages of dismemberment. Some were missing arms or legs, while others had fatal lacerations. A few were already dead and missing their heads. Blood dripped from my body; my hands slickened from it as I dropped the machete. Untouched by the slaughter, Sethe stood in front of me smiling. I felt my body float above, looking down at the carnage that I'd created. I fell to my knees and threw up, then dropped to the floor in such utter exhaustion that I didn't remember being carried out of the room.

13

I'VE GOT WEDDING BELL BLUES

Yuck! I gingerly sat up and looked around. I was on an unfamiliar bed in a ghastly room. The bed was huge, with an over-the-top elaborately gilded headboard. I tried to focus but my eyes must have been playing tricks on me. This room was enormous, painted in garish colors and dripping in cheesy decoration. *Was I in a whorehouse?*

I soon realized I was naked and laying between red satin sheets. *What the hell happened?* I thought. Then it all came flooding back to me in brutal clarity. *Oh god, what was I going to do?*

With my head spinning and my stomach ready to heave, I jumped up in search of a bathroom. I ventured though a huge closet, in which hung dozens of men's slacks, shirts, ties, and suits. I counted the shoes. There were over thirty-seven pairs. I smelled them. Hmm, they smelled of Sethe, and the thought stirred my insides of love and adoration. Wait—what was I—*What the hell?* I was so appalled that I had to be mistaken. Did I actually have feelings for that creepy murderous bastard?

"No fucking way!" I scolded myself, but…

I found a large brash bathroom with red marble tiles on every available surface. Double yuck. I found a pair of jeans and a tank top sitting on the counter. No bra or underwear, great. My reflection in the mirror was jarring to say the least. My hair and face were matted with dried blood, but my neck was perfectly unmarked, and I noticed a slight change to my eyes.

I turned on the elaborate shower to its hottest level because I was frozen inside and out. After shampooing and rinsing off all of the dried blood, I sat on the floor with the water cascading over my body until it ran cold.

I brushed my teeth using Sethe's toothbrush, disturbed that I didn't feel sickened by it. I dried my hair and stood back to regard my image in one of the many floor-to-ceiling mirrors in the room. My god. I was beautiful. My hair was thicker, curlier and gleaming red. My skin was flawless–almost a translucent peach–the freckles all but disappeared. My eyes glowed a vivid green, and my lashes were thick and black. I prided myself on my good teeth, but now they were straighter and whiter, and my full lips were now a beautiful shade of ruby. I must have been seeing things–shit, the ritual, I remembered. Had it worked? Was I now Ah Kin?

I examined my body. My breasts were not larger, but seemed perkier, shapely. My legs were more taut and my belly was so flat that I could see the muscles beneath my now perfect skin, my ass–oh my–was actually firm. No more jiggles. I flexed.

"Holy shit," I whispered. I felt stronger, more alive. My vision was so startlingly clear that I could make out a tiny crack in one of the marble tiles across the room. My hearing picked up a bird singing a sweet song, but there were no windows in this room. I could smell Sethe everywhere, and it horrified me that it soothed my soul.

And then I thought about my family and Declan, especially Declan. I knew he must be frantic with worry, and my heart squeezed at the thought. I would leave here and find him as soon as I got dressed. I felt that nothing could stop me from leaving this place now.

I threw on the clothes left for me. I was not surprised to find a pair of loafers in the closet that fit me perfectly. I took one last look around as I headed for the door, but had to stop midstride. I could feel Sethe drawing closer. I took in a deep breath. It couldn't be, I loathed the very thought of it, but I actually was looking forward to seeing him. Thirty seconds later he walked through the door.

I knew that he was startled at the sight of me, yet he held back and smiled. "So you are up and dressed, and more beautiful than I could have ever imagined." He came to me and held my hands.

Fear–hate–desperation–Sethe's feelings came to me in a wave. Startled at the lucidity of his thoughts, I managed to pull away, but it was a struggle.

"What did you do to me last night?" I tried to stay angry, but that was also hard to do. Just being in his presence gave me a sense of peace and safety. *I must be losing it.*

"I made you mine." And he went to the closet and rummaged for something.

"What if I don't want to be yours?" I looked at my hands so I wouldn't have to meet his eyes, but felt compelled to glance up at him anyway.

He was jovial. "Too late. Now you will accept me as your mate. We will have the mating ceremony tonight, and you will be happy with that."

"And if I'm not?"

He flew over to me, grabbed my neck and squeezed. I didn't make a peep, much to his dismay. I was not scared of him like he wanted me to be, and that made him angrier.

"You will learn to mind me and do my bidding, or you will be dealt with. I am now your master." I just sneered, but wanted to gag from the stale stench of blood on his breath. He squeezed tighter. "I know you now desire me, and I, you. I know how you are feeling; you cannot hide it from me. Bailey, you and I have an unbreakable connection, now and forever. So you'd better get used to it." He finally released my neck and I fell forward.

I felt torn between disgust and excitement. "What about my family? I must go see them. I have to tell them about all of this. And my job? I love my job and I want to continue to work. They are probably worried sick by now."

"You may come and go as you please. I know you cannot leave me, and you will feel at a loss every time you are away from me. So it is no threat. But you will not tell anyone about any of this. This is an order that you will obey. And you will not be allowed to leave just yet. Not until we are properly mated and I take care of some business first. I am hoping to have that accomplished by this morning."

"Properly mated? What is that?"

"It is a wedding. Vampires marry just as humans do."

"Marry? Well, good for you but I'm not a vampire so your rules do not apply to me. Plus, I'm not sure I want to be married."

He hit me so hard, I swore I saw stars. I leered up with fury in my eyes. He winced. I don't know whether he felt my pain or anger. So it was very smart that he left quickly. I walked into the sitting room where he had disappeared, picked up the nearest sofa, and threw it across the room. It hit the wall and broke into several pieces, along with making quite a dent.

"It was ugly anyway," I screamed.

⚇

Declan updated his team and listened to their reports, but the best lead was right in front of them. They all agreed to pretend to keep on looking for Bailey, meanwhile concentrating on shadowing Lily. He could sense their impatience, and knew his team was ready for action.

"I know that all of this waiting is frustrating. I'm about ready to go in there and strangle her. But we must tread lightly. We cannot afford to have her know we are here."

"Do you have any ideas about who would take Miss Bailey?" asked Charles, with concern.

Declan paused, pensive. "Bailey has abilities, as I have already explained to you. I believe someone else knows about her powers and wants to either destroy her, which I believe is not the case, or perform First Blood Rites so she will be in his or her power." He heard an intake of breath and subtle cursing. "But it's too late to save her from that fate. The new moon was last night, so the ritual could have already been performed."

Charles surveyed the building that Lily was using as her den of death. "Do you believe Lily told this vampire about her, or do you think someone had been watching?" Charles looked over to where Lily was holed up.

"I honestly don't know, but I never sensed any other vampire around her besides Mikel that first night in Oak Park, and then her attack on her way home from work. He also followed her in daylight to frighten her." He smiled. "Only it didn't have the desired effect. It only made her angry." He remembered her face, the way her eyes flared. He missed those eyes.

"I believe we are dealing with a very old vampire with a large established network–someone who has been flying under the radar for decades, perhaps centuries. I have researched and haven't found anyone who would know about the history here, but perhaps someone, an elder–someone who knows firsthand." He shook his head. "Nevertheless, we should be very aggressive but careful. We wouldn't want to accuse anyone, especially an elder, without concrete proof." He waited to make sure all of his team members agreed.

"Charles and Shila, cover the back," Declan continued. "I don't want Lily making a move without us knowing. Daniel, you and Thomas keep looking for Bailey in all the wrong places. It's obvious that whoever took Bailey wants us all dead or worse." He met each of his warrior's eyes. "Eyes and ears open, watch your backs, and check in every twenty minutes." They nodded and left.

Declan found a shady corner of the roof to sit and wait. Chances were Lily wouldn't make a move until sunset, but he had to be certain. He felt so anxious and frustrated just sitting there, knowing that Bailey was in trouble, it made him want to kill someone. And that person would be Lily. Yes, Lily would pay for her betrayal.

But first he needed to find Bailey. He had a connection to her from their lovemaking, but she hadn't drunk from him so their link remained tenuous. As much as he tried, he couldn't even catch a whiff of her anywhere other than on himself. But he knew she was in trouble–that she was scared, confused, and angry. He just knew it. So he would sit and wait for Lily to make her move.

Finally, at sunset, he got the call from Shila.

"She's on the move. Heading east down the alley and moving fast." He flew to the next building and over to Lily's roof, where he could just make out Lily's form before she turned the corner.

"Flank me, Shila. Charles behind me just in case, and someone call Daniel and Thomas tell them to get in front of her so she cannot get away from us."

"Yes sir."

Good, finally things were moving. But after several hours of following Lily as she wound her way through the city, stopping periodically to talk to her people, he was still getting nowhere. Periodic waves of pure panic would arise, but he tamped it back and concentrated on his mission. He couldn't afford to make a mistake now.

Declan listened in as Lily gave further instructions to her minions. Clearly they were trying to lead him back to the run-down house on the west side. But this time he picked up one piece of new information: He heard the name of Sethe, and it rang a bell. He had seen it in his research over the years, he was sure of it. He would have Charles check into it immediately. His thoughts were interrupted by Lily's yelling. She was letting one of her subordinates know her unhappiness at their overall ineptitude. He could tell she was getting frustrated, and that only helped increase his own tension. He needed to make things happen, to get her to lead them to Bailey. He thought about it for a while. Well, he might have to accommodate her after all.

He made a few phone calls then hid his cell for later retrieval. There was no way he wanted that found. He left his post and went straight to the west side, where he pretended to snoop around the ramshackle house. He heard them come from a mile away and shook his head. "Embarrassing incompetents." Ready or not, Declan knew he was about to get his ass kicked, but it was worth it if they took him to Bailey. Besides, his team would follow at a distance and help when need be, when Bailey was safe and sound. Going in with no weapons except his natural abilities and his smarts was probably one of the dumbest things he could do. But he had to—for her.

Here goes nothing, he thought, as he braced for what was about to come. It didn't take long to find himself surrounded. Half-heartedly, he tried to defend himself and break loose from the vampires, but they overtook him. He could have easily killed all of these morons, but he chose not to. Instead, hoping they weren't too ambitious and supersede their superior's orders to take him alive. Declan didn't think they were that stupid. So he managed to take a couple of the vampires down, probably killing one, maybe both, before he let them seize him. But he hadn't expected what occurred next. Lily walked straight up to him and aimed a gun at his torso. He felt the bullet enter his chest, tearing flesh and organs along the way. But the worst part was that the bullet contained a surprise: silver nitrate, he guessed from the excruciating pain searing through his body right before feeling nothing at all.

Declan awoke to a nightmare. Silver. The only thing in large quantities that could keep him down. He'd known that they would use something like this, but the realization didn't make it any less painful. And what about his team? Were they close? He wasn't surprised that they hadn't intervened on the west side. He'd given them specific orders to wait until they took him to wherever Bailey was, and they knew that a bullet would not kill him. Not immediately, anyway. So was Bailey here? Hmm. Yes, he could just barely sense her. She was near, but not in this building.

He managed to open an eye and noted that he was in a silver cell. Not unlike what he had in the cave, but this was more crudely built. He was shackled to a wall, and his captor stepped forward and slapped him hard. She was smiling. Lily.

"Well, well, finally you're awake. I thought you were going to sleep all night. Too bad you missed the festivities the night before last."

Declan's heart sank, and his anger did just the opposite. "I will kill you very painfully before this is over," he growled. Every movement was excruciating, but he was so enraged, he didn't care.

"Is that right?" She suddenly stabbed him in the stomach with a silver blade. Pain sliced through his insides. "You have no idea what you are dealing with here, Sir Declan," She spat. "But you'll soon find out. And then you'll be on your knees as my little pet. Yes, you'll become my slave or you'll die."

Declan gathered all of his strength and lunged at her, smiling, since her fear was easily smelled. "We will see, madam, we will see."

She left the room to the burly vampire standing guard. Declan's blood trickled on the floor, and soon it became a puddle. The silver flowing through his veins prevented him from healing quickly, so he could eventually bleed out. But that bitch would have to do better than one little stick to kill him. His team would know exactly where he was and would be planning an attack. But it had to be timed perfectly. They were too late for the ritual, and that sickened him, but he was not leaving without her, no matter what happened–no matter if he had to stand trial for kidnapping and murder in front of the Council. He would not leave her, ever.

ɢʒ

Marry him? How dare he, the bastard. I left the room, surprised that no guard was posted at the door to stop me. I strolled around but saw no one. I could sense Sethe's anger. I knew he was still relatively close, but he was no longer in the house. He was walking down a path towards what looked like a barn. I felt dismayed that I knew so much. My head tightened like a giant balloon ready to explode. I clenched my eyes shut, until the vision dissipated.

This must be the insight ability that Declan spoke of. I swallowed back my fear and concentrated harder, determined to master my new abilities.

I felt beads of sweat forming at my brow as I thought of Sethe. Then I saw him–smelled him–and knew his feelings. He was thinking about the person held in the barn and also his anger at me. He had never had a woman speak to him in such a way. *Good,* I thought. *I knew where he was going now.* How sickening that I felt better knowing where he was.

I snooped around the house. It was an old Romanesque Revival with asymmetrical spaces and nooks and crannies aplenty. It was decorated in the classic 1970s whorehouse style, further marred by broken windows, moth-bitten rugs, and cracked laminate countertops. The furnishings were old but not antique. The place was in need of serious updating and some tender loving care, and maybe about a week's worth of scrubbing. Did I picture myself doing that? Wow, I needed to get out of there.

I saw no one, but I sensed at least five others who were asleep in the house. Downstairs, I believed. I made my way to the front door. Maybe most of his vampires were the changed kind, so were sleeping off the previous night's adventures. I was just happy I didn't need to see the hulk again.

It felt good to be out in the sunlight. I scanned the landscape, wondering where I was. I could see no other houses, smelled no exhaust fumes, and heard no signs of horns blaring or sirens wailing. I was in the country, that was for sure. I counted eight cars parked in various positions along the drive. All had Illinois tags. Interesting. I wondered if anyone had been kind enough to leave keys for me? I meandered down the long winding driveway to the main road. I still couldn't see another house. I did notice plenty of trees, a somewhat hilly terrain, and I smelled a large river close by.

I stretched, then decided I needed to run a bit to loosen my muscles. What? Why the hell was I not running for my life? Why did I not feel like finding the first phone to call home? The realization stunned me. I sensed him then. Sethe was trying to get into my head, probing and prodding. What would happen if I tried to block him out? I decided not to try it for now, not caring about him seeing me here. I took off my loafers and flexed my feet. I wondered if it would hurt to run with no shoes? I decided to give it a try.

As I started out, I questioned why I wasn't trying to find help. Why wasn't I trying to get home, and why did I feel emptier inside the further I ran away from the house? But the big question was why didn't I miss my old life more? And the boys–how were they, and why wasn't I trying to get to them? My boys! I started to panic. Was I really attached to a monster forever and would I never be able to escape this nightmare? Oh, god, what was I going to do?

I stopped and threw up along the side of the road. I seemed to be doing that a lot now. I heaved until I had nothing left in my stomach and then heaved some more. I looked up to see Sethe laughing at me, only it was in my mind. He knew of my anguish, and it entertained him. *Bastard.* I immediately straightened up and ran forward. I was more powerful than he knew, and I would show him just how much soon enough.

I ran past several other estates tucked into pockets of trees, at least a dozen acres with each parcel. I finally found the water I had been sensing, and it was huge and powerful. This had to be the Mississippi River. And then it came to me–Galena. Yes, now that I thought about it, what a great place to hide. Who would ever expect a den of bloodthirsty vampires in the picturesque Galena Valley area? Quiet, secluded, and secure, yet close enough to Chicago and St. Louis for convenience. Yes, good choice, Sethe. I wondered how many people in the area went missing each year, or did his vamps just have their fun in the city where there was plenty to choose from?

I turned and headed back. I was working up a good sweat and hoped I would find a change of clothes on my return. Tomorrow I would find Galena and I would go home. Why did the thought make my stomach clench? Suddenly Sethe was coming towards me fast. I felt it before I saw him.

"What are you doing so far from the house? he demanded.

I sputtered. "I was running to feel better. I thought you wouldn't mind. I saw no one." Why on earth was I groveling to this creep?

"Very well, but you will not leave again until after we are mated."

"Well, about that. I don't want to. Can't we wait and see what happens? I hardly know you."

He whipped around with eyes blazing icy white.

"You will not disobey me!" He gripped my waist and dragged me into the woods. I fought him, but not with much strength. I didn't think he would truly harm me. He threw me to the ground.

"I will show you who is in charge. I'm your master, and you need to be taught to respect me like all of the others. I will bend your will and I will break you. In the end you will be frightened. I can promise you that." He smiled the most vicious smile I had ever seen. He grabbed my shirt and ripped it in two. I screamed and he slapped me.

"You will not harm me, Sethe," I cried.

"I will if you fight me; it's up to you. He lunged for my breasts and squeezed roughly. "You are beautiful, Bailey."

He was all over me, and before I knew it, we were both naked. I tried to hate everything he did to me. My heart said no to his tongue outlining every crevice of my body. But my head wanted more. He ravaged my core, and I couldn't help but feel my release mounting.

I wanted to resist his every move, but I knew he would win in the end. I tried with all of my might not to think of Declan, but I couldn't help it. And Sethe knew, because he turned me over and entered me with brutal force. Tears streamed down my face. I gagged more than once. I loved it and hated it with all of my being. He was an evil sociopath, and I was caught in his web with heaps of useless power at my disposal, because he had my soul. And he knew it.

After Sethe was finished with me he left. I lay for hours on the coarse pine needles in the quiet forest. I watched as squirrels chattered at one another and fought for position on fragile branches. I closed my eyes and dreamed of Declan and my family and how much I missed them. I was frightened for their safety, because Sethe knew where they lived and he would kill them to keep me, if necessary. I knew he would without a second thought. So I was trapped, ensnared by a maniac, with nowhere to run, because I knew he would hunt me down to the ends of the earth.

I was terrified to leave him, and I knew right then that I probably never would. But the thought of staying with this evil man was enough to make me want to walk right into the Mississippi and never come up for air again.

"My god, what am I?" I asked myself. Would I really want to go home now and just pretend nothing had happened even if I could? How could I live with myself knowing that I didn't fight? How could I let my family and Declan ever see me like this; a weak, useless shell of a woman?

So my life was over as I knew it. I needed to tell someone so they could say their goodbyes and properly bury me. How would I explain to them that I would never see them again? Could I find a way to write a letter and mail it? Could I say my goodbyes in just a letter? "Coward!" I yelled at myself. But at least I had an occupation to keep my mind off of other events. I got up, put on what was left of my clothing, and walked back into my hopeless nightmare.

I lay on the shower floor and let the water cascade over my body. I wanted all traces of him off of me, inside and out. He was smart enough to leave me alone for a time to cry for the loss of my family, and all of my friends. I wept for my dogs and my sweet memories of Declan. We'd only shared a few days together but it felt like I'd known him for a lifetime. I mourned the life I would leave behind.

I thought about the letter that I would write, even coming up with a few lines, but the revisions in my head left me feeling weak and sick. I couldn't write it. I just couldn't. So would I be able to live like this? Constantly walking on eggshells, looking over my shoulder, and being with someone who didn't care for me, let alone love me? He was cruel and empty, so how was my life with him going to be? The whole thought made me ill.

That's when I made my final decision. I would not live like this, no matter our connection. I would leave him or die trying, and I was no longer scared to die. With a clarity I hadn't felt in a long time, I knew I would kill myself before I lived like this, before I lived as Sethe's slave, to torture whenever he wanted to. To use me in ways I didn't want to consider. And to harm those I loved. I would find a way to protect my family. I would write the letter, but it would not be in farewell, that was for certain. And then I realized that for these last few hours I hadn't felt Sethe in my head. He had tried on several occasions, but I was so distracted with my plight, I had shoved him away. Hmm. Could I learn to block him out?

I remembered what Declan said about the possibility of my reading and manipulating a vampire's mind. The reading part was easy enough, I had glimpses of what others felt–but the manipulation–could I do that? And how could I even begin to try? What if Sethe found out? I would be dead in an instant, but it would be worth it. I have to get out, and there was only one way to walk out of here without bloodshed, specifically mine. And that was to see if I could persuade my captors to free me, and not to remember doing it. *Wow, not a tall order, Bailey,* I thought. But at least I had a plan forming, and it felt good. I had a purpose, and that was to get back to my family at all costs.

I concentrated and found Sethe going towards the barn once again. Something was in that barn. Good, he was preoccupied with–hmm, I couldn't quite make it out. I would have to practice a bit. Maybe I would have to stay awhile before I could attempt such an escape. Yes, I could put my new skills into practice on the help–the non-human help, anyway. Good, a plan!

I dragged myself out of the shower and discovered clean towels placed by the sink. As I dried off and went into the bedroom, a new slinky dress, cheap shoes, and jewelry were positioned on the bed.

"It's for your mating ritual," the voice of a young girl I had never seen before said from behind me as she closed the door.

Oh, shit. I'd forgotten all about the mating ritual! Now there was no way I could delay. I had to get out of here before the ritual was performed; otherwise legally, I was his property. Vampire legal, anyway. The thought nauseated me. What to do?

I returned to the bathroom to get dressed, when I felt Sethe near. My heart raced from fear. Crap, he did scare me. I couldn't let him sense that, so I concentrated on slowing my heart rate and blocking his trespassing in my head.

He strode into the bedroom and headed straight into the bathroom, dropping his clothes along the way. He entered the shower without even glancing my way. I tried to ignore him as I continued getting dressed. When I was finished he was still in the shower; the glass completely fogged. I could smell something coming from his discarded clothing on the floor. The closer I got, more overwhelming grew the sense of dread. I leaned to pickup his shirt, and it hit me. *Declan.*

I ran into the closet so he couldn't see me. I tried blocking all of my emotions while I smelled the blood on Sethe's clothing. I smelled myself, and our sex, mixed with Declan's blood.

"Shit," I whispered. And then I heard the shower shut off. I threw his clothes in the hamper and tried to contain my emotions. He stalked into the closet and got dressed without saying a word. I went into the bedroom and fidgeted. What the hell was I going to do? I had to find Declan. He was in pain and maybe dying. The thought terrified me.

Sethe came in smiling. He sensed my fear because I forgot to block it, but he had no idea it was for Declan. He went to the door and let in two beautiful brunettes who looked like twins, dressed in slinky royal blue satin. They were human and scared.

"You will escort Miss Bailey to the ballroom in ten minutes. I have to go greet our guests now. And Bailey, darling, try to look pleased." He gave me a quick kiss and left. I wanted to run into the bathroom and vomit again, but I managed to keep my gorge down this time. I'd had no chance to try my abilities on him. I didn't even know how to go about it.

I paced. I had to locate Declan, and I had a feeling I knew right where he was. I probed the girls' minds to see if it could work. I concentrated on them, and their thoughts. I dove deep, seeing purple and then red. I got an instant headache, but I stuck it out. So far I hadn't had to touch their heads like Declan would have done. Slowly images started to appear. Hundreds of them flashed in my mind: an unfamiliar country, children in school, mountains in the background, family dinners, and dates. All normal until–oh– the latest images I got were both horrifying and sickening. Sethe had tortured and killed their family and kidnapped the two, keeping them as his personal sex slaves while slowly draining their blood. They were terrorized and resigned to their fate. But I also caught a glimpse of where Sethe had been going, because one of the girls had accompanied him to his torture chamber. My hunch was confirmed, the barn.

I searched the room for weapons, not caring if there was a camera or what the girls thought. I tore apart the closet and bathroom. Nothing. Maybe he still didn't trust me–with good reason. The girls were smart enough to say nothing and stay away from me. I was just about to search the bedroom when time ran out. Bruiser came in to join the party.

"Damn," I muttered to myself. "Is it time already?"

He only nodded. Well, I wasn't going through with this, so I had to think quickly. I was about to try my mind-bending abilities on the hulk when another vamp came in, so I couldn't risk it.

The five of us entered the ballroom precisely ten minutes after Sethe. How was I going to leave without being noticed now? After all, I was the bride. The thought made my pulse quicken and my head buzz.

The ballroom held about twenty-five vampires seated around a central altar. I guessed these would be the witnesses to this horror show. Two burly vamps guarded the doorways so there was no escape. Shit.

The twins escorted me to the altar, where Sethe was waiting with another man. Who, I presumed would be presiding over the ceremony. I felt panic stricken, but I was careful not to show it. My mind played a beautiful summer's day, driving in my car down Lake Shore Drive. My heart rate was steady and I didn't sweat. I appeared calm, cool, and collected–on the outside.

The women dropped me off with Sethe, and all eyes were on us. Suddenly I heard a commotion by the back doors, which led to the kitchen spaces. In marched two vampires dragging Declan with Lily waltzing in behind them. Oh my god, he looked like he was dying. Blood covered every inch of him, and I could barely recognize his lovely face underneath all of the swelling and bruising. He was so pale, almost translucent, and I could see that he was barely holding on. My heart constricted. I wanted to rush to him and hold him in my arms, and I craved to kill Lily with my bare hands. But I was careful not to show anything. It was the hardest thing I have ever done.

"I wanted to give you a little wedding gift before we begin, "Sethe announced with a palatial smile. "I want you to watch as Sir Declan dies, and your connection to him ends."

I glanced at Lily, who looked surprised and upset at the news. I could barely contain my anger and frustration, and for a split second, I let my guard down.

"What's the matter, my dear bride? I thought you would be pleased to know how well I will take care of you. You see, you will never again need another protector, and this child will no longer bother us."

"But he has not bothered us," I stated in a clear and calm voice, when all I wanted to do was scream. "Release him and I will gladly go through with this. I will be yours forever, and never see him again once this ritual is complete. He poses no threat to us."

Sethe laughed, and I heard chuckles from the crowd. "Silly Bailey, you will go through with this no matter what. So your asking does not matter. Nothing will save this unfortunate miscreant from quite a painful death."

He stepped forward brandishing a huge silver saber. Declan tried to struggle but couldn't do much. He was so weak and in anguish, it made my heart ache. Lily held his head up as Sethe touched the blade to Declan's neck.

"Stop!" I ordered. I was so enraged, fearful, and crazed that my voice was not my own.

Sethe hesitated, open-mouthed.

"You will not harm this man! I will see you both dead before you touch him again." I pointed to Lily and Sethe, and I heard gasps from the crowd.

Astonished and infuriated, Sethe actually lowered the weapon and whirled towards me. "You bitch," he uttered. "You will obey me and you will mind your station! You could never harm me, your master." But I knew he was uncertain, and I could see his confusion.

"Try me, asshole!" I concentrated on the change that I was going to make happen. This time was different. I focused on controlling every cell within my body. I could almost see the shift taking place inside of me. I felt incredibly strong and alive, my senses on hyper-alert. I could hear the heartbeats of everyone in the room, and others who were miles from the property. I knew that the neighboring farmhouse held a family of four, all soundly sleeping in their beds. I could see and hear the United Airlines plane at 30,000 feet above my head. And I knew that Declan didn't have much time.

I sensed my feet leaving the ground and my body hovering in the air. I felt the heat kick on and its warmth caress my skin. I heard a scream, then doors opening, and hesitant footsteps approaching. I heard Declan thinking how beautiful I was and that he was afraid for me. Afraid for me?

Suddenly there was yelling all around me, but I was concentrating specifically on Lily, Sethe, and the saber. And he didn't waste any time on the shock of seeing me perform. He swung back the sword, poised to slice off Declan's head, when all time seemed to slow. I felt a searing heat in my head, then travelling down my neck and into my arms. Somehow I knew instinctively what to do, as I lifted my arms and spewed liquid fire on Sethe's legs. Howling, he immediately dropped the blade. I watched in horror, and a little agony, as the flames slowly rose up his legs. I glared into his eyes, which were filled with pain and loathing. He screamed my name as the flames climbed higher and higher. Lily ducked out of the way and headed towards the door. The two vampires who were holding Declan were now dragging him away. One was reaching for the saber to finish off the job Sethe could not. I lifted my hands once again, and they vaporized instantly. Declan fell to the floor unconscious.

Now there were terrified screams coming from the others, but I was in such a blind rage that I would not stop until they were all dead. I mentally slammed and locked all of the doors, and one by one, I lifted my hands and discharged my fire, my hatred, and my misery. They ran in vain for the exits. A couple had surrounded me for an attack, but before I could do anything, I was surprised to see Daniel underneath me holding a bloody blade in his hands, and the two vampires dead, their heads rolling across the floor.

"Sethe is gone," he yelled up to me over the pandemonium in the room. I looked for him but Daniel was right. I saw no pile of ash where he should have been. I tried to focus on him but I was too angry and distracted to fully concentrate on the task.

"Get Lily," I screamed and pointed as she ran down a long hallway towards the basement.

Daniel gave a signal, and Shila happily ran after her.

I managed to land by Declan and scrambled to gently lift his head onto my lap. Ignoring my dizziness, pounding headache, and nausea, I focused on saving him. He was dying if not dead already, and I had no clue what to do. "Someone help me!" And before I knew it, Charles, Daniel, and Thomas were by my side. Thomas feverishly worked on Declan, injecting him with all kinds of things.

"He needs blood, now!"

I gave him my arm, but Declan did not respond.

"Quick, Thomas, bite me." He did as I instructed and the blood trickled down my arm. A few drops landed on Declan's lips. Nothing. He didn't even stir.

"Help me open his mouth," Thomas said to the others. They complied and my blood dripped into Declan's mouth, but he still had no reaction. He was not swallowing. Now my heart pounded in panic.

"Goddamnit, do something!"

Thomas opened a medical bag and extracted a tube that he put into Declan's mouth and gently probed down his throat.

"I hope he doesn't wake up for this. Hand me that funnel. Okay, now everyone donate. Hurry."

My wound had already healed, even though vampire fangs secreted an anticoagulant.

"Someone bite me again." And Charles complied this time.

We all hovered around the funnel, squeezing our wounds so a steady supply of blood ran down Declan's throat. After about fifteen minutes of this, Thomas put a stop to it.

"That's all we can do for now. He must fight on his own."

"What?" I screamed. "He still hasn't woken. There must be more we can do! Declan!" I shook him. "Declan, wake up." I couldn't stop the tears that were rolling down my face and onto his. "Please, Declan, please come back to me!" I pleaded with all of my heart, but I still got no response.

Rage began to boil inside of me. I was infuriated at Sethe for causing all of this heartache, for ruining my life. I softly placed Declan's head on the floor and stood.

"Take him and get out." I ordered just as Shila came in, struggling with Lily. I walked over to them and sneered at Lily, who suddenly stopped her resistance. I smelled her fear and relished that fact. I hit her so hard we all heard the bones of her delicate face crack and splinter, and her screams of pain, before she passed out. I smiled. "And take this bitch with you."

They left without another word. I noticed confused glances to one another and a couple of smirks, but no one questioned my authority. Continuing to ignore my dizziness and mounting fatigue, I headed to the basement and saw that the security guard had left his post. I walked down the long corridor, emitting my inferno. I wanted everything incinerated beyond recognition. I wanted no trace of Sethe and his band of terrorists. I wanted to destroy him like I had never wanted anything so badly in all of my life. And then I opened my mind just a fraction, just for an instant. To show him how much fun I was having destroying his property and what I hoped was his life. I slowly climbed back upstairs, letting the heat from the flames singe my skin. It didn't hurt; instead it kept me focused. I moved from room to room, burning everything in my wake. I went upstairs where I'd been held captive and looked around. I could smell him in there, stronger than anywhere else. I gathered my strength and entered the closet. I spewed forth such energy that the closet, and the bathroom beyond, exploded, and before I knew it, I was looking at the stars through the smoke and flames.

I could see that Charles had lain Declan's prone form in the back of a van. They all turned towards me as I jumped down and landed without a misstep. I turned and watched with satisfaction as the whole massive structure began to cave in on itself.

I had one last job to do; I headed towards the barn. I entered, and the smell of Declan's blood mixed with pain and torment brought me to my knees. I regained my composure and found that Charles and Daniel had followed me there. I knew where he'd been kept and I descended in that direction. Down and down, deep underground, where one lone vampire stood guard at the cell, unaware of what had happened. I lifted my hands and he disappeared. I heard gasps from behind me. I guess they hadn't caught my earlier act.

I went into his cell and gazed at the blood, so much blood. I dipped my finger into it and tasted his sweetness, his honor, his bravery, and his terror for me. I then knew what they had done to him, as if I'd been standing in the room watching it happen. It disgusted me to witness their depravity as they played with his body, stabbing him over and over again, watching and laughing as his life poured out of him.

I backed out of the room and lifted my arms. The room exploded as though a bomb had gone off. I retreated down the long corridor with wrath and revulsion as I destroyed everything in my path. The others had stayed with me, following and protecting me if need be. I felt their pride, and a little fear as well.

There was a lot more down there than I expected, including computer labs, a library, several torture chambers, medical facilities, and numerous sleeping quarters. I destroyed it all. By the time we got back up, the whole property seemed to be on fire. I could hear sirens in the distance. Someone must have seen the flames or smelled the smoke.

My dizziness and nausea finally overwhelmed me, and I staggered to the grass, gagged, and fell to my knees. I had nothing left to throw-up. The last thing I remember was being lifted and then everything went dark.

14

IT WAS ONLY SEX

was burning up; my arms were on fire, as I ran from the monster who pursued me. I screamed his name, the name of my tormentor–Sethe!...

I was shaken from my nightmare to a pounding headache and cramping in my empty stomach. The image of Daniel solidified, holding my shoulder with concern in his eyes.

"Where will we go to protect him? The cave is damaged, and not secure."

I whipped around to Shila with raised eyebrows and grabbed my head with a moan.

"She's awake."

"Yeah, I wish I wasn't," I mumbled. "My head is killing me."

"Here, take these." Shila handed me three pills and a soda that Thomas had given her. I took them without question, the soda stinging my stomach as it hit emptiness.

"How is he?"

"Still unconscious," Thomas said from the back of the van where Declan lay. "He'll pull through this. He is strong. His body just needs time to heal." He searched through his bag for something. "More damn wounds than I can count," he added in disgust.

"Where is she?" I asked with venom.

Shila raised her eyebrows. "She's in the other van with Charles and a couple of other guards. Don't worry, she won't escape."

"Good, I'm counting on that."

Shila's eyes widened. I guessed my own eyes had started doing their thing.

It was still dead of night. "How long have I been out?"

"About an hour. You needed the rest," Thomas stated. We rode silently for several minutes, everyone deep in their own thoughts.

I eyed Shila. "What were you saying before I woke up?"

"Oh—yes, the attack. That is why we were delayed. We had to stay and defend our home, but some of it was damaged anyway. It was a well-thought-out and coordinated attack. They planned to distract us from finding you, and it worked. We had to fend them off and couldn't get to Sir Declan in time for—this!" She pointed to him, furious and grieved by his condition. "And they killed some of our people."

She and the others felt ashamed and angry. I knew this because I could see it in their minds. Oh boy.

"We caught all of them involved, over twenty. Most are dead, but a couple live—for now." Daniel's face was a mask of seething fury.

"My god—not the library?"

"No, we stopped them before they could infiltrate the sensitive areas."

"My dogs! Where are they? Are they harmed?"

"No, they are safe with Roran. He'll bring them to your house, so you'll see them soon, *mon ami*."

Relief flooded me. I thought about it for a minute. "We will go home, to my home." They looked at me and nodded. "We can defend ourselves if need be, but no one would expect us to go back there. Send someone you fully trust ahead of us to see that no one is still watching the house. I highly doubt that they would continue to do so once we were captured, but just in case. I have an unfinished refrigerated wine cellar in my basement that would make a good interrogation cell for Lily. I'm not through with her just yet. And please send someone to watch my parents' house. Sethe escaped, and I wouldn't put it past him to harm my family to get to me. We'll watch them closely, at least until I have them well hidden." I looked to all of them and they stared back with purpose. They accepted me as one of them now and gladly agreed to do my bidding.

While Daniel made the calls, Shila leaned over her seat. "Here, I want to give you this so you can have it for Sir Declan when he awakens." She handed me his cell phone, and our hands met. I could instantly see that she was fully confident of Declan's recovery. That fact gave me hope, and I felt a ten-ton weight lift off of my heart. I managed a weak smile and nodded my thanks.

I hopped over my seat to get to Declan, sat down and gingerly lifted his head onto my lap. He was not dead, I knew it now. He would live. I studied his beautiful face, which was still covered in blood, eyes swollen shut and nose askew.

"Thomas, can you please pass me that bottle of water, and do you have a clean cloth somewhere?"

He passed me the water and a stack of gauze pads, which I used to clean Declan's face and neck. I washed his arms and chest. I took off what was left of his tattered pants and cleaned every inch of him. His wounds were already healing, but he was a long way from looking healthy.

"It might take him days to recover from this." Thomas took my hand and gently squeezed before he hopped over to my vacant seat.

"I'll take care of him, and I won't leave his side again," I said with certainty. They all nodded their approval. I found a blanket and covered him with it, as I studied his lovely face. His bruising was not quite as bad and the cuts were healing. He looked peaceful and beautiful now, but I knew he would be haunted by the torture he had endured. I lay my head back and closed my eyes. I hadn't realized that I was still exhausted. My arms felt heavy and raw, my head ached, and my body was trembling now that my adrenalin had worn off. If I could just close my eyes for a minute more...

I woke to a gentle pressure on my shoulder. "We have arrived, Miss Bailey." I struggled to open my eyes. Wow, it was morning and we had made it back to Chicago.

Shila gave the thumbs up. "No one has been around for some time."

I managed to shake the cobwebs loose. "Good. Drive to the alley and park in my spare parking place." I glanced down at Declan but he hadn't woken up. I looked to Thomas. "Should I be worried that he's not awake yet?"

"No. It will take his body some time before it heals completely. It's better that he sleeps. It will let him recover faster."

"Okay, please take him gently to my bedroom. It's the fourth level. Use the elevator. There's a spare set of keys hidden under that pot." I pointed to a sad container that was filled with impatiens, which had looked great the last time I was home. The poor things hadn't been watered for—how long had I been gone?

After we all got settled, I showed Charles and Shila the coach house apartment, which held two bedrooms, each with its own bath. I gave them each a key. They seemed pleased with the arrangements. Back in the main house, I showed Daniel to the guest suite in the basement and the unfinished wine closet.

"This is just right for Lily," he said. "Let me make a few adjustments to the lock and we can throw her in it immediately."

"Fine, let me show you where my tools are." I walked to the closet at the far end of the hallway and threw open the doors.

"Excellent. You have almost everything." He was impressed, and that made me happy.

I left him to it and went upstairs to find Thomas. He was in my kitchen all alone.

"Come on up and I'll show you to your suite." He nodded and followed. "I wanted to put you closest to my bedroom in case Declan needs you for something."

"Yes, that is best," he agreed.

I led him to the third floor guest room and bath. He cleared his throat after I showed him his towels and other spare necessities I had to offer.

"Umm, Miss Bailey."

"It's just Bailey, please." I turned to look at his dark eyes. He was a strikingly handsome man whose eyes reflected intelligence and warmth.

"I don't know if Sir Declan would approve, but okay, Bailey. I just wanted to tell you how grateful we all are for everything you have done for Sir Declan and the rest of us. It is difficult for us vampires to be in someone else's debt, and we have not taken a vow for your protection yet, but know that all of us would die defending you and those you love. Vow or no vow."

I was stunned. "I—well, I am very appreciative, but I am the one who got you all into this mess. I should be the one who is thanking all of you." I grasped his hands. He tried to pull back, but I wouldn't let him go. "You are my friends—my other family now."

He tightened his grip and smiled. "Yes, we are. Now let's see to Sir Declan before I get cleaned up."

Declan was laid out on my bed. His battered skin still looked too pale. After Thomas examined him for a time, he looked at me and nodded with a grin. I let out a breath I hadn't realized I had been holding.

"He is resting comfortably and he's in good shape for what his body went through," Thomas reported. "He may sleep for several more hours, but his wounds are healing nicely. He just needs time now." He patted my shoulder and left. I ran after him.

"Thomas, can you please tell the others that I would like to convene at sunset in the kitchen for a meeting?"

He tilted his head in surprise. "Yes, of course."

"Thank you."

I went back into my room, but heard a commotion downstairs. I went flying down to find Roran and the boys standing in my foyer with Charles. I fell on the floor and attacked the boys with hugs, rubs, and kisses. I squealed with delight.

"My boys, oh, my boys. Mama is so happy to see you." I turned to find the whole crew staring at me with smirks and ogles. I guess they hadn't had a chance to inspect me after my change.

I ignored their admiration of my appearance. "Okay, so I love my dogs. Anyone have a problem with that?" No one would meet my eyes. "Roran, where did you go–I mean where you have been hiding?"

After Roran was able to tear his eyes away from me, he came forward and told us his story. He was out with the dogs and heard a commotion by the entrance to the cave. He immediately called Daniel to inform him of the problem and then took the boys to a nearby hotel. Roran went back, and all hell had broken loose. He tried to contact Daniel, but finally reached Charles instead. Charles told him to go back to the dogs and stay put and wait for an "all clear". He'd finally gotten the call about an hour earlier.

"I am in your debt, Roran. Thank you so much for taking such great care of my dogs." He blushed and mumbled something under his breath.

"You will need somewhere to stay. I have a foldout couch in the coach house if you would like to stay there?"

"That would be fine, Miss Bailey. But, can I please keep watching the boys for you?"

"Well, of course! They obviously love you." He blushed even more. "Good; Charles can show you the way. I have sheets and extra pillows in the linen closet by the kitchen there. Please help yourselves to anything you might need."

I gestured to the assembled group. "Now that all of this is settled and I have everyone's attention, I want to show you how to work the security system. It is state of the art." They gawked at me, a couple dubious. "It's true. I dated a guy for awhile who worked for this company designing security systems—anyway, I got it wholesale because it was a prototype and he wanted to try it out." Now everyone had some sort of smirk on his or her face. I cleared my throat and got down to showing them the key codes and where the motion, pressure, and glass-break sensors were located in the main house, as well as the coach house. By the end of the tour, they looked surprised and impressed.

"I can use my print, but you must use the codes. And see how it will detect if someone hops over the brick wall?" I showed them.

"Since everyone is going to bed, I'll activate the security, but remember—if anyone decides to go for a walk it will go off, so deactivate it first. I will put the boys in bed with me so they're not running around. See everyone tonight—sleep well." And we all went to our rooms.

The boys immediately hopped on the bed and were spooked at Declan lying there. They eventually went over to him, gave him the once over, then a quick few licks before they settled down at the foot of the bed. They must have had an anxious few days, because they looked as tired as I felt. I staggered to the bathroom. It felt so good to be home I almost cried in relief. I stripped out of the torn and sooty gown I had on from the night before, and I threw it out in the hallway, along with the shoes and tacky jewelry.

I didn't look as bad as I thought I would. My hair was dirty but still gleamed, and my skin was sooty but unmarred. In the shower I scrubbed until I was squeaky-clean. I threw on a long flannel shirt, brushed out my hair, and braided it for bed. I lowered my shades and closed the draperies from the morning sun. I crawled into bed and spooned Declan, who was nice and toasty. Hmm, vamps cold? It was a total myth. I was just about to succumb to sleep when Sethe's face loomed before me.

"You bitch. You will pay for your deceit and treachery." He was furious and in pain, but he was far away from me. I was perfecting my blocking skills, so he didn't know where I was or whom I was with. I finally went to sleep thinking about Sethe's threats and how I was actually looking forward to them.

ೞ

Hours later and a bit past sunset, Declan stirred, and I immediately hovered over him. He opened his eyes and smiled. It was the best thing I had ever seen.

"Well, welcome back."

He tried to speak, but I covered his mouth with mine and he responded accordingly. I finally let him have some air.

"Bailey, I can't believe it's you! You are the most beautiful thing I have ever laid eyes on!" Then he grimaced.

"What's wrong? Do I need to fetch Thomas?"

"No, no. I'm still running a bit low on blood is all."

"Well, I think I can take care of that." I gave him my neck.

"What are you doing?"

"I'm trying to help you."

"By being my blood patron?"

"Yes. What's the matter? You've had some already."

"But we'll have a stronger connection if I take more of your blood."

"Don't you think we already have a strong connection? Besides, you already have plenty of my blood in you."

"Yes, I can sense it. But I can't tell what you are feeling."

"That's because I'm blocking you. Now just be quiet and bite." He obeyed, but was very tentative. "Don't worry, I won't break." His fangs extended and sank into my neck. The heat it radiated took me by surprise, but it shouldn't have. As he gulped, my whole body quaked with pleasure. My nipples hardened and my core melted. I moaned, and he was hard and pressing against me. I found myself on top of him, grinding into him. I wanted him more than I have ever wanted anyone. Suddenly, he let go.

"Declan," I purred. Why did you stop?" I felt the heat beginning to leave my body, as I studied him closely. His eyes were back to normal, but his lips were still rosy with my blood smeared across them. Hmm, kinda sexy. He looked healthier already.

"He raped you or you let him. Either way, he has been inside of you!" My heart sank. "I can smell him in you. My god, Bailey, why?"

"I–I don't know. I just couldn't help it. I hate him but–needed him."

He pushed me off, and got up unsteadily.

"Should you be doing that? Come back to bed, Declan."

He ignored me and staggered to the shower. After several minutes, and my anger nice and stoked, I stomped into the bathroom and opened the shower door.

"I will not be ignored. If you have a problem with what I had to do, then don't be a coward by just walking away. Talk to me about it!"

"Coward?" He roared and dragged me into the shower and slammed me against the wall. "How do you think I feel when I know you have been with the man who almost killed me? Do you expect me to rejoice in the fact that you allowed him inside of you?"

"But I couldn't help it!" I pleaded.

"Did he rape you?" I only looked at him and then at my hands. I stood mute.

"Did–he–force–himself–on–you?"

"He–um–He–uh–well, yes and no." He glared at me as if I had lost my mind, then released me and turned around to shut off the water.

"Where is Daniel?"

"In the basement," I whispered.

He stepped out, leaving me like the drowned rat I was. He toweled off and left without a backward glance.

15

SOMETIMES THE TRUTH HURTS

I left the shower, peeled off my soaking pajamas, and dried off. He doesn't understand. He can't possibly comprehend what I went through. I went back to bed and curled up in a ball, and cried until I fell back asleep.

Hours later, I awoke to silence so complete it frightened me. I got up and dressed, brushed my teeth, and put my hair up. I noticed the security system was enabled, so I scanned my thumb and turned it off. The boys and I went downstairs. It was just before sunrise, and the house was dark. I left it that way, not wanting to draw any unwanted attention. Besides, I could see just fine.

I suddenly realized that I had slept all the way through the night. I must have really needed the rest. I immediately went to the kitchen and fed the dogs. They were going to have to get used to a new schedule, that was for sure. When they were finished, I let them out in the backyard to do their business while I wandered around the house.

I felt desperately lonely. How could Declan be so angry? *Shit!* I thought. I knew I would get hurt, and I realized that this devastated me more than anything John had done. *Why did I always fall for the wrong guy?*

I walked back into the kitchen and saw a note on the counter I'd completely missed before.

Dear Miss Bailey,
We went to see to the rest of our people and the cave. We will return before sunset.
Please stay inside and keep the security system on. Lily is in your basement room.

Please stay away from her. She is of a foul disposition. Thomas gave her more sedatives to knock her out, so she should not give you any problems. We will make sure that this will be the last evening she spends under your roof.
Daniel

He listed all of their phone numbers in case of an emergency. No mention of Declan. A kick in the gut, but I tried not to think about it.

I let the boys back in and gave them some well-deserved scratching. I looked at their cute little faces.

"Well, guys, what do you say we go to Riverside? It's a little early, but you know they'll be up." If they had tails, they would have been wagging. I gathered them up and tossed them in the car along with their food and beds, just in case. I was frightened for my parents because Sethe was still out there and he would most certainly harm them to get to me. Plus, I needed answers, and they were the only ones who could provide them. I dreaded the confrontation, but it needed to be done.

I passed a 24-hour McDonald's and my stomach growled. It had been a long time since I'd eaten anything. I didn't have much of an appetite, but I needed to keep up my strength. I stopped and ordered a McGriddle, McMuffin, and two burgers for the dogs. They loved McDonalds too. We inhaled our food on the way to Riverside.

I was careful to keep my blocks up at all times so Sethe couldn't see me. A small part of me missed his presence, though that thought made me ill. I didn't know which was worse, Sethe's attentions or Declan's rejection.

As I pulled into my parents' driveway I grew nervous about seeing them. I had been AWOL for how long now? Could it have been a full week? And what about work?

I smelled but did not see the two vampires guarding the house. I nodded my approval, as I knocked on the door. I was greeted with hugs, relief, and genuine happiness at seeing me, even at the ungodly early hour.

"Thank god you are all right. Detective O'Connor phoned us and said you had to be protected for a few days and that you would call us, but you never did."

"Yes, I'm sorry, I meant to call you. I have so much to tell you. I'm glad you both are here." They eyed each other, and suddenly I knew. They were not my biological parents. The thought tore at the last shred of my ruined heart. I couldn't speak. I also knew a couple of Sethe's older vampires had messed with their minds. Shit.

"Come in and let's get more comfortable. Honey, would you like some breakfast?" I could only shake my head. "Tea?"

"Sure," was all I could get out.

"Katherine, I'm going to brew a pot of coffee and heat up some water. I'll be right back." Dad left the room to go to the kitchen. My mom studied me with a worried expression. She fidgeted with her hair and twisted her hands. Hmm, nervous–interesting.

"What happened to you, Bailey?" She finally met my eyes and they widened. She started walking around me. "Your hair is different and you look more radiant–more–alive. And your eyes are so strikingly green this morning. Are those contact lenses you're wearing? What's going on?" Under all of her worry, I felt her guilt.

I sat in my favorite squishy chair. "I'll wait until Dad comes back to explain everything. Is Kristen here?" She shook her head. "Well, that will work out better."

"You're really scaring me now." My mother fell silent as my father entered the room with the cups. We made ourselves comfortable as my mind raced with how I should begin.

I jumped up to pace twisting my hands in anxiety. Eventually stopping when I heard my father clear his throat, then dove right in with my crazy tale. I told them everything, from the evening I went to the Conrad site to the McDonalds I just ate. Well, skimming over the sex parts, of course. By the time I was finished, my mom was bawling and my dad was wiping the perspiration from his brow.

"This can't be true!" She stared at my dad, who could not meet her eyes. "How can this be true? Vampires are real and live within our society? Incredible."

"And have been around since the beginning," I repeated. "Well, almost." My parents were stunned, but overall, taking the news fairly well. I had expected screaming, pulling of hair, gnashing of teeth, and finally, calling the padded wagon to have me picked up. So this was good.

"Oh my god, Henry, we must tell her everything."

He nodded grimly, and my heart sank.

"Let's see." She took another tissue and blew her nose. "It was the summer of 1980 and your Dad and I had just been married that spring." She glanced at my father, who signaled for her to go on. "We had both finished our undergrad degrees and your father was in his third year of his medical school studies."

"I was just finishing up my last semester," Dad added. "I had already won a residency at Rush."

"Anyway. We never took a real honeymoon because we were so busy with school, so we decided to wait until late summer when things settled down. We jumped in the car and headed south. It was our first trip to South Carolina, and we were so excited. We had actually scraped up enough money to rent a beat-up beach house on Folly Beach." She smiled at my dad who was listening intently. "Remember, dear, how the paint was peeling and we had very little hot water? But we didn't care. We only concentrated on each other."

She sauntered over to my father and gave him a kiss on his head. He grabbed her hands and squeezed. I could only smile at the love they shared. How wonderful and rare. Too bad it only emphasized how empty my life was.

"Where was I? Oh, yes. On our last day of vacation we decided to take a drive up the coast, and we ended up on Sullivan's Island, where we decided to stay and have our dinner. Afterwards we found a secluded beach, where we stopped to take a walk before it got too dark to see where we were going. And maybe for a little something else as well." She winked at my dad, who just reddened.

"I remember there were millions of stars out that evening and the ocean smelled crisp. It was a beautiful and peaceful place. We were just about to head back when we heard a terrifying scream coming from an isolated house to our right and up about a quarter mile or so. Suddenly we saw a woman holding something in her arms, running down the beach towards us. As she got closer we could see that it was a child, and they were both covered in blood."

"Oh god." I knew what was going to come next. My mom came to me then and hugged me so tightly that I thought she was going to squeeze me to death. I hadn't expected it, but I didn't resist.

"This woman begged us to take the child and not to go to the police. She was so pitiful and scared that we had no choice but to take the little girl.

The woman disappeared into a patch of woods to our right before we could utter a word. We rushed the little girl back to the beach house on Folly. We wanted to make sure there were no serious injuries, and sure enough, all of the blood was from someone else."

"I'm so sorry we didn't tell you sooner, Bailey." My father got up and joined us. "As you've already guessed, you were that child."

I was not surprised or angry. I felt empty. "So you kept this from me, why? I'm a grown woman, if you haven't noticed. It would have been nice to know that you're not my parents and my siblings are not my siblings."

"Bailey Anne Davis! You are a Davis just as much as your brother and sister are. We never loved you any less. My god, you are our daughter with every fiber of our being, and that will never change no matter what." Now he hugged me tight. When he pulled back there were tears in his eyes, but he did not let them fall. He and mom took a breath and released me.

"What did this woman look like?"

My dad cleared his throat. "You are her spitting image."

I just sat there numb for a few minutes.

"Okay, why then didn't you take me to the police? And how did you explain that you came back from vacation with a child? What did you tell the grandparents?"

"It was weird—as if we just knew where we needed to go. We packed up and left Charleston immediately after I checked you out. I went back to school down in Champaign, while you and your mother went house hunting in here in Riverside. It was as if we knew we wanted to live here. I can't explain it," he shook his head, "but we never had to tell a soul about you, because no one even asked. Including your grandparents."

My mother continued. "We were in the process of leaving Champaign anyway for your father to start his residency in Chicago, so we just rushed it a bit. Your father started at Rush Medical Center in October, and I found a job in Riverside to be closer to home. My parents gave us the money for a down payment on this house. No one knew us here in Riverside. We were both starting new jobs, and we had no connections we couldn't break. Your father's parents were already living in Florida and mine retired shortly after and left the city to settle in Naperville. We all had fresh starts. When we were questioned, which was rarely, we explained that we had been given an opportunity to adopt you and we did. Adoption was much simpler back then. No one ever gave it a second thought." She got up to refresh her coffee.

I concentrated on the china pattern of my teacup, heavy in thought. "Wow. It's hard to believe all of this—my crazy life. But at least I know the truth. You were manipulated into taking me in and not to the police. Somehow she got to the others." Mom grabbed me again.

"We love you and always will, no matter what. You are our daughter, but we will understand if you feel the need to find out the truth—who your biological parents are." After she said it, she burst out crying again. My father wrapped an arm around her shoulders, but I didn't have it in me to do the same.

"So I must be from the Ah Kin line then. I guess it all makes sense now. Holy cow."

My dad turned to me. "One last thing," he said. "We received a mysterious envelope in the mail about two weeks later with a birth certificate in it. It had our names listed as your parents and your name, Bailey Anne Davis on it. It was very perplexing, but we just accepted it and used the name from then on. You became Bailey, our lovely daughter. We still have it if you want to see it."

"Yes, please." He left to go find it.

"Mom, I want you both to be very careful. I have two guards that will be stationed outside of the house and another who will follow you wherever you go. Please try to stay in the house as much as possible. I just don't trust that maniac. I wouldn't be surprised to find out that he had gone after someone I care about just to get to me."

"Bailey, my god. What about you?"

"I'll be fine. I have protection, and a lot of strength." She nodded but didn't believe it. She knew I was in danger. It must be the mother thing. They always seemed to know.

I ignored her worry. "Would you mind too much if I asked you to take the boys? I really hate to leave them, but I don't know if I'll be able to take good care of them on the road. I'll miss them terribly, but I don't know where I'll be, or what's going to happen." I glanced down to my hands, which were white-knuckling the teacup to death. I hated to leave the boys. I regarded them sleeping at my feet with a lump in my throat. These last couple of weeks had been hard on them, and I wanted no more upheaval in their lives. They loved my parents and would be well taken care of.

"Of course, darling. You know we love the dogs. But I'm so frightened for you. What will you do? What about your job? Can you just leave? And your house and Rosa? What about her?"

"I just don't know yet. I'll take a leave from work. It's okay, I have so much vacation time coming that it would probably add up to a whole year. Rosa is at Disney World for the next couple of weeks. I should be home by then, I hope. I just need to take care of the Sethe situation before I return. Please tell everyone to be careful–David and Marny too. Shit, this is such an awful mess."

I could no longer keep them at bay. The tears flowed freely down my face. My mom rushed me, afraid for my safety. We hugged for what seemed like hours, but I'm sure it was only a couple of minutes. I felt better having let it all out.

"Here it is," my dad said as he came in the room and handed me a yellowed envelope. I cracked it open, but saw no "biological parents sign here" or any other indication of where I really came from. Just my name, my parents' names, date and time of birth, and what looked like the Loyola Hospital's logo. What did I really expect?

"Bailey, we'd be happy to take the boys for as long as it takes."

They looked at each other, passing information without speaking. What would it be like to have that powerful a connection to another human being? That much love and respect?

They decided something then.

"We need to tell you something too. As you already know, your dad and I have been thinking about retiring and moving down south. We rented a house on Folly Beach, not quite as shabby as the first one, mind you. But we signed a year's lease. We wanted to test out the waters to see if we would like living down there. We were going to spend most of the winter there, and go back and forth for the year."

She went to the curio. "Here, take these." She handed me a set of keys with a Folly Beach address on the fob. "We have others, and we're not planning on going down until December anyway. I know you will need to go there. Please be careful."

"We were going to tell you all later," my dad explained. "We wanted everyone to join us for the holidays in South Carolina, and then your mother and I would stay until the spring. But now..."

"No! Don't change a thing. You two deserve this. How about I make you a promise? I promise I will meet you there for Christmas. No matter what."

"Yes, we would like that." And we all hugged.

"I love you, Mom and Dad."

We all started bawling, and didn't break it up until we heard the phone ring. My mom ran to the kitchen to answer it. My dad and I waited quietly, he swallowing his tepid coffee, I sipping my cold tea.

"Sorry for the disruption. Where were we?" Mom sat down, elegant and beautiful. I loved her deeply, and then I decided that it didn't matter that she didn't give birth to me. She was my mother in everyway that mattered.

"I guess there is just one more thing I want to do before I leave." They both waited expectantly. I cleared my throat. "I would like to erase where I am going and who I am going after from your memories."

"What?" they roared in unison. "Can you do that?" my father asked, incredulous.

"Yes, I think so, but I've never tried it. I just don't want to put you two in the situation of having to lie about my whereabouts. Maybe I can just manipulate it so you remember that I'm fine so you're not worried. Or that I'm just on vacation or something." I looked from one to the other with confidence I didn't feel.

They checked each other with approval. "We trust you, my dear," my mother said with conviction. Tears began to threaten again, but I sucked it up.

"Okay, just sit down by one another and relax." I concentrated, and soon I could feel my powers emerging. My mother sucked in a large breath. She was scared, but I smiled and she calmed some. I put my left hand on my father's head and my right on my mother's. I closed my eyes, and I could see what they were thinking. I couldn't tell what Sethe and his minions had erased from their minds, or the long ago planted memories from my biological mother. There must have been some reason she led them to Riverside.

I focused harder on the tale of my recent visit, that I'd come to drop the dogs off and say I was just fine, but I needed an extended vacation. I didn't know for sure where, but somewhere warm, maybe by a beach. I thanked them for taking such good care of the dogs. I would call them as soon as I was back. Not to worry, I would be fine. I kept them in a vague state until I said my farewell to the dogs and sneaked out of the house.

I felt so empty inside that I wanted to pull over, roll into a ball, and die. I missed my dogs already, and even though I knew that they would be well taken care of, I felt somewhat lost without their cute little faces by my side. As I slowly drove back downtown, I had to pull over at one point because I could no longer see through my tears.

I knew no one would be around at work at this early hour on a Sunday. I needed to grab some disks and write some important emails before I left town.

I made my way up to my office without seeing anyone, but the security in the lobby. I froze as I unlocked my door. Someone had been in there, and that someone was not human. The scent was fading, so it was probably several days old. I booted up my computer, finished my tasks, and then collected the clothes and shoes that were in my closet, some drawings and disks of projects I still planned to work on, and my laptop. I could submit drawings and go over project details via email. I would need to figure out how they couldn't be traced, but I pushed that thought aside as I headed out. I hoped my clients wouldn't be too upset with me for not being on site for a while.

At home, I scanned my thumb and entered a deadly still house. No one had been there, so I relaxed. I went directly upstairs and blindly started packing, wiping away tears as I diligently worked. I threw in my cosmetics and all of my nail polish. Who knew why—it just seemed like the thing to do. I emptied my closet of over half of my clothes and shoes. Was I really going to South Carolina where it all began, and what was I going to do once I got there? I had no clue. I just knew I needed to.

I dragged my bags downstairs, then went back up to my hidden safe and took all of the cash—about ten grand—and most of the credit cards. I was hoping I wouldn't need to use those because they could be traced, but I wanted the assurance that I had plenty of funds available.

I had packed up my car before I remembered I had one last chore to do. I headed downstairs into Daniel's room and found his machete. I was surprised he had left it behind. Maybe he had just needed his gun for now, or maybe he thought I might need it. Regardless, I was grateful that he'd left it. Finally I went to my wine closet and retrieved the key where Daniel had stashed it. I hesitated by the door, gathering my strength and anger, then went in.

Lily was sitting up, tied to a chair with silver chains. The chains must have been starting to burn her skin; I could smell burnt flesh. They had worked her over pretty well. I saw a puddle of her blood under the chair. Her head drooped to her chest, but she realized I was standing there and she perked up, turning her glassy-eyed stare on me. I wasn't fooled; I knew she was fully alert.

"Tell me why you did it, Lily?" I whispered. "Why did you betray Sir Declan?" I leaned the machete on the wall and crossed my arms to show her I was relaxed and non-threatening.

"You stupid little girl," she spat. "Do you actually think I would tell you anything?" She gave me a wicked smirk.

"No, I didn't think so, but I had to make certain."

I lunged for her head and gripped it between my palms. What I saw was frightening. Sethe was on top of her, screwing her over and over again. She had met him in England over one hundred years ago, when he had raped her and then changed her. She had followed him from country to country over the years as his servant and his whore. She loved him, was devoted to his sick, twisted, mind. In a single rush, I learned of Sethe's entire perverse story: how he was in love with the beautiful redhead I had seen in a vision. How she, Isabol, fell in love and married his brother while they all believed Sethe to have been killed fighting during the last Crusade. How years later Sethe had stunned them all by returning home to find his lover and his brother together, gone into a rage, and murdered them both. He couldn't kill their two children before he was stopped and had regretted it ever since. He had been looking for them and their descendents since his release from prison over four hundred years ago. Yes, Lily knew his whole monstrous history, and still she couldn't stay away from him. She would die for him. I couldn't decide who was more deranged.

But I did decide that I could accommodate her just this once. Before Lily could utter a sound, I grabbed the machete and brought it down with all of my strength, severing her head. It made a loud thunk as it hit the floor. "Thank you for giving me what I needed to know." I dropped the machete, left the house, and turned my car south, toward a place I'd only just heard about.

⊂₰⊃

He had to get up. Yes, his muscles ached, but not as badly as his heart. How could she? He had to get out of her house, because every time he thought of Bailey, he could see that murderous bastard on her, and it made him crazy.

He descended to find Daniel. "It's time to leave but I need clothing first."

"Sir Declan, how are you feeling?" Daniel scurried to gather some clothes.

"I'm a bit sore still, but I'll be fine. I need you to tell me why you were delayed, but first go wake the others. Tell them to meet me in the kitchen in five minutes."

As Declan dressed, he resolved not to think about her anymore. He was going to take care of whatever had happened at the cave, and then he would go back to his life before her. Women were nothing but trouble. And he knew the first time he saw her, that she would be big trouble. He should have listened to his instincts, not his heart.

In the kitchen he found everyone smiling broadly at his approach.

"So what has happened? I can smell it on all of you."

Daniel spoke up. "After your phone call, Shila, Charles, and I met up to go to the west side to watch where they took you. But before we got there, Charles got a frantic phone call from Roran. He had been walking the dogs and was on his way back to the cave when he saw a commotion at security. He heard gunshots and yells, so he ran with the dogs to a nearby vacant warehouse. Then he alerted Charles. I decided to send Shila to follow you, while Charles and I went to the cave." He cleared his throat as the others nodded.

"When we arrived all hell had broken loose. Security tried to hold them back but they had bullets with silver nitrate in them, designed to explode on contact, which proved to be a very effective and costly weapon against us. I called Shila and told her to find someone else to follow you, that we needed her at the cave. She got April to follow because she was one of a few who were not in the cave at the time of attack.

We managed to kill many as we made our way down. They had all but destroyed the entry points and were working on blowing up our main areas when we arrived. They killed several of us, including the Senator."

"Gregory?"

"He's fine; he was shot but has already healed. He is seeing to security and temporary placement of our people."

"Jesus. Who were they?" Declan asked.

"We managed to capture a couple, and they admitted that they were part of Lily's gang. She paid them all handsomely, but they never knew who she worked for. They were just grunts. Apparently, they'd been planning this attack for months. They didn't know why, but they were supposed to distract us from finding Miss Bailey, and you were their bonus. They were ordered to kill everyone but you. Lily wanted you alive. In the end, it was a great distraction from your abduction on the west side and Miss Bailey's—um, turning ritual. I'm sorry sir, we would have come sooner but—"

Declan held up his hand for him to stop.

"No need, the cave and the safety of the others should always come first. You did the right thing. Did any of Lily's crew escape?"

Charles spoke up. "Not once we arrived."

"Yes, and I killed one as I was entering," Shila said.

"I can't believe they would be so bold as to do this," Daniel interjected thoughtfully. "Was it *just* a diversion, or is this the beginning of something larger and more devious? There was no apparent reason for the brutality of the attack. Sure, our policing angered a few, but nothing I can think of that would warrant such an assault. Now they'll have the whole Council and the Provinces to answer to. Are they that idiotic, or is there more to it?"

"Yes, Daniel, I believe you are correct," Declan replied. "There is certain to be more to this, so we keep our eyes open and our noses to the ground."

"And two other things. First, Sethe escaped—we couldn't find him anywhere. We believe he may have taken a secret tunnel that we never got a chance to uncover before—well, Miss Bailey destroyed everything."

"She what?"

"You should have seen her, Sir." Charles glowed. "She was magnificent."

Declan grunted. "And the second thing?"

"We have Lily in the basement. In a wine closet. We interrogated her, but we got nothing of course. Thomas gave her a sedative, so she should sleep for most of the night."

"Fine, I'll deal with her in the morning. I don't like her in the same house as Ms Davis. Right now I need to contact the Council. They must know about this as soon as possible. They will send a team to investigate and decide what to do with the cave now that it has been compromised. And of course, the Senator will need to be replaced. His death leaves us very vulnerable. But you all need to be aware that I will never disclose Ms. Davis' abilities to the Council. Do you understand that she would be a dead woman if this ever got out?"

They all nodded and took an oath to never disclose her secret, and to hunt down those who may now know and could pose a threat.

"Excellent. Let's go see to our people and figure out what we can do to salvage our home here." He stood to leave, but paused when no one got up to follow.

"Excuse us sir. We do not want to overstep," said Daniel.

"Then don't."

"What about Miss Bailey?" Shila stepped up. "We can't just leave her here unprotected."

"She can take care of herself." He heard Shila suck in a breath. "Do you have a problem?"

"Ah—no, sir."

"Oh, all right, leave her a note, Daniel. Let's get going."

Declan made the calls from the car. "The Council is sending a team immediately. Interestingly, they have been looking for a man named Sethe for years. Apparently he has been making a nuisance of himself for a long time. Katrina didn't get into the details. Gregory and I will be sitting down with her as soon as she arrives."

As they passed through the security gate and parked by a seemingly derelict warehouse, the cave's entrance, Declan gasped. It looked as if a small war had been fought here. Presciently, they had located the cave on twenty-three acres of very isolated private property within the neglected far south side of the city. No one took a chance trespassing on property of defunct and collapsing warehouses. Plus, electrified barbwire set on top of ten-foot fencing, and a bit of vampire repellent miasma, tended to keep out the nosy. Not even the homeless or drug dealers came near their little part of the city. So fortunately, no one had alerted the police.

They managed to dodge the debris and stepped towards the entrance, where they were met by a three-man security detail and Gregory. Although Gregory appeared disheveled, filthy, and exhausted, Declan thought he'd never looked happier.

Gregory came at him for a quick hug. "I'm glad you're alright, but I dare say Dec, this is the most action I've had in years," he crowed exuberant. "You really know how to show family a good time."

"Eist do bhéal!" Declan gave him a scathing look.

"No need to get nasty, brother. I'm glad Bailey is all right. When do we go after this scoundrel who harmed our lovely girl?"

Declan chose to ignore him. "How many dead?" he asked one of the security men.

"Thirteen, sir," a young Full Blood replied. "Everyone has been taken care of. The bodies are already removed and family members have been notified."

"Thank you. I want this area boarded up by dawn. We need to find housing for the survivors."

"Most have been placed in area homes; the rest went to the St. Louis and Milwaukee Guilds. Everyone is accounted for, sir."

"Good. I want this place cleaned up before the Council Elders arrive. They're flying in from Rome tonight. They need to arrange for a replacement for the Senator. We will be considered weak until that is taken care of. Daniel and Charles, I want you in charge of securing the facility until the Elders decide what to do with it. I want teams patrolling at all times. No more than ten, no less than six. And make sure the miasma is in place and there are no holes in it. Check above us as well. Gregory, please see to it that the Council members get here in one piece. Find them a place to stay and plan on sitting in on the meetings. We will all look to your counsel and advice. Shila, come with me."

They walked the facility. Three security checkpoints had been destroyed, along with the kitchen, dining room and lounge areas. The fitness area had major water damage from the fire suppressant systems. Many machines were ruined, but they could be replaced. The housing wing had the same water damage problem, and it appeared to have been searched.

"What do you make of this?" Declan pointed to open drawers and rifled closets.

"They were probably looking for money or valuables."

He nodded. "Yes, I'm sure you are right, a little extra for all of their trouble." They continued; Declan was most worried about the research facilities.

"Thankfully they didn't get as far as the archives," she told him, "and of course the separate security and fire suppressant systems were intact."

"Computer lab looks okay, a little water damage, maybe," she yawned. He studied Shila more closely. She looked frayed and tired, a rarity with his team. The past week has taken its toll on his warriors. He made a mental note to see to it that they were all properly fed and rested. But not now; they had too much to do.

"We got things under control and turned the water off pretty fast in this wing," Shila went on.

"Computers can be replaced. Besides, all of our backups are off-site, so everything is safe." He looked at his watch. Five A.M., almost dawn. "So tell me all you know about this Sethe person."

Shila looked startled. "I've only heard rumors, but it's said that he is a very ruthless and narcissistic man. But I don't know where he comes from."

"Let's find out, shall we?"

The emergency lighting had kicked on in the library, and an eerie red glow radiated within.

"The electricians are working on restoring the lighting," Shila informed him. "It should be up and running shortly."

Declan nodded. "Let's split up and start digging."

Their work was slowed, given they had no working computers, but he and Shila found a treasure trove of written information on Sethe. The vampire has gotten away with an alarming number of crimes over the centuries: kidnapping, murder, extortion, and blood trafficking were just a few transgressions Sethe had been questioned about over the years. He'd done a stint in prison for multiple murders and had been implicated in many others. This vamp was certainly bad news, and he had set his sights on Bailey. The thought made Declan's skin crawl.

Sometime during their search, the power had been restored. Good, now they didn't have to sneak out with the precious material. He sent Shila to the copier, where she spent nearly an hour duplicating all of the disturbing information on Sethe. Four hours after they had entered the library, they headed for the exit.

Shila suddenly stopped and put her stack back down on the library table. "Before we leave, I have something to say, sir."

Though surprised, he dropped his load on a different table and sat down.

"Very well, what is it?"

"It's Miss Bailey. May I be frank, sir?" He shifted uncomfortably, but nodded his consent. She sat down opposite him.

"Why are you treating her so poorly? I must admit I didn't like her in the beginning, but she has proven herself as a very trusted friend and ally, and, um, we just left her behind with only a note? I cannot comprehend and neither does anyone else. We have not sworn a protection vow, but we will in an instant if you give the nod."

Declan thought Shila looked about ready to cry. Never before had he witnessed her so–passionate. "You do not understand."

He turned away and looked at the stacks.

"Understand what? If you could have seen her–she was glorious. She saved your life, risked hers for yours! She rescued all of us and then took charge. She brought us to her house, trusted us with her life."

"She betrayed me! You say she killed everyone, but why not him? Why is he still alive?" Declan spat.

Shila's eyes flashed white. "You're acting like an ass, sir!"

He abruptly stood up and started to pace, then moved close to her face, fangs extended. Shila backed off her indignant tone, but continued.

"With all due respect, Miss Bailey was forced into First Blood Rites, and then she was bound to him. You know how that feels–especially in the beginning. She had no choice! Nonetheless she somehow found the courage and power to break that bond and even try to kill him. I've rarely heard of someone doing that to their maker, and I most certainly have never heard of it from someone just turned. I can't even imagine the strength it took to do so."

Declan contemplated Shila's words. He was beginning to feel like an ass. "But, she–"

"She is not Samantha!" Shila's hand flew to her mouth. She had never brought up Declan's past before. She dropped her voice to a mere whisper and concluded. "She chose you, sir."

Declan repressed exploding. He didn't want to hear Bailey's side of things. He certainly did not want to think about Sam. Never again. There was a little place in his heart that was still bruised over her betrayal decades before. He didn't want to care. All he wanted to do was secure his Guild and forget he had ever met Bailey Davis.

"Thank you for your candor," he said with menace. "Now are we finished here?"

"Sir, maybe you should be angry with him. Sethe is the cause of all of this, certainly not Miss Bailey," Shila mumbled under her breath aware he would catch every word.

A crack of uncertainty began to form in his brain.

"What did you say to her?" Shila persisted gently.

He only shook his head. He might be feeling a bit embarrassed about his juvenile behavior toward Bailey now, but he was not about to reveal it to anyone else. He sighed.

"Damn. Let's take this back to her house and I'll talk to her. Call Daniel, Thomas, and Charles, and have them meet us there. We need to go over this information and formulate a plan before the Council Elders arrive."

Shila smiled and nodded. "Good, let's go."

The more Shila told him of Bailey's actions, on their way back, the more chastened he felt. He had treated her like a whore, or worse. He needed to fall at her feet and apologize immediately. He owed her for saving him and his warriors, and all he'd given her was his anger. How stupid was he?

It was almost noon by the time they parked in Bailey's spare parking place.

"She's not here!" he said, panic-stricken. He jumped out of the car and ran to the house.

"Codes, give me the damn codes!"

Shila punched in the codes, opened the door, and stood out of the way. The smell of blood hit him immediately.

"Bailey! Bailey!" He ran from room to room, eventually climbing up to the master level. The smell of blood was fainter here. Relief flooded him, but it was short-lived. Many of her clothes and shoes were gone.

"Her cosmetics are missing! Bloody hell, she's gone!"

Charles ran into the room. "The dogs are nowhere to be found."

"And Lily's head has been detached from her body," Daniel reported matter-of-factly.

They all ran down the stairs to the wine room. The door stood open. Blood covered the ground where Lily's headless corpse sat, still tied to the chair. Her head had rolled, face up with a grimace, and was leering from the corner of the room.

"She did this?" Declan turned to his team who were all smiling.

Shila spoke up. "Yes, she is our ally."

"She should be our Queen," Daniel stated with awe in his voice.

"I don't understand."

"Miss Bailey killed Lily because she harmed you, sir. There is nothing else to understand," Charles said.

He thought for a bit, a lump forming in the pit of his stomach. "We have to find her. She's still in danger until Sethe is captured or killed. I don't smell him or anyone else here, so I believe she left under her own control. Does anyone think she went to him?" He looked to each of his warriors.

They all shook their heads. Charles finally spoke up. "There is no way she would go to the person who is the cause of all of this. Miss Bailey has proven she is stronger than that." The rest of them nodded their heads in agreement.

"Unless—" Shila spoke up. "Unless she intends to kill him, or he finds her to do the same." They looked at one another and fell silent.

Declan's head pounded as he tried his connection. "Damn, she's totally blocked me."

"She knows how to do that?" Daniel asked. "That's amazing for a fledgling. I've never before heard of such control and power. Who is she?"

Declan heaved a sigh. "Let's go upstairs. I have a lot to explain, plus we have some information to put together. Thomas, please arrange for a disposal and clean-up here. Everyone else, follow me."

As the team trudged back upstairs, Declan chastised himself for being a fool. He begrudgingly admitted that he'd pushed away the one person who had meant anything to him in centuries, perhaps his whole life. As all of the facts came to light, he felt more and more respect and admiration for her. Bailey was special, and not just in an intimate way, which she certainly was, but as if she were made of the same mettle as himself. As if she were Centurion, only stronger–better. The thought made goosebumps rise along his arms. If she were as powerful as he was beginning to believe, she was certainly a dead woman. Every frightened vampire in the world would try to hunt her down. And he had promised to protect her. Never had he felt so disgusted with himself.

They sat around her table. Shila pored over the copied information, while Thomas rejoined them after his call. Declan paced as he conveyed all he had learned about Bailey and her abilities, their previous research, and his conclusions about who she really was.

"I believe this Sethe person knows her full family history. He's been watching for her kind, or perhaps just happened to stumble upon her. Either way, he wants Bailey under his control so he gains her power as well. I think he and his group may be the ones responsible for causing a lot of trouble over the decades, especially in Europe. I have reason to believe they have been planning to destabilize the Council."

"But that's impossible!" Charles interjected. "The Council has been in place for over two thousand years. No one could possibly have that kind of power."

"With her abilities under his control, Sethe could do almost anything." Declan declared.

They were all stunned into silence.

"*Dit mon la verite*"! She'll get herself killed! Sir Declan, we must find her." Daniel roared.

"She is completely blocking me, but I have a feeling that she's on the road heading south and someone is following her. My connection is getting weaker as she gets further away. We must move fast."

They all stood, ready for action. "This is what we are going to do, but first we will give her the vow of our protection."

Shila looked relieved, as they nodded their consent and gathered around in a circle. Holding knives, they cut the right wrist of the person to their left. Declan passed a cup, and each offered their blood.

"I, Centurion of Alleah, blood of Reneb, make my vow to protect, with my own life, Bailey, blood of Ahkin, until my death." He lifted the cup and drank. The others followed suit and drank. After all of vows were taken, Declan continued.

"Thomas and Charles, go back to the cave to see what you can do to help. Check in with Gregory and fill him in. I need him to meet with Katrina in my stead. Tell her I have a lead on Sethe and that I will be in touch to report. Do not tell them about Bailey. Gloss over it, if need be. You are the authority there. I want reports every three hours. I will call you when I need you."

"Yes, sir," they said in unison and left at once.

"Daniel and Shila, I want you to research the documents we brought here from the library. We need to find out who this Sethe person is—his history and his connection to Bailey. I will go to her parents' house and her work before I go to the station and check her credit cards and phone records. I'll do a quick search to see if she has used anything. She has to buy a new phone sometime. I just hope she uses her real name."

"This is all just amazing," Daniel said. "I've heard rumors of such a family, but they were very vague and I don't think anyone actually believed it."

Shila ran her hands over her arms. "I've heard the same, and many say it's just a myth. But we all witnessed her power with our own eyes. I still get shivers thinking of it."

"That's the point, Shila," said Declan. "If that's your reaction and you like and respect her, can you imagine what would happen if everyone knew? She would be hunted and killed, and we cannot let that happen. Did either of you see anyone else who may have witnessed her powers and may have escaped?"

"I saw no one," Daniel said, but looked worried. "She destroyed the whole building and the barn where you were held captive, but the compound was much more extensive than it looked. Who knows what happened during her First Rites Ritual? Maybe someone saw something there. We need to find out who witnessed that."

"Or maybe Lily told others," Shila pointed out. "It's obvious that Sethe had a connection or hold over her. He may have divulged his thoughts to her, and she may have talk to others about it. We just can't be sure."

"Well, it is out of our control for now." Declan gave a decisive nod. "Just keep your ears and eyes open. I'll be back in a couple of hours. I want a whole picture of this bastard when I get back. Now let's all get to work. Good luck."

Declan's dismay at the thought of her going off alone was increasing by the minute. Especially knowing someone may be following her. What had she been thinking? She had no clue how much danger she was in. Her connection to Sethe was reason enough for his blood to run cold. If she unblocked for just one second, he would know where she was. Unfortunately, he'd been right about one thing. Bailey Davis certainly was trouble, and he was in deep.

"Jesus," he murmured as he ran to the car. He had to find her, and fast.

16

LOW COUNTRY OR BUST

I t took me two blocks before I noticed someone following me. I stepped on the gas and rounded a few corners, but I couldn't shake the bastard. I looked in the rearview mirror and realized that the figure looked familiar. I slowed down and pulled over, and so did he. Son of a bitch. Is that? I got out of the car, but not before he was standing in front of me.

"What the hell do you think you're doing, John? Why are you following me?"

"Damn it, Bailey! You never returned any of my calls. I've tried for days to reach you. I was concerned, so I came over again to see if you were around. No one had seen you at work, and your parents were worried sick. I was this close to calling the police—my god, what happened to you? You look different. Where were you? At a spa?" He finally took a breath.

At a spa? I would have burst out laughing if I hadn't been so pissed. "John Blaine. Since when do you give a rat's ass about where I go and what I do?" I shook my head. "You know what? Forget it. I don't have time for this shit." I turned to get back in the car, but he maneuvered so he stood in the way, and I didn't want to show him my strength.

He drew close. "You can take off, but I will follow you until you tell me what the hell is going on with you."

I backed up to get some space in between us. "Has it occurred to you that it's none of your business? Now get out of my way!" He met my eyes and moved. I got into the car and took off, but he continued to follow me. *Fine, let him. I don't care anymore!*

I hopped on the Dan Ryan and took it south to Interstate 80 East through Gary, Indiana and then headed south on I-65. John continued to follow right behind me. Unbelievable! I was heading to Sullivan's Island, South Carolina, where I had been given to the Davis's. There had to be someone around who would remember something. If the house was still standing where my, um–family had been living, I could sneak in and use my powers to see what had happened there. If I could even do that. Hmm–a lot of if's. At least I knew one thing for certain. I would stay at the Folly Beach house that my parents rented while I checked it all out. But having John, the pain in the ass, following me was more than I had anticipated.

I stopped in Indianapolis and found an AT&T store, where I bought an iPhone with cash. It worked great, but unfortunately I had to show them my driver's license, so my real name and address were listed. It could be traced back to me, but it couldn't be helped. I needed a phone to make business calls and in case of an emergency.

I filled up before I got back on the highway. I didn't see John anywhere behind me. *Good, maybe he got bored and turned back,* I thought. *Didn't he have a job to go to?* I checked my shields–nice and tight.

I made some phone calls while on the road. The first was to Rosa to see how she was getting along. They were having a blast, and I promised I would call when I got back home. I wished her a happy rest of her vacation and hung up before she could ask too many questions. I called my parents next and informed them, once again, that I was fine and I would be enjoying lying on a beach somewhere. It was odd knowing that we'd had a conversation–well at least part of a conversation–that they would never remember. Next, I called work and spoke to Ron. He had finished with his exams and was anxiously awaiting the results. I advised him to put it out of his mind, because the results could take up to six months. He said the test had been excruciatingly difficult, and many even left the exam before completing it. Wowsa, that session really must have been dreadful. I explained my need to take a vacation and that I would work from the road. He sounded skeptical, but didn't remark. We arranged daily updates, and I asked him to complete several tasks before we hung up. I had already emailed Connie.

I stopped the Tribune delivery and had my mail held. I could get Ron to forward my bills to me later, but I hoped I wouldn't be away from home for that long. I decided not to turn off my water or electricity just in case

Daniel and the team needed a place to stay. I tried not to think about Declan. With all of my calls completed, I relaxed and concentrated on my driving. Shit, John was behind me again. I shook my head. Tenacious bastard.

I drove for hours, until my car was sucking fumes. I looked in my rearview mirror. Still with me. He obviously got better gas mileage. I pulled off at the next exit. It was late afternoon and I had passed Lexington about an hour before, so I was in the foothills of the Appalachians of southern Kentucky. Beautiful. I was filling my tank as John pulled up and popped his gas cap. We ignored each other.

I went inside, used the facilities, and bought a bunch of junk food to last for a few hours. By the time I got to my car, John was patiently waiting in his. Crap. I walked over to him and he rolled down the window. I threw in a couple of Twinkies and a Coke and walked away without a word. Now I was starting to feel sorry for him. Double crap.

Back on the highway, I headed further south. Suddenly my phone rang. I looked at a 312 Chicago area code but did not recognize the number, so I ignored it and kept driving. In Knoxville I took I-40 East and entered the Appalachians about an hour later. It was fully dark but I could still see the outlines of the mountains that surrounded me. My improved vision enabled me to see things I couldn't possibly have seen before, such as the incredibly beautiful landscape before me. I managed to get about halfway through the mountains before I needed another fill-up. It was past dinnertime, and I was tired of junk, so I pulled off at a promising exit that had a Denny's, a couple of hotels, and one gas station. John was stuck to me like glue. He didn't give up. I had to hand him that.

During the last couple of hours, I'd had several more phone calls, all from the same number. I continued to ignore them, wondering if it was Declan. Hoping it was Declan, the bastard. I hadn't set up my voicemail yet, so I had no messages to listen to. I supposed I should do that in case Rosa, Ron, or my parents needed me.

I pulled up to a pump, and filled my tank, then walked over to John, who was also getting gas.

"You know, you are the most annoying asshole I've ever met." He only smiled. "I'm going to check into a hotel and then get something to eat. I have some work to do and then I'm getting some rest. If you want to follow, fine, but don't expect to sleep in my room." He just nodded.

I drove to a somewhat dilapidated motel that advertised a "Good nites sleep for only $49.95" and HBO for only $5 dollars extra. Wow. I checked in and got a room on the second floor, overlooking the mountains. *Not bad for $49.95*, I thought. I dumped my overnight bag in my room, left the annoying phone in the bedside table, locked up and went out to find something to eat. I ran into John in the parking lot.

"Did you check in?"

"Yes." And he held up a couple of shopping bags that I looked at with a raised eyebrow. "I found a men's store and a CVS while you were buying a phone." He proudly grinned.

"Okay, I'll go get us a table at Denny's." I walked down the road towards the restaurant. The quiet was absolute, and the air smelled of pine and the beginnings of fall; lovely. The night was cool but not too cold. Even though my heart was heavy, the mountain air made me feel good, more energetic.

Dinner was uneventful. We mostly stared at one another without speaking. I ate chicken fried steak, mashed potatoes, and biscuits and gravy. John had a burger. I guess I was hungry.

"I haven't eaten much lately," I remarked. He only continued to stare at me with those charming hazel eyes of his.

We walked back in silence. The darkness was complete, but I could make out the birds sleeping in their nests and the deer snacking in the field to our left. I went into my room and he followed.

"What do you think you're doing?"

"I'm seeing you to your room. Jeez, I'm not going to touch you. You've made it perfectly clear that you're not interested."

"So why are you really here then?"

"Because you are in trouble and I'm not leaving you."

I looked into his eyes and knew he spoke the truth. He was sincerely worried about me and concerned for my safety. He only wanted to help me. I opened the door wider for him to enter.

He sat on my bed. "So are you going to tell me what's going on?"

"I can't." I went to my bag to find my flannel pajamas and toiletries. I could feel his annoyance.

"Bailey, I would never do anything to hurt you ever again. The worst thing I have ever done was to leave you. And getting married! I must have been insane."

"But you left me!" I yelled as I entered the bathroom. I slammed the door for emphasis. After brushing my teeth, changing, and doing my business, I came back out to see John pacing. He looked up and his jaw dropped.

"Jesus, you are more beautiful than I remember." He shook his head. "So, yeah, I left. Ah, you scared the shit out of me, to be honest, but I've always loved you. Now more than ever." He slid his eyes to me to check my reaction.

I went to my laptop, took out several disks, and set up at the small table by the window. "Yeah, right. In flannel pajamas, I'm a supermodel," and the rest I just chose to ignore.

"You're more gorgeous than any supermodel I've ever seen."

"Stop piling it on. I'm not buying any of it." I changed the subject. "So do you plan on following me all over the country?"

"Yes, until you confide in me. I'm worried about you, and I plan on helping any way I can." He sat back down on the bed.

"Don't you have a job to go to? And what about Carley? Won't she be concerned about you?"

"I took some vacation time. I don't have anything that is too pressing right now and I do have Sarah, my assistant, who can handle things until I get back. As for Carley, well, let's just say she won't miss me one bit. So sorry, you're stuck with me." He sat back and made himself comfortable.

Oh boy, I had enough to agonize about without worrying about him. I thought of Declan, of my parents, and my new life, and I wanted nothing more than to lie down and sleep for a century. My heart was broken, and it showed no signs of healing anytime soon. The brief time I had spent with Declan had been the most significant of my life, and I cared for him deeply, but I couldn't deal with any more rejection. From him or anyone else, for that matter. I had to go on with my life if I wanted to keep any semblance of sanity. Christ, I had just found out that I'm not exactly human, and that alone would be enough to drive a normal person to drink heavily, if not worse.

"Bailey, are you all right?"

I hadn't realized that I'd moved and now was sitting on the floor rocking back and forth as tears streaked down my face. I began to blubber and he held me as I cried for my lost past, my empty existence, and for my unknown future.

CʒꙦ

I awoke to John banging on my door. Instinctively and without hesitation-I definitely needed to work on that-I jumped out of bed and answered it.

"What's going on, I heard you scream. Are you okay?" He stopped short and gasped. "What's wrong with your eyes? They're glowing!" He grabbed my arms and led me to the mirror above the sink. Sure enough, they were glowing gold.

I was drenched in sweat and shaking. He led me back to the bed and sat me down. "I don't know what's going on here, but it's starting to scare me, Bailey. Tell me why your eyes are gold and why you are scared and running. Tell me why you left your dogs behind and why Rosa is nowhere to be found. Explain to me why your parents are clueless, and why you would just leave a job you love and have spent your whole life working hard for, or I'll go back to Chicago and find out on my own. I swear to god I'll do it!"

"It was just a bad dream. Just a dream."

"No, it's not just a dream! Your eyes do not turn gold because of a fucking dream. Now tell me everything!"

And I did. Lord help me, I spilled my guts to a man who I thought never loved me. A man who had dumped me ages ago and suddenly wanted me back. A human man. I must have been nuts.

He listened intently and got up to pace every so often. He grew visibly distraught when I told him about Sethe and how I was treated, and just as upset when I told him about how wonderful Declan was, and how I'd fallen for him.

"This is just crazy, Bailey. There are really vampires, and for thousands of years? Living here and everywhere else? Right under everyone's noses?" He threw his hands into the air. "It's just too incredible!" He was pacing furiously now.

"I'm not finished yet. Let me tell you about my past." So I told him about how my parents got me, and how I'd always felt different. I explained about my change and strength and powers. I told him everything. When I was finished, I regarded a dumbfounded John. He was very pale and looked faint. His anger had evaporated, replaced by curiosity and some fear.

"Come here and sit down, John. You don't look so well. Here, put your head in-between your legs so you don't faint." He did as instructed. We sat with our own thoughts for several minutes. His heartbeat was now steadying, and his fear was dissipating.

I tried to calm his nerves further. "You know, real vampires are not like in the movies. They're not dead and brought back to life, they just have a different anatomy than you. Changed vampires mutate their anatomy. Anyone can be changed, but there are limitations: sun sensitivity, allergies to certain metals, and consumption of blood more often, among other things. But you don't die like in the movies, just change."

"Oh. I don't know what to say. What are you?"

"I'm not sure yet. I think I'm a combination, or maybe a manifestation–a further metamorphosis, so to speak. I just don't know. My powers are amazing and frightening at the same time. But it could be dangerous to be around me. I may be the only one of my kind, and others don't, or won't, like that. They are afraid of what I can do. That is why you must go home now, and forget about all of this. I can take care of myself."

He only hesitated for a second. "Never. I don't care if you're Santa Claus. You need me. You need to figure out where you come from, and I will be there when you do. And I will help you consider what to do from there. I'm not leaving you, Bailey."

"I could make you forget and go home."

"But you won't do that, because you need me as much as I need you. We are in this together. No matter what."

I felt so touched by his sincerity, that I couldn't help but grab him and hold tight. "You're right, I do need you. Thank you, John."

We lay down together in each other's arms. Nothing romantic, just comforting. The contact felt wonderful, and this time when I fell back asleep, I did not dream.

I woke up the next morning with the sun blazing through the window. The clock read nine A.M. Time to get up. After telling John everything, I felt better than I had in days. I stretched, figuring John must have gone to his room to shower, so I did the same. I had just finished drying my hair when I heard a knock on my door. John was standing there all clean and dressed with Denny's take-out.

"Just what the doctor ordered. Come in with that." We ate in companionable silence while watching the morning news. Sipping my coffee, I strolled out onto the balcony. I took in a deep breath. "This mountain air is intoxicating. And the view is spectacular." And it was. The morning dew still clung to the grass and dripped off leaves that were just starting their fall color change. The mountains in the background held a layer of morning mist, which gave everything a bluish cast.

"Yes, it is beautiful. I wonder why I've never come down here before," John speculated. "I suppose it just wasn't fashionable enough for me. Makes me sick to think of how I used to be, and what I've missed out on." He stared at me with puppy dog eyes.

"Oh, and you've changed that much?" I couldn't help but smile.

"I guess I'm just appreciating what's important. Reevaluating, I suppose."

"Hmm. You and me both." I cleared my throat. "Okay, so what's the plan? Do you still want to drive separately, or do you want to leave your car and pick it up later, or what?"

"Do you want to tell me where we are heading?"

"Charleston."

"As in South Carolina."

"Yep."

"That makes sense. We can start on Sullivan's Island. I'll drive my car to the next airport. What would that be, Asheville?"

"I believe so. There's a map in my bag." I had GPS in my car as well, but having a large map to examine an overall route was a necessity for me. I found where we were. "You're right," I told John. "We're only about thirty miles from Asheville."

"Okay, I'll leave my car in long-term parking. No one will bother with it there."

I started packing. "Let's hit the road. We should make it to Charleston in about six hours."

We followed I-40 East through the mountains and dropped off John's car, then took I-26 out of the mountains and into the piedmont of South Carolina. Once we hit Columbia, the terrain changed again as we neared the lowcountry. We made it to Charleston by mid-afternoon. I got on 17 South and crossed over the bridge into West Ashley and then onto Folly Road. Eight miles south, and we reached the Atlantic Ocean and Folly Beach.

Folly Beach was a beatnik surfing village that sticks out into the Atlantic Ocean. The Folly River divides it from James Island to the west, and the Morris Lighthouse marks its northern boundary. The narrow strip of beachfront has been colonized since the early eighteenth century. It was best known for the shots of fanatical weather correspondents braving the beach during hurricanes.

We turned left onto Ashley Avenue and headed north up towards the lighthouse. After about a mile, the houses started to get larger and were situated further apart. We finally found the house my parents had rented—to my utter surprise, a big, beautiful French-styled beach house. It sat very tall and proud on the isolated beach with wrap around piazzas and large French windows and doors.

"Nice place."

"Yes, it is." I keyed the door to the garage, which was under the house. It didn't budge. "The electricity must be turned off."

"Give me the keys and I'll find the panel."

I handed John the keys, and he slipped through the doorway on the lower level. I didn't have to wait long before the garage door rolled up and John waved me inside. I parked and got out to unpack the trunk. It was warm, probably in the eighties, with a light breeze that smelled like salt, seaweed, and pluff mud. A smell that somehow felt familiar.

"Hey, there's an elevator in here," John yelled from the bowels of the garage.

"Great, we don't have to lug all this luggage up the stairs."

We managed to pile all my bags in the elevator and went up. The doors opened into the kitchen, which was open to the family room and the Atlantic Ocean. Wall-to-wall windows covered the entire east side of the house, and the view was spectacular. There was a piazza off of the north and south sides of this level. The kitchen was bright and airy with white cabinets, stainless steel appliances, and ice-blue glass tiles. I walked around to the front of the house, which contained the front entry, a large library stocked full of books to the left, and a bedroom with full bath to the right. A half bath was located in the hallway leading back into the kitchen, along with a set of stairs leading to the second level.

Where I heard John bellow, "Wow, you should see this. It's very creatively done."

"A true compliment, coming from the best of the best," I said as I followed his voice.

He was right. The front of the house contained two bedrooms, each with its own bath, and a small media room with projection TV. But it was the master suite that most impressed, and encompassed the entire east side of the house on the second level. The wall-to-wall glass made it feel as if the vast Atlantic was at your fingertips. The opposite wall also held glazing in the center for about ten feet, which looked out onto the kitchen area. The king-sized bed fit into a perfect niche to the left of the glass, with the master bath to the right. Both the north and south sides had French doors leading out onto piazzas. The walls and ceilings were decorated in a cobalt venetian plaster. The bedding and draperies boasted crisp white silk. The furniture was Swedish modern and looked fabulous. I peeked into the bathroom. Wow, white marble fixtures and sleek nickel faucets that almost blinded me. The focal point, however, was a huge spa tub right in the center of the room below a turret of glass. Nice.

"I can't believe that my parents rented something like this. It's just too fashionable for them," I said as I stroked the blond wood of the dresser and the magnificent matching tester bed. The wide planked flooring held a luxurious oriental rug, which was about the only traditional touch in the room.

"I vote your parents should buy this house."

"Me too, and I call dibs on this room."

"Not fair, but I guess it's only right, considering your parents' money is paying for it. I'll take one of the other bedrooms up here. But first I'll go downstairs and find the water valve. We will need water eventually."

"Okay, I'm going to unpack."

After about an hour, our unpacking done, we went back into town to shop for groceries. I couldn't believe we were getting along as though nothing had ever transpired between us. As if we were the best of friends. It was a nice surprise, and I was actually happy John was here with me. It kept my loneliness at bay.

We made shrimp and pasta for dinner, then took what was left of our bottle of wine out onto the beach, where we sat and watched the ocean as the sun dipped below the horizon behind us.

"It is beautiful here. Look at the surfers." I pointed south.

"What surfers? I don't see a thing."

"Oh, right. Sorry." And I got up to wade in the surf with my glass.

"Jesus, Bailey, you really do have great vision."

"Yeah, I'm really a freak."

"What are you talking about? You are certainly no freak. Just a little different, and I mean in a good way."

I smiled and relaxed. "It's so weird. I can see everything." I gazed out at the Atlantic. "I can make out shapes of sharks just off shore. It's creepy."

"There are sharks out there? How close? Can you see what kind?"

"I can just see their shadows, but there are several out hunting tonight."

"Should we warn the surfers?"

"Nah. These sharks are too small to harm the surfers. They're just looking for other fish or maybe some crab. The surfers are in no danger."

"Jesus, remind me not to swim out here at dusk." We walked down the beach in companionable silence. The smell of the sea was intoxicating to my heightened senses.

"I'm beginning to see why your parents want to retire down here. It's lovely and peaceful."

"Yeah, it is sure is."

"Well, kids are back in school. It's a good time to be here."

As we walked I noticed that most of the houses sat empty. I couldn't feel anyone around except for the surfers and an occasional dog with its owner. It gave me a little pang.

"The boys would love it here. I miss them." John nodded. I missed Declan as well, even though I'd tried not to think about him. My door was still firmly shut, blocking him out, but I decided to give him just a peek of what I was seeing. I really wanted him to be here with me, experiencing this. Chances were he wouldn't care; besides, he probably couldn't see it. Our bond was not as nearly as strong as mine and Sethe's, which I still kept firmly closed. Believe it or not, there was a tiny empty spot in my heart over our separation. Damn, just great.

"I'm getting itchy to go over to Sullivan's Island. I have no idea what I'm looking for, but I feel that there is something to be found there. Something that's important to my past."

"It's certainly a place to start," John replied. "But do you really want to know what happened? I mean—what if you don't like what you find, or worse?"

"What do you mean?"

"Well, maybe your biological family is crazy, or mean, or perhaps dead."

"I want to know either way. I have to know where I'm from and if I have any family out there."

We walked until it was utter darkness with billions of stars twinkling overhead casting an ethereal glow over the water. It was a magical night, but I still had a heavy heart.

"Let's head back. I want to get a good night's sleep so we can get an early start."

We headed back to the house listening to the surf pound against the sand—both deep in our own thoughts. I was glad John was here. His support and companionship was dear, and I was surprised by the realization that he had become a much better friend than he'd ever been a boyfriend. I smiled and took his hand in mine.

"I just want to tell you that I'm glad you're here. I need a friend."

He looked at me and bent to kiss my nose. "I'll take you any way I can get you." And we went up to our separate bedrooms.

⳩

Sethe entered my room while I was asleep and dreaming of Declan. He slid in through the south side piazza and crawled into bed with me. I stirred, knowing he was there, but I didn't want to leave my dream—my Declan. He started kissing my neck and kneading my breasts. He was so warm—

"Declan." I whispered his name.

Then I was suddenly awake. Sethe had me by the hair and his fangs had entered my neck. He was slashing and gulping, tearing away my flesh while drinking my blood. The pain was excruciating as I tried to scream for help, but was rendered paralyzed from fright. I felt the life slowly flow out of me. Through the fog, I heard a commotion at my door; I was being shaken.

"Bailey, Bailey! Wake up, damn it, wake up!"

I bolted up drenched in sweat and shaking. An unexpected wave of dizziness hit me like a ton of bricks, and I had to lie back down.

"Shit–oh, it was just a dream. It was so real. Oh god, John. I was so scared." I whined while rubbing my temples where a headache was now forming.

"What the hell was it? What could have possibly made you this terrified, Bailey?" he asked while holding me tight to stop my trembling.

"It was Sethe. He was killing me."

"Jesus. Your eyes are glowing again."

"Yeah, crap. I'm beginning to think the only way this will ever go away is if he's dead." John knit his brows.

"I'm afraid that he may now know where we are," I added. "Asshole's invading my dreams. He must know, but I think he may still be healing, so he can't get to me yet. At least that's what I'm hoping." Now John looked scared. "Don't worry, I'm a lot stronger than he thinks." I hid my hands so he didn't see me cross my fingers.

It was five A.M. so I went down and heated up hot water for tea, while John went back to bed. There was no way I was going to close my eyes again. I took my tea out to the beach. The sun was still down and the stars twinkled. The air held a slight chill, but there still was no need for a jacket. I sat and thought, alone for the first time since my escape from Chicago. I knew all about Sethe, thanks to Lily's memories. I realized I wasn't sorry about her death. In fact, I was relieved by it. I guessed that made me a cold-blooded murderer, and I didn't know how I felt about that. I wondered if I was a monster, just like Sethe.

Knowing Sethe could be a distant relative of mine only made me feel worse. I'd been amazed to discover that he is a direct descendant of Reneb, who was his great-grandfather on his mother's side. He is the grandson of one of the children Reneb fathered outside of his marriage to Arabet to keep the fulblood lines intact. Born during the Dark Ages. *How appropriate,* I thought. That was if I could believe Lily's memories, of course. She'd been born centuries later so maybe her information was not entirely accurate. I certainly hoped so. No one, human or not, could be so evil.

Nevertheless, her memories were all I had to go by, and according to them, Sethe was the second child, therefore held less power than his older brother, who was Centurion. Sethe was a spoiled child, as well as being a severely unhinged, borderline sociopath. He had always been jealous of his older brother and his strengths. He'd done everything he could to get attention, even going as far as raping, torturing and killing the thirteen year old princess of Spain so the Royals would leave his family's territory alone. But the heinous act only stoked their anger, which took years and a lot of gold to finally cool. His family often ignored Sethe's transgressions, until the day his parents found him holding a bloody machete, and their eldest son and his wife lying in bed with their heads missing. He had butchered them while their children lay sleeping in another room. His parents had finally had enough of Sethe's sadistic behavior. He was banned from the family forever. But Sethe's narcissism knew no bounds; blaming everything on his father and his long dead great grandfather, Reneb, for his retched and unfulfilled life. The same great-grandfather, who had completely abandoned and ignored Sethe's side of the family, favoring those born to Arabet.

Sethe's Isabol. Reneb's great-granddaughter from Arabet. Lily's memories of her had been vague. She had never met Isabol, who was long dead by the time Lily was born, but Sethe maintained very strong feelings towards her, obsessed with killing every last one of her relations. Though he'd never stated as much, at least not to Lily. But his family had interrupted his plan to slaughter his brother's and Isabol's children, and he had been looking for them ever since—to finish the job. At least that had been what Lily suspected.

After a severe beating by the Centurions who held him for several weeks, he had mended, but did not stop his quest for revenge. On the contrary, for every mark made on his body he burned for retribution. He considered paying the children a visit after his release, but he knew that they were very well protected and his father would be looking for such an attack. Instead, after decades of lying low and recruiting rogues and other discontented vampires who could be easily manipulated, he had garnered a sizable force to do his bidding. To pay his people he sold flesh, loan-sharked, extorted, and promised his protection for their loyalty. It worked, and soon many sought him out. They kept up a diligent pursuit for Isabol's children, who had been very well hidden by his parents. Sethe travelled to Africa,

Europe, and even the far reaches of Asia, but he had never caught so much as a whiff, until about thirty years ago and completely by accident.

Lily, his whore and slave, saw a woman who looked just like the description of the one seared into her brain by her master, shopping at a farmers market in a suburb of Chicago. Lily happened to be there setting up a Midwestern network, and she was at the market that day because she had been following someone else. The woman wore her bright curls pinned up, but Lily could smell that she was different. Lily was old enough that she had powers of her own, so she probed the woman's mind but couldn't get in. Shocked and excited, she'd abandoned the one she was tailing to follow this new one.

She trailed the woman back to her car, where two huge vampire bodyguards flanked the door she entered. They drove to a sprawling estate in the suburb of Oak Park, where the car disappeared down a long driveway secured by a huge iron security gate.

Lily had phoned Sethe to tell him the unbelievable news. He immediately put her in charge of surveillance duties while he flew to Chicago from Madrid. It didn't take long to see that the mysterious redhead rarely left the house, and when she did she was incognito and heavily guarded. Her mate was a full blood and posed as a mafia Don to be feared and left alone. Everyone was glad to comply. Lily also discovered there was a teenage daughter living relatively unsequestered. Her hair was dark and curly. Lily thought her hair was dyed because she could smell her gifts. So she decided to put a close tail on the girl as well.

The daughter, Jasmine, was wild. She sneaked off at night when she could, and smuggled boys and girls into the mansion as well. Lily found it disgraceful that the girl's parents let her get away with such behavior. She also found it hard to believe that Jasmine could get away with it so easily considering who her parents were. That only helped to reinforce Lily's assumption that the girl was more than she let on.

Sethe gave the order to destroy everyone but the red-haired woman, whom he wanted. He no longer sought her death, but now required her for some reason unknown to Lily. She felt a stab of such jealously that it brought her to her knees. Why didn't he obsess over her the same way? Why didn't he fixate on her? She had these thoughts frequently.

They timed the attack perfectly. Lily's team would kill the daughter while the parents were at their vacation house. Sethe would take a couple of his best men and go down to South Carolina to kill the man and capture the woman. Only it didn't quite go as planned. The daughter was easy. But Sethe's team was ambushed in South Carolina, somehow they'd been alerted to his assault. To this day they didn't know who, but they must have been betrayed by someone within Sethe's organization, and they would find that person if it took decades.

They were also stunned to find that there was a second child: a baby girl with red curly hair. But how could it be? Was it this one who had the most power? His men managed to capture and kill the mate, but the woman proved too strong and took out his entire team. She and the child disappeared without a trace, and Sethe was devastated—and angry. Very angry.

The trail had run cold until I stumbled onto the site and the bones—Jasmine's bone's. The girl in my dream's bones: my sister's bones. According to Lily, the press release my firm had distributed about the upcoming renovations of the historically significant property, and subsequent announcement in the local paper and the Chicago Tribune, alarmed them. Sethe insisted that they recover Jasmine's remains and dump them into Lake Michigan, hiding them forever. He didn't want the attention of the authorities. The vampire, Mikel, who was supposed to do the job, found me clutching one of the bones, and tried to erase my memories, but couldn't. Once that fact was reported to Sethe, I became the hunted. And wasn't I a complete surprise to all, when I turned out to be of the same blood.

I shook my head at the coincidence of living near the same town as my biological parents had lived when they were alive. What were the odds—a million to one? Even more unbelievable was the fact that the Conrad Estate was, at one time, my home, and I had won the job of designing an extensive renovation. Crazy! It was too much happenstance for my taste. There had to be more too it, but for the life of me, I couldn't figure out what it was.

It also meant that the bone I'd been grasping belonged to my own sister. Jesus, the thought made me ill. No wonder I had that vision about Jasmine. My god, I had witnessed her brutal death. I tried to concentrate on remembering her, but I couldn't even form a simple glimpse of any of them.

Knowing that my sister and my father had died during the attack made me want to hurt Sethe that much more. But did my mother eventually die as well? And whatever happened to my grandmother? Was she Beatriz? I wanted to know—had to know.

Sethe would never stop his fixation with me, especially given our connection. This was the monster who never took a mate. He'd always preferred torturing, raping, and killing whomever he chose, so he'd never felt the need for a permanent and formal companion. That is, until me. Lily had wanted the position for decades, though he couldn't have cared less about her. At least he wouldn't have to be troubled about her pining over him anymore.

Sethe had already killed my biological father, sister, and possibly my mother. He had kidnapped and tortured both Declan and me. But there was no way in hell he was going to harm anyone else I cared about. I would never just stand by while he continued to terrorize my family and me. I would see him dead first, connection or no connection.

I sighed and watched as the first rays of sunlight slowly peeked over the horizon. What was I really looking for? Why the urgency to find out about my past? I now knew what I was, and who my parents were, so why was I really here? Did I actually believe that my biological mother would still be in the area?

I thought about it some more. I knew I needed to keep my powers a secret, because many would want me dead if they knew what I could do. I hadn't told John that I could read and manipulate a vampire's mind. Declan was the only other person on earth who knew that juicy tidbit.

I took a deep breath. The smell of the ocean mixed with marshlands was intoxicating. I thought of Declan and how much I missed him. I shouldn't have felt this way, I'd only known him a very short time, but I couldn't stop it. I knew he didn't want me, but I still wanted him. Body and soul, I yearned for him—crap.

Damned if I would be hurt again, though. By Declan or anybody else. Which led me to think about Sethe again. I had to kill him. The thought made me nauseous, but it needed to be done, otherwise he would never stop his torment of me, and I could not risk him hurting someone I loved. I would find him after I had exhausted all of my leads on Sullivan's Island.

I watched the sun slowly rise over the Atlantic. The crimson sky morphed to orange, which gave way to yellow, and finally a pale blue emerged, signaling the beginning of a new day. One I hoped would give me the answers I sought. Whatever they might be.

17

WITH A FRIEND LIKE ME, WHO NEEDS A VAMPIRE?

Declan's first stop was Bailey's parents' house. He rang the bell and immediately heard the dogs. *She's been here, and recently,* he thought. *Good.*

Her mother opened the door with a fearful expression. "Oh, Detective O'Connor, please come in. My husband is not here at the moment. Would you like a cup of coffee?" She led him to the kitchen.

"Sure, black, please. I do apologize for calling on you without advance notice, but it is somewhat urgent." He wondered about her fear. "Do you know where your daughter has gone?"

She ignored his question. "Please get comfortable in the living room. I will be there shortly."

He made his way to the living room, but felt too anxious to sit down. Katherine appeared shortly thereafter with a service of coffee that she put on a sideboard. She brought him a cup.

"Thank you. I didn't know if you heard me a few minutes ago."

"I heard you just fine, Detective." He raised an eyebrow. "I believe she has taken some well-deserved vacation time."

"Can you tell me exactly where she went?"

"No." She studied his face, and then decided on something. "She came to us this morning very distraught, Detective. It seems that she has learned about her past."

He almost dropped his coffee cup. She kept talking as if she hadn't dropped a bombshell in his lap.

"She asked us to watch the dogs and said that she would call when she was settled. She said that she might hang out on a beach somewhere."

"How long are you watching the dogs for?"

"Oh, whenever Bailey gets back. I got the impression that she would be gone a while. She wanted us to be mindful of the guards that you posted and not to venture out without them." She looked to him and nodded toward the window. "You know—because of Sethe's threat."

"What? You mean she has told you?"

"Yes, Detective O'Connor. We know that you are a vampire."

They knew, and yet here he sat, talking to her like nothing had happened?

"I'm not scared of you," Katherine confirmed. "Bailey tells me that you have helped her and that you would never hurt us." Her blue sapphire eyes crinkled into a smile.

"Whh—well, of course I wouldn't! I am stunned and somewhat relieved that you know. But I am quite uncomfortable to admit that Bailey and I had a bit of a tiff, and she may be angry with me." He couldn't meet her eyes, so he made himself busy drinking his coffee. He was still too embarrassed about his behavior towards her daughter.

"Oh really? I didn't get that impression. But she did seem pretty sad. As you can imagine, we did plenty of crying. It was a shock for her to find out about us."

"I can well imagine. I don't want to worry you, but it's imperative that I find her. I don't want her alone with Sethe running loose. She needs our protection. Is there anything else you can tell me about your visit with her? Anything unusual or any clue where she could have gone?"

"Let me think. She said that you took Rosa and the kids to Florida, and that she needed some time alone. Other than that, nothing that I can think of."

Declan's heart sank. He could smell her in the room and it made him crazy. He knew that Bailey had probably erased her parent's memories, so he would learn nothing more here. He finished his coffee and got up. He picked up each dog, held him close, and scratched behind each set of ears. Katherine walked him to the door.

"If you hear from her, can you please call me?" he asked, handing her his card.

"Yes, of course. I must admit now that I'm a bit concerned. I hope she calls soon."

"I'm sure she's just fine. Do you have a cell phone?"

"Yes, certainly." She recited a number that he punched right into his own cell.

"Good, I'll check in with you." He grabbed her hand and squeezed. "Don't worry, we'll find her perfectly safe. I promise you that."

She grinned and surprised him by letting go and throwing her arms around him.

"I know you will," she whispered in his ear. She pulled back and he saw tears in her eyes.

Declan left without another word, deeply impressed by Katherine Davis. She knew what he was and still trusted him without hesitation. She had even hugged him without fear. He could see her strength in Bailey, and was certain she was Katherine's daughter, blood or no blood. He gave a final salute to the guards he'd stationed. They had their new orders to stay with the Davises even if they left the city, and to alert him immediately if Bailey herself made an appearance. It seemed he had only missed her by a few hours. He practically ran to the car. Next stop, the Sears Tower.

Security at the Sears Tower was pretty tight post-9/11. Even as a Chicago detective, he was thoroughly searched and his weapon was confiscated until his return. *Fine, he wouldn't need it anyway.*

Declan chose the elevator banks that took him to the Conklin floors. Nice set-up, he thought as he entered the lower suite of offices. He didn't think anyone would be there on a Sunday, but found several people milling about talking, and others hard at work. He approached the first person he saw and gave her his best smile. It seemed to work, because she blushed and babbled. He asked if Mr. Conklin happened to be in, and sure enough, he was. She led him up circular stairs to another level, and to an office in the corner of the building.

"Mr. Conklin, I'm Detective O'Connor, working on the Bailey Davis investigation."

"Of course, come in. What an awful business. Are there any leads about her attacker?" Conklin moved from around the desk to shake hands.

"Her assailant was caught several days ago. But there is a much larger gang at work here."

Conklin frowned, visibly shaken. It was a good opportunity to check his thoughts, so Declan patted his shoulder as a comforting gesture. He immediately pulled back.

Mr. Conklin was definitely not what people thought he was, but he posed no danger to Bailey, so Declan didn't give it another thought. He had quickly probed Conklin's mind and found that Bailey had written him a letter stating that she needed vacation time, and that she would make sure her work was covered. She didn't say where she was going, or for how long. John Conklin was concerned. She had never been so secretive.

Declan touched the older man's head, erased any memory of his visit, and quickly left his office. But before he left the building he couldn't resist going to Bailey's office. He could have picked it out a mile away, her scent was that distinct. He stepped over the threshold and could see she had been distraught, gathering her clothing out of the closet and making sure all was set. He watched as she sat at her desk and wrote several letters and then typed on her laptop. She'd left in a hurry.

Declan sighed and looked around. Bailey's office was beautifully decorated and soothing. He sat behind her desk and let her scent embrace him. God, how he missed her. He had to find her, and soon. He didn't know if he could take Sethe having his clutches on her yet again.

He shook his head and resumed his search for anything that might give him a clue to her whereabouts. Nothing. He didn't want to be seen lingering, so he headed for the elevator while he listened in on several conversations, but nothing that sparked his attention, until–

"I don't know where she could have possibly gone, but I hear John Blaine is also AWOL. He called in to say he was taking vacation time."

"No way, she wouldn't," said a cute brunette.

"I'm not spreading any rumors, but he's so hot she'd be stupid not to go for it," said a mousy woman in her mid-twenties. Then a blond man about six feet tall came up to them both.

"Quit speculating on Bailey. She's a big girl and can take care of herself. I just wish she would call. I'm starting to get a little concerned."

All three nodded at that point and went their separate directions.

Declan took the elevator down. Could she be with John Blaine? The thought twisted in his gut. Well, he could hardly blame Bailey after the way he'd treated her. He definitely did not like the implication, but it did give him another avenue to research down at the station, which was his final stop.

He slid his card through the slot and went directly to his office. He rifled through his messages and threw most of them in the garbage. The others he would take care of later. The squad secretary, Rosemary, stuck her head in and said hello. She had been trying to take him to dinner for months. He kept making excuses, but she was persistent.

He punched in Bailey's vehicle and tag number on his computer. He didn't want to put out an APB because he didn't want the attention, but he wanted to see if she'd been pulled over or anything. Zilch. He called down to Paula, his contact at IT, and left Bailey's information, instructing her to check if Bailey had bought a new cell phone. He told her to concentrate south of the city.

Next he did a trace on John Blaine and got his vehicle information. He checked to see if he had been pulled over for anything. Nothing.

Paula called back. Bailey had purchased a new cell in Indianapolis. She had used her real name because she had to use her driver's license to buy the phone. She had just called her parents, Rosa, the post office, and the Tribune. All of the calls were made within minutes of one another, from the I-65 corridor. Declan got the number but didn't immediately use it. He asked Paula to do the same with Blaine's number, and she'd get right back to him. He marveled at today's technology.

So Bailey was heading south. He pondered it. It had all started when she was assaulted in Oak Park. He opened the file on her attacks. He decided to do a little digging into past owners of the house. The phone rang, and it broke his concentration.

"O'Connor."

"Hey, Detective, I got your information. Blaine used his cell phone several times today along the I-65 area into Indianapolis and later around the Lexington area. He called a few different Chicago numbers—one was an architectural firm he called a couple of times. I'll send over the numbers."

"Good. Do me one last thing. I'm going to call Davis's number right now, and if she answers I want a trace. Can you please email me the position of the call? If she doesn't answer, I'll keep trying, and will check every sixty minutes or so to see if we can get a trace? I appreciate this, Paula."

Was Blaine following Bailey down south? If so, why? He steadied his nerves and punched in the number. Of course, no answer, and she had not yet set up her voice mail.

He went back to his research. He checked any past complaints or problems at that address and what he found was appalling. Why the hell Oak Park hadn't picked up on it was anyone's guess. He hurried down to the archives.

"I need file number 2635794-79, for 1246 Bell in Oak Park." He knew they would have the file because of the Mafia connection. After several minutes the annoyed clerk returned with a box full of files.

"Here you are. Just sign this." Declan lugged the box back upstairs to his office. An hour later he sat back and ran his had through his hair.

"Holy shit," he muttered to himself. He quickly packed up and left to meet with his team at Bailey's house. He had quite a tale to tell them.

His team had gathered by the time Declan walked through the door. They sat around the kitchen table, which was piled high with papers, books, and scrolls. Declan asked Daniel and Shila to begin with their report.

Daniel spoke first. "Shila and I went thought these sources looking for any references to Sethe and got a pretty good picture about this *connard*." He went on to explain the relationship of Sethe to Reneb and his disturbing actions as a child and later.

"Sethe fell in love with a woman—Isabol, with golden red curly hair and emerald green eyes—back during the thirteenth century," Daniel explained. Everyone glanced at one another. "Right before the first plague hit and King Louis IX's last Crusade. Isabol was powerful, but not in a conventional sense. That's all we could find on her. She and Sethe met in Austria, just after the fall of the Babenberg Dynasty. It was a dangerous time in the country, so they left for Spain and settled in Barcelona. The couple had a wild and tempestuous affair for several years there. I found rumors of a marriage, but I cannot substantiate that. She eventually left him, and he went wild trying to find her. He looked everywhere but to no avail. A few years later, he joined up with King Louis IX's army and marched to Jerusalem. And we all know how that turned out."

"He does meet up with her again, however," Shila cut in. "And this is where it gets really ugly." She looked to Daniel, who gestured for her to continue.

"Incredibly, Isabol meets his brother, Gabriel, while visiting friends in…" Shila shuffled through some papers. "Oh, yes, Rouen and she fell madly in love with him. He was more powerful, better looking, and probably much nicer than Sethe. They eventually mated and went back where Gabriel was born, Paris. The happy family resided there for many years. They were very popular in their Guild and within the human community in Paris. It was a flourishing time in the city, and they took full advantage of its popularity and newfound wealth. Gabriel toyed in politics, and Isabol fed the hungry and even opened an orphanage that was highly respected. According to all accounts, they were the perfect family."

"Did Isabol ever connect the two?" Declan asked.

"Oh yes, they knew almost from the beginning, but by that time Sethe had been off fighting for years without a word, and they all presumed he was dead."

Daniel took over the narrative. "A few years passed and they had a child, Beatriz, who looked identical to her mother, and then a son, Marc."

"What are the dates?" Declan asked.

Papers shuffled. Shila spoke up. "Here it is. The mating ritual was performed in 1244 in Rouen. Beatriz was born in 1250 and Marc in 1255 in Paris."

"Oddly, no one mentions anything about any special gifts or powers of either female. Anyway, Sethe returned to his ancestral home after many years of fighting."

They all eyed one another, knowing exactly what the others were thinking. Declan also knew where this was heading, and he had a very bad feeling. He needed to find Bailey, and fast.

Daniel continued. "Sethe found them mated and happy. He flew into a rage and killed them while they slept. But before he could do anything to the children, his parents intervened. They banished him for life, and he hasn't been seen anywhere near his family since."

Declan nodded somberly. It was a terrible thing, to be banished from one's family for an eternity. To be denounced by one's own blood was the worst kind of punishment and humiliation. "They should have contacted the Council," he stated. "Sethe should have, at the very least, been imprisoned for his crimes."

"Apparently, he was incarcerated for several years by his father's orders," Shila said. "There is sketchy information on the subject. No one knows where, or for how long, but it is said that the father was too humiliated to contact the Council. He didn't want to lose his family's standing within their Guild."

"Ultimately word leaked out anyway," Daniel added. "Sethe's whole family has been punished, banned from Province meetings and Council activities."

Declan knew that that would be price enough if they were social climbers. Being punished by the Council Elders was an embarrassment that could not be easily lived down.

"It would have been very hard for a popular family like that to just vanish, Declan remarked. "Someone was bound to find out what really happened."

"We also found that Sethe has gathered a team of very bad vampires, rogues mostly," Shila added, "and a few human men to do his dirty work throughout the years. It is still unclear what his main motive is, but it certainly surrounded the descendants of his great-grandfather's other family–the family of Arabet. He's obviously been a terrorist throughout the centuries. Some say that he and his thugs would destroy whole towns just for kicks. But there has never been any hard evidence." She shook her head in disgust.

Declan got up and cleared his throat. "I believe that Sethe has been searching all this time for the descendents of Reneb and Arabet. More specifically, the child Beatriz, Bailey's grandmother. And he may have found her and her family in Oak Park in 1980."

They all turned to Declan in stunned silence.

"The Tandini's, a supposed mobster and his family, lived a very private life behind huge gates of an estate in Oak Park. Very few people ever saw the wife, but the daughter, Jasmine, was a party girl. She didn't have red curly hair or show any sign of special gifts, so I would assume that her parents didn't believe she was special. She attended public school and was very popular. She was supposed to attend Harvard in the fall of 1980, but she and the entire family disappeared without a trace that summer." He had everyone's rapt attention.

"The family had a summer house in Charleston, South Carolina–Sullivan's Island more specifically–on the beach. The parents went there, leaving Jasmine at home with a housekeeper and a bodyguard. One evening after a wild party, no one could find her. She never showed up at Cambridge that fall, yet a missing persons report was never filed. The police went to the house on several occasions but could never find anyone about. Not even the servants. It was as if everyone had simply vanished off the face of the planet. The entire family was never heard from again.

After the Oak Park investigators contacted Sullivan's Island police, they investigated down there. They found the house in shambles and blood, lots of it, and a trail that led to the beach, but then all clues just stopped. No bodies were ever found, no witnesses. Nothing. It was a secluded house, so there were very few neighbors, but the police interviewed them all. One neighbor said she'd heard screaming the night before, but believed it to be just a child's tantrum, so thought nothing of it. It was assumed a Mafia hit, but killing children is definitely not a Mafia MO. Wise guys do not mess with kids, and that always bothered the investigators. It's been a cold case for thirty years now. The two jurisdictions kept in contact, but nothing ever came of either investigation."

Declan sat back down. "No one ever came forward to claim the houses, so they went to the state and were eventually resold. The money has been in escrow for all these years, just waiting for a long lost family member to claim." Declan paused to survey his team's stunned faces.

Charles spoke up for the first time. "Jesus. Are you sure that the woman and her daughter were of Arabet's blood?"

"Why else would Sethe be interested? Why would he care if the bones were recovered and the police got involved? No, he didn't want the case reopened because it might actually lead somewhere, now that we have a team here in Chicago. We didn't thirty years ago." They all nodded, then fell silent for a minute, absorbed in their own thoughts.

Thomas shook his head. "My god, he found them right here after all of these years. It's crazy. And to think that Bailey stumbled onto it all. The coincidence is too much to be believed."

"Where does she fall into all of this?" Gregory asked Declan.

"I believe that the vampire Mikel was going back to gather the evidence he'd left thirty years before. Sethe definitely doesn't want police attention, and somehow he found out they were doing some remodeling and were excavating the site. Bailey happened to be at the wrong place at wrong time."

"Or someone sent her there," Shila remarked.

Once again, the room fell silent.

"What about Bailey's powers? How can all of this be related to her, other than her being at the wrong place at the wrong time? Do you think she is really blood of Ah Kin and Ix? " Gregory inquired.

"I paid a visit to Katherine Davis today." That got everyone's attention. "The Davises went to Charleston on vacation in the fall of 1980, and came back with a red haired child. They felt compelled to move to Riverside, a suburb close to Oak Park, shortly thereafter, and have lived there ever since.

"She is the child," Shila breathed. "Unbelievable. She is the one–the blood of Ix. She has to be. The stories are true. Incredible."

"Okay, this is what's going to happen," ordered Declan. "Charles, I want the jet fueled and ready to head down to Charleston. Shila, find us somewhere to stay in the Sullivan's Island area. I prefer a house to rent; it's more private. And we need transportation." He looked at his watch. "Shit, seven P.M. already. Gregory, I need an update on the cave and the Elders. Roran, I need you to stay on top of what's going on with the cave. Stay for Gregory's update, and then I want you to assist him with anything he may need. Please tell the Elders that we are on a very strong lead to Sethe. I want a report every four hours. And I want you both to stay here. It's more comfortable and secure right now."

Roran and Gregory both nodded and stayed seated.

"Daniel, you take Shila, go back to the cave, and collect some necessities for everyone. I don't know how long we'll be gone. I'll meet you both at the hangar. Let's say eight-thirty." Daniel, Shila and Charles nodded and left the house.

"Okay, Gregory. Fill us in fast."

C8&0

An hour after Gregory began his report, Declan met up with his team at the remote hangar at Midway International Airport where the Guild stored their private jets and two helicopters. The royal blue and white Dassault Falcon 900LX sat on the tarmac, ready and waiting for them to board. As soon as they did, Charles left the cockpit to tell them airport officials were having problems with the lighting on the runway, so they would be delayed for about an hour. Expected time of departure would be 10:20 P.M. Frustrated, but with their hands tied, they sat down to wait. Declan was just ready to doze after calling Bailey's number yet again, when he got a clear image of her strolling along a beach in the dark. He saw surfers and Blaine.

"Shit!" Everyone looked his way. "She just let me in. She's on a beach with Blaine. Anyone familiar with Folly? Is there a town called Folly around Charleston?"

Daniel opened his laptop and Googled it.

"Why is Blaine with her? Isn't he her old boyfriend?" Shila asked.

"Yes, and he wants her back," Declan spat. "He must have followed her." Shila smirked but said no more.

"Got it. It's Folly Beach, located south of Sullivan's Island. It's on the opposite side of Charleston. Not too far. See?"

Declan and his team gathered around Daniel's laptop to study the Charleston area map. Charleston was on a peninsula that was separated from the Atlantic by two rivers: the Cooper and the Ashley. The rivers converged at the tip of Charleston, called the Battery, forming the Charleston Harbor. Fort Sumter sat dead center with the mighty Atlantic Ocean just beyond it's fortifications. Charleston Harbor had played a hugely important role in both the Revolutionary and Civil Wars. And now Declan could see why. The harbor was strategically a great location for the defense of the city.

Mt. Pleasant sat across the Cooper River to the north, while James Island and Folly Beach lay beyond the Ashley River to the south. Both areas cradled

Charleston proper. Sullivan's Island, on the easternmost point of Mt. Pleasant on the Atlantic Ocean, was separated from the city by the Intracoastal Waterway. It looked to be about four miles long before it ran into the Isle of Palms, by about a half mile at its widest point.

"Shila, can you make sure we have access to a boat?" Declan asked. "It looks to be a short boat ride between Sullivan's Island and Folly Beach. Much shorter and easier by boat than car."

"Yes, Sir. She began to make a call just as Charles peeked out from the cockpit once again.

"You're not going to believe this, Sir, but a tropical storm has gained strength in the Atlantic. They're saying it's about 350 miles southeast of Charleston. It's looking to hit the area in a day or so if it doesn't change course. It could become a hurricane by as early as the morning."

"Great." Declan heard groans from the others, except for Thomas, who looked excited.

"I've never experienced a hurricane. In over three hundred years." His eyes danced.

CŞĐ

They finally arrived at the Charleston International Airport at about eight in the morning after waiting in Chicago for five frustrating hours. Declan had considered using his powers to fly, but decided he was not yet fully skilled enough to make the 930-mile journey.

Shila's contact came through for them and had a courier waiting when they arrived. He led them to a new black Ford Navigator and handed Declan keys to a beach house on Sullivan's Island. He had the address already in the GPS system. They said their thank-you's and headed out.

It was a balmy September morning, and the high humidity felt good against Declan's chilled skin. The clouds were blackening in the east, and the winds were whipping around the palm trees that lined the airport parkway. Charles drove from the airport to Sullivan's Island so Declan could relax and look at the scenery. He had never been in this part of the country before, and he took in the exotic smells of the marsh mixed with salts from the Atlantic. The team dropped their conversation to gape at the Ravenel Bridge that spanned the Cooper River from Charleston to Mt. Pleasant and the islands beyond. Declan marveled at the magnificent structure, and the view it gave of downtown Charleston, the harbor, and the surrounding low country.

"Splendid," he murmured. He continued to take in the scenery as they crossed the bridge and headed down Coleman Boulevard toward Sullivan's Island. *Where is she?* he thought to himself. He was anxious to dump their gear and start the search. Folly Beach. That's where they should begin.

They were stopped by traffic that was backed up getting into a large chain hardware store.

"I guess people are taking the weather seriously," Charles stated. Sure enough, people were exiting with flashlights, tarps, plywood, and other necessities.

"Do we need to prepare?" Daniel asked.

"No." Shila turned to him. "The house was built using steel beams and titanium strapping. It's guaranteed to withstand up to a category-four hurricane and a seven-magnitude earthquake. It also has automated hurricane shutters that engage when the wind gusts hit seventy M.P.H. And they have two back-up generators. The house is fully equipped and stocked for our arrival."

"Good," Declan said with an approving smile for Shila. He looked out over the beaches while crossing the Ben Sawyer Bridge and heading into the tiny downtown area of Sullivan's. The surf was rough, and the surfers were out in droves. He suddenly felt a twinge, an acknowledgement that Bailey was close. He closed his eyes and prayed that was the case.

CઢᏠ

"John. John. Get your butt up; we're heading out. Come on, it's almost nine."

I received no reply and peeked into his room. Hmmm. The bed was made and a note was lying on top.

> I got up early and didn't want to disturb you, so I decided to start digging–off to
> Sullivan's Island to look around. Don't be mad. Call me when you wake up.

"Damn him!" This was my problem, not his. I regretted not ditching him when he decided to follow me. "John, you pain in the ass!" I shouted to no one in particular.

I hurried to shower and dress, then grabbed a banana and my cell phone. I tried calling while I took a bite of banana. No answer. Figured. "John, I'm not a happy camper right now. I'm finding my own way over to the island. Call me back!" I slammed the phone down. Damn him! I considered my maps and discovered that Sullivan's Island was not far by water. I headed out to find a boat.

I walked along the beach until I found a pier where several boats were tied up. Waves were pounding against the pier, and I noticed a few sailors were battening down the hatches, so to speak.

"I need to get a ride to Sullivan's. Who could I ask to take me?"

One man pointed to another boat further down the line. This boat was larger than the rest but needed a lot of work. The paint was peeling in spots, and it looked like it hadn't been cleaned since the eighties. It smelled like dead and long forgotten fish, too. Yuck.

"Hello. Is anyone there?" A grunt was all I could decipher.

"Hello? Could you take me over the Sullivan's Island? I'll pay you for your trouble."

A large man in his mid-to late fifties emerged. He could have been years younger, but he had such weathered skin it was hard to tell. But he had beautiful gray-blue eyes that sparkled, and amazingly white, straight teeth.

He looked out at the open ocean. "Storm's coming in, but I think I can manage okay. Hop in. Can you afford twenty?"

"Yes, thanks. My name's Bailey."

"I'm Cappy. Nice to meet you. Welcome aboard." And he grabbed my hand to help me.

I couldn't find a clean seat so I decided to stand and just watch the scenery. It didn't take long for us to get to Sullivan's Island. It was a bit rough going, but I managed to stay dry. Cappy dropped me off on the creek by the fuel dock.

"Storm's going kick up something fierce tonight and tomorrow too. You best be thinking about getting back early."

"Thanks, Cappy, I will."

He smiled and pulled back out into the creek.

Okay, now what? I wondered as I walked down Station 22 Street towards the one-block business district. There had to be a library where I could to start my search. And then I remembered. I dialed John's number, ready to bite his head off, but my call went directly to voice mail.

"John Blaine, you better have one hell of an excuse for not waiting for me or even calling. Where the hell are you? Call me."

I walked into the Edgar Allen Poe Library on Poe Avenue twenty minutes later with still no word from John. Should I start to worry? A librarian emerged, just about to lock up.

"I'm sorry, I didn't think you closed this early. It's only ten o'clock."

"Well, we thought no one would be in today. The schools are closed because of the storm, and most of the residents are packing up and leaving. We thought we would do the same."

"Oh. Is it going to be a big one?"

"It turned into a category one this morning. Honey, don't you watch TV?"

"I really haven't had much time lately. When is it supposed to hit?"

"They don't know for sure. If it doesn't change course it'll start in earnest tonight, but tomorrow will likely take the brunt of it."

"I see. Is it possible to just look up an address before you close? It's pretty important," I added when I saw her frown.

"Ah, sure. Come on in. What's an extra few minutes?"

She opened the door for me to enter and went to turn on some lights. When she came back I asked for information on the residences in 1980 and before. She led me to a bank of island directories, but they only went to 1985. She then sat me in front of a computer with a disk.

"Go through these and you should find what you are looking for. Let me know if you need anything else."

"Thank you."

I started digging. I was praying that they used the same name as in Oak Park and that their phone was not unlisted. Sure enough after only ten minutes I found it. The Tandini residence was located at 2 Middle Street, phone number "unlisted". It wouldn't have worked by now anyway. I looked on a map for Middle Street, and it was not far from my current location. In fact, I could walk from one end of Sullivan's to the other in about an hour, that's how small it was. I thanked the librarian and left.

The topography had changed a little after Hurricane Hugo in 1989, but it created a spurt in building, and many new homes were constructed thereafter. Sullivan's Island was now a mixture of beach shacks, post World War II barrack housing, and multi-million-dollar beach mansions.

On Middle Street, most of the houses seemed vacant, just like at Folly Beach. A few residents were busy boarding up, but I saw no one else around. It seemed most of the people had gone, leaving their houses to fend for themselves with the impending storm.

As I walked down the deserted street I felt the hair on the back of my neck stand up. I could sense dread and pain. I suddenly heard a moan and knew where it was coming from. I started to run. I ran faster than I thought humanly possible. I felt dizzy yet focused on my hearing, which went into high alert, as well as my other senses. I stopped short of barging into a secluded boarded-up house at the very end of the street, overlooking the Charleston Harbor and Mt. Pleasant. *I must be at the very tip of the island,* I realized. Oh my God. This was the house. I knew it.

I surveyed the area, but saw nothing, although I felt another presence, a vampire presence, and maybe a human. I tore off a couple of boards and squeezed through them to enter the garage space. I ran under the house and found a set of rickety stairs leading up. My heart pounded in my ears as I felt impending dread at what I might discover. I knew right where to go, so I ran up another set of stairs and into a large bedroom. There, lying on the bed, was a prone form with a vampire clamped onto his neck, emptying the life out of him.

"Stop!" I screamed. I was so incensed at what I saw that my vision turned red. I leaped forward and threw the vampire off. He was not happy and shrieked his displeasure, his eyes white, fangs extended and dripping with blood and gore, and his features distorted into a hideous mask.

"It's you!" He pointed and vaulted over me to get to the door. But I was faster and grabbed him before he could make his landing. He went for me then, punching my face and clawing at my eyes. One blow landed on my chest, and it took my breath for an instant–long enough for him to recover and make for the door. This time, however, I jumped onto his back, gripped his head, and twisted, snapping his neck. He instantly fell, with me landing on top of his now semi-dead body. There was only one way to make him truly dead. I raised my hands and burnt the vampire to cinders, then ran to the lifeless body of John.

"John, John! Oh my god," I cried as I tried desperately to revive him. I got a very weak pulse, and almost no breath–I knew he wouldn't survive long.

"John, you son of a bitch, you are not dying on me. Do you hear me?" I cried as tears blurred my vision. I had to get help. I lifted his lifeless body, which seemed to weigh next to nothing, and flew down the stairs. I had planned to rip off the plywood covering the front door when I realized someone had beaten me to it. I gently lay John on the floor and readied myself for the impending fight, but in the doorway stood a familiar form.

"Bailey, are you all right? Bloody woman, you gave me a fright. What the hell happened here?"

"Declan" was all I could get out, as he drew me into his arms and squeezed tight. Shila and Thomas hopped through the opening and hurried to John.

Thomas confirmed my worst fears. "He has only minutes left. I'm so sorry, Bailey."

"Dead." I shucked Declan off me. "Don't tell me that. Do something!" They both looked at Declan. I turned to him. "If you don't do it, I will," I said as the tears fell from my face.

"You don't know what you're asking," Declan stated. "Think of what he would want, Bailey. Do you even understand what you are demanding of me?"

"Yes, dammit," I said. I looked into his eyes and I saw reluctance and pity. "It's my fault, Declan. My fault he is even here, and I won't let him die. Not like this." I ran to the kitchen and found an old steak knife.

"Bailey, stop it! You will not use that knife on yourself. Put it down, now." Declan went over to John and nodded to the others. "Bring the car around and meet me at the house. Bring Bailey." He left in a blink of an eye with John cradled in his arms.

"The process is long and painful. He will need constant oversight, and he will be very grouchy for awhile. His frenzied need for blood will back off after a few days." Thomas was explaining the procedure to me. "And Sir Declan will need a constant supply of fresh blood to replenish his body. After I drop you and Shila off, I will find some."

I froze. "How will you do that?"

Shila glanced at me with a smirk. "He will steal some from the local clinic or hospital. Don't worry; he won't drag an innocent human to the house."

"I didn't think you would do that," I said flushing.

"Humph," was her only response.

"How—um—why are you guys here? Not that I'm complaining, of course."

"Miss Bailey, I'm sorry that we left you like that." Thomas answered. "Sir Declan felt compelled to find you because you are in danger. Sethe is a viable threat, and you need our protection."

"And now Sir Declan will be weakened by the changing process," Shila shot me an accusatory look.

I sighed. "I'm sorry I dragged you guys into all of this—especially John. I've made a mess of everything."

Shila cautiously patted my shoulder. "It's okay. I would've done the same."

Luckily, the island was small, so we reached their rental house in a couple of minutes. It was huge, one of the newer ones right on the beach. The houses on either side were already boarded up and vacant. Shila led me into the house, where they had already set up a couple of computer stations and other equipment, including a lot of firearms.

"I won't even ask you how you found me, but I'm glad you did." I gave her a quick hug and backed away. "Where is he?"

She pointed up, but Shila stopped me before I could move an inch. Just then, a piercing scream filled the house.

"Oh my god, what the hell was that?"

"Like Thomas explained, it's painful. John's organs are changing, and if we were in the cave we could give him some sedatives, but we're not, so he has to bear it."

"Changing, that's right, he's changing." And then it hit me. John would never be the same, and his life as he knew it, was now over. "Oh—what the hell have I done?"

Shila's gaze was kinder this time.

"It will be all right. Come on. We do need to go up and help Sir Declan, especially since we don't have a secured room for the change. You need to prepare yourself though. It's not going to be pretty."

I nodded, and she led the way up. Daniel was guarding the door. Inside the smell struck me like a blow to the head–a mixture of blood, feces, and urine. I covered my nose as I approached. What I saw I wish I had not. Blood covered the walls in splotches. Declan looked white as a ghost and was visibly weak. I ran to the bed. John was tied to the bedposts completely naked. Blood covered his face and chest. He had lost his bowels and was in the process of peeing on the carpeting. He moaned and panted–his body contorted as it rocked from the pain. His eyes were unfocused and glassy. He whispered my name, but then tried to attack me when I got close. I noticed he had sprouted fangs.

"Bailey, get back!" It was Declan's voice but it was weak. I looked him over. He had slid to the floor and seemed ready to pass out. "He's too dangerous right now. He doesn't know what he's doing," Declan stated.

I sat down in front of him. "Please, Declan. Take what you need." He stared at me with fevered eyes, then grabbed me and held close. He moved my hair and kissed my neck. Goosebumps rose on my arms.

"I missed you, Bailey," he whispered as he sank his teeth into my flesh. I immediately went liquid as he drank from me. I couldn't help but moan my pleasure as he restored his health from my lifeblood. It was such an intimate exchange, second only to love making, that I immediately felt self-conscious when I realized there were others in the room.

Declan's face began to look healthier and his grip tightened, signaling his returning strength. He immediately retracted his teeth after he had taken his fill, but didn't let go. He continued to lick my neck and give me little sweet kisses. I was about ready to take off all my clothes right then and there, when another shriek filled the room. Declan pulled away but continued to hold me tight. I felt cold and empty without his lips on me. *Damn.*

"Thank you," he whispered in my ear.

"I'm the one who should be thanking you. What you have done–I mean–I wouldn't have asked anyone but you–you know. Thank you, Declan."

"Don't thank me yet. He's not going to understand any of this for a while, and he will most certainly not be happy with you. His whole life has just suddenly changed. His job, his friends, everything will now be different."

We both looked over to where John lay. He was now sleeping off his exhaustion. Declan helped me up.

"I hadn't thought of that." I considered for a second. "But he'll realize that I just couldn't let him die?" I pleaded to Declan with my eyes.

He nodded his understanding and held my hand. "I need to finish here and then we can talk. I have a lot to say to you."

I gulped. "Okay. I'll leave you to it then. Take good care of him."

Declan nodded. "Please don't go far."

"I won't," squeezing his hand in unspoken agreement. "I'm glad you're here, Declan."

He smiled and turned to his new fledgling.

I headed downstairs. It felt so good to have Declan close. I hadn't realized until then, just how much I had come to rely on him, and his judgment. Sure, I'd left Chicago in a huff, but Declan no longer seemed upset, and I was surprised by the immense relief that gave me.

Then my thoughts turned to John. My heart suddenly sank. What was I going to do about him? If it weren't for me, he would be fine up in Chicago, doing what he normally does. I felt horrible, guilt gripping me. I swore that I would make it up to him. Somehow.

I heard screaming again just as Thomas walked in the door. He acknowledged me and headed up the stairs with a handful of shopping bags. I continued to hear a lot of thumping and yelling until I couldn't stand it anymore. I left the house and walked out onto the beach.

The mid-afternoon sun was trying to peek out through the black clouds, which were increasing and darkening towards the southeast. The wind had picked up, and the gusts were now whipping up sand, which stung my face and exposed arms. The waves came crashing in, spraying me with sea water. But it all felt good. Anything to take my mind off of everything that had gone so horribly wrong. I began to walk, tears streaming down my face. What did I want? What was I looking for? I already knew who and what I was. What more could I possibly want?

I stopped when I found myself in front of the beach house–my biological parents' house–the house I was looking for. This very beach was the one where my mother met my parents. The same beach that I was given away on. And that thought twisted my gut.

I climbed the rickety stairs and entered the house through the exposed plywood. I was amazed the house it was still standing, even after Hurricane Hugo. As I entered, the reek of John's blood, fear, and a little something else I couldn't quite grasp, still saturated the moist air. Through the darkness, I silently crept from room to room, trying to remember ever being there, but couldn't. I found the kitchen and tried to imagine my real family here, laughing, cooking, eating, and playing in the surf on the beach.

I sat on the floor, as once again the tears flowed. I must have been there for hours in my misery, because suddenly I'd realized night had fallen. Tired of being unhappy, I sat up and dried my face. After all, I had wonderful parents who loved me as their own. I had a great job that I enjoyed and was well respected at. And there was Declan. I had hope that he would play an important part of my future.

I knew that Sethe had posted the vamp as a guard in case I came around. I'd read his mind. He'd been bored and attacked John when he came snooping. It only reaffirmed what I had to do, and that was to destroy the one being who had caused me so much grief and threatened my future–and that of anyone else I loved, including John. No way were he and his thugs going to get away with all of this. I opened my mind to him just a pinch.

"Come and get me, asshole," I said out loud. "I'm looking forward to it." Then I slammed the door, hopefully for good.

I got up and surveyed the space. My night vision was just as acute as if it were midday. I spotted nothing out of the ordinary but I walked through the house just to make sure. The wind was now pounding the plywood that was attached to the windows. The sound was deafening to my heightened senses. There seemed to be a particularly loud banging coming from a small closet off the laundry room. I opened the door and noticed for the first time a hatch in the floor under some old, dust-covered boots and shoes. It had come loose from below and was banging wildly. I moved the mess out of the way and lowered my head to see what was below. It looked to be a room off the garage at ground level. Hmmm. *Why hadn't I seen this before?*

I jumped down and landed on a slab of dry concrete in a storage room of about eight by ten feet. There was nothing but the floor, walls and low ceiling–no doors, windows, or anything else in the space. Strange. Suddenly, I felt a slight stirring of the stale air around me as a wisp of wind blew through a small opening behind some shelving, raising the hair along my arms. I bent down to look into the gap and felt lightheaded.

"Holy shit!" As I closed my eyes, I clearly remembered. The monster was coming to get me as I huddled under some boxes in the corner. His face and gleaming fangs hovered right above me. I heard a scream that was coming from my papa. He had the monster by the throat, biting and tearing at his face. Blood rained all over as my mother dragged me out of my hiding place. Crying, she lifted me into her arms, hugging tightly as she wriggled her way into a small cave that eventually led out onto the beach. Covered in blood, my mother ran down the empty beach with me in her arms.

"Bailey, Bailey!"

I came to and saw Declan's face before me.

"Bailey, what did you see? Is this where she escaped?"

"Declan? Oh–yes, yes it is. I remembered what happened now."

He nodded. "Let's see where it leads."

He helped me up, gave me a quick hug, and led the way. It was difficult going for him because he was so large, but he managed to squeeze through the opening. Once through, it led to a larger cavern with many different tunnels. The walls and ceiling were made of stone, and the flooring was compacted sand. A cold breeze blew in from one of the tunnels.

"I guess this is the way." He pointed to the breezy passageway, and I concurred.

"I was getting worried about you because you were gone for so long." He looked over his shoulder and smiled. "I knew you weren't in any trouble, but you were upset, so I decided your alone time was long enough." He looked over his shoulder and smiled.

"Oh really? Nice that *you* decided it was time." I pretended to be angry, but it didn't last long. "Actually I'm glad you came. I was just heading back when I noticed this." I waved my arms back toward the entrance to the cave. "Odd, isn't it?"

"Not really, considering who they were. They had to have another means of escape if they ever needed it. I'll bet the Oak Park house has the same."

"Then you know?"

"Yes, I did some investigating of my own. The cave may be damaged, but the library is intact. We know all about Sethe and his obsession with your family. He will not stop until he has his way."

"I know. That's why I'm going to kill him."

Declan abruptly halted, and I banged into him. "What are you saying? He is your master now, Bailey, he has special powers over you."

"I don't give a rat's ass, Declan. Do I have feelings for him? The answer is yes. But they're not of my making or choice. And my hatred is stronger. I won't hesitate to kill him because he poses a threat to the people I love. Look what his thug did to John. He deserves to die for that alone."

Declan shook his head, his eyes flooded with love, admiration and fear. "I've never heard of anyone turning like that, Bailey, let alone so soon on their own maker. Sethe has great powers and a never-ending network of murderers at his disposal." He paused. "But we have powers too."

I gazed into his eyes—so blue—so beautiful. He took my hands and brought them to his lips.

"We will find him and take care of this so he'll never bother you again. I promise."

After about fifteen minutes we ended up on the beach, a half a mile from the house and not too far from where Declan was staying.

The force of the impending storm almost knocked me over. "Wow, the wind has really kicked up." It was hard to talk and be heard over the pelting rain.

"Yes, the police came by earlier and wanted us to vacate," he yelled. "Daniel had to erase his memory of the visit because John decided to howl. Bad timing."

I trudged after Declan who was aiming towards his rental house.

"Wait, what about my car? Did John have any keys on him?"

"I don't know. I think Shila threw his clothes in the garbage. We can check once we get back."

The relentless rain was assaulting every inch of me with bites of pain, and the wind made it difficult to walk. We finally made it to the house, and amazingly, the lights were on. Declan noticed my surprise.

"Generators. They came on shortly before I left to find you. Luckily there's a large tank of gas on the property."

Once we were inside and sheltered from the storm, I asked. "How is he–and you?"

"I'm fine, just a bit tired. I need to sleep to get my strength back. John is about halfway there. He'll have an uncomfortable night, but by morning the transformation should be complete. The next part is the trickiest. He will crave blood, and lots of it. He will have to learn to curb his cravings; otherwise he will be killed."

"What?"

"Bailey, he must learn how to control himself. Otherwise he would be a danger to humans, and you wouldn't want that on your conscience."

"Oh, of course not. But what are the odds," I asked twisting my hands.

"They are slim, but it happens occasionally."

"Oh. Will there be enough–blood?"

"Thomas has already taken care of that. He'll be fine. You'll see."

I started shivering. My whole body felt cold, inside and out.

"Come on, let's get you into a hot shower and some dry clothes. I'm sure Shila has something you can borrow. I'll send Daniel out to look for your keys."

"Okay, but do I have to wear Shila's slut wear?"

Declan stared at me like I was nuts. "Would you like to go to your place in this weather to fetch some of yours?"

I shook my head in defeat. *Oh brother.* Just then we heard a loud clang, and the shutters of the house began their descent.

"Good," said Declan. "At least we know they work."

"The airport is officially closed, so it looks like we're stuck here for the duration, much to Thomas's delight," Charles said while glaring at Thomas.

Declan chuckled as he led the way up the stairs, where we peeked in on John. He seemed to be resting comfortably. Shila and Daniel were guarding him.

"Daniel, please go through John's discarded clothing and try to find Bailey's car keys. He had them last," Declan said. "Also bring in his wallet and anything else you may find. Everything needs to be destroyed." Daniel nodded and left. "Shila, can you get some clean clothes for Bailey? She needs a hot bath and bed."

She looked over at me and smiled, but it wasn't a pleasant smile. It was one that said, *I can't wait to see this!*

"I'm going to turn in. Take turns watching John and wake me if anything changes. He should be getting hungry around daybreak. And, I want a perimeter set. I'm not sure when Sethe will show up. Please see to it."

He led me up another set of stairs into a large loft space at the top of the house. I could hear the wind banging against the shutters and the loud drumming of the rain bombarding the metal roof. But it didn't scare me like it should have. It felt comforting somehow.

Declan saw that my teeth were chattering and escorted me to a huge bathroom with marble flooring and polished nickel fixtures. The skylights were covered with metal shutters, but I could imagine how beautiful it would be during the daytime. Declan didn't say a word as he went over to the tub and started the hot water, adding some bath salts that were sitting nearby. He came back to me, stopping an inch in front of my face. He carefully started to take off my soggy clothing. There was a knock on the door, but he didn't even pause to see who was there.

"Just leave the clothing on the bed. Thank you, Shila."

He continued to bore a hole in my retinas as he shed my soaked shirt and bra. He sucked in a breath.

"*Ghrá álainn*! My god, Bailey, you are more beautiful than in my imagination."

"Yeah, well, that may be the only good side effect of all of this." I felt pleased by his admiration, but I was instantly sorry that I'd opened my big fat mouth, because I saw him deflate at the thought of Sethe and what he did to me.

"I want to tell you how sorry I am," he said. "How I treated you was inexcusable."

"Will–"

"Let me finish, please." He put a finger on my lips. "I know what that fiend did to you was against your will, and yet I still felt betrayed. I know it's my own issue. I need to deal with the fact that–that maniac laid his hands on you. It still drives me crazy just thinking about it. But Sethe will get what he deserves. I will see to it personally." He gently cradled my head in his hands, lifting it until my eyes met his– igniting sparks within my soul. "Could you find it in your heart to forgive me, and my asinine reaction?"

He spoke with immense emotion, and I knew it was very difficult for him. Declan had probably never felt the need to apologize to anyone in his very long life.

"Of course, but I am the one who should be apologizing for everything–all of this trouble you have gone through," I answered. "And I want you to know that you never left my mind the whole time I was imprisoned by Sethe. You were always in my heart."

He smiled and continued his task of shedding my clothing until I stood before him in all of my goosepimply glory. Then he kissed me like I have never been kissed. Oh god.

"I missed you, Declan," I murmured in his ear. I suddenly felt a lot warmer. He lifted me into his arms and brought me to the tub where he gently lowered me down into the hot sudsy water. He discarded his own wet clothing in a fraction of the time, and stood in front of me naked, an Adonis. Muscles rippled all the way down to his groin, and he was clearly as excited as I was. He entered the water behind me and reached for some shampoo to massage into my hair.

"Oh, that feels so good," I groaned.

He rinsed my hair with clean water from the tap, then continued to massage my shoulders and neck.

"So tell me everything from the beginning. From when my brother took you back to your room to what happened here today." Declan said. "I want to know every detail of what you went through."

So I laid out the whole sordid tale. Everything, even when Sethe took me by the side of the road. I told him how much I loathed Sethe, yet wanted him at the same time. How he was mean, cruel, yet cunning. I recounted how I'd felt when I saw him bleeding and dying and how I'd vowed to kill Sethe for hurting him or die trying. I chronicled how I'd killed Lily and felt no remorse and that I read her mind before I cut off her head. Finally, I explained to Declan the hurt I felt when he rejected me, and how John's companionship helped me through those painful and lonely hours.

"Bloody hell. I'm so ashamed–so sorry you went through all of it." He massaged a little harder. "You are the most incredibly brave person I have ever had the pleasure of meeting. You must be Centurion, Bailey. I'm certain of it."

I could feel his pride at my courage, and happiness that I was once again in his arms where I belonged. Yet he remained worried. Concerned about my abilities and the fact that Sethe knew of them. I reached behind me and ran my fingers through his hair.

"Are you reading my mind, Bailey?" he asked with a smile in his voice.

"Ah, um–sorry," I managed to squeak out.

"We're going to have to set some ground rules, but we can talk about that later." He suddenly turned me around and savagely kissed me.

"I want you, Declan. More than I have ever wanted anyone or anything in my life." I met his smoldering eyes as he gently massaged my breasts. My nipples were about to explode as he began pinching and sucking.

"Oh god, please don't stop!" I heard myself saying. He slowly glided his tongue down my stomach, kissing and licking along the way. He grabbed my ass and lifted me out of the water as he continued his assault on my body. He found my core and suckled until I was panting his name. Gently taking his fingers, he entered me in every possible way, licking and stroking until I was screaming with ecstasy. I came with such an explosion that it rocked us both. He put me down on him, and I shuddered with surprise and delight. I rutted hard until the water sloshed over the side of the tub and soaked the floor. Neither of us cared, lost in the thrill of finding each other's pleasure.

"Bailey," he moaned, and I knew he was close so I paused. He gripped my rear to try and move me, but I stayed rigid.

"What are you trying to do? Give me a heart attack?"

I smiled, got off, and maneuvered so he was behind me. He grunted in appreciation and obliged me immediately. It didn't take long before I was screaming from the pure bliss of having him inside of me, and was about to explode once again, when I cried out for him to bite me.

"Please, Declan, please do it!" And he did. Right on my shoulder. My vision blackened and my core vibrated as orgasm after orgasm rippled through my body. The next thing I knew his bloody wrist was in my mouth and I was drinking in his essence. God, it tasted good. I couldn't speak, could barely breathe, as the rush of pure hot pleasure coursed through my entire body. I saw a jumble of Declan's memories, from his childhood to his current status behind me. Our cells united and our souls converged as one. Utopia, this was it! The current of emotion almost blinded me. Yet it happened so fast I thought I must have imagined it.

His moans snapped me back to reality. Declan's frenzied pounding got more intense as he cried out from his own release and collapsed on top of me, his energy spent. After several minutes his breathing steadied, and Declan groaned.

"Jesus, woman. Are you trying to kill me?" He picked me up and walked me to the shower. He set me on the bench and turned on the showerheads and sprays.

"It seems like we are always wet," and I laughed, a full-fledged laugh that felt good in my soul. I hadn't done it in a long time. He turned and smiled at me, which melted my heart. That was it. I was completely in love with him. *Oh boy. I was in some serious trouble.* I thought.

"Here, let's rinse off and then we can get into a dry bed." He lathered us both up, and then we rinsed. He toweled me off and carried me to the bedroom.

"I think I could have managed to walk."

"I know, but I like to carry you." He moved aside the clothes that Shila had brought. "Here, get in," he instructed as he raised the covers.

"Ohhhh, this feels so good. I guess I'm more tired than I thought."

He went back into the bathroom and returned with a brush and comb. He crawled into bed, sat me in between his legs, and started combing out my tangled locks.

"Is sex going to always be this great between us?" I asked. "Because if it is, I may have to plan my day around it, and of course I'll get nothing done. And my heart—it will most assuredly give out, but I would die a very happy woman."

He stopped breathing for an instant and then burst out laughing until tears rolled down his face.

"You are without a doubt the funniest, sexiest, and most beautiful woman I have ever met. There is absolutely nothing about you that I do not lo…ike." After a moment of silence he added, "And by the way, our lovemaking is not the norm. Even for vampires. It is incredibly–intense." He continued gently picking through the knots until my hair was silky smooth and the curls sprang to his touch.

"I love your hair, Davis. It is truly glorious."

"Good, you can comb it every day. But I warn you, it's a pain in the butt."

"I will do it every day." And he kissed my head.

We lay in each other's arms, listening to the wind howl and the rain splatter against the roof. Once in a while a big gust shook the house, but we weren't concerned. We were happy, if even for a short while. I studied him closely, memorizing his fathomless azure eyes, and the dark eyelashes that outlined them–his adorable cleft chin and his soft perfect ears. His handsomely chiseled face was in need of a shave, but he was amazingly sedate after our lovemaking, and it stirred my heart, and more. I dove into his thick black locks, which were wildly framing his face. I massaged his scalp as he whispered his appreciation. Before I knew it he was on top of me smothering my face and neck in kisses.

"Is it too soon?" he asked in a hopeful voice.

"Never," I replied with undeniable certainty.

18

THE SPELL THAT BINDS

Bam! I jumped up and out of bed to a loud pounding noise and a piercing howling cry. For once it wasn't John or my head, but the relentless wind and rain. I went to snuggle Declan and got only a cold pillow. *What the hell? That didn't last long,* I thought. I reluctantly got to my feet and stretched. It was hard to tell what time it was with the storm shutters covering the doors and windows. I tried to remember where my cell phone was. Oh yeah, in my soggy clothes, which I located on the bathroom floor. Sure enough it was in my jeans pocket.

7:37 A.M. We had slept through dinner and I was now starving. Where was everyone? I sensed only John and one other in the house. I washed my face and brushed my teeth using Declan's toothbrush–I hoped he didn't mind. I ran my fingers through my hair as I checked out the clothes Shila had left for me. Ugh. Black spandex. Didn't she know that spandex had gone the way of the disco ball? I would have to take that girl shopping sometime. At least the shirt covered my private parts.

I wandered downstairs and saw Thomas standing by John's door.

"How's is he doing?" I asked.

"As well as can be expected. He's very hungry now, and it's difficult keeping him in this room. He's resting for the time being."

"Can I see him?"

"I wouldn't recommend it yet. He may try to attack you. He's in no shape for visitors. He's been calling for you though. Maybe you can peek in after he's fed the next time. I'll let you know."

I nodded. "Where is everyone? The house is so quiet." A thunderous banging preceded by breaking glass erupted downstairs. And John started to shriek.

"I'll check out downstairs; you stay with John," I said. "Where is everybody?"

"They went to clean up the mess at the other house and patrol the area."

"In this weather?"

"Yes, isn't it thrilling?" His eyes danced.

I just shook my head at his excitement as I headed downstairs. The top half of a palm tree had crashed through the spare bedroom window, breaking the shutter and the glazing. Horizontal rain, and various debris were cascading in. I hurried to the tree and upended it back outside. It fell with a splash. A splash?

I found a blanket, draped it over my head, and looked out the bedroom window. Holy crap, the beach was gone, and the house was standing in about four feet of water that was rising fast. This must be the storm surge that everyone talked about. The lights sputtered, and went out. Shit.

I turned and spotted Thomas at the door.

"The generator needs a refill of gas. I need it to keep the blood from spoiling, and I also need the microwave to warm it for John."

"Okay, I'll go refill them. Do you know if there's any plywood around so we can board this up?"

"I think I saw some in the garage, but that may prove difficult to get to. The gas tank is buried by the entry to the main road. Getting there is going to be tricky."

"You forget, Thomas. I'm not exactly human."

His eyes brightened. "That's for sure." He grew serious once again. "I'm a bit concerned about the rising water. It must be getting close to the generators by now. They are sitting on a platform in the garage at about six feet. I hope the water doesn't reach them."

"Can we leave and go somewhere safer?"

"The bridge is closed and it's the only way out of here, unless you want to hop in the boat. Which is—well, who knows?"

"Crap. Okay. I'll try to get some gas, and I'll check to see if I can bring up some plywood. I have my cell if you need me. Please just stay with John."

He nodded as John made a screeching sound. "There are raincoats in the closet by the front door. The gas can is under that cabinet in the laundry room." He pointed.

I mentally communicated what was happening to Declan. *"Stay put, I'll be there shortly."* Wow, that really worked. *"Oh please, I'm a big girl. I'm headed to the garage, see you in a bit."* And I closed the door. Last thing I needed was him in my head giving me orders.

I trudged to the closet where the raincoats were hanging and put one on. It was the harsh weather kind that covered me from head to toe. I grabbed the empty gas can and went down to the garage, which was now under at least two feet of water. Crap. I had no boots. As I peeled off my already damp sneakers and socks, and rolled up the spandex, I spotted the generators. We had couple feet to go before water would hit the platform. I hoped that scenario did not happen.

The water was warmer than I thought it would be, but the rain was cold and stung my eyes as I waded into the open garage. I found some plywood, which was soaked, but I managed to heft a piece up the stairs and into the bedroom, where the rain was making a mess of the carpeting. I located some screws and a screwdriver in the kitchen and fought the wind gusts to attach the plywood into place. The molding around the window would need some repair, but at least the water wouldn't further damage the room.

I went back down to the garage. The wind seemed to be settling down a bit, but when I made my way to the doorway, a gust hit me like a hammer and threw me back inside. I landed with a thud on my backside. Thankfully, my raincoat shielded me from the worst of the wetness. I got up and tried it again, bracing myself against the doorway to peek outside.

I called upon my abilities to give me the strength to make it across the property. The wind was deafening, but my keen senses probably magnified the sounds of breaking branches, relentless rain, and pounding surf. I could barely see through the airborne debris, but I managed to locate the general direction of the gas tank, which was further away than I remembered or wanted to travel. Maybe I should just wait for Declan. "What a wimp," I mumbled to myself.

Resigned to my duty, I straightened my back, and my resolve, and ventured out. I was immediately smacked by a powerful wave of wind and rain, but I held steady. I finally made it to dry land, but the tank was still a good fifty yards ahead, to the right of the winding and wooded driveway.

As I maneuvered and stumbled my way down the driveway, I noticed the trees were bent into impossible shapes. Some were broken, but most were surprisingly intact. Debris was flying, and a constant barrage pelted me as I continued my walk. My muscles were starting to protest as I fought against the unyielding wind. I finally reached my destination, wondering how the hell I would get back with the gas can full. *Maybe the added weight would act as ballast,* I jokingly thought. I opened the spigot and managed to fill the can, even though a great deal was blown away in the wind. I was just putting the cap back on when I looked up–right into the face of my nemesis, Sethe.

"Bailey!" Declan screamed in my head.

But time had stopped as I gazed into Sethe's eyes. I could feel his excitement at seeing me again, and unfortunately, and reluctantly, I felt the same–and he knew it. Mesmerized, I watched, in slow motion, his long blond hair whip in the wind. He was letting his beard grow out, and his reddish-blond facial hair gave his chiseled chin a soft appearance. So soft that I had the sudden urge to run my fingers over it. His piercing hazel eyes did not glow white, but remained his natural color to show me he was in total control. And he was; but not for long.

I shut the door to him, and he flinched as if I'd hit him. I chastised myself for allowing him to sneak up on me. I'd been so intent on getting gas that I had no clue Sethe was anywhere in the area. Damn. I wanted a final confrontation, but now was not the time. We were vulnerable with John's predicament and the hurricane bearing down on us. Just as I was about to yell to be heard, the rain suddenly slowed, and the wind died down. I could actually see patches of sun to the east–as if Sethe had called upon the heavens so he could be better heard and seen. *We must be in the eye of the hurricane.*

"Bailey." He said it with so much evil intent that I almost snickered. Almost.

"Sethe. What are you doing he–?"

But before I could get the words out, he snatched my arm and smacked me across the face. It happened so fast I almost thought it was a dream. The other three vampires by his side laughed.

"You bastard!" I yelled, and suddenly I felt my powers straining to unleash. My mind was torn between throwing my arms around him and turning him to ash. He sensed it and chuckled.

"I was very disappointed when you tried to burn me to cinders. Your betrayal hurt me more than you can imagine."

He was desperately trying to get into my head, with no success. He suddenly fell silent and bored a hole into me. His eyes were now flickering bluish white.

"You're an evil sonofabitch who held me against my will. You forced me into First Rites, and almost a mating ritual. What did you expect? That I would actually be okay with that? Are you insane?" I dropped the gas can and took a few steps back. He lunged at me, but I didn't react. I wouldn't let him see me scared.

"No one has ever treated me with such contempt," he spat. "And you will pay for that in due time. In due time, Bailey Davis." He smiled a truly wicked smile.

I suddenly and without warning punched him in the throat. "I'm getting sick of hearing you, Sethe."

He was so shocked he actually sputtered, and his thugs took a step forward.

"Move another inch and I will send you all to hell." I lifted my hands up, ready.

"How dare you, you—"

Sethe's words were cut off, and everyone around me tensed. I could feel Declan nearing. He was close, but I could not hear a thing, even with my sharp senses. In an instant, Declan, Daniel, Shila, and Charles surrounded us. I let out my held breath. The cavalry finally had arrived. *It was about time,* I thought. There was an eerie silence as the wind stilled and a greenish-yellow mist lifted to a lightening sky. The rain had slowed to a drizzle, so I took off my confining coat and let it fall to the ground. No birds sang, and the waves seemed to still, as if all of nature was waiting to see what was about to transpire in the woods by the beach.

"Bailey, you need to leave now. Back away slowly."

"I'm not leaving you, forget it!"

"Bloody hell!"

Sethe's friends did not look happy. On the contrary, I knew their fear. Sethe could smell it too, because he spun on them with a scowl. I couldn't blame them, though. I would be terrified as well to have the likes of Shila pointing some crazy archer's weapon at me. Daniel had pulled out his huge machete–its blade so brilliant it was almost blinding. Charles, I noticed, was just lounging by a fallen tree, pretending not to care, but I knew better. He watched everyone's moves like a hawk. He probably had some nasty weapon within easy reach as well.

Declan moved to my side, not taking his eyes off Sethe. He wrapped his arm around my waist, demonstrating to everyone our current relationship status. Oh brother, vampire men were just like human men. Did they even have testosterone? Who knew, but they seemed to be just as possessive and weren't the least bit reluctant to show it. I gently shrugged him off and drew closer to Sethe.

"I want you to know that I am not interested in ever being with you. I do not want you in my life, nor do I ever want to see you again after this day. If you don't leave me, or anyone one else I care about, alone, I will not hesitate to kill you. On the contrary, I would enjoy it." I gave him a wicked smile.

Sethe's eyes widened, and he paled. I glanced over to Shila, who actually gave me a wink. Sethe quickly recovered, narrowing his eyes.

"Do you think I would ever have you again? I took what I needed and it was not nearly as enjoyable as I had expected it to be. No, Bailey, my dear, you are not as good as you let everyone believe. Quite a disappointment in fact."

Declan was so quick I didn't even see him push me aside and thrust a wicked-looking silver knife into Sethe's chest. "You will never again speak to her. You will never even think of her name, or I will cut out your blackened heart and put it on a spike for all to see. And then I will cut your eyes and tongue out and feed them to her dogs. Do you understand me clearly, Sethe?"

He only nodded, but he also managed a weak smile as he glanced in my direction. I had felt a sharp sensation during the exchange, and now warmth in my chest. I looked down to see my own blood seeping through my shirt. I suddenly felt dizzy and my vision wavered, but I managed to stay on my feet. Declan let go of Sethe and was on me in an instant. Daniel had quickly dispatched one of the vampires, whose head struck my foot as it bounced into the woods. Shila had done the same, and reached me just as my knees gave way. Charles took off after the last vampire, and we all heard a terrified scream cut off abruptly.

"What the hell is happening?" Declan asked Shila. Her eyes were scared and she wouldn't meet mine.

"Daniel!" Declan yelled.

"I'll get Thomas." And Shila was gone.

Declan cradled me on the ground and carefully lifted my shirt. The bleeding had slowed, but he would not stop fussing. I tried to get up, but he held me down. I called upon my abilities, but I was pretty weak and could only manage to produce a sputter of flame. Daniel walked to Sethe, who was struggling to rise from the ground, and punched him in the face. I heard his bones crack from where I was, and I felt my own facial bones cave in. I vaguely remember Declan's panicked voice yelling for Daniel to kill Sethe as blood poured from my mouth and nose.

"Stop!" Someone emerged from the edge of the woods, but I couldn't see who it was, between the blood in my eyes and Declan in my way. But everyone had stopped in their tracks at the voice. Declan abruptly stood up in front of me, guarding so no one could come near me. I couldn't speak because my jawbone was crushed, but I managed to get to my knees and peer around Declan's legs. *My vision must still be blurry,* I thought, *because I could have sworn I was looking at my older twin.*

Daniel was standing over Sethe with his machete at his neck, drawing a fine line of blood. The woman went to him so fast she was a blur. She knocked the weapon from Daniel's hand. "You cannot touch him!"

Daniel rounded on her, about to strike. "Don't, Daniel." It was Declan's order, and Daniel immediately backed off.

I stumbled to my feet and held onto Declan for support. He sucked in his breath.

"Jesus, Bailey, what is happening to you?" I felt his fear for me, and his anger. He touched my neck and came away with my blood. He turned to the woman and Sethe.

"What the fuck did you do to her?" he demanded.

He left me swaying, but Thomas came from behind for support. Thomas bit his own wrist and put it in front of my face. "Here, drink so you can heal faster." I complied, but did not enjoy it as I had with Declan. I immediately felt stronger. I tried out my voice, but it hurt and sounded scratchy and hoarse.

Declan had stalked to Sethe and held his knife to his chest as Shila restrained the woman. Sethe was trying to smile.

"Hurt me and you hurt her." he managed to say with satisfaction as he nodded in my direction.

Declan raised the knife. "What the hell are you talking about?"

"Black magic," Shila said. She released the woman and stepped away from her like she was a leper.

Sethe ignored the statement. He rose slowly past Declan, and went to the woman. "I would like to introduce you all to my mate." he said as his face was visibly healing. "This is Amelia. Isn't she beautiful?" He kissed her deeply on the mouth. She flinched but held her ground. She didn't look like she'd enjoyed it.

I didn't feel jealous, but something about the two of them together bothered me. And I thought it odd that she never took her eyes off of me as all of this transpired.

"What is going on, Sethe?" I croaked.

Declan seemed to snap out of his shock and came to me for support, but I no longer needed it. Thomas's blood had done its work. My face still ached, but the bones were almost healed. I called upon my powers, and Sethe must have seen my eyes change, because he looked surprised that I wouldn't believe him and was willing to kill him anyway. The woman stepped in front of me and laid her hand on my shoulder. Declan stiffened but did not move to stop her.

"Please, Bailey. Don't hurt him. He speaks the truth. You will only harm yourself."

My shoulder tingled where she touched me. I could only stare into her eyes as my anger vanished. Everything stopped, and no one else mattered as we gazed at each other. And I instantly knew. I was standing in front of my mother.

"Mother?"

She smiled and nodded slightly, then clasped my hands and held tight. My vision blurred, and I felt nausea seize my body as I stumbled. I heard Declan from what seemed like a million miles away, but I couldn't make out what he was saying because my concentration was on my mother and her visions. Silently she led me through our family history, and gave me a picture of her own experiences hiding from the powerful forces that wished her and our kind dead. I saw her anguish as she gave me to my parents on that fall night. I witnessed her distress at knowing she was, once again, on the run. Her only consolation was my safety. They called me Emilie—my real name. Oh god.

Amelia had helped my parents pick Riverside; a place close, but not too close to Oak Park, where she could keep a close eye on me. Watching me from a distance for years, she let me live my life in ignorance, as a human, until she thought I was ready to know the truth about my biology. She had arranged the renovations and my winning bid—wanting me to discover my past and my powers. Amelia had no idea who was behind the murder of her husband and daughter, and she certainly hadn't believed anyone was still watching the old house for any signs of either of us. Blaming herself for my abduction, she'd been distraught and angry over her carelessness of my welfare. She should have been watching more closely. I snapped out of it as she suddenly let go of my hands.

"Emilie," I whispered as I staggered a bit, eventually regaining my composure.

Declan was holding me with concern etched on his face. "Bailey, what the hell is going on here? Who is this woman, and who is Emilie?"

"She is my mother," I said to the audience around me, ignoring the latter question. I noticed that Daniel and Charles were guarding Sethe, but he had no plans on going anywhere. No, he loved the show.

"My god, Miss Bailey, she is Ahkin and you are as well," Shila uttered, awestruck. Charles and Daniel appeared just as shell-shocked. But Declan was only anxious about my safety.

Declan turned to Amelia. "What do you want with her?"

"I want her safe and happy. I have accepted Sethe as my mate to protect her."

"But why? How?" I interjected. My mind was on overload.

"He has taken a blood oath." Amelia responded. "He vowed to leave you and your loved ones alone as long as I mated him. Sethe has also agreed to protect me from others who seek my destruction." She smiled at him.

"But he's evil! He kidnapped me and–and hurt me!" I shouted. "He'll stop at nothing to take advantage of you. Just let me kill him and we can all be rid of him forever."

"But you cannot, my Emilie. He cannot be harmed because you will suffer. If he is killed, you will also die."

"I don't understand."

"It's black magic, Bailey," Declan stated as he walked to Sethe, and grabbed him, and shook. "This bastard has made a deal with the devil himself. He has found a witch crazy enough to cast a powerful black spell. One that will protect him from us!" He threw Sethe on the ground and spat in his face. "He is a coward, through and through."

Sethe laughed and sat up, wiping the spittle off with the back of his hand. "He's correct, Bailey. I am a coward, but I'm a smart coward. And one that has managed to stay alive for a couple of thousand years."

His pride in his own despicableness made me even angrier.

"Witches? Now you are telling me there are witches? What's next? Werewolves?" They only stared at me, every one of them, as if I were stupid. "Never mind. I don't want to know." And I shook my head.

"I have agreed to protect him, therefore you. Do not worry yourself," Amelia said when she saw my distress at the knowledge of her sacrifice for me. She took my hands again.

'Do not fret, my little darling. I will find a way to break the spell and free us from him. It is only a matter of time. I will send word of my progress. Patience, little one, patience. We have time to work this out. Go back to your life and to this man who loves you. You are free from Sethe. He will not dare harm you now.'' And she let go of me once again. It left me cold. I looked around, but no one seemed to understand what had transpired between us.

"Mother," I blubbered through my tears. "Please don't leave me again. Please stay."

Just then a sudden commotion came from my left. A familiar figure flew in front of me. John stood with his fangs bared and saliva dripping down his bare chest–his eyes were a wild shade of white and crazed. I motioned for everyone to stay back.

John grabbed me and screamed in my face. "You bitch! You did this to me! You've cursed me for eternity, and I should kill you for it."

I was speechless but managed to shake my head. "No. You would have died!" I pleaded.

He pushed me away, stepped back, and gave me a look of total desperation.

"Oh god, I'm so sorry. Please help me, Bailey," and he took off like a jackrabbit.

Everyone stood motionless–stunned. "John! Wait!" I bounded into the woods after him. I vaguely heard yelling coming from further back, but I was so intent on following his scent and keeping my eye on him that I paid no attention. It didn't take long for me to overpower him. I knocked him to the ground and sat on his chest. He violently bucked, but I held on tight.

"Stop it, John." I slapped him as he tried to bite me. He let out a heartfelt howl that I felt down to my bones.

"I'm sorry, John. Please forgive me." I looked into his wild eyes. He was desperate, scared, and hungry. So hungry.

Declan suddenly appeared and pushed me off of him. Thomas was not far behind with several bags of blood, which John didn't hesitate to tear into and greedily drink.

It was a pitiful sight, and I turned my back to them all to see Sethe beaming with mirth. I stalked over to him, against Declan's protests to stay back.

"You bastard. I will find a way to kill you if it's the last thing I do." I hastily wiped away the tears that were streaming down my face. I was so heartsick and lost that I snatched Declan's silver blade that sat at his waist, and before I could even think about what I was doing, I plunged it deep into my heart. I heard screaming and shouting as the world spun and my vision faded.

"I'm sorry," I groaned as I collapsed. My final breath squeezed out of me just as the rain and wind, once again, pounded the South Carolina coast.

EPILOGUE

M y mother stuck her head out the door, "David, please call the children to dinner."

They were having fun playing on the beach and probably getting into big time trouble, if I knew those kids. My brother rarely reprimanded them, even instigating sometimes. He trudged down the stairs and onto the beach, leaving me sitting on the deck with the boys at my feet, drinking a superb glass of pinot noir.

I gazed out onto the calm winter sea off my parents' porch at their rental house on Folly Beach. I stood and stared in the direction of the place where I tried to take my own life. The thought painfully seared my soul.

The breeze was cool against my skin but not cold. It had been a glorious winter's day in the low country, but it was getting chilly now that the sun was waning. And the boys were getting restless to get back in the house and lay by the fire.

The area had managed to survive the hurricane, but many homes and businesses did not escape unscathed. Rebuilding commenced with a vengeance, and Folly Beach was silent from the barrage of nail guns and buzz saws only because it was Christmas Eve. Luckily, my parents' rental sustained only minimal damage and was back to new. They were now seriously considering buying the place. Who would have thought?

"Mees Bailey, Mees Bailey. *Por favor, venga y coma.*"

"I'm coming, Rosa. Tell my mother I need a few moments. Here, take the boys in with you, please." She nodded and they all left me in peace.

I sighed. It felt good to be back with my family, even if the biology didn't match. The children were loud and obnoxious, my sister had gotten another tattoo, my brother and his wife were constantly fighting, and my grandparents—well, they were just as crazy as ever. No matter, I wouldn't have it any other way. We'd told my siblings of my adoption several weeks ago, and no one seemed to give it a second thought—except for me, of course.

It had taken me a long time to come to terms with what had transpired in the past few months. Between my inhuman nature, my family not being who I thought they were, and the fact that my biological mother was being held against her will, was enough to rattle the most stalwart. And I'd never claimed to be that tough.

After my attempt, and failure at destroying Sethe, the sadness and frustration was sometimes overbearing. It took me a few days, and a lot of blood forced down my throat, to recover from my self-inflicted injury that almost claimed my life. Declan had been furious at my hasty decision, and refused to even acknowledge the whole episode. To add insult to injury, Sethe was still living, and that was unacceptable.

Going back home to Chicago proved difficult. I was happy to be back in my house, even though I had some company for the foreseeable future. Shila and Daniel chose to stay. For the most part the sleeping arrangements had been fine. Vampires are certainly quiet and did not eat me out of house and home. They also gave me my privacy, and I felt secure. Rosa, on the other hand, was a bit of a problem. We were trying to keep my roommates and new "friend's" biology a secret, but she's not stupid. Someday the obvious would happen, and I wasn't looking forward to that day. The thought made me break out in a cold sweat. We would have to deal with it when the time comes.

Charles, Thomas, and Declan declined to stay, instead deciding to secure the cave and help in the search for a good location for a new facility. The Council had decided to repair and secure the current site for most of the Chicago Guild vampires, but would build a new, state-of-the-art facility, which will be much more secure. Because of its library and research facilities, only a select few will have access to it, and security will be top notch. That is also where Declan and his team will live. Meanwhile, the cave was almost complete, and all who vacated were now back. Shila and Daniel would be packed up and gone by the time I returned home—a thought that left me sad and lonely.

I went straight back to work, and for the most part, I didn't have any problems, but at times I found it difficult to concentrate, and I could no longer work on the Conrad project at all. Coming up with a plausible excuse for wanting nothing to do with the job had been challenging–especially since the architect had gone AWOL. But Ron was competent and happy to take over for me, so the transition was a smooth one.

John had called his job to formally resign, and that was all his co-workers knew. The rumors are flying, but no one could even come close to the truth, which is much more frightening than anyone could imagine. Declan took him to an undisclosed location for his "breaking in" period and training. I haven't seen or spoken to him, but I think about him every day, and the guilt was agonizing. I believe it will forever be a part of me.

I dove into my other projects, working long hours and taking any business trip I could, just to stay away. From what, I wasn't sure, but I knew that I couldn't take the rejection I was sure Declan would send my way eventually. He had been avoiding me ever since our confrontation with Sethe. It had been weeks since I talked to him, instead getting all of my vampire information through Shila, who turned out to be a considerate friend. She held me as I cried and consoled me over my anguish for my mother, Declan, and my unfortunate tie to Sethe. She tried desperately to assure me that Declan would find his way back eventually, calling him and all men stupid, chicken shits, etc., etc–although I did notice her cozying up to Gregory, who has decided to stay in Chicago, accepting the position of the Chicago Guild Senator. He was currently back in Rome, packing and tying up loose ends there.

As far as I was concerned, that fateful day when I tried to die, had torn a hole in my connection with Declan, splitting us apart. The thought made me sick. But I had one thing that kept me focused: plotting my revenge against Sethe.

I hadn't heard from Amelia, but I had to find a way to release her from Sethe's bondage and myself from his powerful spell. I would succeed eventually; it was only a matter of time. But first, I had to find a way to get back into the research library at the cave. I had been doing weekly reconnaissance to the local public library, the Newberry, and the Chicago History Museum's archives. I had gathered stacks of information already, including old newspaper clippings of odd and unexplained occurrences, any whispers of the occult, and all of the local Wicca and Witch activities. I was amazed at what I could find, and that there were so many practicing the craft.

But I still needed to get my hands on the unprecedented information held in the cave library. There were sure to be records there that I would find nowhere else in the world.

"Bailey, come and sit." my mom yelled from the kitchen.

My family knew I was forlorn and unhappy. They walked on eggshells around me, and I hated myself for it. This had to stop. I got up, charged into the dining room, and sat at my place, ready to celebrate the holiday. My grandfather walked in with his thinned white hair in cornrows and a sparkling diamond stud in his left ear. He had on a wetsuit that only went to his knees, and his wrinkled and boney shins stuck out like a couple of bleached chicken bones. He was smiling from ear to ear.

"Holy crap!" my brother yelled, as he walked in from the kitchen, then preceded to drop the turkey on the floor.

"Dad! What have you done now?" my mother cried.

My sister and her boyfriend only smiled and looked for food. Rosa laughed and offered some descriptive phrases in Spanish.

"I'm going to be a surfer," grandpa stated matter-of-factly. "What's the problem?" He sat by my grandmother, who beamed at him.

"Awesome, dude," she responded and did something under the table that none of us could see. Thank god.

Then the kids ran in and screamed at their great-grandpa, and at the ruined turkey that Rosa and David were trying to pick up, but kept dropping. My mother was shrieking at my grandpa, my sister-in-law was yelling for the kids to sit down, and my brother was bellowing for calm. Kristin and Jack were demanding food, and the dogs were chiming in as well. I risked a glance at my father, who sat mute, shell-shocked.

I sat back and laughed until tears ran down my cheeks, and then, to my astonishment, I looked up to see Declan's beautiful face taking in the scene and grinning with delight. He had his hands full of gifts, which the kids immediately grabbed to put under the tree. He said his greetings as best he could, considering the mayhem in the room.

I felt as if I were moving in slow motion as I got out of my seat and approached him. I saw my mother out of the corner of my eye give him the thumbs-up with a wink. Rosa was clapping, and David had finally grabbed hold of our dinner. My heart was pounding at the sight of Declan's stunning blue eyes and dark curly hair. I couldn't hear anything in the room but his heartbeat, and my vision took in every detail of his face. I heard him suck in a breath of air as I rounded the corner of the room. His eyes never left mine as I finally reached my destination. I threw my arms around him and gave him the best kiss I could manage under the circumstances.

"Davis, I missed you," he whispered into my ear as I backed off to get a good look at him.

"Merry Christmas, Declan." I murmured. "What a wonderful gift. Thank you for coming."

We smiled at one another, drinking in each other's essence as if we had been apart for years instead of weeks. I turned to see the entire clan staring at us, smiling. My mother stood up.

"Come on in, Declan. We have a seat for you right next to Bailey. Our dinner–well, we have ham."

I couldn't even taste my food, instead concentrating on every movement of Declan's shoulder against mine, and his warm hand on my leg under the table. I watched the curve of his mouth as he talked to my family, and the way he tucked his long dark locks behind his perfect ear when he bent down to shove a mouthful in. I smiled as he cut his eyes to mine, knowing how I was feeling, and his own reaction to my close proximity. We could barely finish our meals before we both excused ourselves and went out to the beach for some privacy.

It was dark now, and the air was chilly. He wrapped his jacket around me as we walked, but there was really no need. I was not feeling cold at all.

"So I assume my mother called to invite you." He just smiled. "Declan, I'm glad you're here. Obviously surprised. I didn't know if you–you–" I was stammering like a teenager. He abruptly stopped and held my arms, while shaking his head.

"Don't. Don't question it…us. It's very difficult for me, um to express how I feel about you. I'm obviously not very good at this."

"It's okay, neither am I," I said giggling as we resumed our walk in silence for some time.

"I've missed you, Davis. More than I ever thought possible. You were all I could think of these past few weeks. Just ask my team. They're all sick of me being so grouchy. They practically begged me to see you, to talk to you. And they were right. I tried to stay away. I don't know if I'm ready for a commitment–I just don't know if I can promise that right now."

"It's okay. I'm not asking for one." I covered his mouth briefly with mine. "I don't know what the future holds for us, Declan, but I would like to try to find out. No strings attached. We both have busy lives."

"Yes, well. To be honest, I was miserable without you." And he embraced me for an incredible kiss that left me breathless and wanting more. Knowing exactly how I was feeling, Declan slowly peeled away my clothing, as his mouth familiarized him with my body once again. It felt so right, like I was finally home.

We made love for god knows how long on the chilly, deserted winter beach, and it was magnificent.

As we hastily dressed, he took my hand and pressed a small box into it. My heart sped up.

"But I didn't–" He put his finger to my mouth to silence me.

"It doesn't matter." He nodded for me to open it.

Inside the box laid a beautiful emerald-encrusted lightning bolt pendant with matching stud earrings.

"To match your gorgeous eyes."

"They're so delicate and stunning. The emeralds flash red. They're spectacular. Thank you Declan."

"Wait until you see them in the light. I had them made for you from an old source. The emeralds are very rare, and can only be found on a tiny island in the South Pacific." He must have seen my astonished face. "The lightning bolt is you, Davis–fiery and glorious. Merry Christmas."

And a merry Christmas it was.

ABOUT THE AUTHOR

M.D. Kenney earned a BFA in Interior Design and a MS in Historic Preservation from the School of the Art Institute of Chicago. She has taught everything from kitchen and bath design to historic preservation while pursuing residential design.

A native of Oak Park, Illinois, Ms. Kenney has been married for over 25 years and has three children. Her and her husband currently reside in Charleston, South Carolina with their beloved Boston terriers, Monroe and Ralphie, and their Maine Coon cat, Sid.

Death By Design is M.D. Kenney's first novel. She is currently working on her next Bailey Davis Vampire Intrigue: *Designs in Blood*.

TURN THE PAGE FOR A SNEAK PREVIEW OF DESIGNS IN BLOOD...AND DON'T FORGET TO VISIT US AT:
MDKENNEY.COM
FOR ALL OF YOUR BAILEY DAVIS NEWS

DESIGNS IN BLOOD

COMING IN 2013

Interior designer Bailey Davis is not entirely human, yet not completely vampire. She's something so rare and unexplainable–thought to be only ancient myth–that very few on earth have an inkling of her true nature. Unfortunately Sethe Rousseau, her master and nemesis, is one of those few. And he will stop at nothing to honor his age-old blood feud against her kind unless Bailey can put a permanent end to his quest for vengeance.

~

Declan O'Connor is Centurion and Chicago Detective. He and Bailey have a somewhat complex relationship, which is made only more difficult when someone from his past shows up at the most inopportune time. Torn between duty and his heart, Declan is forced to make a painful choice, one he hopes that he will not live to regret.

~

Bailey's new client, Aidan LaRoche, seems to have it all, smarts: money, good looks, and charm. He and Bailey make a great team and become close during his new nightclub restoration. But Bailey is convinced that he is too good to be true, and that something more sinister lies behind Aidan LaRoche's attentions. And she is bound and determined to discover what it is before it's too late.

~

Bailey's ex-boyfriend, John Blaine, is gladly a thorn in his new masters side. Having performed the changing ritual at Bailey's insistence in order to save his life, John is now bound to Detective Declan O'Connor in blood and service for many decades to come. However, John will not make it a pleasant coupling. Confused by what he has become, and hurt by Bailey's hand in it, John is determined to fight his inner demons–impulses so deep and dark that they threaten his very existence and the one he loves most.

~

Designs In Blood is the second installment of the Bailey Davis Vampire Intrigues. It places Bailey in the cross hairs of her master–a murdering rogue vampire that she's determined to destroy without bringing harm to her biological mother and herself. But with her love life on the brink of disaster, her ex-boyfriend's sudden lack of communication, and her new client's suspicious behavior, Bailey is continually distracted from her resolution to free herself from Sethe's black magic spell. From Chicago to Charleston to Paris, Bailey is set on a course that will forever alter her life and those that get in her way.

Made in the USA
Lexington, KY
24 April 2012